5 -

MW01133481

EARTH HONOR

EARTH HONOR

EARTHRISE, BOOK VIII

DANIEL ARENSON

Copyright © 2017 by Daniel Arenson
Illustration © Tom Edwards - TomEdwardsDesign.com

All rights reserved.

This novel is a work of fiction. Names, characters, places and incidents are either the product of the author's imagination, or, if real, used fictitiously.

No part of this book may be reproduced or transmitted in any form or by an electronic or mechanical means, including photocopying, recording or by any information storage and retrieval system, without the express written permission of the author.

CHAPTER ONE

Captain Ben-Ari stood on the bridge of the *Lodestar*, storming across space, a fleet of enemy saucers flying in pursuit.

"Full power to our engines!" Ben-Ari said. "We must reach Earth before them!"

Lights flashed across the bridge. The crew was bustling, moving between workstations, manipulating holographic monitors. Alarms blared. Statistics scrolled across viewports. The bridge was dome-shaped, a planetarium showing a full view of space all around them. Even the floor displayed the stars below. In the distance, Ben-Ari could see them. Thousands of them. Dark saucers.

The grays, she thought. *Super-evolved humans from the future. And they want Earth.*

She looked ahead. Sol, Earth's sun, was just a distant speck. Even flying at top speed, the *Lodestar* was still two days away.

And Earth didn't know what was coming.

Earth needed those two days to prepare.

Or Earth would fall.

Ben-Ari spun toward her science officer.

"Professor, how is work commencing on that wormhole?"

Professor Noah Isaac was working at three holographic monitors, typing in equations, mumbling under his breath, and scratching notes into a notebook. His black hair was disheveled. He wore his HOPE uniform, the navy-blue cotton bedecked with insignia and brass buttons. He kept tugging at the outfit, as if he missed his professorial corduroy pants and tweed jacket.

"Progress, progress," the professor mumbled. "Astounding physics, really. To open a communication wormhole—from warp speed! It's never been done. The math is staggering."

Ben-Ari smiled thinly. "If anyone can do it, my dear professor, it's you."

He flashed her a smile, then returned to his work. Professor Isaac, after all, had invented the wormhole, had won a Nobel Prize for it ten years ago. Yet his wormholes had always been static, used for passing faster-than-light signals between two fixed locations. The *Lodestar* had a wormhole generator, but they could only use it while still. They were now flying at warp speed, bending spacetime around them. They could not stop, not with those saucers on their tail. And they needed to warn Earth.

Ben-Ari clenched and unclenched her fists. Earth's fleet didn't know the saucers were coming. Many starships would be in maintenance, others orbiting distant colonies. Earth was asleep.

We need to sound the alarm. We need to rouse the entire might of Earth.

Sudden pain in her arm stabbed her. She winced. She had broken that arm only recently, willingly snapping the bone to escape Marino's grip. The *Lodestar*'s doctor had fused the bone with bio-glue, then sealed the limb in a thin, hardened cast that fit like a second skin. She could move her arm. She could function as normal. But the damn thing still hurt.

Ignore the pain for now, she told herself. *You'll suffer far worse than a broken arm if those bastards reach Earth before we can raise the alarm.*

She glanced back at the saucers. They were gaining on them. Damn.

"Aurora, can you give me more speed?" Ben-Ari said.

The *Lodestar*'s pilot swiveled her seat toward Ben-Ari. Aurora was the only alien crew member. Her eight tentacles reached out to eight monitors, controlling the ship's navigation and flight. Her boneless body was indigo but soon flashed bright blue, and golden dots appeared across it, fading into silver lines. Menorians, intelligent mollusks from a distant world, had no vocal cords; they communicated with colors. A camera attached to Aurora's seat picked up the colors and emitted a robotic voice, translating the hues.

"We are swimming through the cosmic ocean as fast as we can, mistress of dark waters," Aurora said. "We could swim faster, but our Great Shell would grow dark and cold, and our bubbles of air would drain. We have only enough of the small shells for the High Mollusks, not for the podlings who huddle among our tentacles. Even then, we might not swim fast enough."

Ben-Ari contemplated this message. Menorians loved metaphors. Aurora's translation device still struggled.

She means the **Lodestar** *can fly faster if we shut off life support,* Ben-Ari thought. *There are enough spacesuits—small shells—for the bridge officers. The rest of the crew would suffocate.*

Ben-Ari shook her head. "No. We have five hundred people aboard the *Lodestar*. I won't condemn them to suffocation just to gain a little extra speed."

Not yet, at least. She shuddered.

She turned back toward her science officer.

"Professor?" she said. "Progress?"

Professor Isaac winced, bit his lip, ran another calculation, then leaped into the air like Archimedes from his tub.

"Got it!" the professor exclaimed.

Relief flooded Ben-Ari. "You can open a communication wormhole to Earth? From warp speed?"

Isaac nodded. "Yes. Well, not exactly. Not as we are now. We require certain hardware modifications. Right now we're flying inside a bubble of warped spacetime. We cannot open a wormhole—a funnel through spacetime—while inside this bubble. Yet if we leave the bubble, we return to normal spacetime, and we slow down, and the saucers catch us. What we must do, therefore, is open the wormhole along the very edge of this bubble." He raised his notebook, showing a diagram. "Imagine a big soap bubble. We're inside. We dare not pop this bubble. But if we can mount hardware on the thin film of soap forming the bubble …"

Ben-Ari nodded, understanding. "How do we do it?"

"The shuttle," said Isaac. "We must fly the shuttle right to the edge of our warp bubble, extend a generator into regular spacetime, and open a wormhole from there. It'll require extraordinary flying and pinpoint precision. If the shuttle veers too far out, it will fall out of our bubble. The shuttle is likely to shatter. It might even pop the entire bubble."

Ben-Ari nodded. "I'll fly the shuttle. Professor, meet me in the launch bay as soon as you're able. Give me the hardware I'll need."

Aurora flashed a hectic red. "Mistress of dark waters, allow me! I'm the best swimmer in the cosmic ocean."

Ben-Ari nodded. "Exactly. That's why I need you to keep piloting the *Lodestar*. I'll go. I've clocked more hours on the shuttle than anyone else here."

"Your bony tentacle—" Aurora began.

"My arm is patched together quite nicely," Ben-Ari said, ignoring the pain. "Hold down the fort."

She left the bridge.

She walked down the *Lodestar*'s central corridor, shoulders squared.

Inside her, demons howled, ghosts of past wars, of haunting dead. She shut them down.

Earth needs me. I will not fail. I will sound the alarm.

On her way to the shuttle bay, Ben-Ari paused, then took a detour to the armory. This was a military mission. She would dress for war. She doffed her blue HOPE uniform. She replaced it with a black spacesuit; the fabric was flexible enough to let her fight, strong enough to withstand the vacuum of space. She slung a plasma rifle across her shoulder, and she strapped several grenades to her belt. She added a jet pack, standard gear for battles in space, useful in case of ejection. She paused for a moment, her visor raised, and looked at herself in the mirror. Once more—a soldier. Once more—war.

She entered the shuttle bay. The *Lodestar* had already lost one of its shuttles battling the grays. The remaining shuttle stood in the hangar, charred and dented from its past battle. A small vessel, no larger than a sedan.

Ben-Ari tapped her communicator. "Professor?"

"Putting together the hardware, Captain. I'll be there in twenty minutes."

"Be here in ten," Ben-Ari said.

She waited. Every minute—an eternity. Every minute—the saucers growing closer. She could see them through the viewports. She could imagine the creatures within. She could imagine Nefitis, foul queen of the grays, upon her decaying throne, licking her thin lips, craving her prize.

After two devastating wars—first against the scum, then against the marauders—Earth was still reeling. Most of the fleet was gone. What starships humanity still flew were scattered across the solar system.

Earth was virtually undefended.

The grays knew to attack us now, Ben-Ari thought. *Of course they did.* She inhaled deeply. *But so long as I live, I will fight. I am Einav Ben-Ari, a major of the HDF, a captain of HOPE. I fought the scum*

emperor and the marauder hosts. I will face you too, Nefitis. And I will
defeat you.

A pang of guilt stabbed her. Things were different this time, of course. She had caused this war. She had created the grays, marooning the Nefitian monks on a desert planet where they evolved into monsters, nursing their hatred for a million years. She should have slain them. But she had shown them mercy. Now Earth might fall—and it was her fault.

Ben-Ari clenched her fists.

"I started this," she whispered. "I will end it."

Finally the professor rushed into the shuttle bay. He carried a bulky device. It looked like a radio dish with microchips, cables, and motors attached.

"Here you go, Captain," the professor said. "A little wormhole generator. Inside is a small azoth crystal, the size of an apple seed. I took it from our main wormhole generator. It's too small to power a starship like the *Lodestar*. But it can still punch a hole through spacetime. You must fly to the rim of our warp bubble, stick this device into open space, and punch that hole. I already coded the proper coordinates into the machine. It will extend a wormhole straight to President Petty on Earth."

Ben-Ari nodded. "Show me how the controls work. Run a simulation with me. Quickly."

The professor handed her a remote control with a small monitor. He reviewed the functions with her. His voice was gentle, somehow patient even during this mad chase. It was like their lessons back in his quarters again, him teaching, her listening raptly.

I'll miss those lessons, Ben-Ari thought. The hours she had spent in his room, surrounded by his books and model ships, listening to him reveal the wonders of the cosmos, had been among the best hours of her life. *May we have many more such hours.*

"Got it," Ben-Ari said. "I'm ready."

They mounted the generator's dish onto the shuttle's roof, securing it with heavy bolts. Ben-Ari holstered the remote control.

"Fly the shuttle to the top of the warp bubble," the professor said. "Let the dish emerge from the bubble, *only* the dish, while keeping the shuttle inside. Remember: anything heavier than the dish will rip the bubble, so do not fly too high! Do not let the shuttle's roof touch the bubble! When you're all set up, activate the wormhole."

She nodded. "Understood."

She placed one foot inside the shuttle, prepared to fly out.

"Einav." The professor spoke softly.

She turned back toward him. "Professor?"

He stepped closer. He placed a hand on her shoulder. "Godspeed, Captain."

She nodded, smiling, her eyes suddenly damp. She remembered how he had embraced her after Marino's betrayal, had stroked her hair, had comforted her. That too was a warm memory, another moment she wanted to experience again.

"Thank you, Noah, my dear professor," she whispered, then turned and entered the shuttle.

She flew out from the *Lodestar*. At once she engaged her side thrusters, keeping her shuttle close to the *Lodestar*. She inched upward. This would be a delicate operation, a hummingbird flying alongside an albatross. She flew higher, passing along the *Lodestar*'s starboard. Through her porthole, she saw the logo of HOPE emblazoned on the *Lodestar*'s hull: the blue sphere of Earth, her moon circling in orbit.

Ben-Ari raised her chin, the sight giving her strength. She knew that humanity was flawed. Humanity had polluted Earth, had butchered many other lifeforms inhabiting that fragile world. Humanity had butchered its own people, genocide after genocide for thousands of years. Humanity was filled with greed and hatred and violence. But Ben-Ari knew that it could be noble too. She would fight for such nobility, embody it here in the darkness.

She rose to hover atop the *Lodestar*, flying only meters above the starship. She could just make out the bubble of spacetime around them. The bubble itself was invisible, but it bent the starlight, shimmering. Ben-Ari flew her shuttle a little higher. A little higher still. Coordinates flashed on her monitor.

Her communicator crackled to life.

"You're doing well, Captain," emerged the professor's voice. "Nice and easy does it. I'm here if you need me."

She rose several more meters, approaching the rim of the bubble. She adjusted her flight, wincing. Her left arm was still in a cast, stiff, itchy, and hurting badly now. She rose just a meter higher. Another meter. Slowly ... slowly ... One centimeter off, and she would fall out from the warp bubble. If she were lucky, her shuttle would shatter into countless pieces, instantly killing her. It she were unlucky, she would tumble into regular spacetime and float aimlessly. Within an instant, the *Lodestar* would be a million kilometers away, leaving her marooned forever in the darkness.

"All right. I've reached the edge of the bubble," Ben-Ari said. "I'm going to ascend one more meter, so the dish on my roof emerges into regular spacetime."

"Keep it nice and slow," the professor said. "Don't fall out. We can't catch you if you fall."

Ben-Ari smiled grimly. "No safety net. That's how I work best."

"Slow and steady and you'll get it done," the professor said, voice calm through the communicator. "I believe in you, Einav."

She gently guided the shuttle up.

The dish on her roof nudged the bubble's skin—then broke through.

Ben-Ari held her breath.

The dish emerged into regular spacetime. The warp bubble remained intact.

She exhaled.

"Dish has made the breach," she said into her communicator. "Bubble looking steady. My shuttle's roof is still half a meter below the rim. I'm beginning orientation."

She held her remote control. Its screen displayed an animation of the dish. She hit buttons, pointing the wormhole generator toward Earth. The dish locked into place, then dilated.

"Beginning wormhole creation," she said.

She held her finger over the button. She took a deep breath. She was prepared to punch a hole through spacetime, to blast a tunnel toward Earth, allowing instant communication. She was prepared to light the beacons, to rouse Earth's might.

Once more, Earth's best will fly to war. Once more, we—

An alarm blared—coming through her communicator.

An alarm aboard the *Lodestar*.

"Professor!" she cried. "What—"

"Einav, behind you!" he shouted through the communicator.

She stared into the rearview monitor. She saw a flash of red. She couldn't see clearly from here.

"Professor, wha—"

Below her shuttle, explosions rocked the *Lodestar*.

The bubble of spacetime jiggled, jostling the shuttle.

Ben-Ari cursed, gripped the yoke, and lowered the shuttle a few meters. The dish emerged back into the warp bubble. She gazed again into the rearview monitor.

The blood drained from her face.

A dozen saucers—small and red and flashing with lights—had reached the *Lodestar*. Their guns blazed.

Ben-Ari stared in horror. These were not the larger, bulkier saucers, the dark machines of thick metal. These were small, agile fighters, large enough for only a single pilot, moving at terrifying speed. They whirred like tops, ringed with blades.

Ben-Ari sneered. She could not return to the *Lodestar* yet—she hadn't yet opened the wormhole! She had to warn Earth!

The enemy saucers fired again. More blasts hit the *Lodestar*. The starship's shield shimmered, nearly cracking. The *Lodestar* was beginning to turn around to face the attackers. The bubble of spacetime was wobbling madly. There was no way Ben-Ari could now gently guide the dish upward, not without her shuttle falling out of warp and vanishing into deep space

She took a deep breath, eyes stinging.

If those shuttles destroyed her dish, Earth would receive no warning.

She could not wait for the battle's outcome. She had to send the message. Now.

"Professor," she said into her communicator, voice cracking. "You have command of the *Lodestar*. I am sending that signal. Do not come back for me. Continue to Earth. That is an order." She raised her chin. "Godspeed, Noah."

"Einav, wai—"

She soared.

She burst through the wobbling film of the bubble.

Her stomach lurched. Lights flashed across her eyes. She nearly lost her lunch. For a horrifying instant, her consciousness seemed to float outside her body, and images of Nefitis flashed before her, cruel and grinning, her pyramid rising behind her.

Ben-Ari screamed and gripped the yoke.

The shuttle careened madly.

Don't shatter, don't shatter, don't shatter ...

The streams of starlight slammed into points around her.

The *Lodestar* streamed away in a flash, moving at many times the speed of light, crossing millions of kilometers per second. Within an instant, it was gone. With flashes of light, the saucers followed, vanishing too.

Silence fell.

Ben-Ari floated alone in space, lost in the vastness between the stars, light-years away from any world. She sat in a small shuttle without any food or water, with enough air for only a day or two. She was millions of years away from civilization.

But she could still send that signal.

"I can still warn Earth," she whispered. "Even at the price of my life."

She ignored the tears in her eyes. She had always thought she would die in battle. Instead, she would die of asphyxiation, maybe of thirst, lost alone in the darkness.

But she would die nobly.

She hit buttons on her remote control, aiming the dish on her shuttle's roof.

She hit another button—the one to create the wormhole.

She leaned forward, gazing up through the windshield.

Professor Isaac's dish dilated. Lights flashed across it. A luminous ring appeared in space, hovering just above Ben-Ari's eyes. It was beautiful. Even with all this terror, it was beautiful, a little nebula above her. The ring began contracting, glowing brighter, extending outward like a funnel.

"It's working," Ben-Ari whispered, tasting her tears. "It's working, professor. My professor. I wish you could see it. Your invention is working."

A single red light bleeped on the shuttle's control panel.

She glanced at it.

Four more red lights joined it.

Saucers—charging her way.

She ignored them.

She would send the signal.

The wormhole began to form—a thin tendril, stretching out, a rift through spacetime. She checked the progress on her monitor.

Wormhole 50% complete. 60%. 70% ...

She prepared to open a communication channel, to transmit her warning.

80% ... 90% ...

"Come on, come on," she whispered.

96% ...

Red light flared, bathing the cabin.

A second later, an explosion rocked the shuttle.

Ben-Ari screamed.

The shuttle careened through space. The hull tore open. The wormhole fizzled away. Ben-Ari slammed down her helmet's visor. The air shrieked out from the cabin, and more lights flashed, and another blast hit the shuttle. Fire raged.

Ben-Ari hit the ejection.

She blasted out into space.

She saw them ahead: a large black saucer and several small red ones. Their cannons heated up again.

She hovered in the darkness. Her starship gone. Her shuttle burning. The enemy approaching.

Ben-Ari reached down, grabbed the wormhole generator, and ripped it off the crumbling roof of the shuttle.

A second later, a blast hit the shuttle, and it shattered into countless pieces.

Ben-Ari floated through space, a single woman in a spacesuit, a jet pack on her back, the hope of humanity in her hands.

She slung the wormhole generator across her back, using a loose cable as a strap.

She drew her plasma rifle.

As the saucers flew toward her, she sneered.

"I am still an officer of the HDF," she hissed. "I am still a captain of HOPE. I am still a soldier of Earth. I still fight."

She activated her jet pack and charged toward the saucers. She fired her plasma rifle.

The enemy missiles flew toward her. She zigzagged through space, tugging her jet pack's controls. Blasts exploded around her. She kept firing her rifle, screaming as she charged forward.

Her plasma bolts hit one of the small red saucers.

The enemy ship exploded.

Ben-Ari shot upward, dodging the shrapnel. The other saucers loomed before her, several small reds and one massive black mothership. She fired again. She stormed toward them, dodging their blasts. Their missiles streamed around her. She flew onward, taking them head on. She aimed. She fired a bolt into a spinning red saucer, and another, and another, punching holes into it. The small saucer shattered. She flew through the wreckage and soared.

The mothership was lumbering toward her, blasting weapons her way. Ben-Ari kept dodging the blasts. She was a furious wasp flying among eagles. And her stinger was hot. She fired again, and blasts hit the mothership. Fire raged across the dark hull.

She was doing what none had ever done. A single human in a spacesuit taking on a dozen enemy ships.

But I will not die now. Not before sending that signal!

She shoved down the throttle on her jet pack. She flew higher, faster, rising away from the saucers. They flew below her, cannons firing, and she zipped from side to side, dodging the blasts. As she flew, she gripped the wormhole generator. She reactivated it.

Again a ring of light grew.

Again the wormhole began taking form.

The funnel began extending to Earth.

Enemy fire tore through the luminous tube.

Oh for God's sake.

She spun down toward the saucers, prepared to launch another assault, and saw a hatch open on the mothership.

A beam of light blasted out from the hatch. The glow engulfed her.

A tractor beam. And it was pulling her in.

Caught in the light, Ben-Ari aimed her rifle and fired.

Plasma bolt after plasma bolt flew and entered the saucer's hatch. Explosions blasted inside the enemy ship.

But the beam kept tugging her.

Ben-Ari screamed, kept shooting, and more fire blazed in the enemy ship, but the tractor beam kept her in its grip.

She cursed and shoved the throttle on her jet pack. It sputtered. She flew up two meters, but the beam grabbed her again, pulled her with more strength. Her pack rattled.

She yowled in frustration, unable to free herself. The beam intensified, yanking her toward the hatch like a reptile's tongue pulling in a fly.

She tumbled into the saucer.

She landed inside a hangar, leaped to her feet, and fired her rifle.

Her plasma slammed into several grays. The towering, slender aliens were everywhere. They raised prods, and electricity blasted toward her.

Bolts slammed into Ben-Ari, and she screamed.

She fell to her knees. Her teeth knocked together, cutting her tongue. Blood filled her mouth. Electricity crackled across her.

Even through the agony, she kept firing her rifle. She hit another gray, blasting a hole through the wretched creature's chest.

More grays approached. More electrical bolts hit her. Ben-Ari fell onto her side, screaming, banging her hip and ribs and broken arm. The pain was terrifying. Overwhelming. Impossible pain. She nearly passed out.

The hatch slammed shut behind her, sealing her in this hangar.

The grays surrounded her. They loomed like vultures over prey. Their claws grabbed her, dug into her. Their black eyes stared, pitiless, cutting her as surely as their claws.

They grabbed her rifle, her jet pack, and her wormhole generator. They yanked off her helmet and spacesuit, and their claws cut her bare skin. She yowled, kicking, scratching, and managed to hit one in the shin. Her arm was screaming in agony. She ignored it. More electricity slammed into her, and she fell again, losing control of her bladder.

I go down fighting. For Earth.

Smoke wafted across her, and she rose to her knees, panting, prepared to launch into another assault.

I won't be taken alive.

The grays spoke to one another in their harsh, guttural language. When Ben-Ari leaped back toward them, they tossed small pods against her. The spheres burst across her spacesuit and spilled ooze like shattered eggs. The slime bound her, tightening, a sticky cocoon. The grays tossed more pods. More ooze covered

Ben-Ari, coating her hair, her face, her limbs, drying, forming membranes around her. It burned. She could barely see through the translucent material. She screamed, unable to breathe, until a gray sliced a hole in the coating.

They lifted her—this dripping, shouting bundle. She was like a fly caught in their spiderweb.

They carried her through their ship.

They left the wormhole generator—the hope of Earth— behind.

The corridors were coiling, dark, almost organic, like the arteries of a fossilized giant. Ben-Ari struggled as the grays carried her, but she could barely move, barely breathe. The sticky membranes held her as tightly as a python.

She forced herself to stop screaming. She was panting. Her heart was lashing. She was panicking.

Stop, she told herself. *Stop! Focus. Breathe. Think!*

She forced a deep breath.

They want you alive, she told herself. *If you're alive, there is hope. You can still fight. Wait. Bide your time. Think!*

The terror lurked within her, screaming, howling, begging to erupt in panic. Ben-Ari forced it down. She was a soldier. She was a leader. She had faced horror before and overcome it. She would face this too.

They carried her through the bowels of this dark ship. Their claws dug deep. Several of the grays were gripping her, hunched over, their bodies bare, the torsos wrinkled and coated with liver spots, their spines prominent.

They took her into a stone chamber. A surgical table lay in a beam of light. No, not a surgical table—an altar. An altar engraved with ancient glyphs. An altar to a dark goddess.

They slammed Ben-Ari onto the table so hard her spine nearly cracked. They cut through the membranes binding her, tugged out her limbs, and bound them onto the altar with fleshy cords. She did not bother trying to flee. She knew it was pointless. She shoved down the panic.

Wait. Bide your time. Save your strength. Think.

The grays stepped back, vanishing into shadows. She remained alone, bound to the altar, the light from above shining upon her.

A deep, gravelly breath sounded in the shadows. Footsteps shuffled. In the darkness, red lights kindled, deep, glowing, crimson. They materialized into a chain of hearts, pulsing and dripping blood. He stepped toward her—a gray alien, wrinkled and desiccated yet still strong, his eyes narrowed and cruel.

He spoke. His voice was like old death. Like snapping bones. It dripped cruelty like a wolf's jaws dripped blood.

"Hello, ape. I am Abyzou. Son of Nefitis. Prince of the Sanctified Sons." He leaned above her, and his mouth twisted into a grin, revealing teeth like rusty needles. He placed a claw on her collarbone. "I am your agony."

She stared into his black, pitiless eyes.

So there he is. The Prince of Grays himself. Ugly son of a bitch.

"I am Captain Einav Ben-Ari of HOPE," she said. "Commander of the *Lodestar*. That is the only information I will give you."

The creature laughed—a sickly sound like consumption. Saliva dripped from his teeth.

"We know who you are, Captain, and you have no information that we need." Abyzou traced his claw between her breasts. "We know all. All your secrets. We know of Earth's defenses. We know the name and location of every human ship. We know of your life, Einav. Of the bitter, frightened girl, growing up on military bases. Of the scared youth, rebelling against her father, fleeing from her home time and time again. We know of the fear deep inside you, the weakness that you hide there, that ever keeps you from greatness. We know that deep inside, you are still that scared little girl. No, Einav. I do not seek information. I seek only your pain. And after you suffer that pain, Einav, after you have soaked up *so much* agony, your heart too will beat on my chain."

She stared up into his black eyes.

No fear. You are a soldier. You are human.

"Then let us begin," she said.

Abyzou drew an ugly, serrated blade. He pierced her skin.

Ben-Ari arched her back, gritting her teeth against the pain. Her blood dipped. Abyzou smiled.

"Yes, you welcome it," he hissed. "Savor it!"

He pulled the blade downward, etching a line.

Ben-Ari thrashed in her bonds.

He cut again, carving a cross into her skin.

She lashed her body from side to side.

Under her back, it tore free from the webbing—the electrical prod she had grabbed from a dead gray in the hangar.

Abyzou took a hook and sank it into her skin.

Ben-Ari flailed and the prod rolled across the altar. She stretched out her fingers, her arm still bound, and caught the prod before it could fall to the floor.

Abyzou carved her with blade and hook, smiling.

Ben-Ari switched on the prod.

Electricity raced along the prod, across her body, and into Abyzou.

The creature shrieked.

He dropped his blade and hook.

The hook clanged onto the floor. But Ben-Ari caught the blade.

"Wretched ape!" Abyzou cried. He lunged toward her. He grabbed her with his claws. "How you will scream!"

She turned on the prod again.

They both screamed.

As Abyzou fell back, electricity racing across him, Ben-Ari worked with the knife. She freed one arm. When Abyzou lunged back toward her, she drove the prod into his gut and pulsed out more electricity.

As he howled, as he burned, Ben-Ari freed her other arm.

She stumbled off the altar, bleeding, burnt, gasping for breath. Blood and sticky membranes coated her.

Abyzou loomed before her. He rose to his full height, seven feet of fury. He was burning. The hearts around his chest blazed like comets. He reached his claws toward her, a demon risen from Hell, shrieking.

Ben-Ari thrust her blade into the inferno and pierced his chest.

He screamed—a high-pitched, deafening cry—and fell back.

A door banged open. Three more grays entered the room.

Ben-Ari ran toward them and blasted electricity from her prod.

Two grays fell back, crackling. She leaped onto the third, delivering a punch to his chin, knocking back his head. As the beast fell, she vaulted over the creature and ran down the corridor.

The shadowy pathway coiled before her. She ran, ignoring the pain. The grays emerged from doorways at her sides. Ben-Ari grabbed one of the grenades on her belt, pulled out the pin, and dropped it. She raced onward as the grenade exploded behind her. The grays screamed.

She rounded a corner. She dropped another grenade. An explosion rocked the ship. The corridor caved in behind her, crushing grays.

Ahead, she saw the path to the hangar. To freedom.

At her side—another path, sloping downward. Rumbles and heat from below.

She nodded. She chose the second path.

Three grays leaped toward her. She fired her electricity, knocking them back.

She burst through a doorway and beheld a chasm. Engines roiled and boomed and fumed below, churning heat and molten fire. Here was the heart of the mothership.

Ben-Ari smiled thinly.

She lifted her last two grenades and tossed them into the smoldering engines.

She turned and ran.

Fire.

Heat.

Blinding light and deafening noise.

The ship crumbled around her. The walls cracked. The ceiling collapsed. Everywhere—the inferno.

She ran through it.

She burst into the hangar. Several grays were still here. They leaped toward her, firing their weapons. She fired back. She took a bolt to the shoulder, nearly passed out from the pain, but kept firing. She knocked them back.

There—on the floor. Her things were still there. Her spacesuit. Her jet pack. More importantly—her wormhole generator.

She was running toward the items when the floor cracked open. She fell to her knees. Explosions were still sounding deep in the mothership. The entire saucer was crumbling.

Ben-Ari managed to push herself up. The walls fell away around her. Air was shrieking out into space. The floor cracked open, and the last few grays fell into gaping pits. Ben-Ari stumbled onward.

She grabbed her spacesuit and helmet. Ignoring her dripping blood, she pulled them on in a frenzy. She snapped on her jet pack and grabbed the wormhole generator. Her plasma rifle was on the other side of the hangar. She had no time to grab it.

The hangar shattered around her.

The roof caved in.

The hull collapsed.

Ben-Ari ignited her jet pack and roared out into space.

She soared upward. Below her, explosions rocked the gray mothership. The dark saucer split in half. Fire raged from within. A few escape pods were trying to flee, only for the flames and shrapnel to catch them. Shrapnel tore into the red fighter saucers, ripping through them.

Ben-Ari gritted her teeth, soaring as fast as she could, her jet pack thrumming and roaring out fire. All around her, the shrapnel flew, shards of metal and stone streaming faster than her. She kept flying. The stars shone above. The holocaust blazed below.

She soared into the darkness.

She soared into silence.

Below her, the fire died.

The millions of shattered pieces floated.

She switched off her jet pack. She hovered in silence.

She gazed down. Below her, they were gone. The enemy saucers—a gray mothership and her fighters—gone.

I did it. One woman. One rifle. One jet pack. I defeated their ships.

She raised her communication dish. It was charred and cracked, but it still turned on. She calibrated it. She positioned the dish. And she created the wormhole.

A tunnel opened through spacetime, only several atoms wide. Large enough for her to speak through it. To President Petty. To Earth. To all humanity.

She spoke, eyes damp.

"This is Einav Ben-Ari, captain of the ESS *Lodestar*. I am speaking to you from several light-years away. The *Lodestar* is racing back to Earth; it will be home in two days. Fast on her heel are ten thousand enemy ships. Rouse Earth's defenses! Ready humanity's fleet! In two days, the enemy will strike—and strike hard. Across the solar system, rally all human starships to battle! Fight for Earth!"

She closed her eyes and cut off the signal.

She hovered in space.

She breathed deeply.

A lone woman in a spacesuit. Lost in the depths of interstellar space. Millions of years away from any world.

She nodded, a thin smile on her lips.

"So this is how I die," she whispered. "With honor. I did my duty. I raised the alarm. I only wish I could fight there with you, Earth." A tear streamed down her cheek. "I only wish I could see you again, Marco, Addy, Lailani. I miss you. I love you."

She gazed at the stars. They were beautiful. They were so beautiful. She would die, at least, surrounded by beauty. She remembered herself as a little girl, gazing up at the stars with her father. He had told her once, when she was very small, that the starlight was millions of years old, that she was gazing upon the past. The fact still astounded her. Even as the scum rained from the sky, she had seen the stars as magical, had always longed to fly among them.

"And I did, Father," she whispered. "I did."

She thought of the professor. She missed him too. He had become something of a father figure to her—fifteen years older, wiser, a mentor. But no, not a father. Something more. Perhaps even someone who could have become a lover? She missed him too. She wondered if love could have bloomed between them.

Another tear fell. She thought of those precious hours she had spent in his study, listening to him speak of science, learning from him. He had called her his brightest pupil. He had marveled at how she could pick up complex science with ease. Yet how could she not have learned well with such a patient, kind teacher? He could make even the most complicated equations seem simple. Under his tutelage, she had come to understand physics, the properties of light and spacetime and gravity, how azoth crystals could create wormholes but also warp-speed bubbles, how—

She inhaled sharply.

She narrowed her eyes.

"Azoth crystals create both wormholes and warp-speed bubbles," she whispered. She gazed at the device in her hands, the wormhole generator.

There was an azoth crystal inside.

She scoffed. No. Impossible. It was too small! The size of a grain of sand! The azoth crystal inside the *Lodestar* was the size of her fist, perfectly cut, its facades calibrated down to the exact atom, allowing it to bend spacetime just the right way. A crystal like that one, priceless, could create a warp bubble large enough to engulf a starship, to let it travel faster than light.

Ben-Ari took a deep breath.

"But I don't need a bubble that large," she whispered to herself. "Only a bubble large enough for me."

She bit her lip, struggling not to let foolish hope overwhelm her. She ran equations in her mind. The numbers arranged and rearranged themselves, but they soon became fuzzy, fading away. The math was slipping from her. Too complicated!

Imagine the professor, she told himself. *Imagine him here with you. Imagine his voice.*

She brought him to mind—his kind face, his gentle demeanor, his soothing voice. She imagined him at her side, creating the equations with her, making the numbers fit.

And she had it.

With shaky fingers, she typed on the dish's control panel. This time she was not calibrating the device to create a wormhole.

This time she wouldn't punch a hole through spacetime.

She would bend it.

The numbers were inputted. She paused.

"All right, professor," she said. "Let's see if you taught me well. Here goes nothing."

She hit enter.

The dish trembled in her hands.

Light bended around it.

The starlight shimmered.

And around her, the bubble formed.

She laughed and wept as she ignited her jet pack. She blasted forward, flying through warped space. A single woman with a jet pack—and a makeshift warp drive.

She blasted forward, laughing, crying, streaming through space at millions of kilometers per second. The starlight streamed in lines around her. And it was beautiful. It was so beautiful.

She flew for a long time, astounded by the beauty, soaking it in.

Yes. The cosmos was filled with terror and darkness and cruelty. But there was beauty too, she knew. There was so much beauty.

She kept flying until she saw her ahead—the *Lodestar.* Her ship. A starship shaped like an old sailing ship, navigating the cosmic ocean. The enemy saucers were still following the *Lodestar,* ten thousand of them. Ben-Ari had destroyed just one mothership.

But Earth is now roused, Ben-Ari thought. *Earth will now fight. And I will fight too.*

She overshot the enemy saucers, and she lowered herself to hover over the *Lodestar*. She descended slowly, then gently dipped into the ship's warp bubble, coming to fly alongside the *Lodestar*.

She tapped her communicator, and she spoke with a shaky voice, tears still in her eyes.

"Professor Isaac? Would it be all right if I had my ship back now?"

They opened an airlock for her. They gasped. They could not believe it. Ben-Ari stood in the airlock, legs shaking, her spacesuit charred, her body bleeding. She pulled off her helmet, and her hair was wet with sweat and blood.

He came running toward her. His black hair was disheveled. He raced toward her and pulled her into his arms. Her professor. Her Noah.

"I can't believe this," he whispered, holding her close. "I can't believe this!"

"I did it," she whispered. "Like you taught me. You saved my life."

Her knees buckled. He carried her in his arms to the sick bay. He held her hand and stroked her hair as the doctors tended to her, and she slept.

CHAPTER TWO

For most of his life, Marco had considered Addy his best friend, his sister-in-arms, the closest person to him in the world. A kind, wonderful woman who had become more than a friend. Who had become partner, lover, his second half. When he had finally formed this bond with her, it seemed that all his old pain had vanished, that she filled his life with light, joy, and love.

But after two weeks crammed with Addy inside a flying hippie van, he was ready to murder her.

"Addy, for Chrissake!" He pushed her wet laundry away from his face. "Must you hang your laundry all over the ship?" As he trudged across the starship, a wet sock hit his face, and he grimaced. "We have a dryer, you know."

The old Volkswagen looked cheery enough from the outside, its hull painted with flowers, peace signs, and psychedelic swirls. But on the inside, the starship was far less pleasant.

Addy had slung clotheslines across the hold, and her clothes hung everywhere, sopping wet, dripping onto the floor. It was like navigating through cobwebs. Even without the laundry, it was cluttered in here. Addy had crammed the starship full of her belongings: comic books, gun magazines, hockey memorabilia, a guitar she could barely play yet twanged on incessantly, and a real

Japanese katana, her prized possession. At the moment, a pile of potato chips and empty cigarette boxes buried the blade.

She's not fully human, Marco thought. *There's some pig DNA in there or I'm Kermit the Frog.*

"Addy!" he said. "Do you hear me? Dryer!"

Addy was lounging in the corner, reading a comic book and puffing on a cigar. Her bare feet were propped onto a pile of books—*his* books, the ones he had written. Her old helmet from the war, the words *Hell Patrol* scrawled across it, hung askew on her head. A box of chocolate chip cookies lay beside her, half empty. More laundry—these clothes dirty—covered the floor around her.

"The dryer makes my clothes shrink." She reached for a cookie, tossed it into her mouth, and flipped the page.

"Or maybe *you're* growing bigger." Marco grimaced as he ducked under a clothesline, narrowly dodging her wet underwear.

"No way!" Addy snorted. "I'm a petite, delicate rose." She belched.

Marco groaned. "The *Thunder Road* used to be a tidy ship. Now she's a flying garbage bin."

"I told you." Addy glowered. "Her name is *Shippy McShipface.*"

"That's a stupid name for a starship," Marco said.

"Yeah, well, *Shippy* thinks your name is stupid too."

Marco finally made it through the hanging laundry and reached the washroom. He pulled the door open, then closed it again. He spun back toward Addy. "You left the bathroom a mess. The shower curtains are open! You know that creates mold. And there are long blond hairs all over the shower walls. And—"

"Poet!" Addy finally rose to her feet. "For fuck's sake, you're not my mother." She walked toward him, deftly dodging the laundry, and puffed cigar smoke in his face. "You're a twenty-nine-year-old dude, but you're fussier than a stuffy old grandma."

"I'm just trying to keep things neat," Marco said. "This is a small ship, and the windows don't open. If mold gets in here, we—"

Addy groaned. "There's mold on your brain! God! Stop being a pest." She pointed with her cigar around the hold. "So yes, I hang sexy lingerie all over the place, and my beautiful long hair is visible everywhere with its golden radiance, and I leave delicious crumbs all over, but that's what makes this place a home, Marco."

"You forgot all the candy wrappers everywhere," he said.

Addy howled in frustration. "For God's sake!" She reached down, picked up a bunch of dirty laundry and candy wrappers, and dumped them onto Marco's head. "Here!" She picked up more trash and stuffed it down his shirt. "More junk!" She lifted a sweaty old shirt and pressed it against his face. "More laundry! God! Get dirty a little. And get off my ass!"

Marco stood very still, staring at her, her laundry and wrappers hanging across his shoulders. Addy stared back, chin raised, fists clenched, and her eyes shone with fury.

"Come on, take a swing at me," she said, a glint in her eye. "I dare you. I double dare you. Or are you chicken?"

Addy was a tall woman, strong, a warrior. Marco had fought many aliens in his life, and he was a decorated war hero, but he doubted even he could take Addy in a fight. Yet he would not back down. He stared steadily into her eyes, even as she puffed out her chest and brought her face close to his, snarling. They stood like two wrestlers about to brawl.

Finally Marco lifted a dirty sock—one that hung across his shoulder—and draped it across her head.

Addy gasped. She shoved him. "That means war!"

Marco stumbled back. He grabbed her hand, and they fell together onto a pile of laundry.

"War, war, war!" she said, dumping more and more items onto him—laundry, wrappers, magazines, anything that came to hand. When she tried to pull more items off a shelf, he grabbed her hands. He pulled her down.

"Enough, wild beast!" he said. "It's like sharing a spaceship with a tornado. It'll take hours to clean this up."

They lay together on the floor, side by side in the mess. Addy rolled toward him, grabbed his shoulders, and stared into his eyes.

"Clean later," she said. "Now sex."

"Or maybe we can clean first, and then our reward can—"

She silenced him with a deep kiss.

"Yes," he finally said when he came up for air. "Clean later."

They added the clothes they were wearing to the piles. They made hot, sweaty love in the cramped spaceship, leaving them panting, damp, and lying side by side. She nestled against him, her arm slung across his chest. Marco kissed her forehead.

As bad as this journey was, these hours were magical. At first it had felt awkward. They would laugh nervously during their lovemaking. After so many years as friends, it felt ridiculous to become lovers. But it also felt right. It felt meant to be. It felt wonderful.

Marco stroked her long blond hair.

I love you, Addy, he thought. *I've always loved you. Everything that I've lived through—the other women, my marriage, my divorce—it all led to you. You and I were always meant to be. You are infuriating, and messy, and uncouth, and I love you more than anyone I've ever loved. You are beautiful. You are strong. You are—*

He winced. "Ow, Addy, your elbow! It's digging into my ribs!"

She dug it deeper, struggling to reach across him. "I see cookies!"

He grunted with pain as her elbow moved to poke his stomach. "I'll get them for you. God! You're crushing my pancreas."

"No need." Finally, after kneeing him in the groin and nearly suffocating him under her body, she reached the cookies and wriggled back to his side. She stuffed two into her mouth and offered him one. "Cookie?"

"How don't you weigh a million pounds by now?" he asked, dusting off crumbs.

She shrugged. "I burn lots of calories." She swallowed and nodded. "All right. Another round."

"I—"

"Hush and obey!"

Dutifully, he obeyed.

Finally, after a long shared shower—most of it involving Marco spraying her hair off the walls—they headed back into the cockpit. They sat down in the tattered upholstered seats. They were almost at their destination.

"Durmia," Marco said, gazing into the distance. "We're only a few hours away. From peace. From wisdom. From true awareness and spiritual enlightenment."

"And from elephant men with two trunks!" Addy nodded eagerly.

Marco picked up the book, the one Addy had been carrying around for the past year. *The Way of Deep Being* by Guru Baba Mahanisha. It was a thick tome, one Addy had rarely parted from back in Greece. The front cover showed an intricate mandala. The back showed a photograph of the author. The baba was a Durmian, a rare breed of alien. The Durmians had stocky humanoid bodies, four arms, and elephantine heads with two trunks. In his photo, Baba Mahanisha was sitting cross-legged, draped in robes, deep in meditation. Marco had spent the past two weeks reading the book. It was a slow read. Each chapter demanded grueling exercises in meditation and yoga.

"I've been making some progress, I think," Marco said. "But I'm still working my way through chapter five. If the baba agrees to teach us in person, I'm sure I can improve. I have so many unanswered questions."

Addy nodded. "Me too!"

Marco opened the book and flipped through the pages. "This exercise here. Where you have to imagine that you're looking at yourself through another's eyes. He says you're supposed to feel a shift of consciousness, as if you're no longer inside your own head—indeed, that you have no head at all. I can't get it to work. Can you?"

Addy nodded. "Oh yeah, all the time. It's easy!"

"Really?" Marco blew out his breath. "Well, you've been practicing for longer than me. I'm only two weeks into this, and you've been reading this book for a year now. What about chapter four? Have you tried imagining a hole on top of your head, like a whale's blowhole, and the breath passing between your head and toes, until your body disappears entirely, and you're only the breath? The baba says it can take an hour of meditation to reach this stage. I tried for an hour once, and I'm not sure it worked."

She patted his thigh. "You'll get better at it. Soon you'll be an expert like me."

Marco frowned at her. He bit his lip. "How about chapter five? Have you succeeded at staring into a candle's flame until the fire seems to disappear, even though it still burns?"

"Oh yeah, I do that one all the time." Addy nodded. "No problem. I make the fire disappear at will."

"I made up that last one," Marco said.

Addy stared at him. "Bullshit!" She snatched the book from him and flipped through the pages. "Ugh. What happened to the chapter about candles?"

"Addy!" Marco groaned. "For Chrissake. You've been carrying this book around for a year! Have you even read it?" He slapped his forehead. "I knew that the lack of crumbs and stains on the pages was a giveaway."

Addy bristled. "Of course I've read it! What do you think I am? Some kinda illiti … illeta … nonreading person?"

"I can't believe this." Marco stared outside the viewport at the approaching star. "We're almost at Durmia. We spent all our money on this journey to find the baba and study Deep Being. Because *you* recommended it. Because you've been lugging this book around for a year, telling everyone about the elephant baba. And now I learn you didn't even read the book!"

"I read it a million times!" Addy said. "Just … not exactly *that* book." She stared down at her lap, twisting her fingers.

"Addy." He grabbed her shoulder. "Look at me, Addy. What book did you read?"

She winced. "Promise you won't get angry."

"I promise."

"Promise you won't yell."

"I promise, Addy."

She groaned. "Fine. Fine!" She reached into the backpack at her feet and pulled out another book. "*This* is my favorite book. *This* is the one I've been reading all year in Greece. Okay? Happy now?"

Marco took the book from her. His eyes widened. He read the title aloud, incredulous. "*Freaks of the Galaxy.*"

Addy nodded. "Second edition."

Marco's jaw unhinged. The back cover showed the same photograph from *The Way of Deep Being*—a Durmian deep in meditation, an elephantine alien with two trunks. When Marco opened the book, he saw photos of many other aliens, each weirder than the one before. There was a humanoid alien with two heads. A race of conjoined-twin aliens. An alien with lobster claws. A hundred others. He kept flipping the pages, unable to believe this.

"Ooh, ooh, that one is my favorite!" Addy pointed at a page. "The Pillowman!"

The page showed an alien with no limbs, just a torso with a head. The unfortunate fellow was smoking a cigarette.

"The Pillowman," Marco said, voice flat.

Addy nodded excitedly. "He can roll cigarettes with just his mouth!"

Marco slammed the book shut. "Addy, for Chrissake. Do you even care about meditation, or is this all just a freak show for you?"

"I think the freaks are wonderful." Addy nodded. "I love them. And the Elephant Baba is my favorite from the book. Well, my favorite along with the Pillowman. So when I found another book about him, I had to buy it. That's how I found out that the Elephant Baba also teaches meditation, and I thought it would be good to see him in person."

"I can't believe this. I can't!" Marco rose from his seat. He paced the spaceship. "You told me we're coming to study enlightenment. But you just wanted to see a freak from your book!"

"The *best* freak!" Addy said, chasing him. "A real life Elephant Man. Like from my favorite movie!" She raised her chin, held up her fist, and spoke in dramatic baritone, quoting the film. "I am not an elephant! I am not an animal! *I am a human being!*"

"You're a bloody loony," Marco said. "So you don't even know how to meditate?"

Addy shook her head. "Not a clue."

Marco tugged his hair. "But we meditated together! What the hell were you thinking of during those hours with our eyes closed?"

She shrugged. "You know, the usual. Hockey, cartoons, sex ... Sometimes I'd wander off for half an hour, grab a snack, come back, and you were still there with your eyes closed. You didn't even know I left." She grinned. "I liked watching you meditate, being all cute and quiet."

He let out a yowl. "I'll show you cute and quiet! Bloody hell, Addy. This spaceship cost me every last dime I kept after my divorce. We could have bought another house on Earth!"

She nodded. "And then you'd be the same miserable old bastard you always were." She placed her hands on his shoulders. "Look, Poet. Maybe I only found out about the baba from my freak book. But he *does* have wisdom to teach. He can help you— us!—find peace. I believe that. We need that." Her eyes dampened. "I don't want it to be like in Haven. Dealing with shell shock and nightmares. I know you still get nightmares. I do too. We both saw too much shit. We both suffered too much. And if the baba can teach us inner peace, well, it'll be worth it."

Marco sighed. "Oh, Addy. You really are a nut."

She grinned. "That's the way you love me though, right?"

"You're not bringing *Freaks of the Galaxy* with us to meet the baba, you know."

She gasped. "But it's my favorite book!"

"And what if Baba Mahanisha sees it? If he learns he's in a freak book?"

Addy shrugged. "Maybe he'd be happy. He's in the same book as Pillowman! I'd be honored."

"You're a bigger freak than all of them," Marco muttered.

She nodded. "If I keep eating cookies, I will be. Addy, the Amazing Blob Girl! Mmm … cookies." She pulled one out of her pocket and began to munch.

Marco sighed. He looked out the viewport. The planet Durmia was visible now, green around the equator, white at the poles, tan between. A peaceful, Earthlike planet. Wikipedia Galactica's entry on Durmia was only a stub, giving the planet's dimensions and chemistry but nothing more. Marco only knew what Durmians looked like based on the photo on Addy's books. Were these aliens technologically advanced? Urban or rural? Friendly or fearful? As far as he knew, no humans had ever visited this world.

We come as meditation students, but also as explorers, he thought.

He turned back toward Addy. She had torn into a bag of Bugles now, and had put the conical snacks on her fingertips like ten salty claws. He smiled and placed a hand on her thigh.

"I'm glad we're doing this," he said.

She smiled and mussed his head. "Me too."

He cringed. "Addy, you got Bugles in my hair."

Yet despite his groan, and despite Addy licking crumbs from his hair, he was happy. He had never been happier.

I'm with my other half. I'm with Addy.

And yet, just below that joy, terror lurked.

He still remembered Kemi dying in his arms. He remembered the foul Malphas, lord of the marauders, murdering Anisha and his father. He remembered his friends—Elvis, Beast, Singh, Diaz, Caveman, Jackass, so many others—dying around him in the wars. And whenever he was with Addy, whenever they laughed, hugged, made love, that fear was still there. Buried, but still there, always threatening to bubble up.

I can't bear to lose you too, Addy, he thought. *I want to grow old with you, but monsters fill the cosmos, and I'm scared.*

Addy placed her hand on his, and she smiled at him.

I know, her eyes said. *We're together. It will be good.*

And when she looked at him like that, Marco saw that beyond the mask she wore, there was deep wisdom and kindness. On the surface, she was all cigar smoke, cookie crumbs, dirty laundry, swinging katanas, Bugle claws, curses and belches and books about freaks, a crazy little tornado destroying everything in its path. But Marco knew that was just an act. When they gazed into each other's eyes, silent, they said more than words. He saw the true Addy then—the courageous, noble woman he loved. And it eased his fear.

"All right, let's prep this puppy for landing," Marco said. "According to your book, we should land in—"

A light blinked on the dashboard, and an alarm beeped.

Marco frowned and glanced at Addy.

She opened her mouth to speak, and—

The saucer came charging from the darkness, guns blazing. Blasts slammed into the *Thunder Road*, tossing the small starship into a spin, nearly ripping open the hull.

For an instant—panic.

For an instant—frozen dread.

Then Marco gripped the controls.

"Addy, I fly, you fire!" he shouted.

"Roger that!" she shouted, pulled the triggers, and bullets flew from the *Thunder Road*'s front cannon.

She was firing aimlessly. The saucer was out of view. The *Thunder Road* was still spinning madly, and Marco wrestled with the yoke, struggling to steady the ship. Lights flashed all around. More blasts flew their way, and explosions filled space around them. Marco glanced at the ship's radar, desperate to locate the enemy, but piles of comic books and candy wrappers covered the display. With a groan, he swiped them off.

Another blast hit the *Thunder Road*.

The ship jostled, and smoke filled the cockpit. Books and food fell off the shelves. Again they were spinning madly.

"They're destroying *Shippy McShipface!*" Addy cried.

"The ship is called *Thunder Road*, damn it!" Marco shouted, finally steadying them again. "And get those Bugles off your fingers!"

Alarms blared. The front viewport was cracked. He could barely see a thing. He glanced again at the radar, brushing off crumbs.

There.

He saw it.

A bleep on the radar—just one ship.

Sneering, he spun to face it.

"Get 'em, Ads!"

She pulled the triggers again.

Massive bullets flew from the ship's twin railguns, moving at hypersonic speed. Marco kept spinning the prow, and a curtain of their bullets blazed out.

The saucer charged toward them, swerving around the bullets.

Marco sneered and flew toward it, taking it head-on.

Laser blasts flew their way.

Marco swooped, then raised the *Thunder Road*'s nose, soaring toward the enemy.

Addy's railguns pounded the saucer with electromagnetic destruction.

Holes burst open in the enemy ship. Fire blazed. Railguns made regular machine guns seem like peashooters, and their bullets tore through the enemy like meteors ripping through clouds.

"Fuck yeah, I love these guns!" Addy shouted.

She fired again.

More bullets pummeled the saucer. More explosions rocked the enemy ship, and its hull cracked open.

Marco flew higher, dodging shrapnel. He glimpsed several grays float out from their cracked vessel. The creatures careened through space, most already dead, only one still floundering. Marco and Addy watched.

"What the hell are those things?" Marco whispered.

Addy stared with hard eyes, and her lips peeled back with a snarl. "It's the bastards who kidnapped Steve. Who broke his soul. I hate them. I fucking hate them."

She prepared to fire again, to slay the living gray that floated through space. But Marco placed a hand on her arm.

"Let's save our bullets," he said. "He'll be dead in a moment. And more saucers might show up."

Addy turned toward him, and Marco was taken aback. Her eyes were red and damp. Her fists were shaking. Her cheeks flushed a furious crimson.

"I hate these bastards," she whispered, jaw clenched. "More goddamn, fucking aliens after us. Can't they leave us alone? Can't those bastards ever leave us alone?" She looked at the floating alien corpses outside. Her voice rose to a shout. "Who are you? What do you want?"

Outside, the wounded gray stopped moving. He floated among the corpses of his comrades.

"Addy." Marco put a hand on her shoulder. "Addy, it's all right. They're dead. They're gone. It's all right."

Tears flowed down her cheeks. She turned toward Marco and embraced him. He held her in his arms, and he stroked her hair.

"I hate fighting," she whispered. "I hate it. I want it all to stop."

He kissed her forehead. "I know. I hate it too."

He wanted to tell her they would never fight again. That they would finally find peace. But it was a lie. She would know it was a lie. The galaxy was vast, dark, and full of monsters. Life in the cosmos was an eternal Darwinian struggle. He and Addy were the survivors. But every year of life, they had fought, bled, suffered. And perhaps for every year still ahead, they would have to bleed again. He had no words of comfort for Addy, so he only held her in his arms.

When there is no cure for what hurts us, there is still comfort in love, he thought.

"All right," Addy finally said, wiping her eyes. "Let's land *Shippy McShipface* and see how badly her hull is damaged. I—"

The ship jolted.

A thud reverberated through the hull.

Marco frowned.

"That wasn't an attack," he said. "Something hit us. Some debris from the battle, maybe, and—"

A red light flashed on the dashboard. A message appeared on the display: *Airlock Open.*

Marco and Addy didn't waste a second. They grabbed their oxygen masks from under their seats. Addy grabbed the pistol she kept there too. They leaped out of the cockpit, leaving the ship to float aimlessly, and raced into the hold.

The airlock contained two doors around a controlled pressure room. The outer door had opened, letting the air blast out into space. The inner door was rattling.

"There's something in the pressure room," Marco whispered.

"One of them." Addy raised her pistol. "One of those gray sneaky fucks survived the saucer's explosion. You should have let me shoot him."

The door's handle shook madly, then tore free.

The door creaked open.

Damn! The alien hadn't even closed the outer door. Marco was thankful for his oxygen mask. Air began whooshing out of the ship. Candy wrappers, books, clothes, and countless other items flew everywhere, funneling toward the airlock.

Addy fired her pistol.

A creature screamed.

A shadow leaped.

Alarms blared across the ship, and a robotic voice intoned: "Losing pressure, losing pressure!"

Marco could barely see past the storm of debris flying everywhere. He made out a towering creature, easily seven feet tall, clad in a black space suit. Addy stepped back, gripping her pistol with both hands, still firing. The lights died, came back on, died again. The creature reached out toward her, claws glinting.

A gray.

The bullets didn't even faze it. The air kept rushing out of the ship. Addy kept firing until her gun clicked, and the creature reached out, grabbed her, and she screamed.

Marco stared in horror.

No. No. His head spun. *I won't lose you. No!*

Every step was a struggle. The debris flew against him. He reached out blindly, and he grabbed one of the clotheslines Addy had slung across the hold. He shook off her wet clothes.

"Die now ..." the creature hissed, leaning over Addy. "Die, human ..."

Marco leaped forward, vaulted off a fallen shelf, and slung the rope around the gray's neck.

He yanked back with all his strength.

It was like trying to take down a horse. The gray dwarfed him, his massive head grazing the ceiling. The creature thrashed, struggling to tear off the clothesline. Marco clung hard. The gray lurched forward, pulling Marco off the ground. But Marco clung on, pulling the clothesline back, and the creature gurgled, unable to scream. Marco piggybacked, clinging on hard, twisting the garrote.

The gray released Addy. She struggled to her feet. Items were still flying everywhere as the air shrieked out of the ship.

A shelf overturned.

The katana came flying toward the airlock.

Addy reached out and grabbed the sword in midair.

She drew the blade and swung with both hands.

The katana sliced through the gray's belly, and blood and entrails spurted.

Marco released the rope, fell to the floor, and stumbled toward the airlock. He slammed himself against the door, groaning, and slammed it shut.

He fell to his knees, gasping. His oxygen mask kept air flowing into him, but the pressure was so low that his skin was blistering. He shuddered as the cabin's life-support system pumped more air into the hold.

"Addy," he gasped, limping toward her.

She stood before him, eyes hard. The gray knelt before her, clutching his belly, still alive.

And the creature began to laugh.

"You weak, pathetic ape!" the gray hissed. "You do not know the pain that awaits you. You do not know the wrath of my goddess. But you will. You will, ape. You will scream!"

Addy raised her katana high.

"Addy, no!" Marco shouted.

He tried to stop her, but he was too slow. Addy plunged the blade into the gray's chest, and the tip burst out from his back.

Marco stared, panting. Damn it! He had wanted to interrogate the gray. It was useless dead. Anger filled him, but when he looked back up at Addy, that anger melted.

She dropped her sword. She stared at Marco, blood covering her—the soldier again. Her eyes were dry now. Filled with cold fire. Eyes harder than her sword's steel. They were the eyes of a killer.

This is how she looked in the wars, Marco thought. *This is the famous Addison Linden who led the rebellion against the marauders.*

He stepped around the corpse of the gray and held her hand.

"You all right, Ads?"

She nodded. "Yeah. Fucker caught me off guard is all." She snorted. "Chose the wrong ship to break into."

Marco smiled thinly. "Only a ship with two of Earth's most infamous soldiers, right?"

And suddenly Addy was crying. Her body shook with sobs. Marco wrapped her in an embrace.

"I wanted this to be over," she whispered, trembling in his arms. "I never wanted to be that woman again. The warrior. The killer. The veteran with scars on my body, a brand of my slavery on my hip, a heart of steel and fire. I wanted to be silly Addy who eats cookies, who reads comics, who jokes around. Not this person again. Damn it, why do they keep pulling us in?"

Marco wiped away her tears. "They can't change who you are, Addy. Not the person deep down inside you. The person I know and love."

She gasped, and a smile broke through her tears. "So you love how I get cookie crumbs everywhere?"

He shifted uncomfortably. "Well, I didn't say that—"

"And you love how my hairs get on the shower wall?"

"Definitely n—"

"And I know you love how I hang laundry everywhere!" Addy said, grinning now. "And my laundry saved your life. Saved your life, Poet! If not for my clothesline, that creature would have gotten you for sure."

"Actually, the gray was after *you*," he reminded her. He sighed. "But okay. I forgive you for the laundry."

"And the cookie crumbs," she reminded him.

"And the cookie crumbs," he agreed.

"And my book about freaks."

Marco held up a finger, hushing her. "Don't push your luck, Linden."

They blasted the dead gray out of the airlock. Sadly, most of their food and supplies had been lost to space too. But there, just below them, Durmia awaited. A new planet. A place that perhaps could teach them wisdom and peace.

And maybe more about these creatures, Marco dared to hope.

The small, battered ship dived toward the new world, leaving the wreckage of its enemy above.

CHAPTER THREE

Epimetheus barked madly, tail in a straight line, as the saucers pursued.

"I know, I know!" Lailani said. "I'm flying as fast as I can!" She looked over her shoulder. "HOBBS, you still with us, buddy?"

The ESS *Ryujin*, Lailani's small spaceship, was dented and rattling, wounded in battle, fleeing for its life. She had retrieved the azoth hourglass, a powerful artifact, from the jungle world of Mahatek. It was in her backpack, wrapped in cloth, jangling as the ship veered left and right. Yet Lailani could not use the artifact to bend time, not without careful calculations and robotic precision.

And her robot, which contained the hourglass's algorithms, lay dying.

Dying. Yes. For he was no true robot. HOBBS, Lailani had learned, was a cyborg, and inside his chest beat a human heart.

"Hang in there, Hobster!" she said. "All right, buddy?"

The cyborg did not reply. He was a hulking creation, tall like a basketball player and wide like a wrestler, a beast of hardened steel and brute power. Yet now he lay on the floor, unconscious, his eyes dim. His body was dented, cracked open, exposing the arteries within. Lailani had taped shut the punctured arteries, and his blood still flowed, but slowly. Too slowly. His heartbeat was too weak, his body too broken.

I must find his master, Lailani thought. *I must repair him. Only HOBBS can tell me how to use the hourglass.* Her eyes dampened. *And he's my friend.*

Alarms blared on the *Ryujin*'s controls.

"Enemy ships approach," intoned a robotic voice from the starship's systems. "Hostile ships approach. Hostile—"

Lailani switched off the sound.

"I know!" she shouted. "Damn it!"

She saw them in the radar. Sixteen of the buggers. Saucers.

She had met them before. She had fought them at JEX's junkyard, then again in the jungle of Mahatek. She had fought Abyzou himself, their prince, had heard the truth from his own mouth. The grays were no aliens. They were highly evolved humans—humans from a million years in the future, a time when Earth no longer existed.

And they wanted Earth in this timeline. Lailani's Earth.

They also wanted a monopoly on time travel.

"But you can't have my hourglass," Lailani said. "I need it to travel back. To save Elvis, my friend whom I killed." She rubbed her tears. Those goddamn tears. "I'm going to do this. I'm going to escape you, grays. I'm going to heal you, HOBBS. And I'm going back in time to save you, Elvis, Sofia, Beast, Caveman, Kemi, all my friends that I lost."

She shoved down the throttle as far as it would go. She stormed forward, traveling faster than light. Behind her, the saucers followed.

And they were gaining.

Soon they were more than bleeps on the radar. Soon she could see them through the rear viewport. Sixteen massive ships, each the size of a soccer stadium, large enough to easily swallow the RV-sized *Ryujin*.

"Come on, faster, faster!" Lailani said, shoving the throttle. She could barely even reach the damn controls. This ship, obviously, wasn't built for a four-foot-ten woman who drowned in her seat, whose feet didn't even reach the floor.

At her side, Epimetheus growled, ready for a battle. Lailani reached out and gave him a reassuring pat—mostly to reassure herself. Her Doberman was only a year old, but he already outweighed her. He had fought at her side all his life, saving her from sinking into madness and pain. Yet how could Epi help her now?

The saucers flew closer.

Closer still.

"Damn it!" Lailani shouted. Last time the saucers had chased her, she had lost them in an asteroid field. But there was nary a pebble for light-years around this area of space.

Blasts flew from the saucers.

Lailani cursed and dipped, and a bolt skimmed *Ryujin*'s roof. The hull heated up and creaked. Another blast hit their side, and they careened. Lailani gripped the controls with all her might, struggling to steady their flight.

She zigzagged, flew up and down, swooped and spun, but she couldn't dodge the enemy. Not here in open space. Not with those ships faster than her.

A third blast hit the back of the *Ryujin*, and smoke filled the cabin, and fire roared. The engines jolted and coughed and belched out flame. The artificial gravity died, and objects floated across the *Ryujin*. Lailani started to float, grabbed the armrest, and cursed the lack of seat belts.

"Fuck, fuck, fuck!" She groaned. "I have no asteroids to hide behind. I'm flying as fast as I can. I can't fight them all. And there's no world for light-years around. I need to go faster. Faster! Warp speed isn't fast enough. I need—"

A wormhole, she thought, inhaling sharply.

She dipped sharply, dodging another volley. Missiles exploded overhead. The saucers stormed closer.

A wormhole. Of course! During the Marauder War, she had flown through wormholes, traveling the ancient Tree of Light, a celestial network of highways built by ancient aliens. A wormhole could transport her many light-years within instants.

Another blast flew.

A missile burst overhead, raining shrapnel onto the *Ryujin*, nearly piercing the hull.

"Epi, where's my damn tablet?" Lailani shouted. "I have a map of the Tree of Light there. Epi, fetch tablet!"

With the gravity dead, everything was floating through the ship: her pens, Marco's books, the framed photograph of her platoon, her mug, a blob of spilled hot chocolate, an assortment of weapons, and a hundred other items. Where was her damn tablet?

"Epi, tablet!" she said. "Fetch!"

Loyal Epimetheus leaped into action. The Doberman floated through the ship, dog-paddling through zero gravity. With his snout, he sorted through the floating items, finally retrieving her tablet. He swam back toward her, tablet in mouth.

She grabbed it and wiped off his drool.

Another blast flew from the saucers. Lailani swerved, narrowly dodging the blow.

She floated up from her seat—and away from the controls.

Damn it!

She grabbed the seat with one hand, pulling herself back down, but had to release the tablet. It floated away again.

Crap!

She needed at least four hands for this. She couldn't fly, hold herself down, and operate the tablet at once. She groaned, gripped the controls with both hands, and focused on dodging the new volley. The saucers kept gaining on her. Soon they were almost close enough to ram her.

"Epi, hold me down!" she said. "Paws on my shoulders!"

She wasn't sure he understood. He was a genius, of course, but still just a dog. She released the controls for a moment, gripped his paws, and pulled them onto her shoulders.

"Like this! Hold me down."

Thankfully, he seemed to understand. The beast weighed over a hundred pounds, and he pinned her into her seat, shoving against the ceiling with his legs.

Lailani flew with one hand, operating her tablet with the other. A hologram bloomed out from the tablet, displaying the Tree of Light, the galactic pathway of wormholes. Her friend Keemaji had drawn this map for her. She wished he were here; his four arms would have come in handy.

"There!" Lailani said, pointing at a spot in the hologram. "An entrance to the network! Only a fraction of a light-year away." She winced. "Even at warp speed, with a small and fast ship like this, it'll take a good fifteen minutes to get there." She tugged the yoke, changing course. "No choice, Epi. We're gonna have to survive it. Get ready for a hell run."

She twisted knobs, lowering the life support to a minimum.

With a grimace, she shut off all power to the shields.

She diverted every last drop of power to *speed*.

They stormed forth.

Behind, the saucers followed.

When HOBBS had been conscious, he had been able to lean out the airlock, firing missiles at enemies. Lailani still had her front cannons, but she dared not turn around to engage the enemy. She focused on flying forward, just to reach that wormhole, to vanish into the labyrinth.

Another blast grazed them, chipping a wing.

The seconds ticked down.

"God damn it."

She'd have to fight from the airlock herself.

That left her without a pilot. Epi still struggled with *roll over*; she doubted she could train him to fly.

But maybe …

She nodded.

She typed madly, coding a quick algorithm. It would fly the *Ryujin* in a random zigzagging pattern. It wasn't accurate. It wouldn't know how to dodge specific attacks. It largely relied on luck.

It would have to do.

She activated the algorithm, and the *Ryujin* began zigzagging forth, jerking madly from side to side.

Lailani leaped out from her seat, dived through the hull, and swam through zero gravity toward the closet. She pulled on her spacesuit as the ship swerved through space, as the enemy fire flew above and below them.

She knelt over HOBBS. The cyborg was still unconscious.

"Sorry, buddy," she whispered, bringing a screwdriver to his shoulder.

It couldn't have taken more than two minutes. It seemed two lifetimes. Finally she had unscrewed the missile launcher from his shoulder. She raced toward the airlock, leaned out into space, and saw the saucers in the distance.

She aimed.

Her missile launcher locked on a target.

She fired.

The *Ryujin* jerked, her zigzagging algorithm yanking it roughly to the left.

Lailani's missile flew wide and missed.

She cursed.

A laser blast flew her way. She pulled back into the airlock, and the enemy fire raged only meters away, blinding her, melting the plastic buckles on her spacesuit.

She reloaded her missile launcher. She aimed. A beep sounded—locked on target.

She fired.

This time she hit.

An explosion rocked a saucer. The enemy ship veered off course and slammed into another vessel. Lailani fired again, hitting the tilting saucers, and explosions shook them.

The two saucers fell apart, showering shrapnel over the rest of the enemy fleet.

Lailani whooped, raced back to the cockpit, and tweaked her flight. The wormhole was closer now. She was ten minutes away.

Metal shattered.

A blast skimmed the *Ryujin*'s belly, searing through the hull, exposing them to space.

Air shrieked, spilling out into the vacuum.

Fuck!

Lailani raced toward the breached hull, rummaged through the closet, and found her emergency sealing kit. Thankfully, the breach was only the size of a bullet hole. She worked in a fervor, sealing the breach. She was wearing a space suit. Epimetheus was not. She managed to lock in enough air, but she had to race back to the cockpit, to ramp up the air production, and that cost them speed, and more blasts were flying.

She leaped back into the airlock.

She fired another missile. She fired again. She hit a saucer.

She raced back to the cockpit. There was enough air now. She switched off life support, giving them a boost of speed. They roared forth. Three minutes to arrival.

A blast slammed against their back, and the auto-pilot system died.

Lailani yowled in frustration. She gripped the controls and focused on flying. No more fighting for now.

They stormed forth. The saucers grew closer. Closer. Soon they were only a kilometer away. Then mere meters away.

A saucer rammed into the *Ryujin*.

Her tiny starship jolted forward.

Saucers flew all around her, zipping above, below, at her sides.

They want me alive, she realized. *They're just trying to cripple me, not kill me yet*. She sneered. *They won't catch me.*

A saucer dived down before her. Lailani fired her front cannons, blasting her way through.

There! She saw it ahead! The wormhole portal shimmered in space like a nebula.

Saucers moved to block the *Ryujin*'s path.

Lailani screamed as she flew, switching all power to her cannons, leaving her engines dead.

Her ship was small but furious. Her volley slammed into the saucers ahead, knocking them off course.

Lailani diverted full power to her engines, even shutting down life support. She flew forward, barrel-rolling between several saucers. She scraped against their hulls. The *Ryujin* screamed in protest. Sparks flew. Her hull dented. Smoke filled the cabin.

She burst through.

Cracked, dented, leaking fire and smoke, the *Ryujin* plunged into the wormhole.

Lailani switched life support back on, raised her visor, and gulped air.

Lights shimmered around her. The small starship flew through the wormhole, moving at incredible speed through sparkling luminescence.

And behind her, the saucers followed.

Damn it! She had hoped they wouldn't fit. But this tunnel was wide, and at least a dozen of the bastards were now flying after her through the portal.

She traveled fifty light-years within moments.

She burst back out into open space.

She shoved down the throttle, roaring toward the next portal.

The Tree of Light had been built like a subway system, and there were many stations along the paths. Nobody knew who had built this ancient network; the alien architects had vanished long ago. Today many species used these highways, and as Lailani flew toward another porthole, she saw a variety of alien starships. Some looked like massive dragonflies, their wings formed of solar panels. Other starships were bulky cubes. Some were giant spheres of light, spinning madly, while some looked like terrariums, filled with alien plants. A few starships were more like aquariums, built for aquatic aliens. One ship looked like a feathery starfish. Some were giant; other starships were the size of shoe boxes.

Lailani didn't recognize these species. She had no time to pay close attention. She zipped between her fellow travelers, and the grays followed.

Three more wormhole openings hovered ahead. Each portal would lead to another location in the galaxy. Lailani chose the busiest portal, whizzing her way among the other starships waiting to enter. She would have to toss courtesy aside today and cut in line.

"Coming through, coming through!" she shouted, wishing she had a horn to honk.

Behind her, one of the pursuing saucers slammed into an alien starship.

The alien ship—a hulking metal machine, all sharp angles and jagged cannons—did not respond kindly. Soon the saucer and bulky aliens were exchanging fire.

Lailani dived into another wormhole.

She flew through the shimmering tunnel.

Behind her, several saucers still followed.

She burst out thirty light-years away and roared forth, heading toward another wormhole.

Again she flew through a tunnel of light. Again she zipped between alien starships, trying to shake pursuit, and chose another path.

At each intersection, she managed to stir some trouble. She was small and agile, able to whisk around the larger starships traveling the Tree of Light. Again a pursuing saucer crashed into an alien starship. Again a battle raged behind her, the enraged aliens blasting fire at the saucer that had crashed into them.

"That's me, Epi," Lailani said. "Instigator of galactic road rage. Now to finally lose those bastards."

As a battle raged behind her, as smoke and fire hid the *Ryujin*, she chose one of seven shimmering wormholes ahead. The battle, she dared to hope, would hide which path she chose.

She vanished into the tunnel, plunged through light, and emerged by a distant star system.

Nobody followed.

Finally she had shaken the pursuit.

She slumped back in her seat, breathing heavily, and rose to hover in the cockpit.

For long moments, as the *Ryujin* floated in space, Lailani merely floated in the cockpit, just breathing. Her pulse gradually slowed down. Against all odds, she was alive.

"Epi," she said, "we really need to install seat belts here. And some cannons on the back."

The Doberman licked her face in agreement.

She floated into the hold and checked on HOBBS. He was still alive, but barely. He was unconscious, his pulse slow. During the flight, he had banged against the walls, which couldn't have helped.

"Don't worry, Hobster," she said. "I'm going to find your maker. He'll fix you. You'll see. Just hang in there a little longer, buddy."

They flew onward, gliding from wormhole to wormhole, as HOBBS's heart struggled for each beat, as the starship leaked air, and as the saucers filled the galaxy with their evil.

CHAPTER FOUR

The *Thunder Road* flew through blue skies, gliding over the verdant lands of Durmia. The Volkswagen rattled, and the windshield was cracked, but Marco still found the view breathtaking.

"It's beautiful," he said softly. "It's one of the most beautiful places I've seen. I've never seen such—Addy!" He pushed her feet away. "God, feet away from my nose! They stink. And they're hiding my view."

"They do not stink, and they're not on your nose. They're on the dashboard." Addy leaned back, stretching out her legs. "It's not my fault that I'm so tall and have such long, lovely legs."

He groaned and wrestled with her feet for a moment, finally managing to remove them from the dashboard. "God, you must be fucking delightful on coach flights." He gazed back outside. "Now put down that stupid freak book and enjoy the view. We'll be landing soon, and it's our last chance to see the landscape from above."

"Don't call it my stupid freak book. That's offensive." Addy hugged the book to her chest. "It's *Freaks of the Galaxy: Second Edition*. A serious work of literature." She tapped her chin. "You know, Poet, maybe you'd sell more books if you wrote about freaks. People love freaks."

"Fine," Marco said. "My next book, I'll make you the main character."

"That's the spirit!" She frowned. "Hey."

Marco returned to the view, trying to enjoy it—and ignore the sound of Addy popping bubble gum and drumming on the dashboard. Hills rolled below, draped with forests. A river snaked across the land, silver in the sunlight. Golden mountains soared on the horizon. A pristine world, warm and lush.

Yet as they kept flying, his stomach curdled.

"Addy," he said.

She was flipping through her book. "Huh? Are we there yet?"

He frowned. "Addy. Addy!" He pulled her book down. "Look. Look below."

She leaned forward and peered down. She frowned. "Poet!" She turned toward him, face crinkled up. "You took us to the wrong planet!"

He slumped in his seat. "This is the right place, Ads. But we might be too late."

Below them spread ruins.

It had been a city once, eras ago. There was little left now. Most of the homes had fallen, were only scattered bits of walls like a shattered labyrinth. A fortress rose on a hill, two of its towers fallen on the hillside. A villa or perhaps a temple stood on another hill, its dome pockmarked and cracked. Colossal statues lay fallen, half-buried in the earth. Nature had been reclaiming the ruins. Weeds sprouted between the bricks. Trees grew along the streets and through broken roofs, their roots clutching the ruins like wooden fists. If any Durmians still lived here, they were well hidden. Aside from the plants and several birdlike aliens, Marco saw no life, certainly no elephantine humanoids.

Marco looked back at Addy. "Ads, how old is your book?"

"*Freaks of the Galaxy*?"

"Not *Freaks of the Galaxy*! God!" He groaned. "*The Way of Deep Being*. The book by Baba Mahanisha. You know, the reason we're here?"

She shrugged. "I dunno. A year or two maybe?" She lifted the book. "There! Printed 2152. Just two years old."

Marco stared at her, slack-jawed. "Addy! That's the year it was *printed*. When was it *written*?"

She blinked at him. "Those are different dates?"

Marco let out the loudest, longest groan of his life. "Addy! For fuck's sake. Tell me this book isn't as ancient as the Bible, that we didn't come here seeking a guru who died when Confucius was a baby."

"Confy-who?"

He slapped his forehead. "God. God, Addy. Your guru must have died thousands of years ago! We came all this way for nothing. And we lost all our supplies when the grays attacked. We don't even have enough food or water to get us back to Earth."

She frowned. "I'm not going back to Earth. We came all this way to study from the guru."

He pointed at her. "*You* came all this way because you wanted to see an elephant with two trunks. *I* actually wanted to learn something spiritual. Instead I just find rubble."

Her cheeks flushed, and her eyes narrowed. "Hey, don't you point that finger at me. You're the author. You're the one who should know about book dates and stuff. You're the smart one, remember? I'm just the leggy, beautiful, brave, strong, funny, and famous one."

"You're the one with half a cookie stuck on her cheek," he muttered.

She gasped and plucked it off. "Mmm, face-cookie!" She tossed it into her mouth.

Marco wanted to scold her. To roll his eyes. To groan. Maybe even to yell. But when he looked at Addy, he couldn't stay mad.

She's hurt, he knew. *Here is the woman who fought the scum in the mines of Corpus and the hives of Abaddon. The woman who survived captivity and torture on a marauder ship, who had raised Earth in rebellion. The woman who led hundreds of thousands in war, who fought alien tyrants, who saved the world. The woman I love. The love of my life. So let her be silly today. Let her eat her cookies, and put her feet on the dashboard, and be a girl again. Let her find some happiness after suffering so much pain.*

"Why are you looking at me all weird-like?" she said.

He reached out and patted her knee. "I love you, Addy. You know that, right?"

She grinned. "I know."

"Come on, let's land the *Thunder Road*. Maybe we'll find some food below."

"Maybe they have hot dog trees!" Addy licked her lips.

"Addy, you say that about every planet we visit."

She nodded. "Someday we'll find it. A planet with hot dog trees. With billions of planets in the galaxy, I know it's out there. That's just science."

They landed the *Thunder Road* among the ruins, and for the first time in weeks, they stepped out of the cramped spaceship.

"Fresh air!" Marco said, stretching. "Fresh air at last!" He breathed deeply. "It's … too hot." He sniffed. "Smells a bit weird too."

Addy groaned, rolled her eyes, and punched him. "Always complaining, you. You can stay in the ship if you like." She ran in circles around the *Thunder Road*. "Finally I can stretch my long, lovely legs!"

"You've been stretching them all over my dashboard during the flight," Marco muttered.

He looked around, soaking in the landscape. Springy grass covered the ground, sprouting yellow blossoms and serrated leaves. Most of the city was gone, giving way to nature. The shells of old buildings peeked from the soil. Trees, weeds, and moss covered whatever structures still stood. If there had been paved streets here, they were not buried. Animals had made their homes among the ruins: furry little critters that looked like rodents, winged aliens no larger than sparrows, and scuttling insects. On many Earthlike planets, evolution took similar paths. Durmia was the most Earthlike planet Marco had visited so far, certainly more hospitable than Haven, if a lot farther. Walking here, he could almost imagine himself traveling across ruins on Earth, perhaps in humid India.

"What do you suppose killed the Durmians?" Addy said, looking around.

"Time," Marco said softly. "Like most extinct civilizations in the galaxy. Just time." He paused by a fallen column with a decorative capital. A purple snake hissed from atop the column, then fled into a hole in the ground. "As you said, there are billions of planets in our galaxy. Most have been here for billions of years. Species don't have long cosmic lifespans. Most survive for a hundred thousand years, maybe twice that long, then fade away. A blink of an eye to the cosmos. It happened to ninety-nine percent of species on Earth. It'll happen to us. A million years from now, if aliens visit Earth, they'll find only ruins."

They began walking through the ruins, exploring. For a moment they were silent.

Addy bit her lip, then finally spoke. "Dude, you're such a downer. So why even fight to save humanity if we're doomed anyway?"

"Same reason we fight for health if we get sick. Doesn't mean we'll become immortal. We just want to extend our life a little longer."

Addy raised her chin. "Well, I'm not as pessimistic as you are, Poet. We're not fucking dinosaurs or dodos. We're humans.

We're smart. We're capable. We invented sliced bread, infomercials, and *Sweatin' to the Oldies*. We'll survive."

Marco gave her a wry smile. "Even if we do avoid destroying ourselves, we won't survive. We'll evolve. A million years from now, we won't even look like humans, no more than you or I look like monkeys. We'll probably look like, well ... like the grays."

Addy paused. She turned toward Marco, frowning.

"You don't think ..." Addy gasped. "You do, don't you! That the grays are just evolved humans?"

Marco's mouth fell open. He forced it closed. "No. Of course not! Time travel is impossible."

"Um, didn't the yurei travel in time?" Addy said. "Remember those sneaky ghosts that helped us fight the marauders? They were time travelers. And isn't Lailani chasing the hourglass, a time-travel device? Think about it, Poet! The grays aren't aliens. They're humans! Humans from a million years in the future. They're time travelers." She laughed. "I figured it out! I'm a genius!"

Marco wanted to scoff, to tell Addy she was crazy. But she had a point, he had to admit. True, aliens on most Earthlike planets followed similar evolutionary paths. But the results invariable ended up looking like something from *Freaks of the Galaxy*. Meanwhile, the grays were remarkably humanoid. Taller, yes. Their skin a different color. Their heads larger, their faces smaller. But they were still a hell of a lot more humanoid than the scum. Following the evolution of humans down its current path, wouldn't humans end up looking similar in a million years?

"But ..." Marco frowned. "If the grays are humans, why are they attacking us?"

"Beats me," Addy said. "Maybe Earth is a wasteland in a million years. Maybe it looks like this planet, all in ruins. Maybe they want Earth in our time. When it still has hockey and hot dogs and cookies. They probably don't need Bugles, though. They already have claws."

"I can't believe I'm saying this, but you might be on to something," Marco said. "And that scares me more than the grays."

She stuck her tongue out at him. "Admit it, I'm a genius. Way smarter than you."

"Addy, you think that worms are just baby snakes. You told me that once."

She nodded. "They are!" She rolled her eyes. "God, Marco, they only grow scales as adults, like humans with teeth."

"Addy, they—" He sighed. "Never mind."

They passed along a palisade of columns, perhaps once lining a grand boulevard. A palace rose on a distant hill, overlooking the ruins. Once this palace must have been the city's crown jewel. Today its stone domes were scratched and pockmarked; perhaps an ancient conqueror had stripped them of precious metals. A decapitated statue stood in a city square. The head—elephantine, sprouting two trunks—lay fallen several meters away, wrapped in rusty barbed wire.

Addy gasped. "An elephant man!" She rushed toward the head. "Who would do such a thing?"

"Maybe the Pillowman got jealous," Marco said.

"Ha ha, very funny," Addy said, but then she frowned and scratched her chin. "Hmm …" She looked around, as if seeking pillowmen. "Nah."

"An old battle was fought here." Marco knelt and lifted a rusty canister. "This was an artillery shell." He pointed. "And see that fortress? The walls are filled with bullet holes."

Addy shuddered. "That rules out the scum and marauders. They don't use bullets. You think the grays did this?"

"I doubt it," Marco said. "Scientists believe that there are at present ten thousand technological civilizations active in our galaxy. Humans have only met a handful. Could be anyone."

"I hope Baba Mahanisha is okay," Addy said.

Marco placed a hand on her shoulder. "I don't think he is, Ads. I think all the Durmians died a long time ago."

"Well, maybe they stashed some peanuts around at least. I'm famished."

They kept exploring. They found what looked like a silo, but the birds had stolen the grains long ago. In a dilapidated mausoleum, they found skeletons. The skulls were large and sprouted tusks, and bracelets and necklaces still adorned the old bones. Faded murals covered the walls, depicting an ancient battle. The Durmians—Addy still called them elephant men— were portrayed as noble warriors, halos around their heads. They fought a race of twisted, stooped humanoids with faces like lions, ugly and snarling.

"So this is what happened," Marco said, looking at the murals. "It wasn't pillowmen after all. These guys." He pointed. "Humanoid aliens with lion heads. A great war. Presumably, the elephants lost."

Addy was looking at the skeletons. She spoke in a soft voice. "Do you think one of them is Baba Mahanisha?" She knelt and touched an amulet that hung around a skeleton's neck. "A mandala amulet. The same symbol on my book. A Deep Being amulet." She lowered her head. "They studied peace, meditation, serenity. And they got butchered." She looked up at Marco. "Is that how the galaxy works? Only the strong and cruel survive?"

"We survived," Marco said.

"Because we fought," Addy said. "Because we were strong, and we were cruel. That's how we humans are. Maybe we're no different from the scum and marauders in that regard, just another race of aggressive warriors. I came here to find peace. Did we find that peace never lasts?"

Marco raised an eyebrow. "You came here to see freaks, remember?"

She looked back at the skeletons. "I saw them. I think I saw enough."

They left the mausoleum and climbed a grassy hill, hoping to overlook the valley beyond, perhaps spot some game to hunt. Shattered statues littered the hill, mostly buried under the soil, sticking up hands and faces like corpses rising from graves. A portico of cracked columns lined the hilltop, perhaps the remains of an old temple. When they reached the hilltop, Marco and Addy stared into the valley beyond and gasped.

"Bloody hell," Addy said. "The *size* of those things."

Marco nodded. "I saw them from the ship. I thought they were towers. But they're statues. God, they must be taller than the Statue of Liberty."

The statues were carved of stone, but they looked like robots. Giant, hulking, battle robots. Their bodies were humanoid, but their heads looked like the heads of mechanical lions. One was male and held a stone hammer that could have flattened trucks. The other was female and held a sword hilt, its blade fallen.

"Statues of robots?" Marco said.

"They look like giant samurais," Addy said. "With lion faces."

"They're the species that destroyed this planet, I think," Marco said. "Remember the murals in the mausoleum?"

"Yeah. The old war between the lions and the elephants. But there's nothing left of the elephants here. And I just see two giant stone lion robots. Why do you think they carved these statues?"

"Don't know," Marco said. "Maybe they were idols."

Addy shuddered. "You don't think they still have powers, do you?"

He smiled wryly. "They're just statues, Ads. There's no such thing as gods and magical powers."

"Yeah, well, tell that to the Ghost Fleet you found, to the starwhales you rode, and to that goddess the grays speak of." She raised her chin. "Besides, I'm a goddess and you believe in me, right?"

"You're no goddess," he said. "You're more a devil."

"I probably am." She nodded.

A light flared above. A whistle sounded.

"Incoming!" Addy shouted. They leaped back and flattened themselves onto the hilltop. A shard of metal slammed onto the hill, fire blasted, and soil flew. A shock wave scattered stones and uprooted a tree.

When Marco and Addy stood up again, they stared at the wreckage. It was a chunk of metal—a piece of the saucer they had battled in orbit.

"Well, I'll be damned," Addy said. "The fuckers almost had final revenge on us."

Marco approached the wreckage. The metal shard was the size of a hubcap, and it was still sizzling hot. He knelt before it, shielded his eyes, and stared.

"There are hieroglyphics on this thing," he said.

Addy knelt beside him. They looked together. Ibises, ankhs, suns, and snakes were engraved onto the metal. Addy pointed at the snakes.

"Look, adult worms!"

Marco narrowed his eyes. "Fuck me. These are Egyptian hieroglyphs. I used to know how to read them. When I was nine,

I had a box of hieroglyph stamps and a booklet explaining how to write with them."

"Nerd," Addy said. "When I was nine, I was playing hockey."

"Yes, well, once we encounter an alien species that challenges humanity to a hockey shootout, I'm sure that'll come in handy." Marco pulled out his phone. He had no web access here, but he had downloaded most of Wikipedia Galactica—including, thankfully, the entries on hieroglyphs. "I can translate this."

Addy snorted. "I already did. It says: *Worms are baby snakes, let all who doubt this wisdom be crushed under an elephant with two trunks.*"

Marco ignored her. He worked at the translation, brow furrowed. There wasn't much of the wreckage left, but he could make out a few words. He spoke softly.

"… with blood and fire, the children of Nefitis shall return to Earth, their promised land, and their ancestors shall serve as slaves, for the glory of the goddess is …" He let his voice trail off.

"Is what?" Addy said. "Are they talking about me?"

"That's all it says," Marco said. "The rest burned up."

Addy shuddered. "Nefitis. The grays spoke of her, didn't they? Their leader. I knew it. They want Earth. Fuckers."

"And they want their ancestors to serve as slaves," Marco said. "That seems to confirm my theory that they're evolved humans from the future. We're the ancestors."

"*Your* theory?" Addy placed her hands on her hips. "Marco, your theory is that snakes don't have babies. I'm the one who figured out who the grays are."

He bristled. "I never said that snakes—" He groaned. "Enough about snakes!" He sighed. "Let's take this piece of metal with us—once it cools off a bit, at least. I want to show this to President Petty."

"If he's not a slave by the time we return." Addy hugged herself. "Fuck, Marco, another war is coming. A big one. And I never even got to see the elephant baba."

"Maybe we should go back home," Marco said. "To Earth. To help fight. We're good fighters."

Addy stared at him, and her fists clenched. He saw her thoughts in her eyes.

We fought enough, her eyes said. *We deserve to rest. We deserve some peace.*

But then Addy nodded. "You're right. But first, we need some food. I see a river down there, and we have clotheslines to make fishing lines. Let's dig up some baby snakes for bait."

They were walking downhill when they noticed the smoke rising from the mountain.

It was a thin plume, barely visible from the valley, and still kilometers away.

"You see that, Ads?" he said.

She nodded. "What do you think it is? A campfire?"

"I'm thinking another piece of that saucer crashed on the mountain," Marco said. "Maybe with more hieroglyphs. I say we check it out."

Addy scrunched her lips. "All right. But only for the chance that it's a campfire, and that somebody is roasting hot dogs." She nodded. "I'll need a walking stick and a rake."

It was a long hike up the mountainside. They could not fly up; they'd have no place to land the *Thunder Road*. A trail zigzagged up the mountain, perhaps once used by the Durmians. Marco was soon winded and sweaty. The heat didn't help—nor did Addy, who kept jumping onto him, begging for a piggyback ride.

"Addy, get off." He shoved her down.

"But I'm tired!" She groaned. "There better be a Dairy Queen on top of this mountain."

Finally, wheezing, they reached the mountaintop.

The ruins of a temple rose ahead. Much of it had fallen, and bricks and shattered columns littered the mountain. A colossal statue lay across a slope, as large as a warship, depicting a Durmian monk. An orphaned archway stood among the ruins, the walls around it gone. Beyond the archway, Marco and Addy found a courtyard overgrown with weeds. A domed temple rose ahead, dilapidated but still standing. The smoke rose from a chimney.

Marco and Addy glanced at each other.

"Somebody's alive in there!" Marco whispered.

Addy nodded, eyes wide. "Maybe it's a pillowman roasting hot dogs!"

They approached the temple. The door was open. They stepped inside, froze, and gasped.

The room was sparse. A fireplace crackled, and candles shone in alcoves. A mandala of colored sand sprawled across the floor. Behind the intricate artwork sat a Durmian.

A living, breathing Durmian.

The alien was the size of a true elephant. Two trunks grew from his face, decorated with bracelets. His skin was milky white, his body rotund, and four arms grew from him. He wore red robes. The fabric seemed ancient, worn and faded but well maintained, any tatters lovingly mended. His eyes were closed. He was sitting cross-legged, his four hands upon his knees, deep in meditation. Marco recognized him from the photo on his book.

"Baba Mahanisha," he whispered.

The Durmian opened his eyes. He nodded.

"Hello, my friends."

Addy gasped. She hopped with excitement. "Baba Mahanisha! I'm a big fan of yours. I have all your books. Both *The Way of Deep Being* and *Frea*—" She gulped. "Actually, just that one book. I'm Addy and this is Marco. We've come from far away, hoping to learn wisdom."

The baba nodded. "I saw your ship, Addy and Marco. You two are humans. I am familiar with your kind, and I have taught your people before. What questions have you come to answer?"

"All the big ones!" Addy said. "Are worms baby snakes? And do you know any pillowmen?"

Marco rushed forward, grabbed Addy, and pulled her back. "Forgive her, Baba Mahanisha. She fell on her head as a child. Repeatedly. Then had elevator doors close on it. We've

come to learn the way of Deep Being, to seek its wisdom and
serenity."

Addy whispered, "Ask him if he has hot dogs."

Marco shushed her.

Baba Mahanisha gazed at the sand mandala on the floor.
He spoke softly.

"I labored for many months to create this mandala." His
voice was rich and sonorous. "I planted seeds of many colors,
lovingly tended to the plants, and plucked the berries when they
were ripe. I collected stones, ground them into dust, and dyed
them with the berries' juice. I placed the powder into funnels and
gently, grain by grain, created an intricate work of art. Circles
within circles. Dancing figures. Suns and stars."

"It's beautiful," Marco said, admiring the mandala. It
spread as wide as a dining room table, a true masterpiece made of
colored sand.

Baba Mahanisha nodded. "Yet all our toil, our dreams, our
art—the wind blows them all away." The guru leaned forward and
blew air from his twin trunks.

Marco gasped in horror. The guru was destroying his
mandala! All those beautiful figures and symbols, intricate
creations of sand—all blew around their feet. Addy and Marco
stared up at the guru, shocked.

The Durmian rose to his feet. For a creature so large, he
was surprisingly graceful. He stepped over the scattered sand
toward Marco and Addy, his robes swishing.

"To learn Deep Being, you must let its wisdom be like the wind. Let it blow away all that you have learned in your lives. You must begin on a clean floor."

Marco bowed his head. "We are ready to unlearn."

Addy nodded. "I haven't learned much in life, so it'll be pretty easy for me." At a glare from Marco, she bowed her head and adopted a more solemn tone. "I am ready to unlearn, Baba." She glanced up at the guru. "So can you teach us magical powers?"

The guru smiled. "I can teach you inner peace, serenity, awareness, the illusion of the self, and the mysteries of consciousness."

"But no magical powers," Addy said.

Marco gave her a glare so furious she cringed. But Baba Mahanisha didn't seem to mind. His smile widened, and he placed his four hands together and bowed his head.

"Then let us take the path to wisdom."

CHAPTER FIVE

Abyzou floated through the darkness, burnt, bleeding, broken. Half his face had shattered. With trembling fingers, he fished out chunks of bone. The fire had stripped off his skin, leaving sizzling meat. He was a living wound. He was pain put to flesh. He was fury, purified, screaming for vengeance.

You did this, Ben-Ari. You will suffer tenfold more!

Abyzou clenched his fists. A bone in his hand snapped. He screamed.

Blood coated his escape pod. It was the size of a coffin, dented, rumbling. Abyzou sneered. Ignoring the pain, he activated the engines.

Prince of the Sanctified Sons, only son of Nefitis, he flew.

He flew in darkness, alone with his pain.

He flew, his screams a company of demons.

There was no warp engine on this escape pod. He flew, slower than light, for long days. For eras. He did not know how long passed. He placed himself in cryonic sleep, but it worked fitfully. He woke up every year, screaming, still broken. He withered. He slept for a century. He woke, tormented by years of nightmares, thawing, bleeding anew. He slept again.

He flew alone in the vastness, growing thin, growing old. He shrank in his coffin. His madness filled the empty space.

He missed his wife and children. His wife—a human he had chosen himself, had plucked from Old Earth, had impregnated. His children—born with his large mind, with their mother's strength, hybrids who would someday return home, inherit the world.

I love you, my Mila, my sweet wife, Abyzou thought, tears mingling with blood. *I miss you. I miss my children.* He wept. *I miss who I was.*

He flew onward. He slept. He woke screaming. He shuddered in the darkness.

He flew until he reached the portal.

It shimmered ahead, a great metal ring in space, blue shining within. A hundred saucers guarded the portal, faces carved upon them, ancient sentinels. They flew toward Abyzou's escape pod. One saucer pulled him aboard. When they opened the lid of his capsule, when they saw him, fear filled their eyes.

"Prince Abyzou!" they said, bowing.

He saw himself reflected in their shimmering black eyes. He looked barely alive. A desiccated corpse, skin burnt off, muscles red and dripping. Half his face was a ruin, the shattered bone thrusting outward, the teeth gone. Prince? Yes, he was the son of Nefitis, prince to these warriors, yet now he looked like a wretch.

You turned me into this thing, humans, he thought. *You did this to me, Captain Ben-Ari. I will do so much worse to you.*

For the first time in centuries, he spoke. His voice was raspy. Every word was a struggle.

"Bring … me … healers …"

The Sanctified Sons glanced at each other, then back at him.

"She has spoken to us, Prince Abyzou," one said, bowing deep. "The goddess. Nefitis herself, blessed of graces. She knew you would come."

"Healers!" he screamed.

The Sanctified Sons trembled. "Nefitis demands to see you first. Before any healers. We will bring you to her."

She knew, Abyzou thought. *Mother knew I was coming. She let me languish in the pod for centuries. She let me suffer for so many years. She could have sent a saucer with a warp engine for me. But she let me float alone. To suffer.* He trembled. *The punishment for my failure.*

He rose from the escape pod, this coffin where he had languished for so long. Some of his skin had fused to the floor. As he rose, it ripped and fell off. Blood dripped. A bone shard fell and clanged. He stepped out from the pod, sizzling, dripping, stinking. The hearts around his neck had died centuries ago. They lay against his burnt flesh like black, deflated balloons.

"Take me to Nefitis," he said.

The saucer flew through the portal.

They flew through a rift in spacetime.

They contracted, twisted, blasted through time, and Abyzou screamed. His muscles burst. A crack widened on his skull. Lights and shadows danced around him. Demons. Demons.

His life unfurling around him, past and ever-changing futures. In the shadows, he saw himself as a boy, cowering in the corner, his mother striking, beating, ripping. He saw himself as a youth, tying down his deformed brothers, brutalizing, gouging out their eyes, laughing as they died. He saw himself as a soldier, rising high in the legions, leading battalions, commanding fleets. In the visions before him, he bathed the world of Sil Adrianis in blood, slaying the males and enslaving the females, fertilizing their wombs with his seed. In another vision, he lined the roads of Kalatoor with crosses, millions of crosses, upon them the screaming, nailed babies of his enemies. A career of pain, suffering, torturing, always climbing the rungs of agony. He—Abyzou, born of Nefitis, descended of the great priest Harsiese himself. Rising ever taller in the shadow of the goddess. He washed her feet with his blood, and he blessed her name. Abyzou, mightiest of warriors, Sanctified Prince, most wretched of slaves.

They flew over their ruined, blackened world. A world of ash. Of despair. Of hunger. The mouths of volcanoes gaped open, molten fire gurgling within. Rivulets of black, hardened lava flowed toward the pits, frozen into forms like corpses falling into a fiery underworld. Soot rained from black clouds. The despair stretched into the horizons—dark hills, plains of charcoal dust, the bones of great creatures that had once roamed here, that had died like the rest of this world.

We have destroyed a thousand worlds, Abyzou thought, *but ours too is a wasteland. For we crave but one world. We do not crave to live anywhere but in our holy land, to raise homes anywhere but upon hallowed ground. Earth. Earth is our birthright. We came from a good, green Earth. To there we shall return.*

The saucer took him over Gehenna, city of the goddess. Archways rose above the boulevards like dark ribs, draped with banners likes scraps of skin. Obelisks pierced the clouds. The black city looked like the shell of some massive crab, fossilized, deformed, claws sticking into the air. Millions of the Sanctified lived here—thin, scavenging, hungry. Half the babies born into this wretched warren died of starvation. Only the warriors ate well. Only the strongest survived.

But soon we will inherit Earth, Abyzou thought. *Soon we shall live in sunlight, shall feed upon plenty. Soon the Sanctified Sons will be masters, and the humans will be our slaves!*

In the center of this dying, rotting city it rose—Golgalath. The pyramid of the goddess. It was ancient. For a million years it had risen here, the first structure, the pillar around which their empire had spread out. A burnished eye blazed upon its crest, golden, flaming, all-seeing. Beneath it stretched out a platform. And there she sat. From there she ruled.

Goddess. Mother. Nefitis.

Mother of our race, he thought. *My mother.*

The saucer hovered above the platform and extended a ramp. Abyzou climbed out, every step leaving a footprint of blood, every movement tearing his exposed muscles. He came to stand before his goddess. She sat on her throne of rotting flesh, her claws gripping the armrests. Blood dripped from her crown, the iron shards nailed into her brow. One of her pets, a demonic dog the size of a man, nursed at her breast. As Abyzou approached, the hound turned toward him, growling, bloodied milk still on its fangs.

"Abyzou," Nefitis hissed. "My son ... Look what the apes did to you." She rose from her throne, approached him, and caressed his savaged cheek. She plucked out a piece of shattered skull. "My poor son."

He nearly passed out from the pain. He knelt before her. "Mother. Goddess."

She dug her fingers into his open wounds. He yowled. She pulled him to his feet.

"Stand up like a warrior!" she said. "Do not kneel like a cowering child. Where are the apes? I sent you to catch them."

Abyzou's pain was a burning, clawing, screeching demon. He wanted to fall back down. To look away. But Nefitis was staring at him, *into* him, her black eyes seeing all, holding him up like chains.

"I failed," he whispered.

Nefitis sneered. She grabbed one of his loose teeth. Instead of yanking it out, she drove it deeper, digging it into his gum, grinding his nerve. He yowled.

"Where are Marco Emery and Addy Linden, whom I sent you to find? Where is Lailani de la Rosa?"

His blood dripped. His tears fell. "I failed."

"And where is Einav Ben-Ari, she who exiled our ancestors, who doomed us to a million years of privation?"

Abyzou wept. "I faced her in battle. I failed."

Nefitis nodded. "You failed. Again and again, you failed me."

"Forgive me, goddess. Forgive me! I am sorry."

She caressed his cheek. Her eyes softened. "My poor, weak, sniveling worm of a son. If you were not of my womb, I would have slain you here upon my altar. Yet you are my son. You shall live."

He fell to his knees, weeping. "Thank you, my goddess, my mother."

She stood above him, gazing down. Her demonic hound growled at her side.

"Yet you must still be punished," the goddess said.

Abyzou trembled. He looked up at her. He cried out, voice hoarse. "You let me drift for centuries! For long years, I could not sleep. I screamed, I ached! I have suffered enough!"

Nefitis shook her head. "No, Abyzou. Your suffering has just begun." She turned her head. "Bring them forth!"

A portal materialized behind her. Through it emerged soldiers in burnished armor, helmets hiding their faces. They dragged four bound prisoners: a woman and three children.

A human woman.

A woman Abyzou had not seen in years.

His wife.

Abyzou had taken her years ago. He had found her roaming the plains of Old Earth, a daughter of mammoth hunters. Her genes were still pure. Her bloodline was still strong, born from the wilderness. Her hips were wide and made for childbirth, her breasts ample and rich with milk, and she had birthed him three children, blessed hybrids born with the large craniums of his race, with the hardy bodies of hers.

"Mila!" he cried. "My love!"

Abyzou had been floating for many years. But the portal brought him back in time. To Mila, he would have been gone for only days. He had not seen her in centuries.

His wife stepped toward him, barefoot, trembling. They had stripped her naked. They had painted an ankh on her torso, the loop forming a ring between her breasts and collarbone, the pillar running down to her sex. The guards shoved her forward. Her children followed, eyes darting. The oldest—almost a grown warrior. The middle child—a sweet girl, a few years from marriageable age. The youngest—a mere toddler, tears on her cheeks. When they saw him, saw the ruin he had become—a wretched, walking wound—they screamed.

"Mother," Abyzou whispered. "What—"

"Your family," Nefitis said. "The ones you love. An ape woman whom you married against my will. Three hybrid children, twisted and weak." She stepped toward them. She plucked up the youngest and stroked the child's hair. "They stink of ape."

"Mother, do not harm them." Abyzou stepped forward, fists clenching. "I will not let you."

Nefitis sat back on her throne, a smile on her lips. She placed her granddaughter on her lap.

"You do not command me, Abyzou. I am your mother. I am the mother of this world, of this race, of this empire we are building. I am goddess. I am Nefitis. I am wrath and retribution. I am mercy for the servile, vengeance for the disobedient. You have been disobedient, my son. You have failed me again and again. And now you will prove your worth. I give you one more chance to appease me."

Abyzou took another step toward her. His fists trembled. "What would you have me do?"

Nefitis raised a claw. She pointed at his wife and two eldest children. They trembled, still caught in the guards' grips.

"Your wife, the woman you love. Your son, only a year away from joining the military. Your daughter, only a year away from marriage. What do they mean to you?"

"Everything!" he cried.

Nefitis nodded, smiling thinly. "That is why you fail. That is why you are weak. You care for yourself, for your own blood, more than the blood of our race. Sacrifice them! Strap your family onto the altar, carve them open, and hand me their organs so that I may feed. Prove that they are nothing, that I am everything. Do this and be forgiven."

He howled. "I will not!"

Nefitis rose to her feet, still clutching the youngest child. Her eyes blazed with fury. "Then I will have you bound and tortured, your own organs removed. I will trap your soul in my dungeons, leaving it alive and screaming for eternity. Your name will be forgotten, lost to history, and this youngest child shall replace you as my heir. Sacrifice your family! Only your youngest shall be spared. Kill the others. Your fate otherwise will be far crueler."

Abyzou wept. He knelt. He begged.

But Nefitis was a goddess. She was ancient. She was all. She would not be swayed.

Abyzou wept as he worked. He kissed his wife. He whispered of his love to her. And he bound her to the altar with hissing serpents, and he carved her open, and he removed her organs, one by one. A pulsing heart. A dish of entrails. Sweet pancreas. All the treasures inside her, wet and gleaming, served to his mother. He sacrificed his wife. He sacrificed his oldest son. He sacrificed his eldest daughter. Three hearts ripped out. Three times his own heart shattered. Three sacrifices.

Nefitis did not even eat the organs. She tossed them to her dog.

Abyzou stood by the altar, the blood of his family drenching him, mixing with his own blood. The husks of his wife and children lay at his feet. He stared up at his mother.

"I have done as you asked!" he shouted, voice torn with grief. "Release my youngest."

"No." Nefitis shook her head. "Not yet." She stroked the toddler's hair. "Such a precious babe. So fragile. Her bones—so easy to snap." Nefitis smiled cruelly.

"Return her to me!" Abyzou cried.

Nefitis nodded. "I will. Once you've redeemed your honor. Two tasks I give you. First, you must find Marco Emery and Addy Linden. And you must break them." She sneered.

"Then, once Emery and Linden are dead, you will rejoin our glorious fleet. As we speak, it still flies toward Earth. You will lead it. You, my son, will be there to oversee Earth's fall."

Abyzou hissed. "I will not play with time in this way, Mother. I will not chase Emery and Linden across the galaxy, only to come back to the present. The chances for paradoxes are—"

Nefitis sneered. "Do you not think that he, the Tick-Tock King, can manipulate time? Do you not think that he sees all paradoxes, that he is wiser than you?"

Abyzou shuddered. The Tick-Tock King. The Oracle. The Time Seer. The creature had many names, and each one sent shivers through Abyzou. He did not like to think of that creature, that terror that lurked in the darkness.

"Yes," Nefitis hissed. "He knows. He pulls the strings of time like a spider pulling webs. And time moves fast for our brave fleet, for they travel at many times the speed of light. But time moves slowly for Emery and Linden. The Oracle has seen it. A single day for our fleet lasts a month for Emery and Linden. You will create no paradoxes."

"Why should I care about Emery and Linden?" Abyzou said. "They are merely apes. They—"

"They are everything!" Nefitis shouted. "You do not understand. You have not seen their future. I have. *He* has." Blood flooded her cheeks, and fire filled her eyes. "You must kill Emery and Linden. You must, or we will fail. Bring me their hearts! Then go and battle Ben-Ari upon Earth. It will become our domain."

Abyzou did not understand. He could not gaze into the future. Only two had that power. Nefitis was one. The other was the creature that lurked deep inside this pyramid, that deformed beast which Abyzou dared not contemplate.

What role do these apes still play?

"If I do these things, you will return my child?" he said.

Nefitis nodded. "Yes, my son. Do these things and you will be forgiven. I will return your youngest child. I will let you choose another wife among the slaves. You will have my love again."

Abyzou inhaled sharply. Another wife …

"I choose Ben-Ari!" he said. "Her womb will bear my children, and her screams will fill my bedchamber with music."

Nefitis's smile widened, dripping rot. "How soon you forget your old ape and already crave another! Very well. I will grant you Ben-Ari … after I break her. After I spend a long time breaking her. Go now! Go and conquer."

He still needed to see a healer. He was still burnt, broken, and still every movement screamed in agony. But Abyzou knew this mercy too would be withheld. First he would prove his worth. He would conquer Earth. He would enslave the apes.

And then, Ben-Ari, you will be mine. You will be mine to love. To impregnate. To comfort and break again and again. My pain is nothing compared to what awaits you.

He entered the saucer. He took flight. As he flew out on the hunt, he imagined the triumph, the glory, and Ben-Ari trembling in his claws.

CHAPTER SIX

They sat outside upon the mountaintop: Baba Mahanisha, Marco, and Addy. All three wore maroon robes. All three sat cross-legged, hands on their knees. The temple complex rose around them: weedy walls, statues smoothed by centuries of rain and wind, and a copper gong engraved with a mandala. The sun was bright, the sky clear, and Marco was ready to learn.

Baba Mahanisha spoke, voice deep and soothing.

"There are several noble truths along the path of Deep Being. We step toward the first truth. Five simple words. Five words that will take you many days to comprehend." He inhaled deeply and raised his head. "I am not my thoughts."

Marco contemplated this. "Then who am I, Baba?" he said.

"That is among the great mysteries," said the baba. "Before you can learn who you are, you must learn who you are not."

"I am not my thoughts." Marco repeated the five words slowly. "But my thoughts are who I am, aren't they? My reasoning. My planning. My thinking. Everything inside my brain. Isn't that what defines me?"

Addy snorted. "You mostly think about sex anyway. And boring books about hobbits."

Marco glared at her. "Take this seriously, Addy. We're trying to learn wisdom." He took a deep breath and returned his attention to the guru. "So I'm not my thoughts."

The guru nodded. "This is a truth I cannot explain to you in words. You must experience this truth yourself with careful meditation. We will begin to meditate together. As we meditate, focus only on your breath. On the air entering and leaving your lungs. Nothing else. Let your mind be clear, like a pond on a peaceful summer day. Let us begin."

The guru rang a bronze bell.

They took deep breaths and began to meditate.

For a long time, they sat silently, breathing.

Marco tried to focus on his breathing, but soon his mind was wandering. He thought about the grays who had attacked them. He wondered where Ben-Ari and Lailani were. He thought of those he had lost, of his father, of Anisha, of Kemi. As those thoughts rose, he winced, the pain stabbing him. He tried to keep breathing deeply, to understand the lesson here. He was not his thoughts. Then who was he? He glanced at Addy. She seemed deep in reflection, her eyes closed. And she was beautiful. Looking at her, Marco felt his pain fade.

She's a huge pain in the ass, he thought. *But I love her. I love her more than anything. She makes me so happy. I only wish I could have confessed my love to her earlier. During those two years in Haven, when I needed her most, when I drove her away ...*

Now the memories of Haven rose. Memories of being lost in darkness, descending into madness, finally driven onto a rooftop, moments from suicide. Who could blame him? He had seen such terror in the darkness. Scum and marauders and endless violence. Friends dying. He had lost so many. His parents. His friends. Almost everyone he had known—dead in the wars. Their bodies torn apart, and his mother dead in the snow.

His fists clenched. His jaw tightened. The muscles in his back tensed as the memories flooded him.

Addy had suffered too. Marco knew that she joked around to hide that pain. He knew that deep inside, she was different. Strong. Wise. Hurt. He knew she suffered nightmares most nights. Sometimes she woke up screaming. And she still bore the scars of war, scars she tried to hide, scars on her body and soul.

Marco couldn't take this anymore. This damn … silence! He wanted to banter with Addy. To read a book. To make love to Addy. To eat. To run. To do anything but just sit here, thinking, remembering. What did it mean, he wasn't his thoughts? That's all he was! Without thoughts, there was no Marco. There was no pain or joy, just emptiness. Just a body—broken, scarred, no longer soft with youth, and his fingers were trembling now. His breath was too fast. He couldn't focus on it. And—

Baba Mahanisha rang his bell again.

"Our meditation is over." The guru looked at Marco, raising his two trunks inquisitively. "How did it go?"

He slumped. "Not too good. I couldn't focus on my breath. My mind was racing with thoughts."

"Exactly!" said the baba. "Thus is the mind. Perhaps for the first time in your life, you have seen this. Never quiet, the mind! Forever racing with thoughts, memories, fears, worries, dreams, hopes, planning, organizing, fretting ... The mind is like a sky full of clouds. Sometimes there are only several clouds afloat. Sometimes a storm rages, filled with thunder and lightning and gushing wind. But the mind is never completely quiet. Yet is the mind *you*?"

Marco contemplated this for a moment.

"I was thinking about hockey," Addy said. "And hot dogs! And ..." She sighed and lowered her head. "And bad things. The war. And the marauders. And ..." She winced and hugged herself. "Other things I don't want to talk about."

The guru nodded. "You have glimpsed your own minds. Perhaps for the first time, you mindgazed. Yet your thoughts took hold of you! They controlled you, pulled you in. During your meditation, you *became* your thoughts. You *were* your thoughts."

"But I thought we're not our thoughts," Marco said.

"Not when you follow the way of Deep Being," said Baba Mahanisha. "And that is our goal. Thoughts are merely clouds in the sky. You are consciousness. That is all! You are the observer, lying on the grass, gazing up at the sky of clouds. Most people let the clouds seize them. They become entangled in the storm, indistinguishable from their thoughts. They are no longer mind-gazing. But those who practice Deep Being merely lie in the grass, gazing up at the sky, seeing the clouds float by. They see them for what they are: transitory, ephemeral like a mandala of sand. Like clouds, thoughts come and go. They are not you."

Marco nodded, beginning to understand. "How can I achieve this state?"

"Whenever a thought arises in your mind, return your focus to your breath," said the guru. "Bring your awareness to the breath alone. Time and again, away from your thoughts and to your breath. Whenever the clouds grab you, descend back to the grass. Whenever thoughts seize you, descend back to the breath. Let us try again."

The baba rang his bell.

Again they began to meditate.

Marco focused on his breath—the air flowing through his nostrils, into his lungs, out of his mouth.

It felt like breathing through a gas mask, having to focus on each breath. As a child, he used to carry a gas mask everywhere. So many times in his childhood, he had run down the streets as the scum pods rained, spewing poisonous gas, and—

No! he thought. *No thinking! Back to the breath.*

Yet even that command had been a thought. Damn it! He inhaled sharply, shoving all thoughts away. He focused on another breath. Another. Another.

I think this is working. Finally! I'm doing this! He glanced at Addy. *I think she is too. I'm glad we came here. The journey was long, and Addy kept annoying me, and I was going nuts inside that Volkswagen, but if we can find peace here, it'll be worth it. I just hope there's no war on Earth, that those grays aren't attacking. Is Lailani okay? What about Ben-Ari? If only I had a way to contact them, and—*

He winced. Again he was thinking. No thinking!

He crushed those thoughts. He returned his awareness to the breath.

Yet again and again, his mind resisted. He could last one breath, sometimes two or three, before his thoughts seized him. Sometimes he could crush those thoughts quickly. Other times, it was long moments before he even realized his attention had wandered. Finally, when Baba Mahanisha rang the bell again, Marco was frustrated and antsy.

"I tried to push my thoughts away, Baba," he said. "But they kept resurfacing. I remembered what you said. How I'm not my thoughts. But they kept rising, and whenever I pushed one away, another replaced it." He sighed. "I failed."

"Same here," Addy said, shoulders slumped. "I could sometimes go three or four breaths without a thought, but they kept rising, and I couldn't push them away fast enough."

"I couldn't even last two breaths without a thought," Marco said.

Addy rolled her eyes. "Well, good for you, Mr. Smarty-pants."

They turned toward the guru. Mahanisha regarded them.

"You failed because you tried to push the thoughts away," he said. "You saw them as your enemies, as things to be banished. But they are like clouds in the sky. When clouds darken your sky, do you chase them, attempt to wrestle them? When the thoughts arrive, merely observe them. What are they about? How do they make you feel? Do they carry an emotional charge? Do they cause your body to tense? Lie on the metaphorical grass. Gaze up at the clouds of thought. Do not try to destroy them nor judge them. Merely greet them with friendly curiosity, then return your awareness to the breath, and watch the thoughts float away. The Deep Being mind is never blank. Meditation is not about achieving a mind empty of thought. Meditation is about turning your awareness again and again away from thought."

"But ..." Marco frowned. "Who is doing the watching? Who is lying on the grass? How can I observe thoughts? What part of me is observing?"

"That is the first truth you must learn, my pupil," said Baba Mahanisha. "This is the first noble truth along the path of wisdom. Let us meditate."

The guru rang his bell.

They tried again.

For a long time—perhaps an hour—they sat in silence.

Thoughts kept rising in Marco's mind. Sometimes they seized him completely, pulling him in, until he forgot where he was. By the time he refocused on the breath, he realized that many moments had passed, lost in thought. Often he forgot about his breathing completely. Again and again, he tried to focus on the breath alone—the sensation of air in his nostrils, his lungs, his mouth. Again and again, those thoughts, memories, fears, reflections, all the clouds of his mind arose, grabbing him with their hooks, pulling him in.

It seemed a futile battle.

And now I'm thinking about Kemi again, he realized. *Stop it! Stop thinking. Just observe the thoughts. Let them float away. Like the guru teaches. Stop thinking about it! You're thinking again. Just do it without thinking!*

He was frustrated, antsy, his mind a storm. There it was—the memory of Kemi dying. How he had held her in his arms, gazing into her eyes. And he was there, reliving it again, feeling that loss, that pain.

Breathe.

He let the air flow into his lungs.

The memory of Kemi was still in his mind. A cloud in the sky, dark, overwhelming.

He let the air flow out.

He lay on the grass, watching the storm.

He breathed in again, filled his lungs, then released the air.

He gazed up at the dark cloud. It reached down to grab him, to pull him in, to drown him in the memory.

He breathed.

His body loosened.

The dark cloud floated away.

He took another breath.

He spent the rest of the meditation struggling, thoughts grabbing him, and he had to keep forcing himself back to the breath. That one moment of lucidity did not return. When the meditation finally ended, Marco was exhausted. It had been surprisingly hard work. Yet he felt like he had accomplished something.

"I think I experienced it," he said to his guru. "Just for an instant. Maybe a couple seconds. It was like … I was an observer. Outside my thoughts. As if indeed I lay on some grassy hill, watching a thought like a cloud above." His eyes dampened. "I wasn't my thought. I wasn't that pain, that memory. It was there in my brain. But it wasn't me."

He was surprised that tears flowed down his cheek.

The baba nodded, smiling thinly. "You have experienced a moment of Deep Being. With practice, these moments will grow. You will see all thoughts for what they are: ephemeral as a mandala of sand, no matter how intricate. Thoughts are merely activity in your mind, little sparks in the storm. Memories are no more real. The past is gone; a memory is but a shadow of it. Memories are mere echoes. The path to inner peace lies in learning these truths. Learning to connect with the deep well of tranquility inside you, to let your soul, the world, the cosmos itself breathe through you."

Marco thought about this for a long moment.

"Baba," he finally said, "so who was that lying on the metaphorical grass, observing the thought? I was not my thought. Was that the true me, the self?"

The guru smiled. "The self is but an illusion, my pupil. The self is woven of memories, thoughts, plans, dreams, fears, likes, dislikes … all clouds. Only your consciousness is real."

Marco frowned. "But is the consciousness not the self?"

The baba shook his head. "The consciousness observes the self dissipate like the mandala, like the clouds in the wind. Once you can watch all else fade away—the self, the mind, the past, the future, you will simply be. Simply rest in awareness. And all the cosmos will open up around you. And you will be one with everything." Mahanisha inhaled deeply and held out his arms. "That is true wisdom. True tranquility. True Deep Being. That is the light at the end of the noble path. You have taken your first step toward wisdom."

Suddenly Addy let out a sob. She was trembling. Marco rushed toward her and embraced her. She clung to him.

"I'm not my thoughts," she whispered to him, shaking. "I'm not my fear. I'm not my pain. I'm not my memories. All those memories. All those nightmares. They're not me." She wept. "They're not me, Marco. They're not us. They can never be us."

He held her for a long time, and they cried together.

That night, Marco and Addy made slow, solemn love, gazing into each other's eyes. Normally in bed, Addy was something of a wild animal, but tonight she was soft intensity, comfort, a deeper connection. They slept in the temple, wrapped in each other's arms. They had taken a first step, perhaps the most important step in their lives. They would continue along this path together, walking through a valley of shadows to a shimmering light on a distant mountaintop.

* * * * *

They woke up before dawn.

They ate a simple meal. Bread. Fruit. Roots.

They meditated.

For hours, they sat in silence, clad in robes, gazing down at the valleys, deep in awareness.

"Just be," Baba Mahanisha taught them. "Resting in awareness. One with the breath. One with the world. One with everything. Let the self fade. Breathe."

They breathed.

And it was a hard.

And it was a battle.

While Baba Mahanisha seemed tranquil in meditation, Marco and Addy fretted. Their legs fell asleep, their backs ached, their skin itched, but the guru forbade them from moving.

"Be aware of the discomfort," he told them. "Be aware of the pain. View it as a friendly observer, curious. Breathe into your pain. Let it fade."

"Can't we at least get pillows to sit on?" Addy said, twisting uncomfortably in the sunlit courtyard. "These cobblestones are hard."

"At least you have lots of natural padding," Marco said, earning a well-deserved punch.

Their stomachs rumbled with hunger. Yet Baba Mahanisha allowed them no further meals that day. Hours went by, and they did not eat or drink again. Their mouths dried up. Their stomachs grumbled.

"Let it fade," he told them. "Breathe into the pain. Let it be. Observe. Breathe."

The hours went by. Hours of sitting still. Of gazing. Hours—intolerable. Frustrating. Agonizing. Their bodies hurt from lack of movement. The sun beat down, and they couldn't even wipe away their sweat.

"Be still, be calm," the baba told them. "Observe the pain as one observes a cloud. Let it flow away."

Yet worse than the physical discomfort were the memories.

During the past couple of years, Marco had found refuge from trauma in busyness. On Haven, he had brooded too much, remembered too much, and it had broken him. Since leaving that colony, he had buried himself in his quest to defeat the marauders, later in his writing, never allowing himself time to think. The memories resurfaced at night, twisting into nightmares, waking him up in cold sweat, and during the days he suppressed them.

He could not suppress his memories here.

"Let them rise," the baba said. "Do not let them go. You would if you could. Instead, let them be."

"It hurts," Marco said.

The baba nodded. "That is why you are here. Because you suffer pain. The path of Deep Being offers not freedom from pain but power over pain. Not through repression but through acceptance. Let the pain rise. Let the memories hurt. And breathe. Let them be. Let them float away."

Marco tried.

And it hurt.

In the silence, the stillness, his mind open, there were no distractions. And the demons—those terrors that still manifested as nightmares most nights—had nowhere to hide. They twisted under the light, exposed and bleeding.

Memories of his mother dying in the snow. Of the terrors of the scum war. Of his destruction in Haven. Of the marauders and the loss of his friends. Of losing Tomiko, losing his home, losing everything that he had fought for.

Agony.

Despair.

Anger, rage, fury, fear, shame, guilt.

They all rose to play like demons, the seal of their underworld broken.

At his side, Addy struggled too. Marco saw her twitching, clenching her fists, tears in her eyes. He wanted to stop this. To stop the silence! To busy himself. To fight. To run. To build. To do anything but just let this pain resurface.

"Let it rise," the baba said, voice calm. "Observe the pain with compassion. With curiosity. Do not judge. Lie on the grass and gaze upon the storm. It cannot hurt you. The past is gone. The memories are mere visions. They are not real. Only illusions. Only the present is real. Only consciousness is real. Let them be. Let them flow away. Breathe. Breathe into them. Rest in awareness. Let the healing air flow through you. Breathe into every part that hurts, that is tense, that is scarred. With every breath, let the pain flow away. Breathe."

They breathed.

As the pain rose—breath.

As the memories haunted—awareness.

Anger. Guilt. Fear. Storms in the sky, but Marco lay below them. Observing them. Not letting them grab him. They were demons in the mirror, trapped behind the glass.

"I am not my thoughts," he whispered, tears on his cheeks. "I am not my pain. I am not my fear. The self is an illusion. The past is gone. The future has not yet come. There is only now. Only the breath. Breathe."

He breathed.

Air through his nostrils, healing, soothing, filling his lungs.

He breathed into every part that hurt. Into his aching legs. His twisting back. His empty stomach. His dry mouth. His tight jaw. He breathed into the memories, scattering them with breath. He breathed until everything disappeared.

He imagined that he was like an anemone, clinging to the seabed, swaying with the waves, with the breath of the sea. Just aware. Conscious. No past, no future, no thoughts, no memories. Only awareness. Only the pulse of the cosmos.

He breathed.

Often the thoughts claimed him, tugging him into the storm, and he found himself lost within them, sometimes not realizing until long moments later what had happened. Often the physical discomfort tugged at him—the pain in his body, the hunger, the heat, the tension in his muscles—and he forced himself to sink deeper into awareness.

"Let it all be," the baba said softly. "Observe. Breathe. Rest in awareness. Be one with everything. Be present. There is no past, no future, only the now. Be here. Be aware. Breathe."

That night, Marco and Addy again made soft love, and they slept embraced. The baba gave them only four hours of slumber. They rose in darkness. They ate a simple meal. Bread. Porridge. Fruit. They gorged themselves, anticipating the hunger ahead.

They sat cross-legged on the hill.

They breathed.

They let it be.

The hours went by. Hours of struggles, wrestling with thoughts and memories. Marco had never realized how busy his mind always was. How his thoughts were a constant storm. How his demons forever danced—the grief, trauma, nightmares, memories.

Was my mind always like this? he wondered. *For these past few years, did this storm forever rage, and I simply hid from it? Suppressed it?*

Yes, he realized. And for the first time, he was seeing his mind. Not lost within his mind. Not lost inside the illusion of the self. He was outside his mind. He was lying on the grass. He was gazing up at the sky of the mind, observing the thoughts, memories, fears, all just clouds. Ephemeral like the mandala. His thoughts were not him. And they blew away in the breath.

Sometimes Marco felt as if his body disappeared. As if he was nothing but breath, just air flowing from top to bottom, passing through him, as if he were just a sack of skin. And then his skin too disappeared, until he was only consciousness. Until there was no self. Only this mountain, and the grassy valleys below, and the sky above, all one. All a single organism. And he observed.

Those moments of oneness never lasted. A thought would always rise. A memory. Perhaps only a mundane thought, wondering how Addy was doing, perhaps analyzing his own success, perhaps remembering some of the baba's teachings. Sometimes more distressing thoughts arose—about the fate of Earth and his friends. Sometimes their lure was strong. Sometimes the thoughts seemed so urgent that he *had* to think them. He had to plan for the future! He had to analyze the past! He had to invent things, do things, figure things out. It was *important*. He was in danger. There were monsters after him. He was wasting his time here. This was foolishness, just a scam. He had to get back to Earth, he—

He breathed.

Again and again, he took shaky breaths.

Focus on the breath.

Let it be.

Rest in awareness.

He breathed.

He gazed up at that sky, aware, one.

"I am not my thoughts," he whispered that night to Addy, gazing into her eyes.

She gazed back, holding him. "I am not my thoughts."

They slept, holding each other. They rose. They breathed.

They walked along the path, discovering the first truth of wisdom.

CHAPTER SEVEN

Dented, cracked, and belching out smoke, the *Ryujin* trundled
through space. Sitting at the helm, Lailani thought that only her
duct tape was holding the starship together.

"Barnard's Star," she said, pointing at the light ahead.
"We're almost there, Epi. Hope."

Her Doberman made an approving sound and licked her
cheek.

Barnard's Star was a red dwarf, a small and relatively cool
star, barely more than a luminous gas giant. It was only six light-
years from Earth—just around the corner—but few humans ever
visited this place. Barnard's Star was too dim to see from afar, so
unimportant that few humans even realized it existed. A handful
of small, rocky worlds orbited it, desolate wastelands. This was
Earth's neighborhood, but it was the dregs, the back alley of
human civilization.

It was here, HOBBS had once told her, that she would
find Dr. Elliot Schroder. The man who had made HOBBS. The
man who could perhaps repair him. The man who could save
Lailani's quest.

He lives in hiding on a lonely world orbiting Barnard's Star,
HOBBS had told her back on Mahatek. Hiding from what? Or

from whom? The robot had not said, and now HOBBS was unconscious. Lailani would have to find the answers herself.

She tapped her tablet, pulled up the entry on Schroder, and reread it. There wasn't much info. Dr. Elliot Schroder. Born 2107. A robotics pioneer. As a student, he had shown remarkable promise. Professor Ilana Teitelbaum herself, inventor of the azoth engine, had overseen his thesis. His roommate had been Professor Noah Isaac, Nobel Prize laureate and inventor of the wormhole. As a young man, Dr. Schroder had worked on the burgeoning field of artificial intelligence, helping to create the first Osiris models. He had worked for Bai Liu himself, the famous inventor of true artificial consciousness. In the world of science, he had shone like a star among stars.

Yet ten years ago, things had gone sour.

The article didn't say much, only that the police had investigated Schroder, that he had fled Earth in shame. For a decade now, nobody had heard from him. Nobody knew where he was hiding—aside from HOBBS and Lailani, it seemed. According to the article, if Schroder ever returned to Earth, he'd be arrested on arrival.

"I don't know what you did," Lailani said, flying toward the red dwarf. "But you invented HOBBS, and maybe you can fix him. So right now you're the most important person in the galaxy."

She looked back at HOBBS. He still lay in the hold, strapped to the floor with duct tape. It wasn't very dignified, but with the gravity drive busted, it was the only way to keep the cyborg from floating away. He was still unconscious, his heart still beating but his eyes dim. And inside his positronic brain—the instructions for the hourglass. For the time machine that could undo Lailani's shame.

"Hold on to that info, my friend," she whispered. "Hang on to yourself."

She flew closer to the red dwarf. It hovered ahead like a Christmas ornament. Her scanners showed three gassy planets orbiting it, worlds without solid surfaces; she ruled them out. There were a handful of moons too, but most were too small to have any significant gravity, or they were too far from the red dwarf, terrifyingly cold. Finally she found a possible candidate: a large world, roughly the size of Luna back home, close enough to the red dwarf to soak up some energy. It was a barren rock of a world, pockmarked with craters, but the only one where a base could potentially be built. She flew toward it.

She orbited the planet several times, scanning the rocky surface, until she found a source of heat and light—a mere speck on the barren landscape. Thankfully, the atmosphere was thin. Her ship was rattling enough as it was; entering a thick atmosphere would rip her apart. She landed the *Ryujin* in a crater near the energy source she had detected.

The ship had come with a spare spacesuit. Lailani had spent yesterday working on it, cutting and sewing and tweaking. She could now fit it over Epimetheus. It fit horribly; the dog could barely walk in it. But thankfully the gravity was low here, and Lailani was able to carry her pet even though he outweighed her. He lay in her arms, bundled up, peering through his helmet.

They emerged onto the surface of the rocky planet. It was a cold, depressing, shadowy world. Barnard's Star was dimmer and cooler than the sun. It glowed in the sky, small and red, casting crimson light. It was no brighter than moonlight back home.

Lailani walked with her scanner drawn. The energy source should be right ahead, yet she saw nothing. No colony. No other starship. Not even an atmo-tent. Nothing but this sandy valley the color of rust, mountains in the distance, and the red dwarf in the sky.

"What the hell?" Lailani said. "There's nothing h—"

A voice crackled through her helmet's speakers. "Identify yourself or die!"

Lailani spun around, dropping Epimetheus and drawing her pistol.

A hulking robot stood before her. He had seemingly materialized from nothing. He stood even larger than HOBBS, all polished steel, and held a rifle the size of a park bench. His head was bucket-shaped, sprouting an antenna. His eyes were two light bulbs, and his hands were mere wrenches, reminding Lailani of a Lego man's hands. In an era of realistic-looking androids, some indistinguishable from humans, this machine was decidedly retro, like something out of *Forbidden Planet*.

"Weapon identified!" the robot said. Even its voice was quaint, a robotic monotone. "Danger, danger! Drop your pistol and identify yourself!"

Lailani kept her pistol raised, pointing at the massive robot. "I am Lailani de la Rosa!" She considered adding that she was a lieutenant in the army reserves, but decided against it. If this robot served Dr. Schroder, a notorious outlaw, it was likely programmed to dislike the police and military. It perhaps looked like a twentieth-century movie prop, but its rifle seemed real enough.

"State your purpose," the robot said, gun pointing at her head.

At Lailani's side, Epimetheus managed to rise in his bulky spacesuit. The dog growled.

"I've come to seek Dr. Elliot Schroder," she said.

The robot's light bulb eyes blazed. "Target to be destroyed!" His rifle heated up and fired a blast of plasma the size of a heart.

Lailani leaped aside, firing her own pistol. The two projectiles collided in space, shattering.

"I'm not here to arrest him!" Lailani cried. "I'm here with his friend. I—"

The robot fired again. Lailani leaped aside, and a blast slammed into a boulder beside her. It disintegrated. Epimetheus barked and lunged at the robot, but a wrench hand knocked the Doberman aside.

Lailani curbed the instinct to rush to her dog. Instead she fired again, hitting the robot's rifle. The weapon shattered.

"I am tasked with guarding Dr. Schroder!" the robot said. "You must be destroyed. Exterminate! Exterminate!"

He stepped toward her, raising his wrench hands. The robot had no rifle now, but those hands could easily shatter Lailani's bones.

"I've brought HOBBS back!" Lailani said. "Tell your master that HOBBS is with me. One of his creations."

The robot kept walking toward her, metal fingers held out. "Destroy! Destroy! Destroy!"

Lailani raised her pistol again, prepared to fight rather than flee.

The robot loomed above her, and she aimed her gun, and—

Another voice spoke.

"Robby! That's enough now. Stand still."

The massive robot paused, his hands centimeters away from Lailani. The bulky machine looked over his shoulder. His antennae wobbled.

"Must I, Doctor?"

The voice spoke again. "Yes, Robby. That'll be quite enough. Escort the girl and her dog into our home."

Lailani peeked around the robot, pistol still in hand, but she saw nobody. Whoever was speaking was transmitting his voice from hiding.

The hulking robot—Robby—reached out to her. "Come, human. I am to escort you. Disobey and you will be exterminated."

"Was that Schroder speaking?" Lailani said.

"Obey! Obey!"

Lailani rolled her eyes. "Ever heard of the Three Laws of Robotics? A robot shall not harm a human? Isaac Asimov. Read your classics."

The robot gave her a harsh stare. Lailani sighed and followed him, and Epimetheus joined them, swaying and slipping in his oversized suit.

Robby walked several steps, knelt, and lifted a hatch. Lailani gasped. The hatch was made of stone. When closed, it had blended perfectly with the surface. On closer inspection, Lailani saw several vents hidden among rocks, possibly emitting the energy she had detected from above.

Schroder definitely liked his privacy.

"Robby, before we climb down, I need your help," Lailani said. "I have a third passenger on my starship. A fellow robot. Well, not a robot but a cyborg. He has a human heart. Help me carry him inside, please. He's wounded and needs help."

"I am not your servant, human," Robby said. "Follow me! Obey or be exterminated! Obey or—"

"Robby." The voice from earlier rose through the speakers, impatient. "Do as she says."

The sound of grinding gears rose from within Robby. Lailani wasn't sure if robots had true emotions or mere simulations, but Robby seemed convincingly annoyed. With a grunt, he approached the *Ryujin*. When he saw HOBBS lying inside, Robby froze. He looked at Lailani.

"Did you do this, human? Did you hurt him?" His eyes blazed. "Did you duct tape him to the floor?"

Now it was Lailani's turn to fume. "I brought him here to fix him. Help me take him inside, Fisher Price."

Robby snorted but obeyed. He returned to HOBBS, pulled off the tape, and lifted the unconscious cyborg. They returned to the hatch, which led to an elevator. They descended below the surface of the planet.

The elevator reached its destination. They stepped out into an underground warehouse, and Lailani gasped.

"Fucking hell," she whispered.

Robots. Hundreds of robots filled the place, maybe thousands. Robby walked through the warehouse, carrying HOBBS. Lailani followed, gazing around with wide eyes, trying to soak it all in.

In one section of the warehouse stood a dozen battle-bots, tall and burly, mounted with machine guns, grenade launchers, and cannons. Some had caterpillar tracks on their feet. Several robots, she saw with a jolt, looked just like HOBBS, just newer and still operational. As Lailani walked by, HOBBS's doppelgangers gave her dour looks.

But most of the robots were not military. In one corner stood a group of robotic dogs, wagging their tails, hopping up and down, and playfully nipping at one another. Epimetheus gave them a growl, a snort, and then walked on with disinterest. They passed a group of female androids—*very* female androids. They wore lingerie and high heels, and they blew kisses at Lailani as she walked by. There were robotic knights battling a massive dragon the size of a dinosaur. Beyond them, robotic dwarves, halflings, and elves battled one another with swords and daggers. There were robot pirates, robot cowboys and Indians, and robots built to resemble celebrities. On a stage, a robot Elvis was swaying his hips, playing guitar.

Lailani cringed to see that last one. She mustn't forget her purpose. She hadn't come to gape at robots but to save her friend, Benny "Elvis" Ray. The boy she had killed. The boy she would travel back in time for.

She looked up at the unconscious HOBBS. The cyborg lay slumped in Robby's arms.

You're the only one who knows how to use the hourglass, Lailani thought. *How to send me back in time.*

She placed her hand on her pack, feeling the hourglass inside. The time-travel device. Her hope to save her friends. To save herself.

Because just as much as I seek to save Elvis, I seek salvation for myself. Lailani winced, the memory pounding through her. She could still feel her friend's heart in her hand, falling still. Tears burned in her eyes. *After a decade of guilt, I will find redemption.*

They reached the end of a warehouse, where a doorway led to a cluttered workshop. The robots here were incomplete. A gynoid stood on a table, nude and seductive, her skull open to reveal electronic components. Robotic animals crawled in a corral, clicking and clattering, only partly assembled. Various heads, limbs, torsos, and other robot parts hung everywhere. Gears, microchips, cables, wrenches, and countless other components covered shelves, tables, and the floor.

Lailani approached a deactivated android that stood on a platform. It was shaped like a girl, the metal ribs opened like gates.

Inside pulsed a human heart.

"Another cyborg," Lailani whispered.

A red glow caught the corner of her eye. She turned to see several human hearts in jars on a shelf. They were still beating.

Lailani reached for her pistol.

A voice rose from behind a pile of robot parts.

"Robby, have you brought the faulty HOBBS unit?"

The hulking Robby halted in the chamber. "I have the Humanoid Offensive Biometric Battle Soldier. I do not think he is going to make it."

Lailani walked around the table, keeping her hand close to her pistol. Epimetheus walked at her side, tail in a straight line. She glimpsed a figure ahead, mostly hidden behind piles of robot parts. She could just make out a lab coat and a bald head ringed with graying hair.

"You know, Robby, it would be nice if you called me Master." The man raised a wrench, then plunged it down like a blade. "Ah, there we go! This clunky gear will be the life of me."

The man spun around, and his gaunt face split into a tight grin. He dusted his gloved hands against his pants, then held out his arms as if expecting a hug.

"And you must be Lailani!" he said.

Lailani stood frozen, examining him. He was perhaps fifty years old, his cheeks sunken, his nose beaked, his back stooped, giving him the appearance of a vulture. He wore several tool belts across his chest and waist. They were heavy with wrenches, hammers, screwdrivers, and soldering guns. His boots were thick and heavy, and many pockets jangled across his tan leather pants, overspilling with gears and bolts.

"Dr. Schroder, I presume," Lailani said.

Robby cleared his throat—a human tick no doubt coded in as a lark—and dropped HOBBS onto the floor. The cyborg clattered.

"He is your problem now, *master*," Robby said. Lights swirled in his bulb eyes as if he were rolling them. "If you need me, I will be outside guarding again, bored out of my mind. It will probably be decades before somebody else shows up, and you probably won't let me kill them either."

The hulking robot marched away in a huff.

Schroder approached the fallen HOBBS, brushing past Lailani.

"Oh dear." Schroder frowned. "Oh my my my. This won't do. This won't do at all."

He knelt by HOBBS, ran a scanner across the cyborg's shattered body, and tsked his tongue.

"Can you fix him?" Lailani said.

"Of course I can fix him," Schroder said. "He's my son."

Lailani had the hideous vision of Dr. Schroder carving the heart out of his living child, then placing it into a metal body. She pushed the thought aside, hoping Schroder had spoken metaphorically.

"What about HOBBS's memory banks?" Lailani said. "Will he still have his memories, all the data inside him? Things he saw?"

Including the manual for the hourglass, she thought. Only HOBBS knew how many grains of azoth to spill through the hourglass. Only he could send her ten years back in time—just before she had killed Elvis. If she tried to operate the hourglass herself, Lailani was likely to end up crushed by a stegosaurus.

Schroder sighed. "I've seen it all before. Young human falls in love with a robot. It can't be helped! Now you want him to remember you. A tale as old as time."

"Um, yes, that's exactly it," Lailani said. "So, memories. You can save them, right?"

"Too early to tell, my dear, too early to tell. Now be a darling and fetch me a coffee. The dark roast this time. And black!"

Lailani blinked. Had he just ordered her to fetch him a drink?

An android, however, stepped forward. Lailani realized that Schroder had been talking to this machine. The android looked like a Japanese schoolgirl; she wore a sailor suit with a red ribbon, black stockings, and a short pleated skirt. The mechanical girl bowed her head sweetly to Dr. Schroder.

"Would you not care for some nourishing green tea, master?" she said.

Schroder sighed and looked at Lailani. "Do you see this? Even she questions my orders." He turned back toward the girl in the sailor outfit. "Damn it, Mimori. Coffee. Industrial strength. Black. Lailani, you want a coffee too? No, nothing? Fine. Mimori, move, you hunk of bolts, move!" He tossed a sprocket at the android.

Mimori smiled sweetly and bowed her head. "Yes, master." She rushed off.

Schroder returned to HOBBS and began working with a screwdriver, removing panels. "I can feel your frown digging into the back of my head," he said as he worked. "Don't worry, Lailani. They're robots. They can't feel a thing. No emotions, just algorithms. Good outlet for my frustration. Remember, they might look human, but they're just machines. Marvelous, wonderful machines! But they have no more true feelings than a toaster."

Lailani wasn't so sure. HOBBS had seemed to show her true friendship. Had it been merely an illusion, a trick of his programming, no more real than the way Robby had cleared his throat?

Another thought arose. She spoke softly.

"If they're just machines, why do they have human hearts?"

Schroder paused from his work. He looked up at Lailani. "Not all of them do. Some have dog hearts. Bird hearts. I even have a few robotic fish with fish hearts inside. You see, I do not build regular robots here. I build memobots. And that's a trademarked term, mind you, so be careful with it."

Epimetheus growled at the doctor, perhaps understanding his words about dog hearts. Unease crept across Lailani. If Epi distrusted somebody, so did she.

"Memobots?" she said, frowning.

"Memobots!" Schroder returned to his work. "I'll tell you more about them over dinner, shall I? For now, I'll focus on repairing this wondrous specimen. Ah, here comes the coffee!"

The robotic schoolgirl approached, smiled sweetly, bowed, and held out a mug of coffee.

"Enjoy, master!"

Schroder took the mug, sipped, and spat.

"Damn it, Mimori, too sweet! You know I like my coffee black. Did you forget again?"

Mimori laughed. "I forgot, Master! I got you four sugars. I four-got. Do you get it? I made a funny! Did you enjoy my joke?"

Bloody hell, Lailani thought. *She must have Osiris's humor chip.*

Schroder groaned. "Mimori, show Lailani to the living quarters. She'll be wanting a bath and a fresh pair of clothes, no doubt." He looked at Lailani. "I'll keep working on HOBBS. Go, my dear. Rest from your long journey. My pets will take good care of you. I'll also send a robo-mechanic to the surface to tend to your ship. She looks like she needs repairs."

"I'd rather stay by HOBBS, if you don't mind," Lailani said.

"But I do mind, my dear. I'll be performing delicate surgery on HOBBS, and I'm not to be disturbed. Don't worry.

Mimori will take good care of you. Go, Mimori, show our guest downstairs. And no more funnies!"

The android took Lailani's hand—firmly. When Lailani tried to free herself, she could not.

"Come now, Lailani," said Mimori. "We shall be ever such good friends. I will tend to you well. Come, we must leave the doctor to his work."

Reluctantly, Lailani walked with the android. Epimetheus walked with them, his tail still thrust out in a line, a sign of his alertness and suspicion. Mimori took them to a lower level. Here Lailani was shown to a bathing chamber, where tiny flying robots lifted brushes, soaps, and sponges, washing her clean. She felt like a Disney princess, a coterie of birds and mice preparing her for a ball. They even gave Epimetheus a scrubbing, much to his dismay. Two small, fluttering robots brushed Lailani's short black hair, while others wrapped a towel around her naked body.

"We have a variety of clothes for you to choose from," Mimori said. "Master Schroder has collected an extensive wardrobe for his robots. You might need to choose from the children's line—you are very small, did you know? We have many themed outfits. Princess gowns, sailor outfits, kimonos, and—"

"I'm not wearing fucking princess gowns or skirts," Lailani said. "My old clothes are fine."

She pulled them back on: tattered jeans, her belt with her gun holster, and a shirt with the words *Gangsta Rap* printed in Comic Sans over a rainbow. She placed her dog tags back around her neck. Though she only served in the reserves now, she still wore them every day. She was still a lieutenant, given a commission for her heroism in the Marauder War. She was still a soldier of humanity. Even here.

"Let me show you to the smoking lounge," Mimori said. "You can wait for the master there."

The android led Lailani and Epimetheus to a small chamber, no larger than her humble room back home. It was decorated in a Victorian theme—cherrywood divans, an upholstered armchair, and antique lamps with leather shades. Shelves held leather-bound books, pipes, tobacco boxes, and porcelain dolls with glass eyes. Old medical engravings hung on the walls, framed, showing the dissection of corpses. One engraving showed a human heart.

Dr. Frankenstein would be comfortable here, Lailani thought.

"Mimori," she said, "why does Dr. Schroder put hearts inside his creations?"

The schoolgirl gasped. She stared at Lailani, and her eyes narrowed. "That is the forbidden question, mistress! You must never ask." She trembled. "You must never ask!"

"Guess what?" Lailani said. "I just asked. Answer me."

The android took a step back. Did a heart beat within her chest too?

"I cannot," Mimori whispered. "He will know. He hears everything. He ... he is a kind master! He treats me well. He will tell you everything. He knows everything. You must not ask forbidden questions! Remember Eve. Remember Eve!"

Mimori turned to flee the chamber.

"Mimori, wait!" Lailani said.

But the android stepped outside and slammed the door behind her, leaving Lailani and Epimetheus in the Victorian lounge. Lailani yanked the doorknob.

Locked.

She grunted.

"I've had enough of this shit." She drew her pistol, aimed at the lock, and pulled the trigger.

Nothing happened.

She checked her gun. It was loaded. She frowned, opened the gun, and found that a pin had been removed from the inner mechanism.

"They disabled my weapon!" She blinked. "While I was having a bath. Can you believe this shit, Epi?"

Her Doberman growled at the locked door.

Lailani placed a hand on his head. "Epi, where are we?"

The dog leaped onto her, and she hugged him. Against her chest, she felt his beating heart.

CHAPTER EIGHT

"Hey, Baba," Addy said. "What did the Deep Being monk say to the hot dog vendor?"

The elephantine guru stared at her, silent.

"Make me one with everything," Addy said. "Ah? Ah? Nothing?"

Crickets chirped.

"Another Osiris joke," Marco muttered.

The three sat outside the temple, eating breakfast, their only meal of the day. Addy was stuffing herself, cheeks puffed out like a hamster. The food was pedestrian—bread, porridge, and the same fruit every day—but Marco ate heartily, knowing there would be no more until tomorrow. Aside from several hours of sleep a night, and a few moments to eat, they meditated. Day after day of Deep Being.

"This is worse than boot camp," Addy had muttered to him one night.

In some ways, she was right. At least in boot camp, friends had offered some companionship, some relief from the hardship. But in other ways, she was wrong.

"At boot camp, we learned how to kill," Marco had told her. "Here we're learning how to heal."

Days of silence.

Days of raging storms in their minds.

Days when the baba refused to let them suppress their nightmares, their trauma, their haunting memories.

For years, they had struggled to let things go. Here they learned to let things be.

Marco shoveled another spoonful of porridge into his mouth. It was filled with nuts and berries the baba grew in his gardens.

"Baba," he said, "before we begin practice today, I have a question."

Baba Mahanisha sat cross-legged in the courtyard before his meal. Gently, he was lifting fruits with his trunks and placing them into his mouth. For an alien so large—he must have weighed ten times as much as Marco—he ate with surprising grace.

"Ask, my pupil," said the baba. "I am here to provide wisdom."

The question had been gnawing at Marco since they had landed here two weeks ago.

"The other Durmians," he said. "What happened to them?"

Addy gulped down her mouthful of bread. "And what are those giant robot statues down in the valley? And who are the creatures with lion faces we saw painted in the tomb? And did you ever encounter the grays? And why do hot dogs come in packages of ten, but buns come in packages of eight? And why—"

The baba laughed, a sound like rolling thunder, and held up his four hands. "Many questions you have, young ones. Such eager, curious minds! But the Deep Being mind is calm like a tranquil lake, open to whatever winds may blow. I will tell you, for there is no forbidden knowledge for the Deep Being mind. It is a fool who thinks his mind full. A wise mind is like an empty pot, yearning to be filled."

Addy leaned forward. "I'm ready for story time."

And the baba spoke.

At times, his voice was gentle. At other times, it rose louder, deeper, before softening into tranquil water again.

For a long time, Marco and Addy listened.

Baba Mahanisha was old, they learned. Far older than they had expected. For five hundred years, he had roamed this land. For most of that time, he had meditated, sometimes emerging from deep reflection to teach, then sank again into years, sometimes decades of meditation. But as a young Durmian, before becoming a monk, he had been different. Rough. Violent. A soldier in a war.

Millions of Durmians had lived here then, building cities, raising temples and palaces, writing scrolls. They had forged a great civilization—great but unwise. The Durmians grew ambitious, haughty. Forever they wanted, craved, desired what they did not have, forgetting the teachings of the ancient Deep Being monks. They turned away from the Noble Path. They created technology. They built starships. They spread out in conquest. Always desiring. Never living in the present, forever reaching for the future. For a while, they had succeeded, had landed on their moon, had conquered other worlds, had spread their ambition. The conquerors grew mighty. And the monks remained in temples, their voices forgotten, their scrolls collecting dust.

And then, the Durmians met a world they could not conquer.

They met the Taolians.

The Taolians too were an ancient race. They came from a nearby planet, a world orbiting a neighboring star. They too were humanoid, but their faces were those of lions, and they had the pride and fierceness of hunters.

The two civilizations clashed.

Nobody knew how the war began, who had fired the first shot. But once the war ignited, it burned with devastating fury. The Taolians were horrible in their wrath, a civilization dedicated to war. Their weapons savaged the Durmian fleets. Yet the Durmians fought back hard, Baba Mahanisha among them, and would not be cowed. They withstood even the cruelest punishment and rose again to fight. As millions died on both sides, the war showed no signs of slowing. For years, both worlds suffered and lost their sons and daughters to the inferno.

Until the Taolians built their mechas.

"The mechas?" Addy asked, leaping up. "You mean the giant stone warriors we saw?"

"Those are but statues," Baba Mahanisha said. "Mere representations of the true horrors."

The Taolians had built two, the baba explained. Only two. But two were enough. Two massive machines, each the size of a skyscraper. Within each mecha stood a single operator, and the mechas gave them the power of gods. The Taolians had named their twin terrors Kaiyo and Kaji, male and female, god and goddess of fury.

The mechas destroyed the last of the Durmian warships. They landed on the surface of Durmia and destroyed the cities, shattered the monuments, and slaughtered millions of Durmians. The ancient civilization of Durmia collapsed. Its soldiers were put to the sword, and its survivors were placed in chains, forced to serve their Taolian masters.

The masters raised two great statues on Durmia—stone likenesses of Kaiyo, holding his great hammer, and Kaji, holding her fabled Sword of Dawn. Forever these monuments would taunt the Durmians, would remind the slaves of their place. The true mechas returned to Planet Taolian. The stone guardians remained, idols to worship and fear.

Baba Mahanisha was still young in those days, not yet a monk, a mere soldier witnessing the collapse of his world. For long years, he toiled as a slave, mining precious ores deep in the earth for his Taolian masters. For long years, his anger grew, his thirst for vengeance. He had not yet discovered the way of Deep Being.

With a group of rebels, Mahanisha escaped captivity and stole a military starship. He led a mission to Taolin Shi, the planet of his enemies, dodging their patrols. He unleashed an arsenal of nuclear weapons upon the northern pole of Taolin Shi, melting the ice.

The planet flooded.

Taolian cities drowned under the waves.

The ancient Taolian civilization was washed away.

Yet even now, the war did not end. Even from the devastation, soldiers still rose and starships still flew. Survivors from both sides fought on, their planets in ruins. Fleets unleashed weapons of mass destruction. Millions died. For years, the survivors lashed at each other until finally only two soldiers remained.

One Durmian—the bitter, scarred Mahanisha.

One Taolian—a young soldier named Ling.

Of billions, only they remained. Only two. Elephant and lion. Mahanisha and Ling, two old enemies, two last survivors.

Durmia lay in ruin, its cities ground to dust. The neighboring world of Taolian remained flooded, all its treasures lost, all its people drowned.

Finally the last two soldiers shook hands.

Finally there was peace.

Addy shed tears as she listened.

"How horrible," she whispered. "Two entire species— wiped out. All because of a pointless war, and nobody even knows who started it."

Marco lowered his head. "How close we humans came to such a fate."

Baba Mahanisha lowered his head. "For many years after the war, I was angry, overburdened with grief and guilt. My own people had perished. I had caused the extinction of another race. The agony, the loneliness, the anxiety seemed too great. Often I contemplated taking my own life."

Marco nodded. He thought he knew something of such a spiral.

"In the long years that followed," Baba Mahanisha said, "I discovered the wisdom of Deep Being. I read the books of the ancient masters, dug up from our fallen libraries. For centuries I meditated upon their wisdom. I found enlightenment. I then dedicated my life to teaching others. I am old now, nearing the end of my days, but I have passed on my wisdom to many. Now I pass it on to you."

Marco reflected upon this for a moment. In some ways, the baba's story mirrored his own. A soldier who had seen terror, who had exterminated his enemies, who had lived on while so many had died. Who suffered guilt, pain, deep terror, only to seek peace.

Yet can I spend the rest of my life in peaceful meditation? Marco wondered. *Or will my wars continue? Does Earth still face violence, and dare I return to fight? If the grays invade Earth, would I abandon my homeworld for the sake of my own peace, or would I return into the furnace of war?*

He spoke carefully. "Baba, the two mechas. The real ones, not the statues. Do they still exist on Taolin Shi?"

The baba nodded. "They are drowned under the water, rusting away, covered with barnacles, forever relics of that war."

Addy leaned forward. "Do they still work? Can you fight with them?"

The baba shook his head, his earrings chinking. "Those of Deep Being do not fight, do not kill. They find no honor in war, in hatred, in destruction. We are beings of peace."

"But ... Baba, what if we need to fight for self-defense?" Marco said.

"That is what I believed I was doing," Baba Mahanisha said. "Yet in self-defense, we inflict harm upon an enemy, only enraging him to further violence. We retaliate. The enemy strikes again. The cycle spins faster. Violence only begets violence. The student of Deep Being breaks this wheel. The student of Deep Being practices only peace, only love."

"Even love of an enemy?" Marco said.

The baba nodded. "You are not your thoughts. Neither is the enemy. Violence, wickedness, cruelty—these are dark clouds. Yet consciousness is never evil. There are no evil beings, Marco. Only beings who do evil things."

"Oh, there is evil," Addy said softly, eyes haunted. "I've seen it."

"You saw with your eyes, not with your consciousness," said the baba. He rose to his feet. "We are late for our meditation. All will become clear as we keep practicing. All your questions will be answered along your path. You have only taken the first few steps."

Their lessons continued.

For two weeks, they lay on their backs in the courtyard, gazing up at the sky, moving their awareness across every part of their body. On the first day, the baba taught them to focus all their consciousness on their toes, to feel all sensations there, to let the rest of the body fade. Finally they advanced to their ankles, and it seemed ages before they reached their pelvises. Long days of breathing in and out of every part of them, exploring their bodies with their awareness alone, discovering their strengths and flaws.

Marco and Addy did not like their bodies. Both carried too many scars from the war. Addy was still branded on her hip, a mark that shamed her. She still thought she was overweight. Marco still felt too short. Both carried insecurities like yokes. Yet the baba forced them to confront, to accept every part of them.

"Breathe into your toes. Breathe into your abdomen. Let the breath flow through you, healing, filling you."

Finally after two weeks, they could bring the entire body into awareness, feeling every sensation—the sunrays upon them, the cobblestones beneath them, the feel of their robes against skin. Marco had never really spared his body much thought, but for two weeks, he lay here, still, exploring every part with only his awareness. By the end, he could feel the oxygen flow into his bloodstream, could feel that oxygen flowing to every part he focused on, could move his consciousness across his body. Healing. Feeling. Exploring. Soothing. Accepting.

It was hard work. Often his mind was a storm, filled with anxiety, anger, pain. He raged against the generals and leaders who had failed his planet. He raged against the aliens who had butchered so many. He mourned the fallen. Often his mind could not be silenced. Breath after breath, he struggled to focus. To bring his awareness to his body, his breath, his deeper consciousness. It was an act of such concentration that usually he failed, yet he kept trying. It was a war within himself. He had often believed that meditation was simply closing your eyes and relaxing; it was anything but. Not for him. Not for a mind broken and scarred and lost at storming sea. On the outside, perhaps, he seemed to the world to be relaxing. On the inside he fought for every breath, and he battled every cloud of thought. A war fought not with guns but with kindness, with forgiveness, with acceptance.

For another week, they practiced yoga upon the mountaintop. Moving slowly. Stretching. Tilting. Straightening. A languid dance from dawn to midnight. They explored how consciousness could affect their muscles. They learned every joint, every creak, every fluid movement. Nothing but awareness of the body.

"Breathe and move and let be," the baba said. "Accept all parts of your body. Your flaws as well as your strengths. Do not judge. Breathe. Move. Let it be. If thoughts arise, observe them with friendly curiosity, even if they are painful. Let them be. They will float away. Move. Dance. Become one with everything. Be aware."

Every night, Marco and Addy retired to their chamber, an austere room with no furniture, only a single blanket on the floor. Every night, they made love and then slept entwined, warming each other.

After several weeks of practice, Marco noticed something. He no longer suffered nightmares.

For the past decade, ever since boot camp, he had not slept straight through the night. Every night for ten years, he would wake up once, twice, sometimes many times, drenched in sweat, clawing at his blankets. The dream was always the same: he was trapped in tunnels, seeking a way out. Sometimes the tunnels were a scum hive. Sometimes they were the bowels of a great starship. Sometimes the underground streets of Haven. He always felt lost, trapped, desperate to find his way home, creatures chasing him in the darkness.

The first time he had slept the night through, he woke up surprised at how refreshed he felt. The baba only gave them four, sometimes five hours most nights, which Marco had thought cruel, a torture of sleep deprivation. It reminded him of the sleep deprivation at boot camp. But surprisingly, these brief nights filled him with deep relaxation. Addy too slept soundly. She had always kicked, even screamed in her sleep, trapped in her own nightmares. Those nightmares faded here.

"We let the bad memories be," Marco whispered before bed one night, holding Addy in his arms.

She nodded. "We do not suppress them or banish them."

"We accept them," Addy whispered.

"We let them be," Marco said.

"We let them flow away."

"We forgive ourselves," Marco whispered. "We are not our memories. We are not our thoughts. The past is only an illusion."

"The only thing that is real is the now," Addy said.

They slept—deeply, kindly, a sleep of healing and forgiveness.

After two months of their studies, Baba Mahanisha announced a new noble truth they must learn.

"We have learned that we are not our thoughts," he said. "We have learned to bring awareness to our breath, to our bodies, to the cosmos. We have learned to observe as beings of pure consciousness. We have learned that the past and future are but illusions, that only the present is real. Today we will begin to learn kindness."

"I'm already kind!" Addy said. "I'm a ray of sunshine."

"Addy," Marco said, "just this morning, you were twisting my arm and punching me in the ribs."

She placed her hands on her hips. "You deserved it. You ate my last piece of fruit."

Marco groaned. "You offered it to me!"

"Yeah, well, you're *supposed* to say no thank you, here, have my porridge." Addy rolled her eyes.

"Come, my pupils," the baba said, smiling. "To the courtyard. Let us chant."

Chanting? That was new. They had never chanted during meditations before. They made their way into the sunlit courtyard, and they sat cross-legged on the cobblestones. The trees rustled around them, birds sang, and they took several healing breaths, awakening their awareness.

"Repeat with me," said Baba Mahanisha, and his voice was soft and kind. "May I be safe and free from suffering."

"May I be safe and free from suffering," Marco and Addy repeated.

"May I know peace," said the baba.

They repeated the words, softer now. "May I know peace."

"May I have ease of being," said the baba.

"May I have ease of being," Marco and Addy repeated.

Marco felt a little silly repeating these words. It all felt too New Agey to him, too sappy. He had fought in two wars, had seen so many die, had suffered and survived. He had found merit in the silent meditations, but this felt childish.

Yet when he looked at Addy, Marco saw tears in her eyes. She reached out and took his hand, breaking protocol.

"I love you, Poet," she whispered.

"I love you too, Ads," he said, squeezing her hand.

They repeated the mantra all day. Forgiving themselves.

I forgive myself for hurting Anisha and the other women of Haven, he thought.

I forgive myself for killing in the war, he thought.

I forgive myself for neglecting Tomiko, for driving her away, he thought.

I forgive myself for being imperfect. For being flawed. For sometimes being cruel.

He took deep breath by deep breath.

I am sorry.

"May I be safe and free from suffering," they chanted. "May I know peace. May I have ease of being."

Marco added his own words to the chant, whispering them so softly the others could not hear.

"May I be forgiven."

The next day, the baba asked them to think of another person, one they loved.

"I choose you, Addy," Marco said, taking her hands.

"Oh, I, um ..." Addy bit her lip. "I choose you too." She sighed. "I was going to choose the Pillowman, but fine! You're so needy, Marco."

They held hands, looking into each other's eyes, and chanted.

"May you be safe and free from suffering," they said to each other. "May you know peace. May you have ease of being."

Safety. Freedom from suffering. Peace. Yet what of the other things Marco wanted?

"Why not ask for health?" he asked the baba.

"Why not ask for riches?" Addy said.

"Health may come and go," said the baba. "We cannot always control it. Wealth too. Health and riches are as ephemeral

146

as the mandala of sand. Yet do the ill, the poor not deserve peace and ease of being? The winds come and go. They may bring you tragedy: illness, war, the loss of loved ones. They may bring you prosperity one day, take it away the next. You cannot control the wind. But you can adjust your sails. May you be safe and free from suffering. May you know peace. May you have ease of being."

"How can we find safety in a world of danger?" Marco asked.

"You cannot always," said the baba. "Sometimes you must simply ride out the storm. We do not wish to fight the wind, merely to bend and let it blow over us. To know peace. To have ease of being."

On the third day, the baba asked them to think of somebody who had wronged them. Somebody difficult in their lives. Somebody they might even consider an enemy.

"I'll think of Marco," Addy said.

"Hey!" Marco said.

"Well, you keep stealing my blanket at night."

He rolled his eyes. "Addy!"

She groaned. "Fine, fine, I'll think of somebody else."

"Not the Pillowman!" Marco said.

"But—" Addy sighed and crossed her arms. "Fine!"

To choose an enemy? Marco had no shortage of those. There had been Pinky, of course. And Captain Coleen Petty. And the Never War movement that had tried to arrest him. And worse enemies: the scum, the marauders, and the grays. Who to choose?

"Are you ready?" the baba asked.

Marco nodded, settling on imagining a random scum, one among countless centipedes he had fought a decade ago.

"Now," said the baba, "direct your blessings to your enemy. May you be safe and free from suffering."

Addy gasped. "Wait. What?" She growled. "I thought of a marauder! I'm not wishing that fucking thing safety or freedom from suffering. I want it to suffer!"

The baba nodded. "I know, my pupil. This meditation is often difficult. But please, even if you do not feel it within you, repeat the words with me. Even if it's hard. Try. Try to send these blessings to your enemy." He inhaled deeply. "May you be safe and free from suffering."

"May you be safe and free from suffering," Marco and Addy said together, having to force the words between stiff lips.

Marco didn't mean it. The words tasted of lies. He thought of the scum. The creatures that had killed his mother and most of his friends. How could he wish them anything but suffering?

"May you know peace," said the baba.

"May you know peace," Marco said, unable to keep the bitterness from his voice.

"May you know—ugh!" Addy groaned. "Do I have to?"

The baba nodded. "If you wish to learn this noble truth, you do."

Addy groaned and stamped her feet. "Fine! May you know peace, marauder." She shuddered.

"May you have ease of being," said the baba.

"May you have ease of being," Marco said, directing the thought to the scum, not truly meaning it.

"May you have ease of—" Addy stopped. "No." She crossed her arms. "No. Fuck no! Do you hear me, Baba? I won't do it! I won't wish the marauders ease of being, or peace, or freedom from suffering, or anything like that. Fuck them!" Her eyes burned. "They captured me. Enslaved me. Branded me." She pulled up her robe, exposing the brand on her hip. "They murdered millions of humans. They tortured me. And I won't wish them well. Do you hear me, Baba? I won't! What do you know of suffering, of pain? Would you wish well to somebody who hurt you, who tortured you?"

Tears were flowing down her cheeks. Marco rushed toward her and embraced her.

The baba looked at Addy, eyes sad. "You feel pain. You suffer. That is good."

"How is that fucking good?" Addy shouted, struggling to free herself from Marco's embrace. He held on, terrified that she would attack the guru.

Baba Mahanisha lowered his head. "I too was tortured, my pupil. The Taolians had placed me in chains. Whipped me. Scarred me. I still wear the scars on my back, still feel the pain. For many years, I was angry. I wanted revenge. Yet that brought me only more pain, more suffering. Hatred is like drinking poison and hoping your enemy dies. My own hatred poisoned my soul. Only when I forgave my enemies, when I wished peace to my torturers, did my internal torture end."

Addy relaxed in Marco's embrace. "It's hard," she whispered. "I can't truly forgive them. Not ever. I can't wish them well. They don't deserve peace! They don't deserve happiness."

"Perhaps not," said the baba. "But *you* do. And so long as hatred fills you, true happiness will evade you. Only once you wish well to all living beings, even those who had wronged you, will you find your own ease of being. I do not ask you to wish happiness to your enemies for their sake. It is for *your* sake, my pupil. I want your soul to be pure, filled with love for all, not twisted with bitterness or hatred. Only thus will it find true joy."

"Maybe true joy is a luxury for the naive," Addy said. "For those who never saw evil. I saw evil. I suffered evil. I can't just sing 'Kumbaya' and pretend that everyone is good and happy and riding unicorns through fields of cupcakes. The cosmos doesn't work that way. You're asking me to be delusional! To bury my head in the sand! Maybe I prefer the hard truth to the happy illusion."

The baba stepped toward her. He raised one of his trunks and wiped away her tears. "I do not ask for delusion, my child. Only for clarity of thought. Yes, there is evil. Yes, there is suffering. I do not ask you to pretend otherwise. I ask you to extend well-wishes and kindness to all living things. Even those things that are evil, cruel, and wicked."

But Addy just raised her chin and clenched her fists. "I don't believe in loving my enemy. I believe in *destroying* my enemy. If that means there is poison inside me, well, then I am poisoned."

She spun on her heel and marched away.

Marco stood for a moment, still, not sure whether to remain with the baba in the courtyard or rush after Addy.

The baba placed a trunk on his shoulder.

"This meditation is often the hardest for those who suffered greatly," the baba said softly. "It is normal for her to march away. It is not unexpected. Go to her, my pupil. She needs your love more than ever."

Marco nodded. "Thank you, Baba."

He turned and chased Addy.

She was walking down the mountainside, fists clenched at her sides. She ignored Marco's call, and with her long legs, she easily kept ahead of him. He hurried in pursuit, barely keeping up.

"Addy, come on!" he cried, hurrying after her. "Will you wait up?"

She ignored him.

They hiked the entire way, several kilometers, back toward the ruined city. The *Thunder Road*, their small starship, stood among the ruins. Dust coated the flowers and peace signs painted onto its hull and wings. Addy stepped into the Volkswagen, never looking back at Marco.

Winded, he entered the ship after her.

"Addy." He spoke softly. "Do you want to talk about it?"

She stood with her back to him. She stared at the wall. Her fists were clenched at her sides. Her crimson Deep Being robes lay on the floor; she stood in her underwear. They had no more spare clothes aboard. They had lost almost everything when the gray had opened the airlock in space. Only the bed, the stove, the katana, and the fridge remained. The books, the games, their clothes—all had been lost to space.

Marco took a step closer to her. Still Addy wouldn't turn toward him.

"Addy?" He placed a hand on her shoulder.

She spun toward him, snarling, and grabbed him—painfully. Her fingernails dug into his skin. He recoiled, but she wouldn't release him. Her face was a mask of fury, and her eyes were red and damp.

He opened his mouth to speak again, and Addy kissed him, surprising him, taking his breath away.

"Add—" he managed before she pulled him onto the bed.

They made desperate love. Back in the temple, with the baba sleeping next door, they had been quiet, reserved, their sex like meditation, all slow and mindful movements. Now Addy was like a wild beast, shouting in her passion, and her fingernails tore his skin and drew blood. This was sex like a battle, animalistic, raw and primal, and she screamed so loudly Marco thought that even atop the mountain the baba could hear.

When it was over, Marco lay on his back, and Addy sat at the edge of the bed, smoking a cigarette. It was the first cigarette she had smoked since climbing the mountain two months ago.

And finally Addy spoke.

"I can't do this, Poet."

He pulled on his boxer shorts and sat at her side. He placed a hand on her thigh.

"Are you sure, Ads? You've been doing so well. For two months now, you've been acing this."

She placed her hand atop his. "He wants us to love the marauders, Poet. And the scum. And all those enemies. I can't do that." She shook her head. "I can't. I never will." She stared into his eyes. "That's not who I am. I'm a warrior. They made me a warrior. When they hurt me, branded me, tortured me, they made me who I am."

Marco spoke in a whisper. "Maybe you can change. Maybe the baba can help."

She shook her head. "I don't want to end up like him, Poet. The last survivor of a civilization, alone on a mountain. And if the grays attack Earth? I'll fight them." She wiped her eyes and nodded. "I'll fight them, and I'll hate them."

Marco nodded. He held her hands tightly. "I will too. Always. I'll always fight at your side. It still hurts me—every day—that I wasn't there with you. During the marauder war. That the enemy captured you, and that I wasn't at your side that year. I'll never let you go again, Addy. No matter what happens, I'll fight with you. I would follow you to Hell and back. You know that, right?"

"I know." She hugged him. "I know, Poet."

They sat for a long time on the bed, embraced.

"So what say we go back up that mountain and lie." Marco winked. "We'll say the words. Just to get a passing grade. Then keep going with the training."

Addy gasped. Her eyes widened. "You cheater!"

He grinned. "You're one to talk. You always cheated on exams at school."

"I did not! I just copied from you, and *you* didn't cheat, so it was fair and square." She sighed and lit another cigarette. "Do you really think we should? I'm pissed off at that elephant, Poet. Maybe I'll always be pissed off, and anger will always be a part of me. Maybe I just suck at this."

"You're good at this." Marco nodded. "I've seen the change in you. You no longer have nightmares. You yell less. You poke me in the ribs less." He rubbed his side. "You're different now, Addy, in a good way. You're calmer, more focused, more at peace. This has been good for you. For us. I say we go back up there, cheat this one time, then complete our training. We're almost done, after all."

She sighed and mussed his hair. "You really are a silly poet, you know that? And a dirty, rotten cheater."

"I know."

She flopped onto her back. "All right. But not yet. Let's spend one night here." She grabbed him, pulled him down beside her, and stared hungrily into his eyes. "I'm not done ravaging you yet."

"Hmm." Marco nodded. "Yeah, I think I could stand to spend a few more hours in this spaceship with you."

The next morning, they headed back up the mountain.

They chanted for themselves. For each other. For their enemies. For all living beings.

"May all living beings be safe and free from suffering. May all know peace. May all have ease of being."

Their training continued.

CHAPTER NINE

"Why did you disable my pistol?" Lailani shoved her plate of food aside. "Answer me!"

They sat in Dr. Schroder's dining room, deep within his underground complex. Several androids stood against the walls. Yet they were not nearly as realistic as Osiris, the android Lailani had met in the military, or as Mimori, the friendly schoolgirl. These androids seemed older, cruder. Their skin was rubbery, their faces ill fitting like masks that threatened to slip off. The synthetic skin hung loosely around the eyes, revealing their metal skulls. Wet tongues moved in their mouths, too red, too thick.

As Lailani watched these creatures, she had the horrible feeling that these were actual faces, actual human skin peeled off from victims and placed onto the machines. The tongues looked like the severed tongues of animals. She shuddered and shoved that thought away. Nobody was that disturbed.

The robots had placed a feast upon the table: roasted snakes, one of the few lifeforms that lived on this planet, their skin crispy and their eyes glassy in death like the eyes of fried fish. They were like smaller versions of the robots' eyes.

"I did not disable your pistol, my dear," Schroder said. He sat across the table from her, candles lighting his face. "My beloved robots did. They're simply following their algorithms, which I coded long before I met you. We allow no working firearms in this complex. Every armed robot here, even the military ones—their weapons are disabled."

Lailani was not pacified. "And why did you lock me in a room? Are you going to blame that on algorithms too?"

Schroder slumped in his seat. "For that, I must apologize. Mimori was not to lock you in the smoking lounge. As soon as I learned, I placed Mimori in the basement." His eyes hardened. "She will remain there until she learns to behave. Sometimes I must discipline my toys. Sometimes they must suffer."

Lailani peered at him, eyes narrowed. "I thought you said they have no emotions."

For the span of a heartbeat, Schroder seemed speechless. Then he laughed. "Quite astute, quite astute! But come now. We shall not debate the true nature of suffering at the dinner table. Eat, my friend!" He lifted a roasted snake and bit. The skin crunched. "They are delectable."

"Where is HOBBS?" Lailani said.

The doctor slurped up a tail, chewed, and swallowed. He dabbed his lips with a napkin. "The poor fellow was badly damaged." He sighed. "He's an older model. One of my earliest efforts. I'm proud of the boy. Still a remarkable machine, and what spirit! I will save him, but it will take more time, at least a week of work."

"A week!" Lailani leaped to her feet. "That long?"

Schroder raised an eyebrow. "I have other work than simply repairing old robots, my dear. Important work."

She stared at him, still not touching the food. Below the table, Epimetheus was reluctantly nibbling a roast snake. The poor pup seemed unhappy with the fare, but hungry enough to keep eating.

"What kind of work?" Lailani said. "Why do you put hearts into your robots? Mimori said that's forbidden knowledge. Like Eve and her apple."

Schroder blinked, then burst out laughing. "You misunderstood her, dear! Our friend Mimori did not mean the biblical Eve, feeding upon the forbidden fruit of knowledge. Eve was the name of my wife." Schroder sighed, and his voice softened. "Her heart now beats within Mimori's chest."

Lailani grabbed a knife from the table. She held it out like a dagger. "What game are you playing here, Schroder? Are you some kind of butcher? Is this why they exiled you? I'm going to—"

The robotic servants lunged toward her. Their glassy eyeballs peered through the holes in their loose, rubbery masks. They grabbed her with twisting fingers of many joints, wrenching her blade away. Epimetheus barked and tossed himself into the fray, biting the robots, his teeth clattering harmlessly against them.

"Let go of me!" Lailani cried, floundering, kicking the air as they lifted her. "Schroder, damn it!"

The engineer rose to his feet and raised his arms. "It's all right, friends! Let her be! She is right to be suspicious."

The robots unceremoniously dumped Lailani back into her seat. She rubbed her sore arms.

"You owe me some answers," Lailani said, glaring at Schroder. "No more bullshit. And if your robots attack me again, I'll summon the wrath of the HDF onto this planet."

For an instant, fury filled Schroder's eyes. His fists clenched. His lips peeled back. But his moment of anger vanished. He nodded and sat back down.

"Of course, my dear. Let me explain, please. There is no need for fighting. No need to call anyone over. My wife died of natural causes, I assure you. She fell ill at the tender age of forty-three. She died here on this planet." Schroder lowered his head and wiped a tear away. "I preserved her heart inside Mimori, my beloved android. Thus do I keep Eve's memory alive. As I told you, I build memobots. Robots to preserve the hearts of loved ones, to keep them still beating forever."

Lailani grimaced. She looked at the rubbery-faced servants.

Schroder laughed. "Oh, no, my dear, not them. They're merely heartless machines who tend to my table. Though they too have the capacity to contain a heart. DF3, open your chest cavity. Show her."

One of the robotic servants stepped forth. His leathery face jiggled with each step, sliding around the metal skull. He swung open a door on his chest, revealing a cavity shaped like a human heart.

"Someday, I dream to have a heart inside me," said the robot, thick tongue sloshing in his mouth. "It is what I pray for every day."

Schroder nodded sadly. "They desire it, you see. I programmed them that way. To have a heart is their dearest wish." He sighed. "I used to sell my memobots all over Earth. Lost your beloved pet? Simply place Fluffy's heart into a robotic animal! Lost a beloved family member? You can choose from a variety of robots of all shapes and sizes, and they will keep your loved one's heart alive."

Lailani narrowed her eyes. "People will pay for this? It seems so ..."

"Morbid?" Schroder said. "It does at first. Yet is it any more morbid than burial, letting the heart rot underground, letting the worms consume it? Is it any more morbid than cremation, letting the heart burn? Is it any more morbid than burial in space, letting the heart float forever in the vacuum, cold and frozen for all eternity? With memobots, the heart beats on. The heartbeat—the very basic indicator of life—preserved! Someday, when I'm dead, my heart will beat in a memobot too. My robots have instructions to preserve my heart, to implant it in one of their chests. I've not yet chosen the robot I will become."

"I hope it will be me," said the serving robot with the rubbery face. "How I yearn for it!"

Lailani shuddered. She had signed an organ donor card when joining the military—not that much was left to salvage from most dead soldiers—but to place a beating heart inside a robot? When human patients could use it? It seemed not just creepy. It seemed callous.

She frowned. "What about the battle-bots? Like HOBBS? Weren't they built for the military?"

"They have the hearts of soldiers!" Schroder took another bite of snake. "When soldiers fall, sometimes their families wish to see their battle completed, their war won. They place the heart of their fallen warrior into a memobot. The young soldier's heart goes on to fight—to win! Truly the hearts of champions."

Lailani placed her hand on her chest. She felt her heart beat behind her thin ribcage. She shuddered at the thought of her heart beating inside one of these machines. Did people truly even place the hearts of loved ones into the robotic burlesque bots? And Mimori—poor Mimori, docile and sexualized—with the heart of his wife?

"In the warehouse, I passed by thousands of robots," Lailani said. "Do they all ...?"

"Oh no," Schroder said. "Most are like our friend DF3 here. Their chests are empty. I sell them empty, you see. Or used to, at least. I sold HOBBS empty as well, back when my business still operated on Earth. I don't know whose heart beats inside him, though I've been doing my best to save it." He sighed and looked around him. "I don't sell many memobots these days, only to the rare, discerning client. But they keep me company. They are my beloved pets. I am never lonely."

Lailani bit her lip. "But don't you ever miss human companionship?"

"Robots are better than humans," Schroder said. "Humans will hurt you, betray you. Robots are always loyal."

Lailani thought back to her life back in the Philippines. She herself had few human companions. There were Marco and Addy, of course, but they lived on the other side of Earth. And Ben-Ari didn't even live on Earth anymore. Mostly Lailani just shared her life with Epimetheus.

Humans will hurt you, betray you.

She thought of how she had betrayed Elvis, slaying him. Perhaps Schroder was right. She looked back at him. Somebody had hurt him. Or he had hurt somebody. She dared not ask. HOBBS would know.

Whatever sin Schroder committed, Lailani thought, *he's helping me now. And surely his sin is no greater than mine.*

"I apologize, Dr. Schroder," Lailani said. "Thank you for your help." She lifted one of the snakes. "And your hospitality."

She bit down deep. The skin crunched. The doctor smiled.

* * * * *

"Goodnight, Mistress!" Mimori said. The android smiled brightly, cheery as ever.

"Goodnight, Mimori," Lailani said, smiling in return.

The schoolgirl bowed her head and closed the door behind her. Again she locked Lailani in the smoking lounge, leaving her to spend the night on a divan.

Lailani waited, ear pressed against the door. Once the android's footsteps faded into the distance, Lailani reached into her pocket. She pulled out the forks she had stolen from the dining room.

She worked at the lock. She had grown up on the rough streets of Manila, a hungry orphan, scavenging and stealing to survive. She could handle a rusty, Victorian-era lock.

The lock clicked.

Lailani knelt by Epimetheus and hugged him.

"I need to do this alone, Epi," she whispered, patting him. "Will you wait for me here?"

The dog gave a huff of objection.

"Guard our den, Epi," Lailani said. "I'll be back soon."

Leaving the Doberman behind, she crept into the hallway. It stretched before her, paneled with hideous wallpaper. The entire underground complex was a mishmash of styles, each room and corridor decorated differently. This corridor gave Lailani the impression of some abandoned hotel. She half expected to see a pair of twins in the distance, inviting her to come play with them.

She crept down the hallway.

I need to find answers, she thought. *I need to find HOBBS.*

In the distance rose strange sounds. Laughing babies. A titter, then a scream. The sound of muffled gunfire, perhaps a television set. Pattering. Clanking gears. The sounds were all dim; Lailani could barely hear them. Yet as she kept walking, she felt as if this entire underground complex was alive.

She froze.

A robot was walking ahead. Lailani inhaled sharply.

Ugly fucker.

The robot moved on six serrated legs like a spider. But it had a humanoid torso, an oval head, and blazing blue eyes. A guardian of these halls. Lailani pressed her back to the wall.

The spider had not yet seen her. It clattered forward. Blades tipped its legs.

Lailani's heart thudded. She dared not even breathe. That spider was the size of a cow. Any one of those blades could slice her in two.

The spider took more steps forward. Its head was turning toward her.

Lailani reached behind her back, felt around, and found a doorknob. She opened a door and retreated through the doorway.

She found herself in shadows. She stood hidden, watching the hallway. When the mechanical spider walked just outside, she slunk deeper into the shadows. Her heart beat so powerfully she was sure it would give her away.

The spider paused.

Its head creaked, turning toward the open doorway.

164

Fuck!

Lailani retreated deeper into the darkness, heart pounding, sweat dripping. The spider gazed into the shadows.

Please walk on. Please walk on.

The mechanical spider turned away. It walked on down the hallway.

Lailani breathed out in relief and wiped the sweat off her brow.

She glanced around her, unable to see through the darkness. She drew her phone from her belt and switched on its flashlight mode. Where was she? Her beam of light pierced the shadows, and her eyes widened.

Dolls.

She was in a room with hundreds of Victorian-style dolls.

They were robots, she realized. She could see the rivets and bolts. Thankfully, they were shut down for the night. Schroder obviously had an obsession with dolls; they filled the room, a collection that would not shame a museum. Perhaps Schroder had daughter on Earth who enjoyed them?

"They give me the creeps," Lailani muttered, gazing at the porcelain faces, frilly dresses, and dead eyes.

She walked through the chamber, moving between the dolls. They lay on the floor, sat on shelves, and hung from the ceiling. Their glass eyes followed Lailani, but they made no other movement. She paused by a doll that was roughly her size. The robot wore a purple gown heavy with ribbons, a frilly scarf, and a wide hat adorned with flowers. Lailani undressed the doll, then put on the gown and hat. They smelled of mothballs, and she sneezed.

Thank God I'm tiny, she thought. Her friends had sometimes mocked her that she looked like a doll. Now it was finally coming in handy.

She stepped back into the hallway, her gown rustling, her wide-brimmed hat pulled low. She carried the doll's matching purple purse. There wasn't much Lailani could do about her face—her olive complexion would not pass for porcelain—but thankfully the hat was wide enough to shadow her, and she pulled up the frilly scarf as a veil.

She continued down the hallway.

She had taken only ten steps when another arachnid robot emerged from around the corner.

This time there were no doorways nearby for Lailani to slink through. She froze for a moment, then steeled herself and kept walking. Her Victorian gown rustled.

The mechanical spider approached her. By God, it was massive. Its legs were the size of her, and guns gleamed on its back. It turned six swiveling camera lenses toward her.

Lailani gave what she hoped was a convincing robot movement. Thank goodness for that evening on the HSS *Marilyn* she had spent practicing the robot dance.

The spider's six eyes narrowed, scrutinizing her. Lailani kept walking, passing it by, struggling to calm the thudding of her heart.

The spider emitted mechanical sounds, and Lailani cringed, expecting a hailstorm of bullets to tear through her. But the spider kept walking, leaving her behind.

She released a shaky breath.

Finally being doll-like pays off, she thought. *I'll never wish to be tall like Addy again.*

At the end of the corridor, she found a shaft leading to a lower level. She climbed down into a dingy, cluttered basement. Countless items filled the place, hanging from rafters: wrenches, hammers, gears, robot clothes wrapped in plastic, cables, and many robotic limbs, faces, and torsos. Several operational robots were here too. A robotic snake rose from the floor, gazed at Lailani with a single eye like a cyclops, then slithered away. A humanoid robot, so thin he looked like a metal skeleton, approached her, recognized her as a fellow machine, and moved aside, muttering about doll-bots belonging upstairs.

"That's right, boys," Lailani whispered. "It is I, Laila-bot, one of your own."

The basement was dark, but among the shelves and chests, Lailani found a flashlight, its beam more powerful than her phone. She walked deeper, moving between a hundred legs that hung from the ceiling. Mechanical mice moved across the floor, squeaking. A massive robotic gorilla loomed at her side, staring with shining eyes. Beyond the creature, a few plastic torsos hung from meat hooks on the wall. Hearts beat inside them, connected to tubes that ran up to the ceiling. Lailani cringed but kept walking.

She paused.

Bloody hell.

Jars stood on a shelf ahead. Inside were brains.

"This isn't a robotic workshop," she muttered. "It's Frankenstein's lab."

Past the jars, she found what indeed looked like a Victorian laboratory. There was a bloodstained table topped with scalpels, saws, a rib spreader, and various vials and tubes. Old medical books were open between them.

The results of these surgeries filled the room. A collection of lamps stood on a shelf, made from human skin and bones. The lampshades still had nipples, bellybuttons, and tattoos. Severed human hands stood on another shelf, mummified, arched and twisted with anguish, as if the victims had died trying to stave off assault. Shrunken heads hung on a wall, peering with glass eyes. There was an armchair embroidered with a hundred human faces, ripped off the skulls, the mouths and eyes stitched shut.

These are all real. Real human remains. Nausea filled Lailani's belly. *The robotic servants who served me dinner—their faces had been actual human faces, peeled off corpses.*

Lailani looked away from the remains toward several framed newspaper clippings. She pointed her flashlight and stepped closer. She read the newspaper headlines.

Dr. Death Sentenced!

Famed Doctor Caught Mutilating Captives!

Schroder's Wife and Children Still Missing

After Scum Destroy Prison, Dr. Death Flees Earth!

Schroder's Family Found Dead, Faces Missing

Dr. Death Still At Large; Reward Money Grows

Victims' Families Demand Justice!

Every newspaper clipping—lovingly framed and hung on the wall.

The room spun around Lailani. She struggled for breath. She should never have come here. She should have fled the instant they had disabled her pistol. She had delved into the lair of a serial killer, light-years away from Earth.

Do not panic! she told herself. *You are a soldier. You are an officer in the Human Defense Force. You have fought worse than him.*

A weapon. She needed a weapon! She would fight her way toward HOBBS, steal him back, and leave this cursed place. She would find somebody else to repair him, perhaps an engineer on Earth.

"We're leaving this damn place," she said aloud. "Me, HOBBS, and Epi."

A voice answered from behind her. "I'm quite afraid I can't allow that, my dear."

She grabbed a scalpel from the table. She spun around, pointing the blade.

Schroder stood there, smiling thinly. He had removed his lab coat and goggles, and instead he now wore a dark suit. He looked less like an engineer, more like an undertaker.

Lailani kept her scalpel pointing at him, still clad in her frilly gown, like a homicidal doll.

"You're going to return HOBBS to me," Lailani said. "And I'm flying away. We go our separate ways. I keep your little lab secret. End of story."

The doctor shook his head sadly. "Do you remember what I told you, Lailani? Humans cannot be trusted. They will betray you. Hurt you. If I release you, you will betray me."

Lailani snarled and stepped forward, scalpel pointing at him. "Like you betrayed your wife and kids? Like you carved out their hearts with a scalpel? Maybe I'll do the same to you."

The doctor sneered. He raised a fist. "I gave them immortality! My wife was getting old. Gray. Withered. I made her forever young. My children—they too were growing. Soon they would have turned against me. Hurt me. Betrayed me. As all humans do. As robotic dolls, they are forever small, forever loving, forever loyal."

"Only their hearts live!" Lailani shouted. "What about their brains—their memories, thoughts, personalities?"

"I tried!" Schroder shouted, face red now. "For years I tried! To connect brains to machines. To create true immortality. And I would have succeeded! I was close. So close!"

"And you would have gotten away with it too, if it weren't for us meddling kids?" Lailani said.

"Humor," Schroder said. "Another human failing." He grinned luridly, exposing yellow teeth. "Here is a little humor of my own. I think you will become a nice little schoolgirl android. Just like Mimori. It will suit you, my little Oriental flower. I will enjoy carving out your heart."

"Pro tip: use a spoon. It's dull, it'll hurt more." Lailani tossed off her hat and ripped off her gown, remaining in her jeans and shirt. She gave him a crooked smile, scalpel raised. "If you can reach me first, that is. I might look like a doll, but I'm a combat officer in the HDF. And I'm bringing you back to Earth to face justice."

She lunged toward him.

"HOBBS!" Schroder said, stepping back. "Grab her!"

From the shadows he emerged—HOBBS, her robot, her dear friend.

Lailani skidded to a halt. Relief flooded her. HOBBS was healed! His armor had been patched up, a few of the older parts replaced. He had been washed and waxed. He looked brand new.

But his eyes were different. They no longer shone blue but an angry red.

"HOBBS!" Lailani cried. "Thank God. Let's get out of here, and—"

The cyborg grabbed her. His eyes blazed, pitiless.

"HOBBS!" Lailani struggled in his grip, unable to free herself. "Hobster, it's me—Lailani!"

"Don't bother, my dear," Schroder said, watching with a thin smile. "He doesn't remember you. He doesn't remember anything. I wiped his memory clean. He obeys me now."

Lailani's heart seemed to stop in her chest. She couldn't breathe.

No, she thought. *No. Not his memory. The algorithms for the hourglass ... The only way I can save the fallen ...*

She screamed and tossed her scalpel.

Schroder leaned aside, and the blade slashed across his cheek, cutting a red line.

Lailani thrashed, desperate to free herself.

"HOBBS! HOBBS, it's me!" Tears streamed down her cheeks. "You have to remember!"

Schroder clutched his wounded cheek, hissing. "Take her to the dungeon, HOBBS. Lock her in the containment cell. Leave her alive and conscious. I'll enjoy cutting out her heart as she screams and begs."

HOBBS nodded. He spoke in a deep, metallic voice. "Yes, master."

Lailani took a deep breath.

Nightwish, she thought, deactivating the chip in her mind. *Let me become the beast.*

Her consciousness expanded.

The dormant alien within her awoke.

She reached out her mind, attempting to seize Schroder, to command him like she had commanded the dragons of Mahatek.

She hit what felt like a brick wall.

Schroder laughed. "Your psychic abilities won't work here, girl. As soon as you landed, I recognized you. I activated a jamming signal across this station. Truly, yours is a fascinating brain! Part alien. I will enjoy dissecting it as you still live." He touched his bleeding cheek. "But first, Mimori will tend to my wound. HOBBS, carry out your orders."

The hulking robot carried Lailani through the laboratory, and she kicked and shouted until he covered her mouth. She couldn't breathe, and tears filled her eyes. He carried her down, down into the belly of the planet, and he tossed her into a dark cell. All was shadows, pain, and despair.

CHAPTER TEN

They trekked through the forest. Baba Mahanisha led the way, trampling over bushes and bending trees. The massive alien fed from the land as he walked, plucking grass and leaves and rushes with both trunks. Behind him followed Marco and Addy, clad in orange robes, walking sticks in hand. Despite being slimmer and lighter on their feet, both humans were falling behind the Durmian. Soon Mahanisha was walking far ahead.

"Hey, Poet." Addy elbowed his ribs. "Where's he taking us?"

"How should I know?" Marco shoved her elbow aside. "I'm not a mind reader."

Addy looked around her. "Maybe he's taking us to a Hot Dog Shack. Or a Dairy Queen. Maybe a nice Happy Cow Shawarma. Damn I'm hungry."

"You can try eating the rushes like Mahanisha." He poked her hip. "It would do you good to eat some salad."

She growled and raised her fist. "You can try eating a knuckle sandwich."

The trail was long. They walked for hours. But Marco was thankful for the journey. Over time, he came to see the hike as a form of meditation. He focused his awareness on every footstep, on the sounds of insects and birds and rustling leaves, on the feel of sunlight. When his legs began to ache, he let his breath flow into them, easing the pain.

Even Addy was surprisingly quiet. The old Addy would not tolerate a long, silent walk like this. He knew this; he had gone hiking and camping with her on Earth. The old Addy would sing, dance, joke around, climb trees, throw rocks, wrestle him, and do anything to fill the silence. Marco understood why now. It was to silence the demons.

Yet now Addy was able to walk silently. Instead of battling those demons with endless energy, she simply breathed. She experienced. She was in Deep Being. As they walked, she slipped her hand into his and smiled. They walked hand in hand, one with nature.

Finally they reached a river, and here the baba stopped, and they drank from the cold water. The river was filled with orange fish and many stones of various colors.

For the first time that day, the baba spoke. "Today we will learn about the mind. Today we will balance stones." He lifted one large white stone. "The white stone symbolizes our awareness. It is the foundation of the mind." He placed it in the shallow water, then lifted a blue stone. "The blue stone symbolizes our physical senses—what we hear, see, taste, feel. The ache of old wounds. The warmth of an embrace. The taste of food or the smell of a rose." He placed the blue stone atop the white stone, then lifted a green stone. "The green stone symbolizes our memories, be they kind or painful." He added it to

175

the pile, gentle, then lifted a purple stone. "The purple stone symbolizes our emotions—love, anger, joy, despair. Often memories birth our feelings." Gingerly, he placed the emotions stone atop the memory stone. Finally he lifted a stone of many colors. "The stone of many colors symbolizes our thoughts, which are woven of all the stones beneath it. Our stone of thought completes the tower."

Delicately, he placed the memory stone atop his construction. The tower of five stones rose in the shallow water: a large stone of awareness and above it stones for senses, memories, emotions, and thoughts.

"Thus is the mind built," said the baba. "Of five components. Awareness is the foundation of the mind. Awareness is the most basic, purest, primal form of being. It is what we call Deep Being. All other components rest atop it. When we meditate, we retreat into our awareness stone. Into a state of Deep Being. From there, from within the river, we can observe the other stones above us. We are aware of our physical sensations, our memories, our emotions, and our thoughts. We do not suppress the other four components. We do not hide them, do not seek to silence them. We let them be. We support them in our awareness."

"What does the river represent?" Marco said.

"Life," said the baba. "Life flows around us. And if our tower is not balanced properly ..." He nudged his tower of stones. It collapsed into the water. "Now let us practice. Let us balance stones. Let us balance our minds."

Marco and Addy got to work.

It was hard.

Balancing two stones was easy enough—a large white stone for awareness, above it a blue stone for senses. When Marco tried to balance the third stone, the green stone of memory, it kept slipping off. He had to start over, this time with a flatter white stone and larger blue one. Finally he managed to stack three together. Yet when he added the fourth stone, purple for emotions, the entire construction collapsed.

Addy was less patient. Soon she was cursing and throwing stones. She couldn't even get three to balance together.

"You're placing them down too quickly," Marco said. "Hold on to the stone for a while. Feel it. Sense its weight."

"You'll be sensing my weight when I hold you under the water," she muttered.

They kept working at it, choosing stones, delicately balancing them. Baba had made it look easy, but Marco and Addy made many attempts and still failed. Yet as they worked, trying again and again, this task too became a meditation. They could feel the stones. Breathe into them. Be one with them. Understand their shape and weight and movements. Build with them. Bring balance to the river.

Finally Marco got a tower to stand. Awareness at the bottom, the stone underwater. Above it: senses, memories, feelings, and thoughts. Around it flowed the river of life. It took Addy several more attempts, but finally she balanced a tower too.

She beamed at Marco. "My tower is taller than yours."

Marco rolled his eyes.

"Remember, my pupils," Baba Mahanisha said, "to always live in Deep Being. A life of Deep Being does not mean being empty of thoughts or feelings or memories. It is a life of awareness. A life where thoughts, feelings, memories, or sensations do not claim you, control you, become you. A life of observing, of being. The deepest part of your mind is awareness. Dwell there. Observe from there. Keep your tower strong, no matter how fast the river flows."

It was dark by the time they returned to the temple. Marco and Addy retreated to their bedchamber, a simple brick room with two piles of straw instead of mattresses. They lay down to bed, so weary after the march they fell asleep at once.

Sometime in the night, a scream woke Marco.

He leaped up, heart racing, sure that the grays had found them, that war flared. He whipped his head toward Addy.

She was thrashing on her straw bed. She screamed again. Her eyes were still closed.

"No," she whimpered. "No. Orcus, no! Don't hurt me. Don't brand me." She clutched her hip, covering her old brand, and screamed again. "Please don't. No. Don't hurt me. Don't kill them. Don't kill them ..."

She jolted up in bed, and her eyes snapped open. Tears were on her cheeks.

Marco was with her at once, soothing her, embracing her.

"Only a dream," he whispered, stroking her hair. "Only a dream, Addy. I'm here with you. It's all right."

She trembled. Sweat soaked her body. "Not a dream. A memory." She grimaced. "I still feel the pain, Poet." She screwed her eyes shut and wrapped her arms around him. "It still hurts so bad. All of it. What they did to me. What they made me see. The scum. The marauders. What the grays did to Steve. All of it. From my parents dying to the marauders torturing me to …" She wept. "The nightmares are still inside me."

He caressed her cheek. "Addy, look at me. Look into my eyes. It's not real."

She looked at him, eyes red. "What do you mean? It's real. I'm still scarred. I still have nightmares. It's fucking real."

"A memory," he whispered. "Just a memory. Just a memory stored in your mind. Just neurons firing in your brain. The only thing real is now. The present moment. Remember the stones."

She nodded and took a deep breath. "I remember."

"Let's retreat into Deep Being," he said. "Into awareness. Let's be the foundation. The white stone in the water. Let's observe all the other stones from there."

Addy nodded and took another deep breath, still embracing him. "I'll try."

They took several more deep breaths, sinking into Deep Being. They became their foundation. From down here, they could see the other four components above. Senses—the warmth of each other, the cold sweat, Addy's tickling hair. Their emotions—fear, grief, love. Their thoughts—of seeking solutions, of figuring things out, worrying, analyzing, overthinking. Their memories, coming and going. The nightmares—just memories. Just another stone.

"Only the now is real," Marco whispered. "You are not your thoughts. You are not your memories. You are not your feelings or senses. You are in Deep Being. Observing. Let them be."

She nodded. "Let them be," she whispered.

They lay on their backs, breathing, being aware. Just being. Resting in awareness. And they watched the memories flow away. They observed the fear fade. Until only the present moment remained.

Addy held his hand. "I lied, Poet."

He looked at her. He gasped. "You mean that time you claimed to see a pigman in High Park, you were lying?" He covered his mouth. "I'm shocked."

She punched him. "Not that! That was true. I did see a pigman in the park! Snout and everything, and he was wearing overalls and sniffing for truffles."

"You saw a fat drunk," Marco said.

"Pigman!" she insisted. "He should be added to *Freaks of the Galaxy*. But anyway, I'm talking about something else now. When I said my tower was taller than yours. I lied. I'm a sore loser."

"It wasn't a contest, Ads."

She grinned. "But I'll beat you next time! And even if my tower was shorter, *I'm* still taller than you."

He rolled his eyes. "You are not. We're the same height. I think I'm a centimeter taller, actually."

She snorted. "You wish!"

He kissed her cheek. She kissed his lips. They made gentle love, then slept in each other's arms until the morning.

CHAPTER ELEVEN

Marco and Addy knelt in the Deep Being temple upon the mountain, deep in concentration, creating a mandala.

Jars of colored sand stood around them, a hundred different colors. Marco and Addy both held *chak-purs*, bronze tools of Deep Being used for this holy task. Each chak-pur was conical, a slender bronze funnel filled with colored sand. Ridges lined each funnel. When tapped with another tool—a metal stick—the chak-pur released a sprinkling of colored sand. Tapping different ridges released the sand in different patterns.

"It's like decorating cakes with icing," Addy said. She licked her lips. "Mmm ... icing."

"Except this cake is the size of a dining room table, and the icing is as intricate as a Persian rug," Marco said.

They had been working for days, spilling out colored sand, creating circles within circles, rings of decorative patterns, human figures, and animals, expanding the artwork from its center outward. The baba had asked them to add a personal touch, images that mattered to them. Marco had chosen to create little books of sand, done in reds, blues, and greens, symbolizing his love of literature. Addy, in her mandala ring, created little hot dogs.

Slowly it was taking form. The first day, the mandala had been nothing but chalk sketches on the temple floor. By now, it was a beautiful work of art, dazzling with its colors and patterns. Every few moments, Marco and Addy had to pause, refill the chak-purs with another color of sand, then return to their work, always moving outward from the center.

"Is this what it feels like when you write a book?" Addy said. "Lots of slow, careful work?"

He nodded. "It does, actually."

Addy rubbed her back. "At least you get to sit down while writing. All this kneeling is killing my back and knees. Will you give me a massage later?"

"Addy, last time I gave you a massage, you started ripping off my clothes two seconds into it." He thought for a moment. "All right. I'm definitely giving you a massage later." He sighed. "Unfortunately, we still have ten hours of work left today on this mandala."

Addy groaned. "Ten more hours? The little sand hot dogs I'm making are going to turn into little sand d—"

"Addy!" Marco flushed and brushed away her sand. "Keep the mandala civil."

"What?" Addy bristled. "It's a fertility symbol!"

"Addy."

She sighed. "Fine."

"Remember, we're not even supposed to talk while doing this," Marco said. "This is meant to be a silent form of meditation. Let's try to focus."

They kept working, creating symbol after symbol of sand, expanding their mandala.

Day after day, they entered the temple, refilled their funnels of sand, and toiled at their work.

They slept in the temple on the stone floor. They woke, ate their single meal of the day, and worked again. Meditation through sand. Creating. Adding beauty to the world. To Marco, this indeed felt a little like writing a novel—day after day of creation, building toward a final work of art. To Addy, who had never created art, this was new and frustrating at first. Often she fretted, groaned, felt trapped, but gradually she sank into the trance of it, adding each day to their creation.

Days turned into weeks, and still they worked, their mandala expanding across the floor, filled with figures, coiling lines, squares, triangles, a dizzying array of colors and shapes, rings within rings.

Marco found that, in many ways, this was the most pleasant time he had ever spent with Addy. Their childhood had been fragile and painful, living under the constant threat of the scum. Their youth had been filled with agony, battling the aliens on the front line. Their twenties had been filled with trauma, two homeless veterans, struggling with loss and shell shock, exiled from Earth, slowly going mad in Haven.

But now, almost twenty-nine years old, Marco was here with the love of his life, learning peace, creating art. He looked up from his work at her. Addy was kneeling before him, deep in concentration, tongue thrust out, spilling out blue grains of sand.

I love you, Addy, he thought. *Fully. Completely. Eternally. I came here to study peace. And with you I found joy. I wish we could stay here forever. You make my life full, complete, joyous.*

She suddenly stood up and groaned. "Jesus Fucking Christ, I'm bored! If I have to spend another minute in here with you, Poet, I'm going to strangle you."

Marco sighed. *So much for the feeling being mutual.*

"What did I do?" he said.

"You're too silent! I want to sing and dance and run around and wrestle. Wanna wrestle?"

He kept working, spilling out sand. "This is meant to be meditation practice, not wrestling practice. Come on, Ads. We're almost done. Just a few more hours of work."

"I'd rather spend a few hours wrestling," she muttered, settling back down.

Finally, after a month of work, they finished.

The mandala was complete.

It sprawled across the temple floor, as large and intricate as the finest oriental rug. Baba Mahanisha came to view it with them, and he smiled.

"It is beautiful, my pupils," the Durmian said. "Grain by grain, you have spread the sand into a work of holiness, of great art. This mandala symbolizes the cosmos, its balance and beauty, for the cosmos is an eternal circle, ring within ring, forever turning. It also symbolizes your dedication to peace, to transcendence, and to the Noble Path of Deep Being."

"And our dedication to processed meat," Addy said, pointing at the little red hot dogs she had added to one ring. Marco gave her his best scowl.

The baba smiled. He was, to his credit, far more tolerant of Addy than any of their sergeants.

"We learn in Deep Being," the baba said, "that all is ephemeral. The seasons come and go. We are born and we die. Within our life, suffering is temporary. So is joy. All comes and goes. All is like clouds in the sky, and we live only for the present moment. Beauty is created. Beauty is dismantled." He held out two thick brushes. "Let us see this mandala too fade."

Marco and Addy looked down at their creation. It was special to them, a work they had created together, had labored over for so long. And it was beautiful. It was precious.

"Baba, I can't," said Addy.

"Often this is a difficult lesson," said the baba. "But it's an important one. We do not live for material things. We do not live to preserve the past. When we brush the sand away, we are making a powerful statement. That our peace is not tied to the physical. That our joy is not tied to remembering past labors, only to our awareness in the present."

They took the brushes.

Addy cringed. "Can I at least take a photo first?"

"Addy, take this seriously," Marco said.

She winced. "I hate this. You go first, Poet."

He knelt, brush in hand. "Come on, Ads. Together."

She sighed. "All right." She knelt too, holding the brush above the sand. "Three ... Two ... One ... Go!"

Marco brushed away a long stroke of sand, destroying the intricate creations, mixing the radiant colors.

"Ha ha, made you go first!" Addy said, then winced and brushed her own path of sand. "Damn that's tough to do."

It had taken a month to create the mandala. They dismantled it within moments. A pile of sand rose in the center of the temple, a hundred colors all blended together.

They placed the sand into buckets, carried it down the mountain, and released it into a river. Colors streamed through the water, then flowed away.

That night, for the first time since beginning their training, Baba Mahanisha cooked dinner. There was more than bread and gruel too. In a hundred clay bowls, he served a feast of lentils, vegetables, fruits, grains, and other delicacies. Outside the temple, it was raining after a long, dry summer, but indoors a fire blazed in the hearth, and warmth and light filled the stone chambers.

"Normally we live as ascetics," said the baba, sitting cross-legged before the meal. "But tonight, in gratitude of the milestone you passed, we will feast."

"Hell yeah!" Addy said. "I don't even care that it's vegetarian." She inhaled deeply. "It smells delicious."

The baba nodded. "First, let us chant a prayer of loving-kindness. To all living things, we wish safety and freedom from suffering. We wish them peace. We wish them ease of—"

Outside the temple, a rumble sounded.

Marco and Addy leaped to their feet.

That was no thunder.

"Starship engines," Marco whispered.

And even here, in the temple of Deep Being, terror flooded him.

Starships. War. Death.

* * * *

Outside the temple, the engines roared.

Marco and Addy ran toward the arched doorway, abandoning their meal. They stared outside.

Rain was falling outside in sheets. Dark clouds filled the sky. Wind shrieked. And there, in the storm, they saw it. Descending toward the mountain. A dark round starship. Its engines rumbled, belching out smoke and fire. The ship spun, revealing golden glyphs carved into its hull. Thundering, it came to hover outside the temple.

A saucer.

Standing at the temple doorway, Marco sneered and clenched his fists.

Several figures emerged from the saucer onto the mountainside. They were shadowed, clad in black robes and hoods, tall and slender.

Addy hissed and bared her teeth. "Grays," she spat.

Baba Mahanisha stepped toward the doorway too. He moved ahead of Marco and Addy, shielding them, and raised three of his hands in peaceful gestures. But in his fourth hand, he clutched his walking staff, its edges heavy with metal rings.

"Greetings, friends!" the baba cried out. "Please, come find shelter from the storm and food to fill your bellies."

"Baba, no!" Addy said, eyes flashing. "These are enemies."

"Baba, these are creatures who've attacked us before," Marco said. His belly twisted, and his pulse quickened. He wished he had a weapon. His chest felt tight. He forced himself to breathe like the baba had taught him, to control the terror.

The cloaked grays drew nearer. The rain streamed over them. No light penetrated their hoods.

They came to stand outside the doorway. Lightning flashed behind them. There were six of them, tall and powerful, hidden in their robes, even their hands covered. A coppery odor rose from them. One among them stepped closer.

"Step back, my pupils," the baba said softly.

The lead gray spoke, voice hissing, creaking, dripping malice. "Allow us passage, monk. We seek the apes you hide."

Marco and Addy stood within the temple, tense. Their guru was far larger than them, blocking the doorway.

"This temple is a place of peace and safety," the baba said, voice still friendly, but now that voice also carried authority, was deeper, stronger. "All are welcome here aside from those who seek violence."

The hooded figure sneered. He was thinner than the bulky baba, but he exuded power. He raised one hand. The sleeve rolled back, revealing four knobby fingers tipped with claws.

"Step back, Durmian," the gray said. "We seek no violence here. Though if you resist us, we will not hesitate to become violent."

Hissing, the gray doffed his cloak, revealing a cadaverous, scarred ruin. His skin was burnt and peeling. His head was massive, one eye black and pitiless, the other eye crushed. Half the gray's face was shattered, caved in, flaked with dry blood. Yet still the creature lived. He gave a hideous grin, revealing teeth like rusted needles. Around his chest, the gray wore human hearts on a metal wire, a lurid necklace that pulsed and dripped blood.

Marco's breath quickened. He wanted to run, to fight. He wished he had a weapon and body armor. He was just wearing robes, had nothing but his fists. Addy stared at the gray, her cheeks red with fury. Hatred simmered in her blue eyes. They were no longer the eyes of the trickster or joker, no longer the eyes of a woman in love, no longer the eyes of a Deep Being pupil at peace. They had become the eyes of Addy the warrior, the heroine who had raised Earth in rebellion against the marauders, who would not hesitate to fight again.

"Name yourself!" said the baba, voice booming. "Do not come here skulking in the night as a thief. Who are you?"

The gray hissed out a horrible laughter, a sound like sizzling flesh. His comrades echoed the sound, raising their claws.

"I am Abyzou!" said the gray. "Born of Nefitis. Lord of Hosts. Prince of the Sanctified Sons."

Addy stepped forward, snarling. "Yeah, well, I'm Addy, Lady of Fuck, Princess of You. So why don't you get lost before I bash in those weasel teeth of yours?"

Abyzou looked at her, and his eyes crackled with internal fire. "Addy Linden," the creature hissed. "I know you. I've known you since you were a child. I watched from under your bed. From your closet as you slept. Over your shoulder as you suffered, as your father beat you, as your mother sank into a stupor, as the other children tormented you, as they locked you away in the classroom for the freaks. As they broke you in the war, branding you, fattening you up like cattle. You think you know pain. But you know nothing, Addy Linden. My goddess will teach you true pain."

Addy could only stare. She seemed frozen. Tears filled her eyes. Her mouth opened but she could not speak.

Marco took a step forward, fists clenching, and Abyzou turned his eyes upon him. Those eyes seized him like claws. Marco could not move. His legs would not obey. That black gaze wrapped him in agony, penetrated him, dug through him, unearthed all his secrets, and pulled them out like talons pulling out entrails.

"Marco Emery," the creature said, voice slithering. "The boy who hurt so many. Who let his friends die while he lived on, a coward. The boy who fathered the marauders, whose own blood formed their twisted king. Yes, Marco. I know. I know that Lord

Malphas was built of your flesh. That he killed your beloveds. That he killed your father. That their blood is on your hands. I was there, Marco. Watching. Laughing. I was with you in Haven as you stood on the roof. And your pain has only begun, Marco. My goddess will see you along your path of agony, and it will last for all eternity. None of your race, not in all your faiths, have imagined a hell as torturous as what awaits you."

Marco could do nothing but stand, transfixed, held by that gaze as surely as by manacles. And in his mind, he saw nightmares taking form. Visions of a black pyramid in an alien city, an eye upon its crest. A rancid goddess upon it, a crown of metal hammered into her brow. And he saw the creatures, the Sanctified Sons, descend upon Earth, enslave humanity. He saw them shatter the bones of his loved ones. He saw Lailani, Ben-Ari, and Addy broken upon wooden ankhs, still alive and screaming as the enemy pulled out their organs. Hell. Hell on Earth.

Yet if Marco and Addy were paralyzed, Baba Mahanisha was not.

The guru seemed to grow taller. He took a step onto the mountainside, and the lightning flashed, illuminating his massive form. He raised his staff with two hands, and his trunks rose, revealing tusks. For the past three months, Marco had known a gentle giant, kind and loving.

Now he saw a warrior.

"Twice I have offered you kindness, and you have rejected it," said Baba Mahanisha. "Leave this temple! You profane it. It is forbidden to you. Leave now!"

192

The grays all doffed their robes. They raised metal batons, the tips crackling with electricity, and they laughed. The creatures pointed their weapons, and thunderbolts flew toward the baba.

Marco cried out, the spell breaking.

Baba Mahanisha swung his staff.

With its metal tips, he deflected bolt after bolt, casting them back into the storm.

"Leave this place!" the baba boomed.

But Abyzou cackled. "You cannot harm us, monk. I know your order. You are forbidden to kill. I will not kill you either. I will delight in keeping you alive. And screaming. For many long centuries."

The grays leaped forth, claws lashing.

Mahanisha swung his staff. It whirred so fast it appeared like a disk. The massive baba, the size of an elephant, moved at incredible speed. One gray lunged toward him, and the staff slammed into the creature's head, knocking it back. Two more grays attacked, and the staff whirred, sweeping out their legs. The creatures kept trying to enter the temple, to slay the guru, only for the staff to hold them back, cracking their bony bodies. Their cries echoed in the temple.

As the battle raged, Addy grabbed Marco's arm.

"Poet." She pulled back her robes, revealing her legs. She wore a pistol strapped to each thigh.

He gasped. "You brought weapons into a temple of peace?"

Addy nodded, eyes hard. "A precaution. One I'm glad for." She drew the pistols and handed him one. "We fight."

Marco took the pistol. It was heavy and comforting. He glanced back toward the battle, where Baba Mahanisha was still holding the grays at bay.

"Wait," Marco said. "Let's see if the baba can still resolve this without killing. Shedding blood in his holy temple would be devastating to him."

Addy sneered and raised her pistol. "I'm not waiting long."

A gray leaped onto Mahanisha and sank his teeth into his shoulder. Another gray lashed his claws, ripping into the guru's leg. Blood spurted. The grays attacked like wolves on a bison. Baba Mahanisha bellowed, enraged, ripping them off, tossing them back onto the mountainside. Their bones shattered. Yet still more grays attacked, tearing into the burly monk.

The guru gave a mighty swing of his staff.

Abyzou caught the gnarled wood in his claws.

"Your torment begins, monk," the gray hissed. "I exile you from this hall."

Abyzou tightened his grip, shattering the staff. Wooden shards flew, slamming into Baba Mahanisha, cutting his skin. The grays shrieked and laughed, biting deeper, clawing.

The baba gazed upon his enemies, his eyes damp. He spoke softly even as they ripped into him.

"May you be safe and free from suffering." A gray tore into his legs. "May you know peace." The grays ripped off his cloak and lacerated his chest. "May you have ease of being."

The mighty baba fell to his knees.

Addy and Marco screamed and fired their guns.

Bullets slammed into the grays, shattering against their skin, barely fazing the creatures. They seemed made of boiled leather over steel bones. The creatures walked around the fallen baba, advancing into the temple, reaching out their claws. Marco and Addy kept firing, hitting the grays' heads, knocking them back, drawing some blood, but unable to kill them, to stop them. The desiccated humanoids stepped into the temple, bloodied claws raised, eyes dripping hatred.

Those eyes tugged at Marco.

Visions invaded him.

The dark city. The black pyramid. The wretched queen.

Come to us, Marco. Worship her. Scream for her.

He was in a daze. The nightmarish visions tugged him. He couldn't move, couldn't fight. Addy too stood frozen, the grays controlling her. The creatures were gripping Marco's mind, as surely as claws could grip flesh, filling him with their terrors. They were controlling his thoughts, controlling his body, and he took a step toward them, and—

You are not your thoughts.

The wisdom resurfaced.

You are not your nightmares.

He took a deep breath.

Breathe. Let your thoughts be. Let them flow away.

He sank into deeper consciousness. He watched the nightmares float away. He let the alien thoughts fade.

He fired his gun and hit a gray in the eye.

The creature howled, raised his hands, and blood spurted between his fingers.

"Addy, come!" Marco grabbed her wrist, snapping her out of her paralysis.

They ran deeper into the temple, and the grays followed. They entered the central hall, the place where they had spent a month constructing the mandala. Abyzou and the others raced after them, raising their electric prods.

Marco had only a single bullet left. Addy's gun was already clicking, empty.

As the grays advanced, Marco knelt and grabbed a bowl of colored sand. He hurled it with all his strength.

Sand flew into the grays' large black eyes.

Addy joined him, tossing bowls of sand, shattering the vessels against the aliens.

A storm of colored sand filled the air, blinding, swirling. The grays fired their bolts but missed.

Marco charged toward the blinded enemy, pulling Addy with him.

As he raced by Abyzou, he fired his last bullet, hitting the creature.

As Abyzou fell, Marco and Addy barreled through the group of grays. They raced through the clouds of colored sand. They burst outside onto the mountainside. The rain fell and lightning flashed.

Baba Mahanisha knelt on the mountainside, bleeding. He was barely alive.

"Baba, we have to run!" Marco said.

The guru nodded and managed to stumble down the dark mountainside. Marco and Addy ran with him. The wind roared through the night, the clouds stormed above, and rain fell in sheets. Behind them, in the temple, the grays were shrieking. They emerged onto the mountainside.

Marco and Addy kept running, holding Mahanisha's hands, guiding their baba onward.

Before them, it rose from the shadows.

The alien saucer.

It was forged of dark metal, and glyphs were engraved onto its hull like brands into flesh, searing red with internal flame. The vessel hovered before them, the size of the temple, rumbling, spewing fumes. Perhaps it was an alien starship. Perhaps, as they suspected, a time machine from humanity's dark and wretched future. But here it appeared as a deity of wrath, a chariot of fire, a weapon of retribution.

Its cannons turned toward Marco, Addy, and their baba.

The cannons fired.

The companions ran.

The laser blasts flew over their heads. The inferno slammed into the Deep Being temple behind them.

The columns shattered. The archway collapsed. The roof caved in. As the temple crumbled, they ran. Bricks cascaded. Dust flew. Fallen columns rolled. Marco and Addy were fast, but the wounded baba was slower, and bricks slammed into him, knocking him down. A column fell onto his back, and Baba Mahanisha fell. Bricks hailed onto him.

"Baba!" Marco cried, kneeling by his master.

"Poet, we have to run!" Addy shouted.

The grays were descending toward them from the ruins, Abyzou leading the pack, his necklace of hearts flaming. Before them, the saucer descended until it grazed the mountainside. Its front hatch opened, and more grays emerged, bearing electrical prods. Marco and Addy knelt on the mountainside, trapped. Grays stood behind and before them. At their sides lay fallen bricks and columns. They were surrounded. Nowhere to run. No way to fight.

Marco reached out to Addy, to die holding her.

But she ignored him. She stood tall, sneered, and held up a small device. At first Marco thought it was her pistol, but it was smaller, slimmer.

"It's time to meet your goddess, apes!" Abyzou cried. "Your torture begins."

Addy inhaled deeply.

"There's one thing you're forgetting, Abyzou!" she said. "I learned to wish my enemies peace and health. I learned to never harm another." A crooked smile tugged at her lips. "I cheated."

She hit a button on her device, and finally Marco recognized it.

A remote control.

With roaring fire and thundering fury, the starship *Thunder Road* roared forth through the storm.

Its cannons blazed.

Massive bullets the size of daggers, raging at hypersonic speed, slammed into the saucer.

Explosions rocked the grays' starship.

The saucer fell. It slammed into the mountainside. Metal shattered. Stones cracked. Shock waves rippled outward. Fire roared skyward.

Dust. Shards of metal. Boulders and bricks. All flew everywhere. More bullets raged, slamming into grays. The mountain trembled.

"Addy, you are a bloody maniac, and I love you!" Marco shouted, ears ringing.

She laughed. "A girl always has some surprises in her purse. Mints, coupons, a remote control for a flying hippie van with mounted railguns ..."

She hit more buttons, and the *Thunder Road* came to hover above the mountainside. Addy raced into the airlock. Marco hesitated, then knelt by Baba Mahanisha. The guru was bleeding, but he was still alive. Marco strained, shoving against a fallen column that pinned the guru down.

"Poet, we don't have much time!" Addy shouted. "There are still grays on the mountain."

"Addy, he's still alive! Help me!"

Addy joined him, and they rolled off the fallen column. They managed to pull Baba Mahanisha to his feet. The guru, wheezing and bleeding, stumbled into the starship, barely squeezing through the airlock.

Grays charged toward them through the rubble.

The starship rose.

Grays leaped and caught the rim of the airlock.

"Addy, grays on the *Thunder Road*!" Marco cried.

"The ship is named *Shippy McShipface*!" Addy shouted, racing to the airlock. "Fight them as I fly."

The Volkswagen soared, cannons blazing. The grays dangled from the airlock, claws digging into the metal. They began climbing into the rising starship. Marco cursed. He had no rifle here, but he saw Addy's katana on the floor. He drew the blade as a gray leaped toward him.

Marco screamed and swung.

The blade slammed into the gray's stomach. It nicked the skin and sank no deeper. It was like trying to slice a block of boiled leather.

The gray laughed. The beast lashed his claws, and Marco pulled back, narrowly dodging the assault.

Marco thrust, howling. The katana's tip perforated the gray's skin, driving a centimeter into the flesh. Marco roared with fury, shoving deeper, leaning into the sword, piercing the creature. He kept shoving until the gray hit the edge of the open airlock.

Marco pulled back the blade and kicked. The gray tumbled out of the airlock, falling to the mountain below.

The ship kept soaring. Baba Mahanisha lay on the floor, still bleeding, not moving, maybe dead already.

Two more grays still clung to the airlock, dangling and struggling to climb in. Marco swung the katana, cleaving one's fingers. The other gray made it into the ship, and claws lashed, slicing Marco's shoulder. He cried and fell back, holding the katana before him.

He swung the blade. The gray caught the sword and wrenched it free. Blood spurted between the gray's claws, but he seemed not to notice. The creature grinned. Half his face was gone, and hearts pulsed around his neck. Marco recognized him: Abyzou, prince of the grays.

The creature stepped closer, clutching the katana. The ship's bullets had slammed into his chest. Marco could see them embedded in the wrinkly flesh. A rib was exposed, a bullet lodged into it. Yet still Abyzou stepped toward Marco. The gray raised the katana. Marco retreated, his back to the wall.

Abyzou spoke, voice thick with mirth.

"You have children in the future." Abyzou's thin lips peeled back. "They will scream for us too."

Marco stared into the oval black eyes, unable to move. Terror. Pure terror filled him.

Yes, they were human.

Yes, they were time travelers.

Yes, Marco would scream and beg for death.

Abyzou took another step, claws reaching out to grab him, then stumbled and crashed down.

The wounded Baba Mahanisha knelt behind the gray, clutching the creature's legs.

Marco lunged forward and grabbed the fallen katana. Before he could stab the gray, Baba Mahanisha yanked mightily. The monk swung Abyzou like a rag doll, hurling the rancid creature out of the airlock. The gray's screams rose from outside, then vanished into the storm.

"I could have killed him!" Marco shouted. "He might still survive this fall!" If that creature could survive bullets to the chest …

The baba only stared at him sadly.

Marco stumbled toward the airlock, bleeding, limping. He pulled the door shut, but not before glimpsing several more saucers outside, flying toward them.

"Addy!" he shouted.

"I see 'em!" she cried from the cockpit. "We're ditching this planet."

Marco was about to run toward her when the baba collapsed. The Durmian lay on the floor, robes soaked with blood. His eyes glazed over.

"Baba!" Marco clasped his master's hand. "Don't leave us. Not yet."

His guru gazed upon him with kindness. "Marco …"

Marco leaned closer. "Yes, baba."

The guru raised one of his trunks and touched Marco's cheek. His voice was weak, growing weaker. "Do not let them fill you with hatred. Remember your teachings. May you be safe and free from suffering. May you find peace. May you have ease of being."

"May you be safe and free from suffering," Marco whispered, holding his master's hand. "May you find peace. May you have ease of being."

The baba's eyes closed. For centuries, Mahanisha had taught the holiness of breath. Lying on the floor of the starship, he breathed his last.

Addy's voice rose from the cockpit. "Poet, get your ass over here and help!"

He ran and joined her. She was still flying in the atmosphere, the storm surrounding them. He hopped into the seat beside her.

"You all right, little dude?" Addy said.

Marco nodded. "Got another battle scar. Killed a couple grays. Same old." He lowered his head. "The baba didn't make it."

Addy stared ahead, lips tight, eyes narrowed. "The storm is thick and hiding us for now. There are more of those assholes not far behind. I don't dare breach the atmosphere, or they'll see us."

"Thank goodness the *Thunder Road* is small. Hard to detect."

"Her name is *Shippy Mc*—" Addy began.

"I know, Addy." He placed a hand on her knee. "I know. And your little remote control—and your pistols—saved us. Even though you sneaked weapons of destruction into a temple of peace." Suddenly his eyes stung. "We came to study peace. We brought war and death."

"Not us," Addy said, eyes hardening. "More thugs. More monsters. More evil. And I knew it, Poet. I knew evil was still after us, that we had to fight, that—" She forced a deep breath, and she spoke in a whisper. "I am not my thoughts. I am not my emotions." Another deep breath. "Baba Mahanisha taught us well. He made us stronger. And we'll keep fighting, Poet. Until we win."

"Until we win," Marco said. "We fight together. Always."

Addy shoved down the throttle, increasing speed. "I'll put more distance between us and those assholes, then blast into space and hit the warp drive from orbit. If I curve our flight right, I can adjust for the planet's gravity. Old trick Kemi taught me. We'll be in warped space before those sneaky gray fucks know what happened. Their friends are hitting Earth. When they stared at me, I ... I saw it. A vision. A fleet of saucers heading to Earth, and the world burning. We'll fly there now to join the fight."

Marco shook his head. "No. We're not flying to Earth, Addy."

She looked at him, eyes flashing. "Poet! I'm not going to hide from this fight. This is personal now. I'm still a soldier, and—"

"We'll fly to Earth, Addy, but not yet. Not before taking a detour." Marco smiled thinly, gazing out at the storm. "We're flying to Taolin Shi. To the world Baba Mahanisha flooded centuries ago. And we're going to find those mechas."

Addy's eyes widened. She grabbed Marco's hand.

"Fuck yeah!" She took a deep breath. "I mean—this is the path we must walk, for to reach light and wisdom one must first pass through darkness and despair. But also: Fuck yeah!"

They soared through the clouds and breached the atmosphere. Below them, the saucers were still lost in the storm. Within seconds, Addy entered orbit and fired up the azoth engine. They blasted into warped space. They streamed through the darkness, leaving Durmia behind—the place where they had learned wisdom, awareness, and strength. They flew toward the watery world where perhaps hope awaited.

May we find hope there, Marco thought, holding Addy's hand as they flew. *May we find the weapons we seek. May we find an end to war. May we find ease of being.*

CHAPTER TWELVE

Lailani pounded on the cell door, screaming.

"Let me out of here, you fucking scumbag!"

Nightwish, she thought, deactivating her microchip.

Her scum side awakened, giving her strength, speed, power. She grew claws and scratched at the door. It was thick iron, but her claws were sharp. Yet when she scratched too deep, electricity pulsed across her. She fell back, hissing, shaking. She yowled in her rage, a monster trapped in flesh.

Serenity, she thought, reactivating her chip before she lost her sanity, lost her own memory in the depth of scum thought.

Deep underground on this distant world, buried beneath Schroder's lab, Lailani paced her cell. Hours passed. Maybe days. She languished.

Schroder wants to cut out my heart, Lailani thought. *But first he wants me to suffer.*

She curled up on the floor, drifting in and out of sleep. Her belly rumbled with hunger, and her mouth went dry with thirst. It was cold. It was so cold. She found a dispenser and nozzle in the wall; they gave her dry pellets and brackish water. She was like a hamster in a box. Going mad. She imagined herself a creature, a weird animal losing its fur, eating its young.

She found letters etched into the walls. She could barely make them out in the dim light.

I am Jasmine. Age 12. I love you, Mom and Dad. I love you.

Farther down the wall, more letters.

It has been a year now. I'm scared.

More words across the walls.

I am pregnant.

Blood stains.

He took my baby.

Words scratched with fingernails. Finally becoming mad, senseless marks. Final words.

He wants my heart. I love you.

Lailani hugged her knees, shivering. She closed her eyes.

Time flowed by.

She languished.

She scratched onto the walls.

I am Lailani. I love you, my friends. I'm sorry. I'm sorry for the bad things I've done.

She took a deep breath.

"I must keep fighting," she told herself. "I am a soldier. I will not give up."

The time flowed by. She slept. She withered away in the dark.

Until finally the door opened.

He stood there at the doorway, seven feet tall and broad as a prizefighter. HOBBS. Her friend. His eyes blazed red. His memory was wiped. He was now a servant of evil.

He grabbed her arm, his grip a vise. "Come with me."

The robot dragged her out of the cell. The bright corridor burned Lailani's eyes.

"How long has it been?" she whispered, squinting. "Where's Epi?"

HOBBS ignored her, dragging her down the corridor. She stumbled after him, as small as a toddler by her father. She was so weak. How long had she been living off those animal pellets? Days? Weeks? Months, even? Time had lost meaning in the darkness. Her limbs seemed so thin to her.

"HOBBS," she said. "Hobster, it's me. Don't you remember? It's your Lailani. We traveled to Mahatek together. We saw dragons. We—"

He smacked her. Hard. His metal hand left her bloody.

"Silence."

The hulking cyborg walked on, dragging her along. Her blood dripped from her nose, leaving a trail. On the corridor walls hung framed photographs of surgeries. Victims lay bound on tables, mouths open in silent screams, as Schroder carved out their hearts. Some of the photographed victims were children—*his* children. Lailani remembered their faces from the newspaper clippings.

Below each photograph, upon a pedestal, rested a skull.

Sick bastard, Lailani thought. *He collects trophies from his victims, even from his own family.*

"HOBBS, listen to me," Lailani said as he dragged her onward. "Your memory has been wiped. Schroder is not your master. I am your—"

He struck her again.

He kept dragging her down the corridor.

There was no use reasoning with him. She knew enough about computers to realize that she could not restore his memory, not with all the pleading in the world.

So I will have to fight.

Down the hallway, she saw double doors with large windows. Through the windows, Lailani could see a surgery room. She glimpsed an IV drip, surgical tools, and a masked figure in scrubs—Elliot Schroder, waiting to carve out her heart.

I am a soldier. I've faced worse than him. I will fight.

She took a deep breath.

Nightwish.

The scum awakened.

At once, she felt the pulsing, jamming signal Schroder filled his lair with. Her consciousness slammed into it like a wall.

She growled and shoved through, shattering it.

Her consciousness spread. She could see through the eyes of every burrowing snake. See the trophies of skin and skulls. See the dismembered corpses in the freezer. See the altar below her feet, the skulls arranged in a pentagram. She screamed with them. Screamed with them all, the women and children Schroder had imprisoned here. The lost souls who had wandered toward the spider, who had fallen into his web. The rib spreaders breaking them open. The scalpels cutting. The doctor smiling as he pulled out the still-beating heart.

She raced through the tunnels, a centipede with a human face. She lived among the stars and under the soil.

She grew her claws, and she lashed them with fury.

They slammed into HOBBS's arm. They cut through his bad joint, the one that had broken so many times before.

His arm, still holding Lailani, fell.

She ran.

She raced back down the corridor, passing the portraits, passing her cell. She was racing down tunnels, seeking, feeding, one among a billion centipedes. She hungered for flesh. She hungered for death. She would eat the skulls. She would eat the hearts. She served the horde! She would mate in the hot shadows and lay her quivering eggs, a great queen, beloved, and—

Lailani clenched her teeth.

Serenity, she thought, reactivating her chip, restoring her humanity.

Behind her, she heard HOBBS following, his feet pounding the floor. She whipped around a corner, leaped into an elevator, and the doors shut an instant before HOBBS could reach her.

The elevator descended.

HOBBS remained above.

Lailani allowed herself a few deep breaths and wiped sweat off her brow. She realized that HOBBS's hand was still gripping her, attached to his severed arm. She yanked it off.

The elevator dinged and the doors opened. Lailani jammed HOBBS's arm into the doorway, preventing the elevator from rising back up.

Panting, she stepped out of the elevator into a warehouse.

Hundreds of robotic dolls filled it.

None were moving. They filled the warehouse, crowded together, wearing frilly gowns. Their porcelain faces gazed blankly. A single light flickered above.

Lailani cringed.

Footsteps thudded deep in the complex; HOBBS was taking another route down. Lailani would have to find her way to her starship—fast.

With a deep breath, she took a step into the warehouse.

The Victorian dolls did not move.

Lailani walked between two of them, pale things her height. Both wore funeral gowns, complete with veils. Ahead, hundreds of other dolls still stood in the shadows. Lailani wormed her way between them, step by step, fearful to even touch them.

A bark sounded.

Lailani froze and gasped.

Epimetheus came running through the shadows toward her, knocking into the Victorian dolls. He leaped onto her.

"Epi!" She hugged him. Tears flowed down her cheeks. "Oh, Epi, I missed you. Come on, boy, we're—"

A creak sounded.

One of the dolls moved its head.

Lailani stared. Epimetheus growled at her side.

Another doll turned its head toward them, creaking. Its eyes opened, shining lavender.

Across the shadowy halls, hundreds of heads turned toward Lailani and Epimetheus. Hundreds of eyes opened, shining.

Lailani stood frozen, daring not even breathe.

Epimetheus barked.

The hundreds of robotic dolls lunged toward them.

Porcelain hands grabbed her. Tiny mouths opened, filled with real human teeth, perhaps yanked from the jaws of screaming victims. Those mouths bit. Those teeth cut Lailani. She shouted. She kicked and punched. Her fist slammed into a doll's face, shattering the porcelain, and her knuckles bled. She kicked another doll, knocking it down, only for several more to leap at her. They tugged her hair. They scraped her skin. They ripped her clothes. They chanted around her, laughing, singing. Their voices were shrill, growing higher and higher in pitch with every verse.

> *Hickory, dickory, dock.*
> *The girl ran up the clock.*
> *The clock struck one,*
> *The girl ran down,*
> *Hickory, dickory, dock.*

Lailani shouted as they bit her, as her blood spilled. One doll tore out a clump of hair. Lailani kept punching, shattering their faces, exposing the gears within. Their eyes blazed red now, and maniacal grins twisted their faces.

> *Hickory, dickory, dock.*
> *The girl ran up the clock.*
> *The clock struck three,*
> *The girl did plea!*
> *Hickory, dickory, dock.*

Lailani fell to her knees, bleeding. Epimetheus was fighting at her side, but the dolls were tugging him, ripping him. They knocked the dog down, laughing, patting him violently, twisting his jaw. They kept singing all the while, hundreds of voices echoing in the warehouse, growing louder and louder, shriller and shriller.

> *Hickory, dickory, dock.*
> *The girl's in for a shock.*
> *We tore her apart,*
> *And stole her heart!*
> *Hickory, dickory, dock!*

Lailani managed to rise. She fought through them, but more hands grabbed her. The dolls pulled her arms behind her back. They grabbed her cheeks, tugged her eyelids, laughing, laughing, singing.

"Soon you'll be one of us!" said a doll.

"One of us!" the dolls chanted.

A shattered girl, her face spilling gears, swung open her metal ribs. Inside her torso beat a human heart.

"You will join us soon, Lailani," the creature said, then cackled, showering sparks. Its human heart pounded.

I'm already like you, Lailani thought, staring in horror, caught in the grip of the dolls. *I'm already part human, part monster.*

Her heart thumped in her chest. The dolls placed their hands over it, feeling, whispering, nodding.

"Hickory dickory dock," they said. "You can't escape the clock. Tick tock. Tick tock. Clockwork. Tock-work. Hickory tickory tock!" They lifted her overhead, carrying her as a sacrificial lamb, and her blood fell upon them. "Tick tock, tiptoe, tick-tock dolls! Coin-operated princess! Tick tock through the tulips with us. Soon you will know the Tick-Tock King!"

They carried her through their kingdom. They carried her up coiling tubes. They carried her toward double doors and into a room full of knives and saws. There he waited, wearing bloodstained scrubs. Grinning behind his surgical mask. Gloves on his long, long hands. He held a scalpel.

"I have been waiting for you, Lailani," Schroder said. "Now you become one of us. My precious doll. Forever."

They strapped her to a tabletop. She struggled, screamed, could not free herself. Beside her, she saw a porcelain doll sitting on a shelf. Lifeless. Her chest was open, an empty chasm awaiting. A sweet doll, made to look Asian, her lips like a heart, her eyelashes long and dark. A coin slot on her head. Coin-operated princess. Tick-tock girl. Hickory Dickory Dock. Lailani's new clockwork body. Her new monstrosity.

"Are you ready, HOBBS?" the doctor asked. "We will not use a rib spreader with this one. I think we will rip out her ribs, one by one. I would like to hear them snap. I would like to hear her scream. Your hands are strong enough for the task."

He stepped forward, her massive battle machine, all dark steel. He had reattached his arm, and his eyes shone red.

"Yes, master," HOBBS said.

Lailani looked for Epimetheus. He was gone. All was gone. Hickory Dickory Dock. Where, O Where Has My Little Dog Gone? Old songs. Old rhymes her mother had once sung her.

A tear streamed down her cheek.

"I'll make the first incision," Schroder said.

He brought his scalpel down. It was so sharp it didn't hurt. Lailani barely felt a thing as the blade entered her chest.

Another tear fell.

She gazed into HOBBS's eyes. Long ago, so many years gone that Lailani could barely remember, her mother had sung her a song. A song to comfort her on those long nights in the dark, nights alone by the train tracks, cowering as the junkies and whores and cutthroats moved around them. A song of having no home. Of a single light in the darkness. A song she had sung for HOBBS in a jungle world, cradling him as he faded away.

As the scalpel moved, she sang that old song again, tears flowing.

How many miles to Babylon?
Three score and ten.
Can I get there by candlelight?
Yes, and back again.

HOBBS stared at her. She gazed back into his eyes, crying.

"If your heels are nimble and light," she whispered.

His eyes faded. They gave the fainted flicker of blue. He spoke, his voice soft, organic, mournful.

"You may get there by candlelight."

His massive metal hand reached out and grabbed Schroder's wrist.

His hand tightened, shattering that wrist.

The doctor screamed.

HOBBS twisted Schroder's arm. Bones snapped. The second metal hand grabbed Schroder's throat. HOBBS lifted the man, squeezing, suffocating him.

Lailani lay on the table, strapped down, the scalpel still inside her.

"Don't kill him," she whispered. "Show him mercy."

But HOBBS kept his metal hand around Schroder's throat. The man kicked, his feet not touching the floor. His face turned red, then crimson.

"He must die," HOBBS said. His eyes were now blue. He was back. He was HOBBS again. He was her friend.

"No," Lailani said. "I've killed enough people. Let him live."

HOBBS released the doctor. Schroder fell to the floor, gasping, and cradled his shattered wrist.

They bound him. They gagged him. But they let him live.

I already killed Elvis. I will not kill another.

Lailani walked through the complex, weak, pale. Stitches ran down her chest. Epimetheus and HOBBS walked at her sides.

"Your memory?" she whispered.

"Restored, mistress," said HOBBS. He turned his head toward her. Though he had no mouth, his eyes seemed to smile. "I remember the dragons of Mahatek. I remember the hourglass. I remember our friendship." He lowered his head. "I am sorry, mistress, that I betrayed you."

She shook her head. "You did not. Schroder did. Humans cannot be trusted. He told me that once. But he lied." She placed her hand on HOBBS's arm. "He lied."

He held her small hand in his massive, metal grip, warm and protective.

HOBBS knew how to find all the robots here who had hearts. Seventeen of them, the hearts of their victims pulsing within. The doctor's wife, his children, his lovers, others he had slain. Seventeen victims. Seventeen beating hearts in metal machines. They took them into the *Ryujin*. They left the other robots behind.

Once the starship was far enough, the heartless robots of Elliot Schroder would wake up, would free their master. He would remain in his underground playground of madness. But nobody else would visit him. Nobody else would fall to his evil.

Lailani updated Wikipedia Galactica about this distant world.

Warning: Extreme Danger. Keep away.

They flew into the darkness. One woman. One dog. Eighteen robots with human hearts. Holding the hourglass to her chest, Lailani gazed at the rocky world.

"Remain with your toys," she whispered. "Remain with your madness." She closed her eyes, and the tears gathered. She whispered, voice trembling. "How many miles to Babylon? Three score and ten. Can I get there by candlelight?"

HOBBS placed a hand on his shoulder. He spoke gently. "Yes, and back again. If your heels are nimble and light, you may get there by candlelight."

She opened her eyes, gazed at her friend through her tears, and smiled.

The rocky world vanished in the distance. They flew onward.

CHAPTER THIRTEEN

The *Lodestar* burst out from warped space ahead of Earth, flying into a sea of human starships.

A thousand of them flew ahead. A thousand starships small and large. The fleet of humanity. The hope of Earth.

I roused them in time, Ben-Ari thought, standing on the *Lodestar*'s bridge. *Now our great battle begins.*

She gazed upon the fleet. Three massive starfighter carriers flew here: the *Sparta*, the *Athens*, and the *Thebes*. All three were new, built since the marauder war two years ago. All three were among the mightiest ships humanity had ever built, containing weaponry unknown during the previous wars. Among these three terrors flew thirty warships, nearly as large, lined with cannons, their shields thick, their holds containing enough munitions to destroy civilizations. Finally, among these behemoths, flew hundreds of smaller vessels, ranging from space-tanks with crews of five to agile Firebird starfighters with a single pilot.

Even more inspiring than the military ships were the civilian ones.

Hundreds had risen to fight too, a fleet of volunteers.

Mining vessels. Trading barges. Pleasure pontoons. Racing ships. Even an antique space shuttle from the twentieth century, now owned by a collector. Cannons were mounted upon these ships. Civilians piloted them. No, not civilians, not today. Today they were soldiers. Today they were among the bravest of humanity.

In total, the human ships numbered a thousand.

It was inspiring.

And it was nothing.

It was but an echo of humanity's lost glory. During the Scum War only ten years ago, Ben-Ari had flown among a *hundred thousand* starships toward Abaddon. Two galactic wars had devastated humanity. A decade of fire had nearly destroyed them. Earth had beaten the scum and marauders—but at a horrible cost. Only one percent of humanity's might remained today.

But it will be enough, Ben-Ari told herself. *It will have to be. We are the survivors. We are the mightiest of our race. We will overcome.*

She did not wear her fine captain's uniform today, the navy-blue fabric bedecked with polished brass buttons. Instead, she had raided the security guards' wardrobe. She stood now on the bridge clad in black, body armor protecting her—a hardened vest and pads for her elbows and knees. She wore a helmet too, and she carried her plasma rifle. She had insisted on dressing for battle, even inside a nonmilitary starship, even as the other officers had exchanged uneasy glances. Ben-Ari had fought enough space battles to know that even here, even aboard mighty starships, war often came down to hand-to-hand combat. Even for the captain. She would be ready.

Aurora extended her tentacles, guiding the *Lodestar* toward the head of humanity's fleet. The pilot then turned the ship around, and they faced the depth of space.

From that darkness, they came flying.

The enemy armada.

Ten thousand charging saucers, only moments away.

Some were small red saucers, each with a single gray pilot. Some were motherships that dwarfed even the human carriers. All were flying death. All promised the destruction of old humanity. All would see Earth burn.

Then we must kill them all, Ben-Ari thought.

"Mistress of dark waters," said Aurora, speaking to Ben-Ari. "Like beads of light in a murky sea, the song of sharks reaches our shell. Shall we gaze into their light?"

Ben-Ari had to contemplate that for a moment. *I think she's telling me we're receiving a transmission from the enemy fleet, and she's asking if she should patch them through. We really need to upgrade her translator.*

Ben-Ari clenched her jaw. She nodded. "Central viewport."

A screen before her came online. Ben-Ari inhaled sharply. Around her, the bridge crew cursed.

A hideous visage appeared on the monitor before her. It was a gray general, half his face shattered, the rest burnt, his skin peeling. Shards of broken skull thrust out from his cheek, and several of his teeth hung loose. He stared at her with cruel black eyes, one bulging out and blind. Around his chest hung his hearts, withered and dripping, no longer pumping.

"Hello, Einav," Abyzou hissed. "Did you think me dead?"

"I'm still not sure you're alive," Ben-Ari said. "I've seen month-old corpses in better shape."

The wretched, dripping creature cackled. "You cannot win, Captain. You have a thousand ships, most of them weak, fragile vessels not geared for war. I fly to you with ten thousand machines of might. Surrender now. Surrender and become our slaves. Serve Nefitis. And live in chains."

Ben-Ari stared into that dark, black eye. She squared her shoulders. "We have lived in chains before. We were slaves to the marauders. Never again. You face a small fleet, that is true. But you face free warriors, noble and proud. You face humanity. Know that the scum and marauders have tried to defeat us before. They both failed."

Abyzou laughed—a deep, gurgling laugh that brought blood to his shattered teeth. "We are no alien race, Einav. We are the true humans. Evolved. Supreme. You are but apes, embarrassing ancestors. Earth is ours. It has always been ours. You will serve us as slaves. Or you will die in fire, and your ashes shall feed our fields!"

Ben-Ari frowned. "Sorry, I missed those last couple of sentences. Transmission garbled. Something about how you're embarrassing?"

She glanced at Aurora and swiped her finger across her throat. With a nod, the mollusk cut the transmission.

"I've never been one for smack talk," Ben-Ari said to her crew.

Humor. An attempt to hide her fear, perhaps. To comfort her crew. Inside, she was ice and fire.

Fish came to stand at her side. The Australian was finally wearing his uniform, though he had kept his shark-tooth necklace. His long blond hair was tucked behind his ears. He stared at the gray fleet, eyes hard with determination and haunted with fear.

"Crikey, look at those drongos," he muttered. "I'll be stuffed, it's chokers out there, and they're mad as thirsty mozzies." He turned toward Ben-Ari. "Are you sure about this, sheila? Maybe we should chuck a sickie. Sit this one out. The *Lodestar* is no warship."

"She is now," Ben-Ari said. "Every ship of humanity is now a warship."

Professor Isaac came to stand at their side. "And today we are all soldiers. Even the scientists. Today all humanity is an army." He gave Ben-Ari a soft smile. "And I'm glad that you lead us. I'm proud to call you my captain."

She smiled back at him. She placed her hand on his arm. "And I'm proud to call you my friend."

The enemy fleet flew closer. Within minutes, the saucers would be upon them.

A raspy, baritone voice emerged from her communicator. "Welcome home, Captain."

Even with the looming battle, Ben-Ari couldn't help but smile. "Hello, Mr. President."

"I heard you destroyed a few of these ships on the way here," President Petty said. "Nice of you to leave us a few."

"I wanted to share some of the fun," Ben-Ari said.

James Petty had been her commanding officer during the Marauder War. Gruff, stubborn, and courageous, he had always reminded her of an aging lion, still king of his pride despite his advanced years. The general had risen even higher after the war, winning a landslide election to become the new president of Earth's Alliance of Nations. Until now, presidents had always commanded battles from bunkers. Ben-Ari did not ask Petty for his location; she knew he would not reveal it over the communicator. But she had a feeling he was commanding the *Sparta*, the largest of the warships.

Of course he is, she thought. *The old general wouldn't miss a chance to fight. Truly an old lion, proud and stubborn. And this lion's fangs are still sharp.*

"Will you speak a few words to the fleet before the battle?" Petty asked her.

Ben-Ari nodded. "Patch me through."

Lights appeared on the viewport before her, one by one, as the fleets of humanity came online, as they connected to her communicator. A thousand lights, large and small. A thousand candles in the dark.

Ben-Ari clasped the professor's hand. His grip was warm and comforting. Surprising her, Fish took her second hand, his grip equally confident.

She took a deep breath. And she spoke.

"To the fleet of humanity! This is Einav Ben-Ari. You all know who I am. You all know of my service in the Galactic Wars. Some have called me a heroine. But today I will not speak of myself but of you. For today you—every man and woman in this fleet—are all heroes. Today you are all afraid. But today you will all do your duty. You will all fight. You will be tempted to flee! In the heat of battle, as starships explode around you, as flaming corpses rain toward our blue planet, your fear will call you to fall back. But you will charge forth nonetheless! You will fight onward! You will fight with all your strength, you will do your duty, and you will win!"

She paused for a moment. She took a deep breath. She spoke again, more softly now, but her voice grew stronger with every word.

"We have suffered unimaginable horrors. Everyone among you has lost loved ones. Ten years ago, the scum slaughtered tens of millions. Only a few years later, the marauders slaughtered many millions more. We watched entire cities crumble. We watched nations fall. We watched a hundred thousand starships vanish from the sky. Today we fly again into battle. And today we are accompanied by the spirits of millions of our martyrs, our loved ones burned, slaughtered, consumed, mutilated, millions who perished in the hellfire of battle and the inferno of the alien slaughterhouses. Today we fly to battle remembering our fallen mothers, fathers, siblings, spouses, children. Millions who suffered and died so that we may live." Her voice rose to a loud cry. "Today you *will not* join them! Today *you will live*! Today we will defeat the enemy! Today we will bring freedom and victory to humanity! Today we save Earth!"

She cut off her transmission. She raised her chin.

The saucers charged toward them.

Ben-Ari nodded. She turned toward Aurora, and she smiled thinly, tears in her eyes.

"Forward," she whispered. "To war and glory."

The alien lifted one tentacle in salute. Her body flashed gold. "To war and glory."

Across the bridge, the other officers—scientists, engineers, pilots—saluted too. Today they were all soldiers.

"To war and glory."

The engines rumbled.

Ben-Ari stood at the viewport, facing the wrath of the enemy—ten thousand saucers storming forth.

The *Lodestar* blasted forward to meet them, leading humanity's charge.

The enemy opened fire. Thousands of blazing bolts streamed toward Earth's fleet.

Ben-Ari nodded and hit a button on her controls.

The *Lodestar*—a tiny light before the dark horde—unleashed her fury.

The heavens burned.

Explosions rocked the *Lodestar*. A viewport cracked. Across the ship, the hull dented, then tore open. People spilled out into space. Fire raged.

Ben-Ari fired again. They took out one saucer. Hundreds more stormed toward them.

They kept charging forth.

"They're tearing us apart!" Fish cried.

"Onward!" Ben-Ari shouted. "Charge! For Earth!"

The *Lodestar* kept flying forth.

More blasts hit them, tearing into them. Another deck was breached. Flames filled the bridge.

Ben-Ari raised her chin and took a deep breath.

Firing all their guns, they slammed into the gray fleet.

Their figurehead, shaped as the Greek goddess Eos, plowed through the enemy. Saucers shattered. Their cannons kept firing, blasting bolts from port and starboard, knocking enemy ships back. No, the *Lodestar* was not a warship, but she had been built to survive the dangers of space, and she fought with a fury few vessels could match.

"Onward!" Ben-Ari cried. "Humanity, onward!"

They charged onward.

Blasts hit them.

Fire engulfed them.

More decks shattered, and flailing men spilled into the void.

They kept charging, knocking aside the buzzing saucers, tearing through the enemy ranks.

Ahead loomed a massive dark mothership, a hulking disk of dark metal, many times the size of the *Lodestar*. Hieroglyphs were engraved upon it, leaking red rust as if they bled.

Forward.

Onward.

The *Lodestar*'s cannons blasted.

They charged toward the enemy

With fury, with shouts and blood and blazing fire, they rammed into the mothership. The goddess Eos, forged of sharp steel and larger than life, plowed into the enemy and shattered the glyphs and pierced the hull with raging flame.

The *Lodestar* shook.

The mothership careened, cannons blazing.

The two ships detached, and Ben-Ari fired everything they had, sending the wrath of the *Lodestar* into the gaping hole in the gargantuan saucer, the hole they had torn open.

Their shells flew into the enemy ship, and the mighty saucer—a vessel the size of a town—shattered.

The holocaust filled space.

Shrapnel flew everywhere.

Shards the size of oaks rained toward Earth.

The *Lodestar* hovered in the middle of the enemy formations, a single small ship, damaged, cracked, burning. Around them spread the thousands of enemy saucers.

Perhaps this is our death, Ben-Ari thought. *But we die killing many of the bastards.*

She sucked in air, prepared to release another volley of fire, to die in glory.

With streams of light and thrumming engines, hundreds of other human starships crashed into the battle around her.

Warships tore through saucer formations. Firebirds streaked forth, all guns blazing, whipping between the motherships and engaging the small red fighters. From the distance, the great carriers—starships the size of skyscrapers—were blazing their cannons, shelling the enemy.

All was light and flame and shattering metal.

Ben-Ari sneered.

"We fight," she said. "We stand. We will win! Forward and fire!"

The battle raged for hours. All around them, the small fighters zipped, careened, shattered. Firebirds exploded. Saucers cracked open. The motherships sent forth beams of light, searing through human warships and starfighters alike. From below on Earth, it would seem that the sky was burning, that the stars were weeping.

"Ships of Earth, fight!" Ben-Ari cried, broadcasting her voice to the fleet. "Do not let one saucer pass! Fight! Hold them back! Charge into them and fire everything!"

And they fought. Warships. Starfighters. Civilian vessels. Merchants, cargo haulers, miners, racers—they fought with the same fury, same valor as the soldiers. Not one ship fled. Their cannons kept blazing. Every moment another human ship collapsed, torn apart by the enemy fire. Every moment more warriors perished. Yet here in Earth's orbit, they kept fighting. Defenders of their planet. Heroes of humanity.

"Captain!" Fish shouted. "Captain, look at those tossers! Approaching off the starboard! And we're exposed like a shag on a rock."

She spun and stared. Her heart sank.

She clenched her fists.

"Divert power to starboard shields and cannons! Fire all we've got! Take those bastards down!"

A dozen of them were charging forth: dark enemy ships, conical, tipped with drills. They were not saucers, but they were still gray ships. Bullets flew from them, hammering into the *Lodestar*'s shields. But Ben-Ari knew these ships intended more than shelling.

Those were boarding vessels.

The *Lodestar* answered with a volley. Shell after shell flew from the starboard cannons. Explosions rocked the enemy drills. Two, three, then ten of the drills shattered.

But two of the conical vessels reached the *Lodestar*. They slammed into the ship, drove hooks into the hull, and started drilling.

"Bring up a map of the *Lodestar*," Ben-Ari told her computer. "Show me the hull breaches."

A hologram appeared before her, showing the decks where the drills were working.

"All security guards!" Ben-Ari said. "Make to decks D7 and E4! Now!" She turned toward her new security officer, an erstwhile HDF battalion commander. "Man the cannons and keep us fighting."

With that, Ben-Ari rushed off the bridge.

She raced down the corridors, her armor clanking, her rifle clutched in her hands. She made her way to deck D7, and ten security guards burst into the room with her.

Her heart sank.

It was the ship's nursery.

The *Lodestar* was, of course, not a military vessel. They had only just returned from deep space, hadn't yet evacuated the civilians. The nursery was filled with babies.

The enemy drill, a screaming terror the size of a shark, was tearing through the wall. A nurse lay on the floor, dead, pierced with shrapnel. A baby shrieked in her arms, bloodied. The lights were flashing, and the room alternated between blinding white light and pitch-blackness.

"Henson!" Ben-Ari barked. "Walt! Guerra! Get the children out!"

Three security guards rushed forth. They grabbed babies, one under each arm, and began evacuating them from the deck.

Ben-Ari faced the spinning drill, gun raised. Seven other officers stood with her, holding their own weapons.

The drill shrieked, spraying sparks and metal shards. The massive machine kept shoving into the room, crushing the empty cribs, grinding the dead nurse to a pulp. When the hole was the size of a doorway, the drill began pulling back.

"You are warriors of Earth!" Ben-Ari said. "You will fight well! You will defeat the enemy. Today you will live!"

The drill vanished, exposing a tunnel from the enemy ship.

And the creatures charged into the *Lodestar*.

Officers screamed.

They were grays—but not the grays Ben-Ari had fought before. Not humanoid. These ones scuttled on eight legs like spiders. They towered eight feet tall, strange centaurs, their claws like swords. Their mouths opened in shrieks, and their black eyes blazed with dark fury.

Ben-Ari stared in horror, for an instant frozen.

Then she screamed and fired her gun.

Her plasma washed over one of the towering, deformed hybrids.

One creature burst through the flames, shrieking, and lashed its claws at her.

A blast hit the *Lodestar*, and the lights went dark.

Backup power kicked in, and the light returned, revealing the massive, twisted head of a beast only centimeters away from Ben-Ari. Its jaws opened wide, teeth bared, shriek deafening.

Claws slammed into Ben-Ari, denting her armor, and she flew through the air. She hit the wall, screamed, and fell to the floor.

More of the creatures came charging into the *Lodestar*, scuttling on their many clawed legs.

The lights vanished again.

Ben-Ari roared and blindly fired her plasma rifle. Blue bolts flashed forward, filling the room with light, slamming into the creatures.

The monsters kept advancing, shrieking, jaws unhinging and widening like the jaws of serpents. Guards shouted and fired their guns. The creatures advanced through the hailstorm of bullets, grabbed guards, and ripped them apart. Severed limbs hit the walls. Blood showered. Entrails splashed onto the floor.

Ben-Ari fired again. Again. She trudged through the gore, switched her plasma rifle to automatic, and gushed forth a mighty torrent of flame.

The inferno washed over one of the creatures, and it screamed. Its skin and flesh melted, revealing the bones beneath, but its heart still pulsed behind exposed ribs.

Two more monsters advanced around their burning comrade, and their claws grabbed Ben-Ari, denting her armor. They lifted her off the floor.

As laser blasts shook the *Lodestar*, the power died again. The room plunged into darkness.

Pain blazed on Ben-Ari's shoulder.

She yowled and swung her rifle, slamming the barrel into something hard.

The lights came back on, revealing two drooling, bloated faces, the craniums draped with wrinkly gray skin, the eyes deranged, the jaws red with blood—her blood.

Darkness fell.

Teeth slammed into her armor, punching holes through it.

Ben-Ari drew a knife from her belt and drove it upward with all her strength.

When the lights returned, the blade burst through a creature's jaw and into its mouth.

The claws released her, and Ben-Ari fell to the ground, raised her rifle, and fired.

Plasma sprayed upward, a geyser, bathing the room with heat. She screamed as the flames cascaded and showered her helmet. She kept firing. The two creatures above her fell back, faces melting.

She rose to her feet. The twisting creatures knelt before her, ablaze, flesh dripping off the bones. Across the nursery, monsters and humans lay dead. Two living beasts still remained.

Her rifle was drained. Ben-Ari drew twin pistols and fired with each hand.

Bullets slammed into the creatures.

They leaped forth, skin blistering.

Ben-Ari stood her ground, firing again and again.

Her bullets drove between their exposed ribs and into their beating hearts.

The creatures crashed down onto her, burying her beneath them, showering her with blood as they died.

She shoved them off and rose to her feet. The rest of the guards lay dead around her. The monsters gave a last twitch, then fell still.

She spoke into her communicator. "This is Ben-Ari. Get an engineering team to deck D7. Hull breach."

She left the chamber, swayed, and nearly fell. She forced herself to keep walking. Medics rushed toward her. They bandaged her wounds as she marched through the ship. The corridor shook. She tilted, nearly fell. Blasts sounded everywhere. She kept walking. Through the portholes, she saw the battle raging outside, the shells flying, the starfighters battling. Saucers slammed into a warship, and the mighty vessel shattered, showering the *Lodestar* with shrapnel. The ship shook, and the lights vanished for an instant before returning.

She made her way back onto the bridge.

"Status!" she barked.

Fish turned toward her, face dour. "Half our fleet is gone, Captain. Our ships have taken out a thousand of those buggers, maybe more, but they've got thousands to spare."

"We'll keep fighting to the last ship," she said. "We can't let them reach Earth."

The bridge swayed as the enemy fire slammed into them. The *Lodestar* was limping, barely able to stay flying. Thousands of starships still battled around them. Earth filled half their viewports, its forests burning as the husks of ships slammed onto the surface.

"Professor!" Ben-Ari said. "Can you open a communication channel to Earth's HDF headquarters?"

He nodded. "Yes, Captain."

"Patch me in."

The professor worked, opening the channel.

"Earth, this is Captain Ben-Ari," she said. "I'm going to send you a live feed of the battle with coordinates of every ship. I want you to begin firing artillery from the surface."

The professor's eyes widened. "Captain! Missiles from Earth to space are notoriously inaccurate. With so many moving targets up here, they won't be able to aim. They'll be firing blindly. They might hit our ships too."

Ben-Ari nodded. "Yes, Professor, I'm aware. But we have only five hundred ships left. They have thousands. The odds are in our favor."

The professor gasped. "Einav—"

"There are tough choices in war, professor. Sometimes commanders must sacrifice the few to save the many. Our task is not to bring everyone home alive. It's to keep that home safe." She returned to her communicator. "Earth, are you receiving our live feed?" She nodded. "Good. Commence shelling when ready." She glanced out the viewport at her disintegrating fleet. "I suggest you hurry."

She stood on the bridge, hands behind her back, watching thousands of starships fly and fight and burn. Watching another human warship shatter. Watching hundreds of Firebirds wink out and rain to Earth like comets. Watching thousands of saucers still fly.

Ahead flew the flagship of the enemy, a mighty saucer with a golden ankh upon it. It still flew high above, overseeing the battle. Ben-Ari knew that Prince Abyzou was there. Waiting for her. She could feel him staring. Even without a communication feed, she felt his eyes boring into her. And he knew she was staring back.

Another human warship shattered.

A carrier fell.

Ben-Ari stared up at her enemy.

Taste our fire, she thought.

And from Earth below soared thousands of missiles.

From here, they seemed almost delicate, tipped with red fire, leaving trails of smoke. Yet they grew larger. Thousands. Soon tens of thousands. A forest. A cathedral. The columns of fire rose, and the missiles soared into the battle, and space itself seemed to shatter.

Mushrooms of flame bloomed across space.

In the sudden silence, it was almost beautiful.

Missiles drove into saucers like flaming needles. The vessels shattered. Red and orange and golden fire blazed across them, a thousand shimmering lights. Another volley rose from below, gentle arches of smoke, and space shook, and saucers fell, cracking, falling apart, spinning, blazing, hailing down into the oceans, onto the ravaged plains and cities of Earth.

With them, human ships fell.

Careening saucers slammed into Firebirds. Errant missiles drove into warships. Storms of shrapnel tore into civilian ships. Only one carrier, the mighty *Sparta*, still flew.

But we're hurting the enemy. Ben-Ari stared at the devastation unfolding around her. Standing in the domed bridge, she felt as if she hovered within the battle, as if again she were fighting in nothing but a spacesuit. *We're holding them back. With the last of our strength, we're defending Earth.*

She checked the *Lodestar*'s arsenal. They still had some fury left. With a thin smile, she unleashed a volley of missiles, directing her wrath toward Abyzou's ship above.

The mighty saucer trembled.

Cracks raced across its hull, and chunks of it fell, emblazoned with its bleeding hieroglyphs. Around the mothership, missiles from Earth were ravaging the smaller red saucers.

"I failed to kill you last time, Abyzou," Ben-Ari whispered, ready to release another volley. "I will succeed today."

She prepared to fire the killing blow, to finally slay Nefitis's son.

Across the bridge, red lights flashed and klaxons blared.

"Ben-Ari!" Petty's voice emerged from her communicator, raspy, gasping for Earth. "The other side of Earth!"

She spun back toward the blue planet. Her heart froze.

"Tell me," she whispered.

But she saw them rising over Earth's horizon. Now her heart shattered.

More saucers.

Hundreds more.

Thousands more.

A monitor crackled to life, and Abyzou's ravaged face appeared there, smirking.

"My second legion has orders to take you alive, Einav." The creature licked his shattered teeth. "Soon we'll be together again."

She screamed hoarsely and fired her missiles at him. Abyzou laughed. The thousands of new saucers slammed into the battle with blinding light and shattering steel.

CHAPTER FOURTEEN

"Poet!" Addy whined. "Writing is boring."

He didn't look up from his notebook. "Boring for you maybe."

She groaned. "I have nothing else to do here. *Shippy McShipface* is tiny. And we lost all our games and books and movies when that damn gray blasted them out of the airlock. I'm bored!"

Marco shrugged, trying to focus on his writing. "I'm keeping busy. Also, our starship is called *Thunder Road*."

She tugged his shirt. "Let's make out."

He held up a finger. "One moment. Let me finish this paragraph."

She gasped and placed her hands on her hips. "You did *not* just choose your book over my lovely self."

He looked down at his notebook. He looked up at Addy. He put down his pen.

"Yes!" Addy said and began tugging off his clothes. "I knew I was better than some silly story about evil robots."

"Actually, Addy, *The Clockwork Rose* isn't about evil robots. It's about robots who are enslaved. Who are sentient and have feelings. Who rebel against their human masters, and—"

She silenced him with a kiss. "Be quiet, robot slave, and do your duty."

An hour later, Addy was asleep, sprawled out on the bed. The damn woman always took up the entire bed, never knowing how to share. Marco wasn't sleepy anyway. He entered the cockpit. The ship was still on autopilot, but he took over the steering for a while, just to feel the movement in his hands. He gazed out at the stars. Tomorrow they would reach their destination: the flooded planet Taolin Shi. The planet Baba Mahanisha himself had destroyed as a young warrior, melting its polar caps. The planet where perhaps they could still find the drowned mechas Kaiyo and Kaji, find these great weapons for Earth.

Marco sighed. He didn't want another war. All he wanted was some peace and quiet to work on his books. He was excited about *The Clockwork Rose*. He had gotten the idea on Durmia while studying meditation from Baba Mahanisha. When seeking to understand his own consciousness, he had realized that robots probably had a form of consciousness too. Did that make them slaves? He had only ever known one robot, the wisecracking Osiris, and she had seemed pleased enough with her lot in life. Yet what if someday the robots rebelled? In *The Clockwork Rose*, the robots were the heroes, slaves seeking freedom, the humans their oppressors.

And yet now Marco was being drawn into his own story, his own war.

"All I want is a quiet place to write," he said softly, speaking to nobody. "To be with Addy. To meditate. To be at peace."

Perhaps he should find a little planet, a place far from everything, and settle down with Addy. Be like Adam and Eve on a virgin world. He didn't even care if he never sold another book; Tomiko and her new boyfriend were entitled to half the earnings anyway. Yes, he could find a little planet, farm the land, live a happy life with Addy.

He sighed. But no. He knew he couldn't do that. He wasn't Baba Mahanisha, the last of his kind. His homeworld was still out there, and it needed him. He would not just flee to safety while the grays destroyed Earth.

I'll come back to you, Earth. I'll bring help with me. I spent the past decade fighting for you, and I won't stop now.

A few hours later, they saw it in the distance. A blue planet wreathed in clouds. Addy joined him in the cockpit, hair tousled, wearing her old *Wolf Legion 2127 World Tour* shirt.

"Taolin Shi," Marco said, watching the planet grow nearer. "Five hundred years ago, it was similar to Earth. Can you believe that Baba Mahanisha—our guru, the same wise old monk who taught us peace and kindness—flooded this planet? It's hard to believe he was once a warrior, a killer, a destroyer of worlds."

Addy looked at him. She raised an eyebrow. "Is it?" She placed a hand on his knee and spoke softly. "Poet, we destroyed the scums' planet. And we're nice."

"*I'm* nice," Marco said. "Just last night, you knuckled my head and gave me an Indian burn."

"You deserved it!" She poked his chest. "You ate the last frozen taco."

"Addy!" He rolled his eyes. "We had three tacos left, and you ate two for dinner."

She pouted. "I wanted all three."

They entered orbit around Taolin Shi. The blue planet spun lazily below, shimmering and ringed with a glowing band of atmosphere. Marco kept seeking some land, even an island, but saw only clouds and water. A mighty empire had risen here, a civilization that had traveled the stars, had conquered Durmia. It was all gone. All underwater.

"How easy do civilizations fall," he whispered. "Even the mightiest are but kingdoms of sand when the tide comes in."

Addy raised an eyebrow. "Shakespeare?"

"Emery," he said. "I just made that up."

She mussed his hair. "Smarty-pants. I have a saying too." She cleared her throat. "How easy do civilizations fall! All are like tacos when Addy's around."

How easy do civilizations fall, Marco thought with a pang. If his travels had taught him anything, it was that they fell quite easily. He only hoped Earth was not next.

He pulled out his tablet and opened Wikipedia Galactica. He brought up the entry on Taolin Shi. There wasn't much info. The planet had flooded centuries ago, after all, back around the time of the French Revolution. Yet blessedly, some intrepid graduate student had visited Taolin Shi a few years ago. The man hadn't attempted to dive into the ocean world, but he had charted it from orbit using sonar. His thesis was uploaded to Wikipedia Galactica, providing a map of what Taolin Shi must have looked like before the flood, including its cities.

"I reckon the Taolians would have parked their mechas in their capital city." Marco tapped the map. "Here."

Addy raised an eyebrow. "You reckon? What are you, a cowboy?"

He glowered at her. "It's a British word."

She snorted. "There are no cowboys in Britain. Even I know that."

"Well, you're right that—"

"That's where Vikings are from!"

Marco sighed. "Never mind."

They entered the atmosphere. The *Thunder Road* was still rickety, and Marco cringed as it rattled, but they made it through in one piece. They glided over the endless ocean. For a long time, they gazed silently at the water.

"It's sad, isn't it?" Addy finally said. "An entire civilization—drowned under the sea."

"Two civilizations," Marco said. "Taolin Shi, this flooded world. And Durmia, a world of ruins. Baba Mahanisha was the last of his kind, of that old war. Two worlds—gone."

Addy nodded. "It really makes ya think."

Marco scoffed. "What are you thinking about? Pillowmen? Pigmen? A pillowman and pigman having a baby?"

"Hey! I'm serious." Addy bit her lip. "God, Poet. Look at that world below—a whole civilization wiped out. Earth got close to this. Twice. Three times if the grays are already attacking. Even if we find the mechas, who's to say they can save Earth? They couldn't save Taolin Shi."

He patted her thigh. "They didn't have the famous Addison Elizabeth Linden, defeater of the scum, queen of the Resistance, slayer of marauders, devourer of tacos."

She didn't smile back. "I know who I am on Earth. I know I'm famous. But I don't feel like a heroine." She lowered her head. "Heroines don't wake up screaming from nightmares. They're not so afraid all the time." She looked at him, eyes haunted. "I'm just a woman, Poet. I'm ten years from youth, twenty scars from pretty, and thirty pounds from thin. I'm no legendary superheroine. I'm not who Earth thinks I am. Maybe not who you think I am."

He held her hand. "Addy, I know who you are. And you amaze me." He leaned over and kissed her. "You are fucking amazing."

"And amazing at fu—"

"Don't ruin the moment, Ads."

She grinned. "So hey, Poet, what do you think a pillowman and pigman baby would look like? A pig in a blanket?"

Marco sighed. He checked the controls. "What I think is that we're hovering over the drowned city now. Ready for some underwater exploration?"

She nodded. "Always. But are you sure *Shippy McShipface* can handle it?"

"*Thunder Road* can handle atmospheric entry and space battles. She can handle water." He patted a bulkhead. "At least, I hope she can. Don't crumple and crush us like a tin can, dear girl."

"Hey!" Addy bristled. "I wasn't that heavy when I sat on your lap at breakfast! Just because I ate all the bacon doesn't mean that—Oh. You mean the ship. Never mind."

Marco could see it below: the vague, dark outline of the underwater ruins. They weren't deep. He lowered the *Thunder Road* until they skimmed the water, then plunged in. The ship creaked. For a terrible moment, Marco was sure the water would crush the hull and come rushing in, but the ship remained airtight. If the city had been any deeper, the weight of the water might have done them in. Thankfully, they only had to plunge down several meters before reaching the ruins.

"The ruins are beautiful," Marco said softly. "And sad. Like a symphony played at its composer's funeral."

Addy nodded thoughtfully. "Like the wrapper of a frozen taco, carelessly tossed into the trash while you enjoy the meal."

"Like the words of dead authors," Marco said, "echoes of their souls, forever immortalized on the page."

"Like a pillowman's baby," Addy said, "crying in loneliness for arms that can never hug him."

Pagodas rose across the city, many stories tall, each floor with its own tiled roof. Those roofs curled up at the corners, draped with seaweed. Mossy statues still guarded doorways, shaped as snarling lions. A colossal archway rose along a boulevard, and as the *Thunder Road* flew through it, Marco saw octopuses and snails clinging to its stones.

There weren't streets left. Sand and shells covered the seabed. Fish flitted everywhere. Forests of seaweed rose among the ruins, filled homes, and swayed upon the pagodas. Coral clung to the husks of homes. A massive starship lay fallen nearby, a hundred times the size of the *Thunder Road*, coated with coral of every color, home to countless fish. A raylike animal swam overhead, shimmering with blue lights, its fins flapping; it was the size of a swimming pool. Eels peeked from old windows, electricity racing across them. Statues still stood outside temples, shaped like the native Taolians—humanoids with lion faces. Some statues wore mossy armor, while others wore robes and sported long mustaches.

"Why do these animals look so much like Earth animals?" Addy asked. "Even the Taolians look almost human. Their bodies, at least."

"Ever heard of Panspermia?" Marco said.

"Poet, we get it, you're the smart, brainy one. Stop showing off."

He ignored her. "Panspermia is a theory that suggests that microbial life travels between planets, hitching rides on asteroids. An asteroid might hit one planet, collect some microbes, and glance off and fly back into space. The asteroid then lands on another planet, which it seeds with those microbes. Panspermia might mean that many planets have the same evolutionary ancestors. It's possible that we on Earth share a microbial ancestor with Taolin Shi and Durmia. We evolved separately but from the same seed. That's why we're similar."

Addy nodded. "Perfect! So that means they'll have invented a Hot Dog Shack too, right? Let's find one."

"Right after we find the mechas," Marco said. "Saving the world is more important than hot dogs."

"Says you."

He stared out at the city. "I still don't see mechas. They should be huge. As tall as these pagodas. Let's swim a little higher."

They rose higher. Below them, the roofs of the city rose from the forest of seaweed. Above them, the ocean surface shimmered with light. Marco scanned the horizon. Underwater, he couldn't see far, but he saw the distant outlines of large structures—perhaps more pagodas, perhaps the mechas he sought. He navigated toward them, the ship's headlights piercing the water.

"Aww, look, Poet!" Addy pointed. "That cute little fishy is coming to say hello."

Marco looked. A fish was swimming toward them, its fins long and blue. Barbels extended around its mouth, tipped with glowing lights, and sharp teeth filled its mouth.

"Um, Addy?" Marco said. "I'm not sure that fish is so small."

The fish swam closer. Closer. Closer still. Soon it was only meters away. It was larger than a blue whale—large enough to swallow their starship. And it was opening its jaws.

"U-turn!" Addy cried, leaned across the cockpit, and grabbed the controls from him.

They spun around.

"Addy, let go!" Marco shoved her aside. "Let me—"

A shadow fell across them.

The jaws engulfed them.

Marco cringed and hit the throttle, and they blasted out from the fish's mouth an instant before its jaws slammed shut.

The fish chased. Its jaws snapped again, missing them by centimeters.

"Faster!" Addy said.

"I'm going faster!" Marco shouted.

The fish chomped down. A tooth scraped against them, denting the hull. Addy screamed.

"Poet, damn it, let me drive!"

"Get back!" He shoved her away and gripped the yoke. He veered left down a boulevard, shooting between pagodas. The massive fish chased, roiling the waters, knocking into buildings. A pagoda collapsed, shattering coral beneath it. Seaweed and bubbles flew.

"Poet, turn left!"

"Will you stop backseat driving?"

He veered down another boulevard. The fish pursued. Its scaled body scraped against a pagoda, and the ancient tower collapsed, burying houses beneath them. Marco flew onward.

"Poet, not that way!"

"Will you stop?" Marco said, glaring at her. "I know where I'm going! I—"

"Poet!" she screamed. "Eyes on the road!"

He looked back ahead and cringed. The *Thunder Road* flew into a forest of seaweed.

The leaves tangled around them. Fruit the size of watermelons slammed against the windshield, splattering juice. Marco shoved down on the throttle but the ship slowed down, then jammed.

They were still.

Clouds of sand hovered around them. The forest of seaweed obscured everything. Marco shoved the throttle as far as it would go. Their engines rumbled, but the ship would not budge.

"Good job, Emery," Addy said. "Real good job! If only you had listened to me."

"I meant to do this," Marco lied. "We're concealed here in the forest. We're hidden. The giant fish can't hurt us."

"You should have just blasted it with our cannons."

Marco shook his head. "I don't want to kill the local wildlife. Remember what the baba taught us? Peace and kindness, Ads."

"I'll kiss every bullet before you fire it into that bastard, if it makes you feel better," Addy said.

"No need." Marco leaned back. "We're hidden in the seaweed for now. We'll just wait until the fish swims away, and—"

Jaws slammed down around them, tearing through the seaweed. Marco and Addy screamed.

The fish tore them free from the algae, along with a chunk of leaves. It began to swallow.

"That does it!" Addy said. "Fuck peace and fuck kindness!"

They were inside the fish's mouth. The teeth towered before them, a closed portcullis. As the *Thunder Road* began sliding down the fish's throat, Addy reached over and hit the photon cannons. A blue bolt blasted forward and knocked out one of the fish's massive teeth.

Marco hit the throttle, and as the fish opened its mouth to roar, they blasted out. The ship shot out of the forest, spun in the water, and raced back toward the city. The fish chased them. Its injury only seemed to enrage it.

"Poet, damn it, stop running away!" Addy tried to grab the controls from him. "Turn around and let's blast that fucker."

"Wait," he said. "I have an idea."

He dived lower until they skimmed the seabed, racing between pagodas and statues. The archway rose ahead, the one coated with octopuses and barnacles. The fish chased them down the boulevard, roaring. Its fins knocked down columns and houses. Marco grimaced and flew through the archway, barrel-rolling to protect their wings.

The fish followed ... and lodged itself into the archway.

Marco spun the ship around. They faced the fish. It wriggled in the archway, stuck.

Addy burst out laughing. "That's right, Moby Dick! You ate too many spaceships, you fat bastard." She spun around and wriggled her backside at the fish. "You lose! Eat our dust!"

"Addy, you don't have to gloat."

She bristled. "Gloating is a proud human tradition, our way of life! It's who we are as a people." She sat down. "Fine. But hey, you're the animal lover. You're going to leave the fish stuck in this archway forever?"

"It won't be forever," Marco said. "He'll lose some weight and free itself. By then, we'll be off this planet. Now come on. Let's find those mechas."

"It won't be in this city," Addy said.

"How do you know?" Marco said, guiding the *Thunder Road* alongside a temple. Thousands of statues rose in the courtyard, shaped like ancient warriors with lion faces, a mossy army. "We've only searched one neighborhood."

"Because the mechas were military machines," Addy said. "They wouldn't just stand around in the city. They'd be in a military spaceport. You don't see humans placing our best warships in the middle of a city, right?" She tapped the map. "Look. There's a spaceport just outside the city. That's where we need to go."

Marco frowned. "Why didn't you suggest this earlier? We could have avoided nearly becoming fish food."

She shrugged. "I was hoping to find a Hot Dog Shack."

"You—" He groaned and tugged his hair. "Addy, I saw a hot dog under that patch of seaweed. Why don't you go swimming after it?"

"Ha ha, very funny," she said. "I know you made that up." She glanced at the seaweed. "Pretty sure you made that up." She leaned forward and squinted. "Seriously, where? I can't see it."

Marco sighed. He rose higher and piloted the ship away from the city. They glided over the seabed. Fields of coral spread below, and thousands of fish swam around them, shimmering, creatures of all colors. As they flew, Addy sang a song, and even Marco was relaxing, enjoying the beauty, and humming along. But soon they fell silent. Below them they rose, row after row, thousands of them, maybe millions: tombstones.

They were old stones, coated with moss, barnacles, and crabs. But there could be no doubt: here was a cemetery.

"The cemetery is larger than the city," Addy said softly. "This is a military cemetery."

Marco nodded. "Millions of Taolians died in the war against Durmia." They kept flying, passing over the fallen. "Even Baba Mahanisha could not remember which world had started the war. So many died for nothing."

Several kilometers farther out, the tombstones gave way to mass graves. These pits had once been covered with soil, perhaps, but the flood had washed the coating away. The bones were now exposed to all. Crabs and fish lived among them. Once this place must have fed countless bottom-feeders. Today only the old bones remained. The bodies were humanoid, but the skulls were feline, long of fang. The skeletons wore rusty armor. They held what might have been guns. Countless soldiers lay below in the pits, crumbling away. In a few years, perhaps, they would be nothing but dust.

Past the mass graves, the land sloped downward. As they descended, the water pressure grew, creaking the hull. The light dimmed, and the sun was a distant sparkle above. Stranger fish swam here, glowing bulbs dangling from their barbels. Their bodies were blobby to survive the greater pressure, and they had faces like grumpy old men, noses bulbous, lips fat and pendulous.

"This is how you'll look in thirty years, Poet," Addy said, pointing at a blobfish.

Marco pointed at something resembling a manatee floating nearby. "That one's you."

She punched him. "You did not just compare me to a manatee!"

"Look at it!" Marco said. "With a blond wig? Come on!"

"You'll be having sex with the manatee tonight if you don't watch out." She raised her fist.

Marco felt it best to change the topic. "Look, Ads. Down there in the valley." He squinted and increased the brightness on their headlights. "That looks like the spaceport."

They flew closer. The husks of starships lay below them, rusted and cracked. Some starships were barely larger than the *Thunder Road*. Others were warships the length of several city blocks. Barnacles and moss now covered them, and fish flitted in and out from holes. Eels nested in the barrels of cannons, and an octopus's tentacles emerged from an exhaust pipe. Coral grew atop the ships, tipped with glowing stalks.

"Death gave way to new life," Marco said. "One civilization fell. But a new society rose here."

Addy licked her lips. "A delicious society. Can we go fishing?"

"Can you stop thinking about your belly for a second?"

She shook her head. "Nope. I'm like a fish. Always hungry."

"Tell me something I don't know," he muttered.

"Did you know that you look like a blobfish, and I look like a beautiful mermaid?"

"You need a tail to be a mermaid. I'm well familiar with your big feet. They keep kicking me in my sleep."

She gasped. "My feet aren't big! They're petite and delicate and smell like roses." She glanced down at her bare feet, which rested on the dashboard, and gasped. "Ooh, there's a potato chip between my toes!" She plucked it out and ate it.

Marco nearly gagged.

The *Thunder Road* glided between a tilted control tower and a ravaged warship coated with starfish. Skeletons still sat in the ancient warship's cockpit. Fish nested in the empty eye sockets of skulls. They passed by warship after warship, dozens of them lying on the seabed, half-buried in sand. Many were shattered. Marco couldn't tell if they had been blasted from the sky or had simply disintegrated over time. He supposed that much of humanity's fleet looked the same now, scattered across the galaxy or sunken in Earth's oceans after years of war.

We barely have any ships left, he thought. *We need those mechas. We need those weapons.*

"These ships look horrible," Addy said. "All cracked and full of holes. Even if we do find the mechas, won't they be a mess, rusty and filled with snails?"

"Maybe," Marco said. "We're about to find out." He pointed. "Look."

Ahead, they could just make them out. They were still distant, kilometers away. Two dark pillars rising from the seabed, so tall they nearly reached the ocean surface.

Addy gasped. "The mechas?"

Let's take a closer look." He gently increased the *Thunder Road*'s speed.

They thrummed over the ruined port, heading toward the two towers, when the starship rose before them in the water.

Marco hit the brakes."

The ship ahead was ten times their size, bulky and cracked and covered with barnacles. At first Marco thought that some Taolians must have survived, were piloting a starship here underwater. Then he saw the tentacles. One huge tentacle, large as a bus, reached out from an exhaust pipe. Another tentacle, coated with suckers the size of manhole covers, emerged through the airlock. Two claws, large enough to crush the *Thunder Road*, thrust out from cracks in the hull. Stalks peeked from the ship's shattered bridge, topped with eyes.

"Fascinating," Marco said. "It's like a giant hermit crab. But instead of finding shelter in a discarded shell, it's using a starship."

"And it's coming our way!" Addy said. "Poet, blast that thing!"

The crablike creature charged toward them, tentacles propelling itself through the water. Its claws extended. Marco grimaced. He didn't want to kill this wonderful animal, but he had no time to turn and flee. He fired the cannon.

A bolt flew toward the crab.

The creature retracted its tentacles, eyes, and claws into its starship shell.

The blast hit the starship's armored hull, doing it no harm.

The tentacles reemerged, and the creature leaped toward the *Thunder Road*. The claws snapped.

Marco yanked the joystick, and the *Thunder Road* veered aside. The claws—they were as large as the starship—clattered shut, missing them by centimeters.

Marco drove the *Thunder Road* upward. The claws snapped beneath them. Again. Again. The creature swam after them, and the claws grazed the starship. Marco cursed, barrel-rolled, spun the ship downward, and released a volley of photon bolts. The blasts slammed into the enemy hull, barely denting it. Marco aimed at the tender parts—the tentacles and stalks emerging from the ancient starship—but the creature withdrew into its shell again. The instant Marco lay off the cannons, the creature reemerged and attacked.

"Marco, aim at the tentacles!" Addy said.

"I'm trying!" He fired again. Again. The tentacles kept pulling back, then reemerging. One tentacle slammed into the *Thunder Road*, and the small starship rolled through the water. A claw clanked shut, grabbed their wing, and shattered it.

"Poet!" Addy screamed.

"I know, I know!"

"We need that wing to fly out of here!"

"I know!" He fired. His blasts hit the enemy hull. Its armored plates took the punishment with ease.

A tentacle hit the *Thunder Road* again. The ship careened through the water and slammed into a coral reef, shattering its azure tubes.

"We're getting out of here!" Marco said.

He pushed down on the throttle, trying to escape. They would have to find another route to the mechas, one not passing through this creature's territory. Yet the massive hermit crab chased them. The claws grabbed their exhaust pipe, cracking it.

"Poet, damn it!" Addy cried.

He struggled to spin the *Thunder Road* around. He managed to face the crab, to fire. He tried to aim at the holes, to get a blast inside the ship. Twice he managed to shoot through holes in the hull, but the creature squirmed within, hiding from his bullets like a magician's apprentice contorting in a box of swords.

"Here, grab the wheel!" Marco said, hopping out of his seat.

"Finally!" Addy grabbed the controls. She released another volley, but the bullets slammed against the enemy hull, barely even leaving a dent. "Poet! Hey, Poet, where are you going?"

"I'm going out there!" he cried from the *Thunder Road*'s hold. "Try not to shoot me."

"You're *what?*" Addy said, but Marco ignored her. He grabbed a spacesuit from their closet and tugged it on so quickly he placed both feet into one pant leg at first. It was an agonizing few moments to strap everything on, suit and boots and gloves and helmet. All the while, the *Thunder Road* shook. A tentacle thrashed them, and Marco crashed down. He shoved himself up. He grabbed his rifle.

"Addy, keep it busy!" Marco cried.

"Poet, what the fuck are you doing?" she shouted from the cockpit, firing the cannons at the creature.

He leaped into the airlock and shut the door. He opened the outer door, and water flowed in, thick with sand and fish, slamming him against the inner door. He hadn't even paused to consider the pressure down here. He just hoped his suit could withstand it.

He swam out of the *Thunder Road*, rifle in hand.

Damn.

From out here, the creature seemed even larger.

The rusty old starship loomed ahead, the size of a jumbo jet. The tentacles and claws thrust out, flailing. Marco watched the claws grab the *Thunder Road* and dent the roof, only for Addy to release a volley, sending the creature back into its shell. Before

Addy could retreat, the tentacles reemerged from the starship and grabbed the *Thunder Road.*

Marco swam through the dark, dense water. The surface was far above, the sunlight dim. Most of the light now came from the *Thunder Road*'s remaining headlight; the giant crab had already smashed the second light.

Marco swam toward the alien starship. One of the tentacles reached for him. Marco fired his rifle. The bullets thrummed through the water, but the pressure slowed them down. The bullets thumped into the tentacle, doing it no harm. That tentacle—it was the width of an oak—slammed into him.

Marco careened through the water, the breath knocked out of him.

He righted himself. He swam back toward the alien crab. It had grabbed the *Thunder Road* in its claws, was squeezing, crushing, denting the hull. He glimpsed Addy screaming inside.

He reached the alien.

A tentacle reached toward him, extending through the Taolian starship's exhaust pipe.

Addy fired the *Thunder Road*'s cannons.

The tentacle retreated into the starship, and Marco swam in after it.

He swam through the exhaust pipe, a cavernous tube. The tentacle writhed inside. Before it could shoot outward again, Marco pressed himself against the rounded wall. The tentacle shot past him, its suckers larger than his head. Marco swam deeper, the flashlight on his helmet illuminating his way. He swam into the

Taolian starship's engine room. The engines had rusted away eons ago. The giant hermit crab's body now filled the cavern. Marco kept swimming, pressing himself against the wall, moving deeper into the dark ship.

The crab's body filled the place, clinging to the ceiling and floor. On the outside, the tentacles were coated with hard skin, the claws in shell. But on the inside, the creature was gelatinous. It was no wonder it had taken up residence in the armored starship.

Marco swam deeper.

"Poet!" Addy's voice emerged through his communicator. "Poet, it's crushing me! I can't break the ship free!"

"Get into a spacesuit!" Marco shouted.

"But you took the good one! You left the ugly pink one. I hate pink!"

"Just do it!"

He swam up a staircase and into a cavernous chamber— perhaps once a mess hall. The skeletons of Taolians lay here, fused into the walls, coated with barnacles. There, in the center of the chamber, Marco saw it. A bulbous, quivering mound rising through the floor, taller than Marco.

The crab's head.

He swam closer. The head had no skull, only translucent skin. It jiggled inside—the creature's brain.

"I'm sorry, buddy," Marco said softly. "You're truly a marvelous animal."

He placed his rifle against the creature's head.

The brain inside quivered. An eye opened within it and stared at Marco. It filled with fear.

Marco fired.

His bullets tore through the brain, tore through the eye in its center, and the entire head shattered.

Chunks of brain and flesh flew everywhere.

Grimacing, Marco swam, making his way back through the engine room. The tentacles twitched, then fell still.

Marco reemerged back into the open water.

Behind him, the massive creature sank to the seabed. The starship, its shell, tilted over and was still.

I'm sorry, friend, he thought.

He spun back toward the *Thunder Road* and grimaced.

The small starship was crushed. Its engines had fallen out. Its cockpit was shattered. It would never fly again.

"Addy?" he whispered, dread leaping inside him.

"Poet! Poet, you stupid idiot!" She came swimming toward him, wearing a pink spacesuit. "I look like a goddamn Disney princess."

"Oh thank God." Marco exhaled in relief and swam to meet her. He clasped her hands. "Thank God you're all right."

"Give me your spacesuit!" She began tugging at it. "That one's mine! You know I like the white one."

"Addy!" He shoved her away. "Lay off. You look fine. You don't look like a Disney princess."

"No?"

He shook his head. "You look more like Miss Piggy."

"That does it!" She began karate chopping him. "Hi-yah!"

"We have more pressing concerns than the colors of our spacesuits." He watched the *Thunder Road*'s wreckage sink to the seabed. "You smashed our ride."

"I'm going to smash your skull." She pounded his helmet. "But don't worry, little dude. We have a better ride." She pointed at the distance. "See those two giant sea-dicks ahead? Those are our mechas. And our new rides."

Marco stared toward the distant, murky towers, able to make out no details. Were those indeed the mechas? He hoped Addy was right. Otherwise it would be a slow, agonizing death here underwater. They had only enough oxygen in their tanks for another couple of hours. Panic began to rise in him. Two hours— to find air. Two hours—to find hope for Earth. Two hours—and their homeworld could become just another desolate planet. He began to pant. His head spun.

He breathed.

Remember the tower of stones.

He pulled himself into the lowest level, into awareness, like a crab retreating into its shell.

From there, he observed his panic. It hovered above like a storm cloud. It no longer controlled him.

He and Addy swam, leaving the ruined *Thunder Road* behind, heading toward the distant towers.

CHAPTER FIFTEEN

Earth's orbit burned.

Hundreds of humanity's starships shattered.

Thousands of Earth's missiles slammed into the enemy, filling space with fire and metal.

And the enemy kept storming forth.

Saucers flew everywhere—large and dark, small and red, spinning and spraying out plasma bolts. Death filled space.

Ben-Ari stood on the *Lodestar*'s bridge as her ship shuddered, cracked, burned, and she knew that she would die this day.

But so long as she lived, she would fight as if she were immortal.

"You will live!" she shouted to her fleet. "You will live, warriors of Earth! They will die! Cast them back into the darkness!"

The last human ships fought. Only a hundred left. Then fifty. Then a mere handful.

Perhaps it is our lot to forever fight, Ben-Ari thought. *Perhaps it is humanity's fate to forever live by the sword. My family has known this for generations. If I am the last Ben-Ari to raise a sword, I will swing it well. If I am the last human to rise up in rebellion against the darkness, I will shine bright.*

As the bridge shook around her, as monitors shattered, as officers fell, Ben-Ari kept fighting. Aurora fell to the floor, her boneless body crushed under a fallen beam, but she reached out her tentacles and still piloted the ship. Fish stood at a doorway, battling a gray invader that had made it aboard. The professor desperately raced between three workstations, sealing breached hulls, diverting power to life-support systems. Their new security officer lay dead, pierced by gray claws, and Ben-Ari stood over his corpse, manning the cannons, firing from port, starboard, and prow. They stormed through the enemy lines, taking more fire, crashing gray formations, ramming into saucers. All around them, the last Firebirds burned. The shells from Earth exploded around them, a blast every second.

"There are too many!" Fish shouted after finally slaying the gray.

"They're going down to Earth, Captain!" the professor warned.

She knew. She knew! Through the viewports she saw them. A hundred saucers or more descending toward the planet.

"Earth, keep those missiles flying!" Ben-Ari said. "I'm feeding you coordinates. Blast those bastards out of the sky!"

If Earth was short on starships, she was well stocked with missiles. Rockets kept soaring from below and slammed into the descending saucers. The ground-to-air artillery caught the saucers in the stratosphere, and fire filled Earth's blue sky. The descending saucers shattered, but a hundred more were soon swooping toward the planet. A barrage of missiles rose to meet them. Saucers exploded, but several made it through and streamed toward the surface.

Ben-Ari looked around her, surveying the battle. All around her, the missiles were slamming into saucers, barely able to dent the enemy fleet; thousands of saucers still flew. Barely any human ships remained. The *Lodestar*. The *Sparta*. A handful of Firebirds. That was all.

And Abyzou's ship was still flying.

The gargantuan saucer, several times the *Lodestar*'s size, came barreling forth. Missiles from Earth slammed into it, barely denting the dark hull. The mothership unleashed its fury, a hailstorm of shells, thrusting hundreds of missiles into the *Sparta*.

Ben-Ari watched, chest tight, as the mighty *Sparta*—the flagship of humanity—shattered.

"Petty!" she cried out.

Before her, the *Sparta*—a ship the size of the Empire State Building—split in two. One half still hovered. The other dipped down toward Earth and began plunging toward the Pacific. Missiles from below slammed into the collapsing remains, desperate to break them into smaller chunks. Humans—some still alive—leaped out from the wreckage of the *Sparta*, only to die in flames or careen into the depths of space.

"Aurora, charge!" Ben-Ari cried. "To Abyzou's ship! Take it head on! Ram it! Now!"

The *Lodestar* charged.

Around them, hundreds of saucers were making their way down to the surface. Ben-Ari ignored them. The ground forces would have to handle them now. Her target was one: Abyzou.

She shoved down the throttle. The *Lodestar* thrummed. Her crew stared ahead, eyes narrowed.

They flew through a rain of light and the husks of dead ships. Corpses thudded against their hull. They flew through hailstorms of plasma bolts, their shields cracking, their decks breaching. They flew through hundreds of floating corpses. They flew above the good blue sky of Earth.

Abyzou's ship loomed ahead, hovering over the ruin of the *Sparta*. The saucer's cannons fired. The *Lodestar* flew through the barrage, losing more decks, flying onward. Their ship became a missile.

Like a wolf charging at a bear, the *Lodestar* shot toward Abyzou's dark saucer.

The professor reached out and clasped Ben-Ari's hand.

Their figurehead, the goddess Eos, drove into the enemy's hull.

The cosmos seemed to shatter.

She tightened her grip on the professor's hand. She looked up into his eyes. He smiled at her. They stood together as the bridge splintered. Their figurehead plowed deeper, tearing into the enemy ship, and from the crumbling bridge, Ben-Ari stared into the innards of the saucer. Grays perished before her. All the monsters of hell screamed, lashed against her ship, shrieking, clawing, laughing, dying, a horde of demons all around her. She was floating through the underworld.

Pinned under the beam, Aurora reached out a tentacle. Most of their workstations were gone. Most of the viewports had fallen, exposing spurting cables and dented steel. The mollusk grabbed a lever and yanked it down.

The *Lodestar* pulled back, detaching from the massive saucer, exposing a hole the size of a house.

Ben-Ari swayed across the crumbling floor and fired their last missiles.

The missiles flew into the hole.

They exploded deep inside the enemy mothership.

Fire.

Fury.

Flaming shrapnel and shattering glass and bending steel and melting flesh.

The great saucer, the largest ship in the battle, cracked open like a rancid egg, spilling its innards.

The *Lodestar* pulled farther back, and Ben-Ari watched, eyes damp, holding her professor's hand. It was like watching a supernova. It was a thing of beauty. Several escape pods jettisoned the saucer, but most of the grays perished in the fire, and their charred bones flew. The last of the Firebirds flew toward the wreckage, firing missiles, tearing apart the larger chunks. Millions of shards, all that remained of the enemy's flagship, rained into the atmosphere and burned up.

Ben-Ari allowed herself a single deep breath.

Most of the *Lodestar*'s hull was cracked, falling apart. They hovered, barely still alive.

Most of her bridge had shattered, the viewports gone. She couldn't see much, but she logged into one monitor that was still working. Only a dozen human ships still flew, the *Lodestar* the largest among them. Hundreds of saucers still fought, but they were descending toward the planet now, leaving the remnants of humanity's fleet behind. Nobody was attacking the *Lodestar* at the moment; perhaps they thought the ship mere wreckage. Reports came in from Earth, flashing across her screen. The saucers were landing, and thousands of gray warriors were emerging to fight.

Her communicator crackled to life.

"Captain Ben-Ari?" the voice emerged.

She could almost weep from relief. "President Petty! I thought you were ..."

"Aboard the *Sparta*? I was. I jettisoned in time." Gunfire sounded in the background. "We're fighting on the plains of Earth. If the *Lodestar* is still capable, I want you to fly into deep space. Leave Earth."

She gasped. "Sir! I will not!"

"You will!" Petty said. Background screams and shrieks sounded through the com. "I have an important mission for the *Lodestar*. You must flee the battle for now. You must live to fight another day. I have a new mission for you. I will send details when I can. For now, fly at warp speed and get the hell out of here."

Ben-Ari looked around her. But there were still hundreds
of saucers flying toward Earth! She needed to fight them!

"I am a soldier," she said. "I will not tuck my tail and—"

"The *Lodestar* is to depart Earth's orbit, flee to deep space,
and await further instruction," Petty said. "That is an order,
Captain. Obey it."

She inhaled sharply. She nodded, eyes damp. She couldn't
speak louder than a hoarse whisper. "Yes, sir."

She cut off the communicator.

She turned toward her bridge crew. Only three remained
alive. Fish, leaning against a control panel, bleeding from gashes
on his leg and forehead. The professor, hair in disarray but eyes
hard with determination. Aurora, her chair smashed, wounded but
still holding the controls. A dozen other bridge officers lay dead
around them among shattered viewports, bent steel, and the
corpses of grays.

"You heard the man," Ben-Ari said. "You are to fly the
Lodestar into deep space. Professor, you have command of the
ship. Godspeed, my friends."

She turned to leave the bridge. The professor raced after
her. He took hold of her arm.

"Einav! What—"

She turned back toward him. She smiled shakily and
placed a hand on his cheek. "I cannot abandon Earth, professor.
Never. I'm not a scientist like you." Her tears flowed. "I am a
soldier. I always will be."

His own eyes dampened. "But how?" he whispered.

"I will not disobey Petty's orders. The *Lodestar* will still fly away. But I won't be on it." She smiled shakily. "We have flight suits in the armory. I practiced space jumps in Space Territorial Command. I can do this." Her voice dropped to a choked whisper. "I can still fight for Earth."

The professor pulled her into an embrace, and he kissed her lips. For a moment, as sparks rained around them, as outside the demons flew, they kissed. A single light in darkness.

When they pulled apart, he gave her a salute.

"Godspeed, Captain."

She left the bridge.

She walked through the devastated corridors of the *Lodestar*, moving between corpses and shattered chambers.

She pulled on her flight suit.

She dived through the battle, falling through the wreckage and death. She blazed into the atmosphere, a comet of fire. She burst into blue sky. She plunged down toward her planet, toward the world she loved. Toward war. Toward beauty.

Someday perhaps I will dedicate my life to science, to exploration, to love. But not today. Today I fight.

She dived toward the plains of Mongolia, sprawling grasslands where warlords had once raised an empire. A battle was already raging below. A hundred saucers were hovering over the plains, and thousands of grays were emerging. A battalion of HDF tanks was roaring toward them, while infantry troops charged, firing their guns.

As Ben-Ari plunged down headfirst, she held out her rifle. She aimed at one of the saucers and blasted down a barrage of plasma bolts.

Her weapons slammed into the saucer's roof, and the ship tilted and slammed down, crushing several grays.

Ten meters above the ground, Ben-Ari activated her jet pack and leveled off. She swerved from side to side, dodging the enemy fire, and rained down plasma. She rose higher. She flew over the enemy hosts toward the charging human infantry. She was still an infantry major in the reserves; today she would fight with the infantry again.

Below, the HDF troops saw her. A private raised the call.

"Ben-Ari! Ben-Ari! The Golden Lioness fights with us!"

Lioness. Yes, that is what the young soldiers had begun to call her. Her surname, Ben-Ari, meant "lion's child" in her mother tongue. Her golden hair, she supposed, supplied the rest of the nickname. She had become famous after the Scum War, the commander of the platoon that had killed the scum emperor. After the Marauder War, when she had returned with the Ghost Fleet to secure Earth's victory, she had become a legend. The Golden Lioness. A heroine of Earth.

Today I better not become a martyr of Earth, she thought.

"Be brave, soldiers of Earth!" she cried, flying toward them. "The Golden Lioness fights with you! Onward! To victory! Drive them back! Show them no mercy! Fight for—"

A hailstorm of fire rose from the gray ranks.

Ben-Ari cursed and swerved sideways.

Electrical bolts flew around her, ionizing the air. She swerved right, leaning sideways on the curve, and more bolts flew, and one slammed into her jet pack.

She screamed as the jet pack shattered.

It caught flame and she plunged downward.

She careened madly through the sky, her teeth knocking together, her jet pack sputtering.

She slammed into the ground and plowed forward through the dirt, shattering stones, uprooting grass. Her hardened jump suit cracked, dented, turned red hot. When finally she came to a halt, she was deep behind enemy lines, struggling for breath. Inside her hard suit, her body felt like a beaten sack of meat.

She ignored the agony.

She leaped to her feet, gun firing.

They surrounded her. Thousands of them. The gray warriors.

Their armor was vaguely Egyptian. Crimson ankhs were engraved onto their breastplates, symbols of their goddess. Dark helmets coated their massive heads, the visors cruel masks. Each warrior carried a rod, eight feet tall, topped with a generator for firing bolts. Sickle swords hung at their sides. Already some of these grays carried lurid trophies of war—human heads, hands, and hearts that dangled from their belts.

Ben-Ari spun in a circle, howling, firing her plasma rifle on automatic, spreading a ring of fire.

All around her, gray warriors fell, burning. More stepped up to replace them. She had charged her rifle before her jump, but it would not last long on automatic. She kept spinning, cocooning herself in flame, desperate to hold back the horde. The grass blazed around her feet. The shards of broken starships lay around her, still sizzling hot. She slew another line of grays, but more advanced.

A gray raised his electrical rod. A bolt slammed into Ben-Ari's shoulder, denting her armor. Another bolt hit her chest, shoving her back, charring her breastplate and knocking the breath out of her. A third bolt hit her back, and she fell to her knees.

They closed in all around. They drew their swords.

"Ben-Ari," a gray rumbled, voice deep and demonic. "We have orders to take you alive." His eyes narrowed with glee. "But you can live without your limbs." He raised his sword.

Ben-Ari raised a shard of broken starship and hurled it. The sharp metal slammed into the gray's chest, cracking his armor and impaling him. His sword fell. Ben-Ari lifted the weapon.

"You will not take me," she said, staring around her at the creatures. She held her rifle in one hand, her sword in the other. "You will not take this world! I am Major Einav Ben-Ari! I am human! This world is not yours. You will not take it!"

She would fire her plasma gun until the last drop of flame, then plunge her sword into her heart.

She pressed the trigger, and her plasma roared out.

Around her, the enemy burned.

The great ring of fire crackled around her, her shield, her fury, her death in light and glory.

Her gun sputtered. A last flicker of fire emerged, then died. She stood alone, clad in her charred armor, hundreds of dead grays around her. And thousands of living beasts climbed over the corpses, advancing her way. She raised her chin. She raised her sword.

Farewell, Earth. Remember me in victory. She took a shaky breath. *Be brave.*

She placed the tip of her blade against her chest, prepared to plunge it through her heart.

Roars tore across the land.

Cannons blazed.

Clouds of dust flew.

With the might of gods, the tank battalion plowed into the gray lines.

Ben-Ari lowered her sword. She gasped, her eyes damp.

She stood in the field, watching as the great machines of war crushed the enemy beneath their caterpillar tracks. The tanks' shells sailed overhead, shrieking, deafening. Phoenixes were emblazoned on their hulls, symbols of the HDF, and pride filled Ben-Ari. Here was human might.

She ran, swinging her sword.

She was still alive. And she could still kill.

A gray lashed a bolt at her. She deflected it with her blade. She leaped toward the towering creature—she didn't even reach his shoulders—and swung the sickle blade into his legs, cutting them out from under the gray. Another gray fired, hitting her with a bolt, knocking her down. When he loomed above her, she leaped up, and her sword slashed through his neck. She wrenched the rod from his hands, aimed, and fired a bolt into another gray. The beast fell, crackling with electricity.

"The Golden Lioness lives!" cried a voice. A tank rumbled up toward her, and a soldier reached down a hand. She took it. She climbed onto the tank. They charged onward.

The tanks crested a hill, and from here, Ben-Ari could review the battle.

She lost her breath.

She had fought in two galactic wars, but she had never seen a battle like this. Hundreds of thousands were descending upon the plains. Saucers hovered everywhere, fading into the horizon. Human transport jets were releasing company after company of paratroopers. Artillery brigades were shelling the saucers, and fighter jets were flying overhead, battling the enemy's red dogfighters. Entire infantry brigades were charging into battle, slamming into countless gray warriors. Blood drenched the fields of Earth. The husks of starships, some small Firebirds and some massive warships, smoked upon the plains.

The words of an old song returned to her.

"We're putting out the fire with gasoline," she whispered, and a sad smile touched her lips. "It's been so long."

As a younger officer, Ben-Ari used to scoff at fools who rode atop tanks instead of hunkering within their shells. Today she was a fool. Today she remained atop the tank, charging at the lead of the thousands of lumbering machines of war. Today she wanted them to see her—her soldiers for inspiration, her enemy for fear. She was the Golden Lioness. She had defeated the scum and marauders. She was the scion of a military dynasty. She would let them see her. She *would live.*

The sun set, but the battle lit the darkness.

Tonight we are free. Tonight we live.

Throughout the night, the horrors kept descending from space. More saucers arrived, runes blazing red upon their hulls, and they cast down death from their cannons. The clouds broke, and countless chariots of fire descended, their wheels scythed, their riders firing bolts into the lines of infantrymen. Armored pods fell from the sky, cracked open like eggs, and spewed out monstrosities the grays had engineered: towering warriors that raced on six legs, charging insects with wicked black eyes, and scaled beasts with humanoid faces that could lift tanks in their claws. The gates of a hellish future had opened, and the terrors spilled forth.

Not alien terrors, Ben-Ari thought. *The terrors of humanity, of the monsters we will become, which I must prevent us from becoming.*

And again the guilt filled her.

I banished the monks. I created this.

Her tank charged into a line of grays, and she cried out and fired an assault rifle taken from a fallen soldier.

I will make this right.

"The chariots of fire!" she shouted into her communicator. "Black Rose Brigade, take them on! Destroy the chariots!"

Hours ago, over two hundred tanks had rumbled in Black Rose Brigade. Only half now remained. Their commander had fallen; Ben-Ari now wore that mantle. The hundred tanks charged downhill, cannons blazing.

Ahead, the enemy chariots were tearing through the lines of human infantry. Each chariot was larger than a tank, terrible machines of dark steel, glyphs shining upon their sides. Fire crackled across them, and scythes thrust out from their wheels, tearing into soldiers, ripping men and women apart. Instead of living horses, robotic beasts pulled these chariots, stallions of dark steel and gears and engines. Nefitis had first revealed herself to the ancient Egyptians, and here was that civilization reborn, mechanized and ruthless.

The ancient Egyptians enslaved my people, Ben-Ari thought, *as these creatures seek to enslave us all. We will not let them.*

"Charge ahead!" she cried. "We do not stop. We do not surrender. We do not turn back. We do not slow down. Charge! Full speed ahead, and tear through them! Send these bastards to hell!"

The tanks charged, crushing corpses beneath them, and plowed into the lines of chariots.

Flame met metal. Bullets met flesh. Blood soaked the soil.

Fire and gasoline, Ben-Ari thought. *Despair and hope. War and glory. Human nobility and the evil we cannot become.*

As the battle raged, she knew that this was different than any war she had fought. This was a war against herself. A war against the demon inside—the demon she must cast back.

Her tank slammed into a chariot and fired its cannon, knocking the massive vessel aside. Mechanized horses galloped, and another chariot slammed into their tank, and fire engulfed them. Ben-Ari ducked into the hatch, and they charged onward through the battle, ramming into gray warriors, battling for every meter. The wall of tanks and the wall of chariots met where life ended, and the earth shook.

She rose ahead atop the tank to survey the battle, and she saw that all around her, tanks burned and humans lay dead, ripped apart, many merely piles of bone and blood.

Screams rose from a living company. Soldiers turned to flee. Ben-Ari stared and lost her breath. She placed her hand against her chest, seeking the comfort of the Star of David medallion she kept hidden within her armor.

By God.

Three monstrous cyborgs were scuttling their way. They were the size of whales. Each was formed of segments, and they raced on many clawed legs. They were organic flesh yet coated with metal plates. Their torsos thrust upward like those of deformed centaurs, and each creature sprouted several bloated, wrinkled heads with massive black eyes. They were grays, genetically twisted, hellishly formed, integrated with machines. Guns were mounted on their backs, and they fired hailstorms of bullets into the fleeing infantry.

For the first time in the battle, Ben-Ari wanted to flee too.

For the first time, pure terror filled her.

She tightened her lips. Eyes damp, she nodded.

"Take them on," she said into her communicator. "Black Rose Brigade, take them on! Charge! To victory!" She grabbed a megaphone and shouted across the battle. "Soldiers of humanity, I am the Golden Lioness! I fight with you! Take them on! Charge! To victory!"

"To victory!" the soldiers repeated her cry.

Tanks and infantrymen charged.

Shells flew toward the colossal cyborgs. The creatures swatted the shells aside as if they were mere flies. The many-legged creatures screeched, louder than missiles. They raced forth, and their clawed legs slammed into soldiers, piercing them, ripping them apart. Ben-Ari howled from atop her tank, firing her assault rifle, emptying magazine after magazine, but bullets glanced off the cyborgs. She might as well have been tossing pebbles.

The infantry charged at them with valor Ben-Ari knew would become legendary should humanity survive. Yet they could not harm the cyborgs. The creatures grabbed soldiers, lifted the screaming men and women, and feasted upon them. Soldiers screamed as the cyborgs pulled out their entrails, guzzling them down. Blood rained. And the cyborgs charged onward.

The tanks fired again. Shells burst against the cyborgs, denting armor but not harming the flesh within. One of the monsters reared before Ben-Ari's tank.

God, the size of it, she thought. She had thought it the size of a whale before. It was larger. It was a god.

The cyborg raced toward her tank, and the cannon fired, and the creature barely slowed as the shell slammed into it. It reached the tank, stretched out claws the size of oak roots, and lifted the vehicle overhead.

Ben-Ari clung on, firing her rifle, trying to hit an eye.

The cyborg hurled the tank through the air.

Ben-Ari screamed, spinning.

She fell off the tank.

She still wore her light suit, though her jet pack was cracked open, badly damaged. In midair, she ignited the pack. It sputtered, sprayed out a burst of fire, and she soared. She fired down a volley onto the cyborg. Below her, her tank slammed down and exploded, and the shock wave tossed Ben-Ari into a tailspin.

She had no time to mourn the dead inside.

She stared down at the cyborgs. One had cracked open a tank, was picking out the soldiers from inside and devouring them.

Ben-Ari sneered.

This ends now.

Her jet pack gave a last flicker, then died. She fell. She managed to kick-start it again, to fly, to sputter a kilometer away, passing over the line of battle. Her pack finally gave up the ghost. She fell and landed on a pile of corpses. Thousands of dead spread around her. There they lay: the noble men and women of the HDF. Privates and corporals, most of them. They couldn't have been older than eighteen. Some were barely old enough to shave.

She knelt by the corpses. She placed her hand on a boy's cheek. The dead private looked so much like Marco that for a second Ben-Ari was sure it was her friend. But no; Marco was ten years older now, a lieutenant, and far from this world. How had so many years passed so soon?

"I'm sorry, friend," she whispered to the fallen boy. "I need you now. Even in your rest."

A chariot stood overturned nearby, the grays inside slain. Four mechanical horses had once pulled the chariot. The tanks had smashed three, but the fourth horse still stood. The robot was larger than a regular horse and forged of black steel. Levers thrust out from its neck.

Ben-Ari slung the dead private, the one who looked like Marco, across the horse. She added two more corpses, then strapped them down. She climbed up and sat between them. She grabbed the levers.

It was a crazy plan. It was a crazy war.

She pushed on a lever, and the robotic horse burst into a gallop.

It took a few moments to get used to the controls. But soon Ben-Ari was driving the mechanical stallion with ease. The robot was *fast*, far faster than a tank. Its metal legs blurred, and it could leap several meters in the air, vaulting over corpses and the husks of armored vehicles. Ben-Ari kept riding, galloping toward the front line. The corpses she had slung across the horse jostled.

She galloped toward the cyborgs. The three massive beasts stood in a sea of human soldiers, rearing, roaring, feeding upon men. They stood like titans among mortals. Cannons were firing at the cyborgs, unable to take them down; their armor was too thick.

Ben-Ari rode closer, charging between lines of infantrymen. She tugged a lever, and her horse reared.

"Angels of Nefitis!" she cried. "I am Einav Ben-Ari! I am the Golden Lioness! And I have come to worship you!"

Each of the three cyborgs sprouted three heads. All those heads turned toward her. The black eyes narrowed.

The colossal beasts ran toward her, stomping over soldiers and tanks. The battlefield shook.

Ben-Ari struggled to calm her racing heart.

She unslung the corpses off her horse.

She tossed them to the ground before her.

"Accept my offerings to your glory!" she shouted. "Feed upon this flesh, oh mighty lords!"

The cyborgs paused for a moment, staring.

Ben-Ari only hoped that they were less intelligent than their masters.

Thankfully, their hunger overpowered their prudence. The cyborgs took the bait. They leaned down and devoured the corpses—flesh, clothes, and the explosives Ben-Ari had planted inside them.

The cyborgs rose, gulping down the meal. They stared at her again. Still hungry.

Ben-Ari sat astride her horse, facing the giants. She smiled and lifted a remote control with a large red button.

"I am the Golden Lioness," she whispered. "And this is *my* world."

She pressed the button.

Inside the cyborgs, the explosives detonated.

The cyborgs' bellies bulged. Smoke blasted from them. Their armor cracked, and fire burst out from within. Grenade after grenade detonated, and even though Ben-Ari wore a helmet calibrated to protect her ears, she instinctively raised her hands to cover them.

Before her, the cyborgs burst open. Their armored plates flew. Their soft flesh splattered across the battlefield. Their spines rose like morbid trees, dripping blood. Still the creatures lived, shrieking, lashing their claws.

Ben-Ari fired her assault rifle into their exposed flesh. Across the field, hundreds of other soldiers fired too.

The bullets tore into the wretched monstrosities. Their spines shattered. The creatures fell with thuds that cracked the ground. They rose no more.

Ben-Ari rode her horse up a hill, and she gazed upon the battle. Flares hung in the night sky, keeping the field as bright as day. The human fighter jets were battling the saucers above. Tanks were still crashing into chariots. Hundreds of thousands of warriors battled on the fields: human soldiers in dusty fatigues and grays in ritualistic armor. A soldier lay fallen beside Ben-Ari, but his radio still operated, speaking of other battles around the globe.

War is hard, but we are fighting harder, Ben-Ari thought. *We can withstand this enemy. We can win.*

Rumbles sounded above.

Ben-Ari looked up to see a huge black saucer descend, ringed in fire. It came to hover upon the hill before her.

She sneered. Her horse reared, and she loaded her rifle.

A hatch on the saucer opened, and a ramp extended toward the hilltop.

A cyborg emerged. No—not a cyborg but a mecha suit, a wearable machine. The suit was shaped like a scorpion, all spinning gears and clattering chains. It was three times the size of Ben-Ari's horse. A stinger rose behind it, large as a cannon, and two claws extended from the machine.

Inside the mechanical scorpion stood a gray, operating the machine with levers and buttons. Half the gray's body was burnt away, and half his face was shattered, chunks of skull clinging to raw flesh. A chain of hearts beat around his chest.

"Abyzou," Ben-Ari spat, prepared to fire.

The Gray Prince laughed. "Fire your gun, Einav! But then watch him die."

Abyzou moved his right arm, and the scorpion extended its right claw.

Ben-Ari frowned. The claw was holding a human prisoner. Inside the mecha, Abyzou opened his hand. In tandem, the mecha suit opened its claw, and the prisoner fell to the ground. The man was clad in rags, beaten, haggard.

"Look at her, slave!" Abyzou said to the man. "Look at your Einav."

Slowly, the bloodied prisoner raised his head and gazed at Ben-Ari.

Her heart shattered.

Tears filled her eyes.

"Father," she whispered.

CHAPTER SIXTEEN

Marco and Addy swam in their spacesuits, their oxygen slowly running out. Behind them, their shattered starship was already too far to see. All around them spread the endless ocean of Taolin Shi, this flooded world at the edge of the unknown. Ahead they loomed—two dark figures in the distance, towering from seabed to the ocean's surface.

"These better be the mechas," Addy said. "And they better work. Or we're fucked."

They had only an hour of air left. After that, they'd be forced to swim on the surface, to try to breathe there. But what if this world's atmosphere was toxic to humans? And even if they could breathe the air, there was no land. They would have to swim until exhaustion pulled them to a watery grave.

"Unless we can find a mechanic crab," Marco said. "One who knows how to fix *Thunder Road*."

Addy nodded. "And one who tastes delicious. Because after he fixes *Shippy McShipface*, I'm eating the fucker. I'm starving."

"When are you *not* starving?"

Addy thought for a moment. "Sometimes when I'm asleep. No, actually, even then I dream about hamburgers. Once I dreamed that you turned into a pizza! You were delicious."

He rubbed his shoulder. "So that's why you were biting me in your sleep last night."

It felt good to joke. To banter. To forget the terror. Death loomed. The grays were heading to Earth, perhaps were already attacking.

Maybe humor is like Deep Being, he thought. *A way to stave off the horror of existence.*

As they swam closer, the two towering smudges came into focus. Finally some hope filled Marco. The obelisks began to take form. Barnacles, moss, and seaweed covered them, and their forms were rough—but yes, these were humanoid shapes. One seemed to be male, and he held a great hammer, its head the size of a house. The other was female, and she held a sword as long as a skyscraper, the blade coated with barnacles and seaweed. Both male and female had lion faces, and both seemed to wear armor.

"The mechas," Marco whispered. "They're real."

"I call the boy one!" Addy said.

"Addy! I'm not flying in the girl."

She bristled. "What's wrong with girls?"

"Nothing! But—oh, shush, Addy. Let's find a way inside these things and see if they still work."

They swam closer, passing through a school of fish. Below, ancient pagodas lay fallen on the seabed, and eels nested in smashed starships. Finally they reached the mechas. They were massive. They could dwarf the Statue of Liberty. If these things could still fly, still fight ...

Marco tried to curb his excitement. All the starships they had encountered here were ruins, far too rusty and broken to ever fly again. The war had ended centuries ago. Odds were the mechas wouldn't work. Odds were they would die here. Earth would die. And—

Breathe. Don't let your thoughts control you. You are not your thoughts.

The baba's voice spoke in his mind. Marco breathed and observed. He continued swimming, no longer hostage to his fear.

Marco and Addy both swam toward the male mecha. They came to float before its head, only a few meters below the surface of the ocean. Just the mecha's head was larger than the *Thunder Road*. It gazed back at them, coated with barnacles and moss, its features barely visible. Starfish clung to its eyes, and limpets filled its mane.

"Now this looks more like me," Marco said. "Noble and strong. Not like those blobfish."

Addy patted his helmet. "Sure, my sweet little blobfish."

"Let's look for a door." Marco's excitement was slowly growing. "I imagine that the command center would be inside the head. Maybe we'll find an airlock. Let's start chipping off these barnacles and clearing off all this moss."

"It needs a shave." Addy nodded. "But don't you think the airlock might be by the feet? After all, these things were meant to land. The Taolians would have entered from below, then taken an elevator up to the head."

Marco nodded. "Yes. That's smart, Ads. Let's check the feet."

They began to swim downward.

"You mean I'm smarter than you?" Addy said as they sank.

"Let's not go that far," Marco said.

"But you admitted it! You thought the airlock would be on the head. I had the smarter idea! Which means I'm certainly smarter than you."

He groaned. "Addy, you once thought my thesaurus was a book about dinosaurs."

"Oh yeah?" Addy said. "Well, you once didn't believe me that green apples existed."

"That was you!" Marco said. "I had buy a crate of Granny Smiths to convince you, remember? And even then you kept insisting they were pears."

"Well, how should I know?" She scoffed. "I only eat apples if they're in a pie. With a big slice of cheese on top. And there's ice cream on it. And somebody scooped out the apples."

Finally they reached the statue's feet. The grime was even worse here. A thick coating of barnacles, coral, and moss covered the mecha's legs and feet. Marco and Addy both had their rifles. They chipped away with the barrels, cutting off centuries of buildup.

"Crustier than a whore's crotch." Addy slammed at a cluster of limpets. "This is worse than that time we had latrine duty at boot camp. Remember that, Poet?"

He nodded. "Yeah. We got latrine duty because you were mouthing off to Sergeant Singh."

"I did not!" She gasped. "My mouth is always polite and clean like a—" Her barrel slipped off a stubborn limpet. She growled and began slamming the gun against the cluster. "Fuck you, you fucking pieces of goddamn space shit!"

It was slow work, and it used up lots of precious oxygen. Marco kept one eye on his oxygen meter. Pretty soon they would have to rise to the surface, hoping to find enough oxygen in the atmosphere. Yet even if they could breathe this planet's air, how long could they possibly drift at sea before exhaustion killed them? Perhaps death by asphyxiation would be kinder. He shoved the morbid thoughts aside and concentrated on his work. Finally they carved their way through the thick layers of moss, barnacles, and mineral buildup.

They reached stone.

They frowned.

No metal hull. No airlock. Just polished stone.

"What the actual fuck?" Addy said.

They kept working, chipping off more layers of crud, revealing what lay beneath. More stone. A giant foot of stone standing on the seabed.

"It's … a statue," Addy said. "It's another goddamn statue! This isn't a mecha at all, Poet!" She grabbed him and shook him.

"Poet, it's a fucking statue like the ones on Durmia. We wasted our time! We lost our ship! We're going to die here underwater for a fucking giant stat—"

"Addy, wait," he said. "Breathe. Let it be. Remember Deep—"

"Fuck Deep Being!" she shouted. "Poet, we're dead. We're fucking dead! These aren't mechas. Mechas are metal machines!" She let out a wordless howl and fell to her knees. "Fuck!"

"Addy, conserve your air."

"What's the fucking point! We're dead!" She yowled and slammed her fists against the seabed. "We're dead, Poet. Oh fuck. Oh fuck."

Marco too felt the panic rise. It tugged at him, threatening to claim his mind. Without much air left, breathing was difficult, but he forced himself to take deep breaths, to try to clear his spinning head.

A few months ago, I would have fallen apart, he thought. *Let me examine this from Deep Being.*

He returned to the stone surface, which they had cleared of barnacles. He placed his gloved hand on it. His flashlight was already fading. The light was dim. The air was almost gone. He squinted, struggling to see better. He tapped the stone with his gun's muzzle. It was hard to breathe. It was hard to think. He forced his mind to keep working.

Just a statue, he thought. *Another colossal statue. Like the ones on Durmia.* He frowned. *But why would they build massive statues here— in a spaceport?*

Addy rose to her feet. Howling, she began slamming at the stone with her rifle. "This goddamn fucking thing!" She stepped back, cocked her rifle, and fired a bullet at the stone. "Fuck you, you asshole statue, I'm going to—"

"Addy, wait!" Marco said. He gasped. "Gun down. Look!"

She lowered her rifle, and Marco examined the bullet hole. He fished out the bullet, then tore out a chunk from the statue. He looked at her.

"It's not stone," he said. "It's clay."

"Same difference!"

He frowned and crumbled the clay between his fingers. "You wouldn't build a statue this size from clay. You'd use clay to waterproof something."

He slammed his rifle again, tearing out clay, and used his hands to rip off more chunks.

Behind the clay, he saw it.

Metal.

It was made of metal.

"The mecha," Marco whispered.

Addy gasped. She rushed forward, pressed her helmet against the metal surface, and began kissing it. "I'm sorry I hit you! I'm sorry!"

Their air was almost gone. There was no time to keep chipping away with their barrels. They stepped back and opened fire. The water slowed down their bullets, but they stood close enough to shatter the clay. Great chucks of clay, a foot thick, crumbled off the mecha, revealing the metal machine within.

A giant machine. A starship shaped like a Taolian warrior. They only saw its foot, but it was real, and it stood before them, tall as a skyscraper.

Their air kept dwindling. It was agonizing work to chip off more clay, to find an airlock. Marco was lightheaded. At one point, Addy fell and he had to help her rise. He breathed deeply, but his breaths felt empty. He saw stars.

He fired on automatic, ripping off chunks of clay, not even caring that he dented the metal beneath. And finally—there. A doorway.

They pulled it open. They stumbled into an airlock, flooding it with water. They couldn't breathe. They gasped like fish out of water. They had to wait, sucking up the last drops of oxygen, until the airlock drained of water and they could stumble through the second doorway.

They found themselves in a dark, dry room. They fell to the floor, pulled off their helmets, and gulped down air.

For a moment, Marco was worried. After being sealed up for centuries, would the air be breathable? Had the Taolians even breathed the same air as humans? Yet it felt good in his lungs. It cleared his head. For long moments, he lay in the dark, just breathing.

Addy breathed beside him. She kicked off her boots, peeled off her spacesuit, and lay on the floor in her shorts and Wolf Legion band T-shirt. Her hair was damp with sweat.

"It's a good thing I shot the clay off, right, Poet?" she said when she had caught her breath. "You just panicked. I thought and came up with a plan. Because I'm the smart one."

He was too exhausted and thankful to argue. He patted her. "Thank you, Ads. That was quick thinking."

She beamed.

They stood up. Their flashlights were almost out of power, casting only dim, flickering beams. They found a light switch, and to their surprise, it still worked. Golden light bathed the chamber, revealing two tasseled swords hanging from a wall, a framed painting of sunset over a pagoda, and a creature in the corner.

Marco frowned. "What the hell is that?"

Addy's eyes widened. "A freak!" She stepped closer. "I need to take a photo! He needs to be in the next edition of *Freaks of the Galaxy*."

"Don't touch it, Ads." Marco grabbed her.

She shook free. "What? He's cute."

Marco shuddered. "It looks like a giant deflated balloon with eyes."

He stared at the creature. It lay sprawled across the floor, eyes blinking. Its bulbous nose hung over its pendulous lips. Its pink, wet flesh glistened.

Addy patted it. "Ooh, slimy!" She thrust her face closer to the animal. "Just what I always wanted. My own little cutie-freak! I will name you George, and I will hug you, and pet you, and squeeze you, and—"

The creature leaped up and wrapped around her like a wet, sticky blanket. Addy screamed and stumbled back, flailing.

"Looks like it's squeezing *you*," Marco observed.

She shouted, voice muffled. "Help me tear off this fucking thing!"

She flailed around, wrapped in the alien, looking like a woman trapped in a giant plastic bag.

"All right, I'll shoot it off," Marco said. "Hold still."

"Don't you fucking dare shoot me, Poet!" Her voice was stifled, barely audible. "If you shoot me I'll—" She screamed. "It's biting me! The fucker is biting me!"

Marco sighed. He grabbed the alien and began peeling it off. It struggled a bit, but when Marco used the barrel of his rifle as a crowbar, it came free.

"You all right, Ads?" he said.

She stood, arms held to her sides, dripping slime.

"It bit me! Right in the leg!" She showed him the tooth marks.

Marco frowned. "Looks like it bit you in the butt."

She growled. "That's my upper thigh!"

"Didn't a jellyfish once sting you in the ass too?" he said.

"That was my leg too!" She looked at the creature which hung draped across his rifle. "Toss that thing out."

He gasped. "Toss out George? But I thought you wanted to hug him, and kiss him, and pat him, and squeeze him, and protect him forever and ever and—"

She grabbed the alien and hurled it into the airlock. They blasted George out into the sea. They stood at a porthole, watching it. Once it was back in the water, the alien inflated. Soon it was round, filled with water, and its face looked young again, no longer like a wrinkled, grumpy old man. It looked like any other blobfish.

"Asshole," Addy muttered, watching the fish swim away.

"More like ass biter," Marco said.

"Watch it, or your ass will be kicked halfway across this ocean." She limped toward a doorway at the back of the chamber. "Come on, Poet. Let's explore this mecha."

"Wait." He held her hand, then pulled her into an embrace. "Just a moment. Hug break."

He stood holding her. She wrapped her arms around him. They embraced silently for a long time.

"We did it," Addy whispered. "We did it, Poet. We found it. We found the mecha."

He touched her cheek. A tear shone there. "We did much more. We studied Deep Being. We faced monsters and overcame them. The grays who attacked us on Durmia. A giant fish that swallowed our ship. An even larger crab that shattered it. And George."

She laughed, eyes damp. "The dreaded George, mightiest of monsters." She squeezed Marco tightly.

"We did it together," Marco said. "And we'll keep doing it. We'll keep defeating our enemies. We'll defeat the rest of the grays. I know it. We can do anything together."

She bit her lip. "We'll keep doing it?" She reached down and began tugging off his pants. "Ooh la la!"

"You know what I mean."

She grinned. "Let's do it."

Marco looked around him. "Here? Now?"

She nodded. "You started hugging and patting me and stuff! Got me all hot and bothered. Now pay the price!" She began tugging off his shirt.

He nodded. "Okeydokey."

She paused and stared at him. "Never say that again."

"Never," he promised.

She kissed him. And it was more than just sex; it was love, relief, hope. It was new life after coming so close to death. It was Marco with his other half. And as they made love, he looked her in the eyes, and he whispered, "I love you, Addy. I love you more than I've ever loved anyone. You're the love of my life."

"Such a poet." She laughed and mussed his hair. "Now less poetry and earn your keep, lover boy! Put some back into it!"

Poetry? Perhaps. But Marco knew those words were true. He had loved other women before. Lailani. Kemi. Tomiko. Many women on Haven. But none had been through so much with him. None had ever understood him so well. Addy and he were fire and water. He could not imagine anyone more different. He could not imagine anyone else he preferred to be with.

I had a house by the beach, he thought. *I had fame and fortune. I had everything I wanted. But I was miserable. Here with you, fighting monsters, exploring worlds of danger and wonder—I'm happier than I've ever been. Because I'm with you, Addy. Because you and I are meant to be.*

They made love, and they lay holding each other for a while. Then they got dressed and prepared to explore the mecha. A doorway opened to reveal an elevator. Inside, they found a control panel. But instead of numbers representing floors, they saw a diagram of the mecha. Glowing buttons appeared on various locations on its body.

"The control center must be in the head," Marco said.

"If this mecha is anything like you, it'll be in the crotch," Addy said.

"Ha ha, very funny," Marco said. "If it's like you, it'll be in the stomach, because all you think about is food."

She patted her stomach. "I do." Then she pressed a button on the diagram's head. "But as you wish, milord. We'll check the head."

The elevator began to rise. It creaked and jangled, but considering it was five hundred years old, Marco couldn't complain. As they traveled up the colossal statue, Addy began to hum "The Girl from Ipanema."

After a moment of silence, Marco said, "Ads, I've been thinking."

"Me too," Addy said. "My mind is working a mile a minute." She kept humming the tune.

"That creature down there that bit your bum," he said. "George. He wouldn't have survived inside this mecha for five hundred years. That's when Taolin Shi flooded and the mechas were sealed up. George must have sneaked in recently. There must be another entrance to this place. We might encounter more life in here."

Addy nodded. "Makes sense. This time I won't squeeze it."

A glowing dot was moving up the diagram, showing the elevator now in the mecha's chest.

"And what was it you were thinking of, Addy?" Marco said.

"Huh? Oh. I was just imagining the *Space Galaxy* movie, only with a cast of dogs instead of humans." She laughed. "It's hilarious!"

Marco sighed.

"No, seriously, think about it!" Addy said. "They're all pugs, and have little uniforms on, and—"

"I get it, Ads."

The elevator reached the top of the mecha. The door opened, and they stepped into the mecha's hollow head.

"Well, this is certainly the command center," Marco said, looking around.

Monitors, control panels, and gleaming diagrams filled the place. Lights shone on the ceiling and walls. Holographic stats flickered. Pipes, fans, and grills covered the walls. It looked more complex than any starship cockpit Marco had ever seen. One viewport displayed the outside world; he saw a school of fish flit through the water. Nearby, he could make out the second mecha, the female one.

In the center of the room rose what looked like an exoframe, the mechanized armor Marco had worn in the army. Cables ran from the exoframe to the floor and ceiling. The mechanical suit held a war hammer, a smaller version of the mighty hammer the actual mecha held.

"You probably have to get in there to pilot the mecha." Marco bit his lip and couldn't help but smile. "I want to try it out."

Addy nodded. "Sure. Might want to ask for permission first."

"Addy!" He rolled his eyes. "This mecha has been standing here for five hundred years. The civilization that built it is extinct. Who am I going to ask permission from? George?"

She shrugged. "Sure, if that old Taolian dude is named George too." She pointed.

Marco looked. He nearly jumped out of his boots.

Jesus Christ.

It was a Taolian.

A living Taolian.

CHAPTER SEVENTEEN

"All right, boys. It's time to fuck up the spacetime continuum." Lailani grinned. "Ready to destroy the universe?"

Her boys stared at her. Epimetheus, her dear Doberman, tilted his head and gave a confused bark. HOBBS, her hulking battle-bot, shifted uncomfortably with a clatter of metal plates and gears. The *Ryujin* was a small starship, no larger than an RV. With their supplies, weapons, and all the robots they had rescued from Dr. Schroder's lair, it was a tight squeeze.

It's cozy, Lailani thought. *Cozy like chickens in a cage.*

She was wearing her spacesuit. Unlike battle spacesuits, which were heavy and covered in armor, she wore a black, skintight suit used for stealth missions. She carried her helmet under her arm. Several weapons hung from her belt: a pistol, a blade, and a handful of throwing stars.

Today I'm like a ninja, she thought. *Sneaky. Fast. Moving in shadows.*

"Mistress," HOBBS said, "while it's true that time travel can rupture spacetime, fraying the fabric of the universe, I've run and rerun the calculations. The mission has an eighty-three percent probability of success. Even if we fail, we'll likely destroy

merely this local arm of the Milky Way galaxy, not the entire
universe."

"HOBBS, I was kidding!" Lailani rolled her eyes, then
frowned. "Wait a minute. Eighty-three percent chance?
Destroying this arm of the Milky Way galaxy? When I asked you
about the odds earlier, you said they were excellent, and there's
nothing to worry about!"

HOBBS nodded. "Indeed, mistress. I am not worried.
Considering how dangerous time travel is, eighty-three percent of
complete success is excellent. In fact, there is only a one percent
chance of destroying the entire cosmos. Quite good odds."

Epimetheus mewled.

Lailani felt queasy.

"So let me get this straight," she said. "If I travel back in
time to save my friend, I might actually—no joke, for real—
destroy the universe."

HOBBS nodded. "If you create a paradox. Yes."

She cringed. She looked at the framed photograph she
kept in the *Ryujin*. Taken a decade ago, the photo showed Lailani
in her old platoon. They were all so young, wearing dusty olive
drab, rifles slung across their backs, posing over the carcass of a
dead scum. Einav Ben-Ari, then only an ensign, stood at the head
of the group, stern, strong, the quintessential officer. Marco was
trying to look serious, but Addy was raising rabbit ears behind his
head. Caveman, Beast, and Sheriff were still alive, showing off
their muscles. Lailani was making a silly face, cheeks puffed out
and eyes crossed. She had her arm around her friend—a young

recruit with long sideburns. Benny "Elvis" Ray. Her brother-in-arms. The boy she had killed.

For a decade now, she had struggled with guilt over killing Elvis. She had been only eighteen. Only a kid. A pawn of the scum. And those nightmares still haunted her.

It wasn't my fault, she thought. *The scum were controlling me. Moving my limbs. Making me evil.*

She winced. Perhaps that was a lie. The scum had not controlled her like puppeteers. She was part scum. There had always been a beast inside her. All they had done was awaken that part of her.

I grew claws, and I drove them into his chest, and I ripped out his heart. It's my doing. The blood is on my hands. She took a deep breath and tightened her lips. *And I will find redemption.*

Sensing her anxiety, Epimetheus nuzzled her, licking her tears away, making soothing noises, until she calmed. She embraced her pet.

"Thank you, Epi," she whispered. "You always bring me back." She wiped her eyes and looked up at HOBBS. "Tell me about these paradoxes."

The bulky robot sat with his knees pulled to his chest. On the battlefield, he struck an imposing figure, a giant of metal and fury, a grenade launcher on his shoulder and retractable guns on his forearms. He looked like some medieval knight, all in armor, his eyes two blue lights in his steel head. Yet here, crammed into the *Ryujin,* he struck almost a comical figure.

Perhaps it was the other robots that crowded the small spaceship. Seventeen robots. Seventeen machines with human hearts beating inside them. Seventeen Lailani had rescued from the dungeon of Elliot Schroder, the madman who had plucked out the hearts of his wife, children, and anyone who strayed too close to his world. He had also scarred Lailani's chest in an attempt to steal her own heart. The wound was still stitched up, still aching.

Lailani could not have left these machines behind. They were not human. But perhaps they qualified as cyborgs—humans merged with machines. And yes, perhaps they were a comical lot. One robot, the one who contained the heart of Schroder's butchered wife, was shaped like a Japanese schoolgirl in a sailor outfit, cute and smiling and docile. Three others were shaped like Victorian dolls with porcelain faces and elaborate gowns; inside them beat the hearts of Schroder's children. There was an assortment of others—a couple shaped as courtesans, one shaped like a metallic dinosaur, and a few whimsical robots made from gears and pipes and goggles, and they emitted steam as they moved.

My motley crew of friends, Lailani thought. *Surely we're the oddest group of travelers in this galaxy. This galaxy I might destroy.*

She realized that HOBBS was speaking, that her mind had drifted. She forced herself to focus on his words.

"... for example, if you were to go back in time and kill your grandfather as a baby, surely you would not have been born," HOBBS was saying. "But if you were never born, how could you have killed your grandfather? So your grandfather survives after all, and you are born, but then you do kill him, and … well, mistress, there's a paradox. There are many other examples."

Lailani nodded, trying to ignore the assortment of robots around him. "And that can destroy the cosmos?"

"Well, the cosmos is sturdy," said HOBBS. "A paradox like that would rip a hole through spacetime, though not a very large one. The universe would then patch up the hole. Imagine creating a bubble of vacuum on Earth. As soon as you expose it to air, the vacuum fills up. Nature hates a vacuum, and it also hates paradoxes in spacetime. But when the universe fills the holes in spacetime, it can wipe out anything nearby. People. Planets. If the paradox is large enough—galaxies."

Lailani gulped. "Got it. So I just have to avoid killing my grandpa."

"Not that simple, mistress," HOBBS said. "Paradoxes can be tough to predict. You change one element in the past, and you can change the entire flow of time. For example, let us say you save Elvis. That means your younger self will not be plagued with guilt. If you are not plagued with guilt, why would you travel back to save Elvis?"

Lailani's jaw unhinged. "So I can't save him? Not without creating a paradox? And then universe goes kaboom?"

"To minimize the chance of catastrophe," HOBBS said, "you must make it *seem* like Elvis died. You must make sure that you—the young you, ten years ago—*believes* that she killed Elvis.

Marco witnessed the original killing, correct? And so he must witness a killing again, so that his own timeline maintains its integrity. That moment changed the course of both your lives. If the young Lailani does not kill Elvis, is not racked with guilt, she will never seek the hourglass. She will never fight the grays in the jungle and summon the dragons of Mahatek. She will never go back in time ten years later. We will never be here now on the *Ryujin*, having this conversation. Paradox. The only way to avoid this catastrophe is to save Elvis—but make the younger you think she killed him."

Lailani sighed. "This is getting more complicated by the moment. Fine. So I have to fake his death."

HOBBS nodded. "Yes, mistress. And you must do this alone, to minimize the risk of more lives affected by paradoxes. You must not alter the past in any other way. You must not speak. You must not reveal your present form to Marco or to your younger self. You must not save anyone else. You must move quickly. Any wrong move, any other change to the past, and you can destroy the fabric of spacetime. I cannot go with you, not without risking further damage. You must do this alone. Flawlessly."

"All right," Lailani said, trying to hide the tremble in her voice. "I can do this. I've pulled more dangerous stunts before. I fought the scum emperor. I fought the lord of the marauders. I've eaten military Spam. I can handle a little tampering with the fabric of reality. No problemo." She gave a nervous laugh. "Not like the fate of the cosmos is on my shoulders or anything."

She looked back at the photograph. At herself and Elvis. That guilt was forever a demon curled up in her belly, worse than the scum inside her.

I can do this, she thought. *I must do this.*

She returned to the *Ryujin*'s cockpit. It was a crammed little space, filled with old taco boxes, a handful of books to read during long flights, and bags of dog food. There were two seats, the leather upholstery cracked. Lailani took one and Epimetheus hopped onto the other. She turned on some music—good old classic hip hop from before the Cataclysm—and grabbed the controls. In the distance, she could see it, growing brighter.

"Beta Ceti," she whispered. She couldn't help but shudder.

She had flown here before.

Over ten years ago.

And she had found evil.

She winced. The images flashed before her. She had been only an eighteen-year-old private, a pipsqueak, the smallest soldier in her platoon, four foot ten and ninety-five pounds and always so terrified. They had come here, seeking a moon named Corpus, following a distress signal.

We crashed, she remembered, wincing. *I sabotaged the ship. We fell. We burned. They made me do it.*

She was trembling now. Tears flowed down her cheeks. She could still remember screaming as the *Miyari*, their warship, had crashed onto the dark moon. How the infantry company had plunged into the mines to seek hope. How the terrors had awoken. How the monsters had risen.

"So many died," Lailani whispered. "Because of me. And Elvis, I killed him with my own hands, and ..."

The terror was too great. She was panting. Her hands were shaking too badly to grip the controls.

Epimetheus was there at once, licking her cheeks, nuzzling her, making soothing sounds. She held him until she calmed.

"I'll do this, Epi," she whispered. "You believe in me, right?"

He licked her face.

"What would I do without you, Epi?"

He answered by nuzzling her neck. He was a mighty Doberman, heavier and stronger than her, and he could fight when necessary. But he was also her sweet therapy dog and best friend.

She kept flying. Beta Ceti grew larger, a massive orange star. Lailani kept a safe distance from its crackling, searing radiation. She kept flying. She was far from home now, a hundred light-years away, deep in the darkness. Even with the best warp engines, Earth was weeks away.

She saw it now. It rose ahead, half in shadow—the gas giant Indrani, a great red blob in space, larger than Jupiter.

And orbiting it—there.

Lailani shuddered.

A small dark moon.

"Corpus," she whispered. The azure mine. The place where she had found hell.

The images flashed before her. The giant centipedes in the tunnels, scurrying forth, descending from the ceilings. The human prisoners, glued to the ceiling, bellies bloated and filled with honey, and the scum sucking on them. The hybrids in the alien lab, twisted humans with the bodies of centipedes. Her friends dying. Beast. Sergeant Singh. Corporal Diaz. So many others, the people she loved—the scum cutting them, their blood spilling, their—

She took a deep breath. She held her dog close.

"I'll make this right," she whispered. "I can't save them all. But I can save one life."

She entered orbit around Indrani. The gas giant swirled, filling the viewport. It looked like a planet of blood, thousands of times the size of Earth. The radiation baked the *Ryujin*'s shields. Corpus hovered ahead, so small by comparison. Last Lailani heard, the mines had reopened, and the extraction of azoth crystals had resumed. Even with all the death, the terror, the monsters, and the nuclear waste still clinging to that moon— Earth needed its azoth. In many ways, Corpus was the most valuable world in human civilization.

Azoth crystals—the only known substance that could bend spacetime, refracting it like a normal crystal refracts light. There was an azoth crystal inside the *Ryujin*'s engine, letting them fly at warp speed. There were azoth crystals inside wormhole generators too.

And there were tiny azoth crystals inside her hourglass.

Lailani pulled out the ancient artifact. It was small enough to balance on one palm. She had fought monsters and tamed dragons to retrieve it from the jungles of Mahatek, and it was a thing of beauty. Inside she could see them: countless grains of lavender sand. Sand made from azoth crystals. Sand that, when spilled through this hourglass, could bend time. Could send her back. Could save her friend.

"I don't remember exactly where the *Miyari* was ten years ago," she said. "It had just entered the storming sky of Indrani when I ki—" She swallowed. "When Elvis died."

She let the controls rest, let the *Ryujin* orbit the gas giant. To one side spread the stars. To the other—the roiling red-and-orange surface of Indrani, an immense world of endless storm.

"Ten years ago, at this place, I lost my soul," she whispered. "I will reclaim it."

She turned back toward the hold. "HOBBS?"

The robot could barely squeeze into the cockpit. Epimetheus had to jump into Lailani's lap—and the damn dog outweighed her—and HOBBS took the second seat. But Lailani wanted to be in the cockpit for this. To see it happen.

"Are you ready, mistress?" HOBBS said.

Her throat tightened.

No, she thought. *No, I'm not ready to go back. To see myself as a confused teenager, possessed by the scum. To see so many of my comrades dead. To see me strangling Marco, nearly killing him. To see my claws reach toward Elvis. To see the scum all around us, the horrible monsters from the darkness—the monsters that live within me. To see the nightmares that have haunted me for a decade. No, HOBBS, I'm not ready. But I'll do this nonetheless.*

She nodded. "Let's rock and/or roll." She handed him the hourglass.

HOBBS took the artifact from her. He tilted his head. "Mistress? Rock and—"

"Let's do this," she said. "I'm ready."

HOBBS nodded. "I must spill out just the right number of sand grains. One grain off, and we will fail. Thankfully, Dr. Schroder fixed me well and calibrated my gears. My hands are steady. I will perform the necessary calculations, mistress, adjusting to the gravitational pulls from Indrani, Beta Ceti, and Corpus, both in the present moment and according to their positions ten Earth years ago. This is a very accurate science."

His eyes dimmed, and for long moments, mechanical sounds rose from inside his processors. Lailani gazed at his chest, thinking of how a human heart beat there, powering the machine. How hearts beat inside all the robots she had saved. The scar on her chest ached, and she placed a hand there, remembering how Schroder had almost carved out her own heart.

As HOBBS was busy calculating, Lailani reviewed herself again. Black spacesuit, sneaky and silent—check. Weapons—check. Jet pack—she grabbed it from a shelf and slipped it over her shoulders. Check. Helmet—she placed it on her head. Check. Her lucky cross—hanging around her neck, inside her suit. Check.

She glanced at her reflection in HOBBS's polished chest. A space ninja indeed. She almost looked tough. Thankfully, nobody knew how terrified she truly was. Well, nobody but Epimetheus. Her Doberman curled up against her. He always knew.

HOBBS's eyes brightened. "I am ready, mistress."

Lailani's heart thumped. It was all too real. Her throat felt so tight. Her belly felt so empty, so cold. She could barely speak.

"Do you need to be outside, or—"

"I can open a portal from here, mistress, directly ahead of the *Ryujin*."

She nodded. "Do it," she whispered.

HOBBS had no true mouth, only a thin opening for his voice box, but somehow she could swear he was smiling.

"It is time to rock and/or roll," he said.

The robot hit a button and turned a few gears, activating the hourglass, opening the bottleneck between the two bulbs. Next he tilted the hourglass. Gently. Slowly. A handful of grains spilled out—shimmering, lavender, glowing bright. Azoth crystals, each no larger than a grain of sand. As they fell through the hourglass, they ignited, burned up, and faded. HOBBS tilted the hourglass back and shut the bottleneck.

For a long moment—silence. Shadows.

"Did it work?" Lailani whispered. "Did—"

Light caught the corner of her eye. She looked at the front viewport, and she saw it. Her eyes dampened.

A portal was opening ahead, glowing blue, a ring of shimmering crystals.

A portal back in time.

She tightened her lips and guided the *Ryujin* forward. The starship was small—just small enough.

"Rock and/or roll," she whispered, eyes moist, and flew the *Ryujin* through the portal.

Light shimmered.

And reality unfurled around her.

The stars bloomed, bursting into beams. Her consciousness flowed outward, seeing all. The *Ryujin* cascaded down a tunnel of twisting space. Stars, nebulae, galaxies—all danced around her, expanding, contracting, a great dance of space and time.

She huddled under a sheet of tarp, weak with disease, clinging to her mother. Her mother, only a youth, sang to her softly.

How many miles to Babylon?
Three score and ten.
Can I get there by candlelight?
Yes, and back again.
If your heels are nimble and light,
You may get there by candlelight.

And her heels were nimble. Her heels were light. She ran. She ran as the men chased her, laughing, reaching for her dress, lust in their eyes. She ran and huddled by the train tracks, a hungry orphan, knees skinned, so hungry. Her heels were nimble. Her heels were light. She crawled over the landfill with a hundred other orphans, covered in filth, waiting for the garbage trucks. As the great machines spilled their precious cargo, she rummaged, fought a boy, found an old rotten fruit.

She huddled by the train track at night with thousands of other souls, trembling, and she had no candlelight.

Her heels were nimble. Her heels were light when she ran across the desert, when hell rained upon Fort Djemila. She fought the scum, and their pods lit the darkness like a thousand candle flames.

Her heels were nimble. Her heels were light when she raced through the tunnels of Corpus, when the monsters rose in darkness, when she had no candles, no light, no hope. When her friends died. When all was death, and the monsters grabbed her, sniffed her, recognized her as their own.

She wept.

She was eighteen, her head shaved, the monster inside her. The darkness that had driven her to cut her wrists. To sabotage her ship. To kill. Kill. Kill!

Kill them all.

The centipedes laughed inside her. The centipedes nested in her belly.

Kill! Kill! Eat them! Slice them open! Lay your eggs inside them!

"No," she whispered, clutching her temples. "No. No. I'm not her. I'm not that girl. I'm twenty-eight. I'm me. I'm me." She wept. "Serenity."

Serenity.

She took a deep breath.

Serenity.

I'm me.

My heels are nimble. My heels are light.

"I'm me," she whispered, tears on her cheeks. "I can get there by candlelight. There and back again."

She breathed deeply. She opened her eyes, not realizing she had closed them. And she gazed upon the stars.

She was back in the *Ryujin*. Epimetheus was on her lap. HOBBS sat at her side. They floated through space. The red gas giant swirled to their right, and Corpus floated ahead, a dark moon.

They were back where they had begun.

As far as Lailani could tell, they had not moved a meter. And the portal was gone.

"Did it work?" she whispered. "Are we … back in time? Ten years ago?"

HOBBS stared at her silently. In his eyes she saw the answer: *I don't know.*

Epimetheus whined.

Lights blazed overhead, drenching the cockpit. A burst of exhaust blasted across the *Ryujin*, nearly blinding them. Their ship shook. Lailani gasped.

A warship blazed overhead, missing them by mere meters, then charged forward toward Indrani.

Lailani stared, unable to breathe.

It was an Olympia-class warship, emblazoned with the golden phoenix of the Human Defense Force, large enough to carry an infantry company. It looked like it had just flown through hell. It was battered, dented, cracked, barely flying. It didn't look like it had merely seen battle. It looked like it had crashed and risen again, spilling bolts and spewing smoke.

Tears filled Lailani's eyes.

She trembled.

She knew that warship. She had served on it. She had sabotaged it. She had lived through hell within its halls.

She *was* on that ship—right now, her younger self.

"The *Miyari*," she whispered. "We're back."

* * * * *

We're back.

Lailani took a shuddering breath.

We're back in time.

The *Miyari* flew ahead, growing smaller and smaller, soon only a speck against the roiling storms of Indrani, a gas giant that could dwarf Jupiter.

"That's it." Lailani couldn't hide the tremble from her voice. "That's my old spaceship. Where I was a teenager. Where I *am* a teenager." She had to blink away tears. "I'm in there right now. The old me."

"We do not have long, mistress," said HOBBS, sitting beside her. "Every moment that we remain here, ten years away from our normal time, we increase the chance of creating paradoxes. We must hurry."

She nodded. "Let's go."

She shoved down the throttle, and she followed the *Miyari*.

HOBBS leaned forward in his seat. The lenses on his eyes dilated. "Where is the ship going, mistress?"

"Into the storm," Lailani whispered. "Into the hellfire. To fight the Scum King."

She flew faster. She remembered that day so long ago. The *Miyari* was battered, barely able to fly, nearly all its crew dead. They were too damaged to detect the pursuing *Ryujin*. Only a handful of Lailani's friends were still aboard, the people she loved most in the world.

"Kemi is there," she realized. "My dear friend Kemi is still alive here. Maybe I can save her too, I—"

"Mistress, the danger of creating a paradox would be too great," HOBBS said. "Kemi was a part of your life after this day. Your friend Benny, whom you call Elvis, was not. Perhaps you can save him. Bring back Kemi, and you'd be preventing her from appearing during the past decade of your life."

Lailani nodded. "The whole destroying the arm of the Milky Way galaxy stuff."

"Yes, mistress. I would caution against it."

Ahead, the *Miyari* reached the gas giant and dipped into the red storm. The dilapidated starship vanished from view. Lailani shoved down the throttle, picked up speed, and cringed as the *Ryujin* dived into Indrani's atmosphere.

She might as well have flown into Hell itself.

The storm grabbed them. There was no solid surface to Indrani. There was only this massive ball of gasses in space, containing more mass than Jupiter and Saturn combined. Winds rattled the hull. Red dust buffeted the windshield. The storm roared. Funnels swirled left and right, deep crimson fringed with furious gold. Lightning flashed, and deep below roiled a sea of red-and-orange gas, swirling, rumbling, belching up fire. The storm was deafening, all-consuming, threatening to crush the *Ryujin*. From behind in the hold rose the terrified cries of the robots—porcelain dolls and burlesque dancers and mechanical dinosaurs.

The situation was so absurd that Lailani laughed.

"I'm not sure we can handle this storm, mistress!" HOBBS said. "It's crushing us! And—mistress? Why are you laughing?"

She kept flying, navigating around funnels and blasts of flaming gasses. Lightning blazed all around. She could just see the *Miyari* ahead, sinking deeper into the storm. She followed.

"I'm flying inside a gas giant," she said, "a hundred light-years from Earth, ten years in the past, I'm talking to a robot with a human heart, and behind me a bunch of Victorian dolls and go-go dancers are screaming." She laughed again, so hard she shook. "This isn't rock and roll. It's goddamn calliope music."

HOBBS tilted his head. "Calliope. A musical pipe instrument, similar to an organ, popular in nineteenth-century circuses. Mistress, you are not suggesting that we travel back to the nineteenth century and—"

"Jokes, Hobster. Jokes. I—"

A roar pierced the storm.

Lailani's heart nearly stopped in her chest.

Ahead she saw it, coiling through the fury.

"My God," she whispered, eyes stinging. "It's him." She trembled, and her voice dropped to a whisper. "The Scum King."

She had seen him so many times in her dreams. She had heard his voice, whispering to her. She had felt his tongue, licking her. She had felt his fury, filling her with rage and hatred. The creature that had coiled inside her, tormenting her, pulling her strings. He had died ten years ago. They had killed him, the lord of the Corpus hive. Yet here he was, still alive, filling the storm with his malice.

He was a massive beast, larger than the *Miyari*, all black, hardened skin and spikes and claws the size of men. A great insect, flying in the storm, a demon, a spawn of evil. He was cruelty taken form. And with his massive tail, he whipped the *Miyari*, knocking the warship into a tailspin.

Lailani remembered. She had been on the *Miyari* when that tail had lashed them. She *was* on the *Miyari*.

"It's only moments away. Fuck! I'm going to kill Elvis in only a few moments—right as the *Miyari* is battling the demon. We have to hurry!"

She shoved the throttle down. The *Ryujin* roared through the storm, whipping around the clouds and funnels, racing toward the *Miyari*. The warship was trying to fight back, but its power died. It listed. Of course. Lailani herself had sabotaged it, shutting off the power, obeying the Scum King's voice in her mind. The alien gripped the warship, twisting its hull, biting into the steel.

Soon, she remembered, Marco would manage to restore power to the ship, to blast its cannons, to kill the alien.

But not before I kill Elvis.

She bared her teeth.

But that won't happen now.

She charged forward. Ahead of her, the Scum King clawed at the *Miyari*, tossing it through the storm, cracking its hull. The *Ryujin* too was being battered, its hull bending under the fury of the red storm. Bits of the hull tore free. Alarms blared. Lailani ignored them and flew faster. She placed a hand against the framed photograph, the one showing her with her arm around Elvis.

"I'm coming for you, buddy," she whispered. "This ends now. A decade of guilt and terror—it ends."

She roared forth until she was only a kilometer away from the Scum King. The alien loomed ahead, wreathed in lightning, roaring. The storm raged around him, and the red lights reflected on his horns and fangs. The *Miyari* was stuck in his claws, struggling to break free on backup power, its cannons dead.

Lailani hit the brakes.

"HOBBS, grab the wheel." She hopped out of her seat.

HOBBS replaced her at the controls. He gave her a blue stare. "Godspeed, Lieutenant Lailani de la Rosa."

He saluted her. It was the first time he had called her by name.

She nodded, eyes damp, and returned the salute. She closed her helmet's visor, adjusted the straps of her jet pack, and ran into the hold. She grabbed a heavy backpack filled with a spare spacesuit, helmet, and jet pack. She slung it across her chest.

She took a deep breath, steeling herself.

Rock. And. Roll.

She raced into the airlock, opened the door, and leaped out into the storm.

* * * * *

Lailani plunged through the red storm of Indrani, wearing nothing but a spacesuit.

The rage, fury, and heat of Hell blazed around her. She screamed.

I should have worn an armored battle spacesuit, not this bullshit ninja outfit.

She grimaced. The storm whipped her. Blazing gas rose all around. Lightning crashed.

She gripped the controls of her jet pack, swerving left and right. A funnel slammed down ahead of her, casting out terrifying winds that knocked her into a tailspin. She managed to right herself, to fly onward. A geyser of sizzling hot gas burst ahead, tall as a skyscraper. Lailani swerved around it, spraying out flames. Her head rattled in her helmet. The jet pack thrummed against her back, slamming into her spine. The storm was deafening. Lightning crackled. When a splash of gas burned her leg, she couldn't even hear herself scream.

She saw him ahead. The Scum King.

By God, the size of him. Here in the open, Lailani could barely believe how large he was. He loomed ahead, the size of goddamn Godzilla. He roared, fangs the length of lamp poles. He kept lashing at the disabled *Miyari*, denting the mighty warship as if it were a tin can.

In just a few moments, Lailani knew, Marco would get past her younger self, would reactivate the power. The warship's cannons would tear through the great alien.

Lailani flew faster, roaring forth, charging through the storm.

The Scum King whipped his tail. The scaled appendage shrieked over Lailani's head, scattering red clouds, and slammed into the *Miyari*.

The mighty warship cracked and spun through the air, helpless, only for the alien to grab it again.

Lailani gritted her teeth, adjusted her jet pack, and stormed toward the warship.

She grimaced, shouting wordlessly, and slammed into the hull.

The impact knocked the breath out of her. She clung to the metal. As lightning flashed and the storm roiled, the Scum King lashed his claws. Lailani scurried across the warship's hull, dodging those claws. She crawled across the golden phoenix painted onto the *Miyari*, desperate to reach the airlock.

Above her rose the head of the Scum King, roaring, gullet filled with molten fire, eyes like cauldrons. Its wings spread out, black curtains of night draped with flame.

For a moment, all Lailani could do was cling to the hull, to stare.

Lailani …

His voice was speaking inside her! Dark, deep, a voice like thunder. No. No! Her chip was activated! It should not be able to penetrate her mind!

We know you, our daughter … You are one of us …

Clinging to the hull, she trembled. She wept.

"Father," she whispered.

Daughter of centipedes … Mistress of malice …

"Let me pass," she whispered. "Let me in. I will make them bleed!"

Enter, child. With his great claws, the creature tore open the airlock. *Bring them to heel.*

She leaped down the hull, gave a single spurt of fire from her jet pack, and flew into the airlock.

She landed inside the ship, banging her knees. Ahead of her loomed the airlock's second door. Behind her the storm still roared.

She paused for just a moment, taking deep breaths.

He knew me. He called me daughter. He is about to die.

She tightened her lips, rose to her feet, and drew her pistol.

"I am human," she whispered, tears in her eyes. "That is where my loyalties lie. I am a hybrid. But I fight for humanity. I fight the alien outside and the alien within me."

Leaving her backpack in the airlock, she opened the inner door. Clad in black, singed, holding her pistol before her, she entered the *Miyari* for the first time in a decade.

A narrow corridor stretched before her, tilted. A single fluorescent light flickered above. Bloodstains covered the floor. A dead scum twitched in the corner, its nervous system giving a few last spasms. A severed human arm still bled in its jaws.

Lailani walked down the corridor, struggling for balance as the ship swayed. A roar sounded outside. The *Miyari* jerked and spun, and Lailani swayed and hit the wall. She ignored the pain and kept moving, faster now.

A shout rose somewhere above.

"Emery, damn it! Get the power back up!"

Lailani recognized that voice. It was Major Ben-Ari! No, she wasn't a major now, only a young ensign.

In this ship, she's only twenty, Lailani thought. *She's eight years younger than I am now. She seemed so old back then, an adult, while I was just a kid.*

"He's tearing us apart!" Ben-Ari shouted somewhere in a higher level. "We need that plasma, soldier!"

From deeper in the ship, she heard shouting.

"On it!" rose a voice. Marco's voice.

"There, red pipes!" answered another voice.

Lailani inhaled sharply.

"Elvis," she whispered.

She ran, following the voices. She raced along the corridor, leaped down a stairwell, and saw a round door. There, beyond it—the engine room full of pipes, turbines, and steam.

And she saw them.

Marco. Elvis. Two eighteen-year-old privates in bloody fatigues. She could only see their backs, but she knew it was them. Tears streamed down her cheeks.

Marco. The boy she loved. The boy she had made love to. Elvis. Her friend. The friend she had killed.

No. Not killed. Not yet!

"I see it," Marco said, racing with Elvis toward the plasma generator. "We're turning it back—"

A figure emerged from the shadows, blocking their way.

"No."

Marco and Elvis skidded to a halt.

Between them and the plasma generator stood a young girl, barely larger than a child. Her head was shaved down to stubble. A crooked smile played on her lips. Madness danced in her eyes.

It's me, Lailani thought. *Me ten years ago. Me possessed by the scum. And in a few seconds, I'm about to rip out Elvis's heart.*

She took a deep breath.

Nightwish, she thought. Her code word to deactivate the chip in her head, the chip that kept the alien at bay.

Her chip shut down. Her consciousness expanded. The alien part of her, only one percent of her DNA but so powerful, began to rise, to fill her with cruelty, with might.

Elvis breathed out in relief, still facing the younger Lailani.

"Damn it, de la Rosa," the boy said. "You scared the shit out of me. Help us turn this fucker back on."

The young Lailani didn't move. Her voice rumbled out. Low. Guttural. Demonic. "No."

"What the fuck is wrong with you?" Elvis said, trying to walk around her, to reach the pipes and turn the *Miyari*'s weapons back on.

The young Lailani smiled crookedly.

Her hand thrust forward, growing claws.

The older Lailani, twenty-eight years old, her heart pounding against her ribs, reached out with her mind and grabbed Elvis.

Like a puppeteer tugging a string, she yanked him a step backward.

The young Lailani's claws scraped across Elvis's chest, tearing open the skin, ripping the muscle … but missing the heart.

With her mind, the older Lailani slammed Elvis onto the floor.

Play dead! She forced the thought into Elvis's mind, keeping him down. *You're dead, damn it. They must think you're dead!*

The young Marco stood, frozen, eyes wide.

"God, no," he whispered. "God, no, God, no. Elvis!"

Neck creaking, the young, demonic Lailani turned her head toward him. Her smile stretched into a grin. Elvis's blood dripped from her claws.

"Hello, Marco," she said, advancing toward him.

"Who are you?" he whispered.

Lailani licked the blood off her claws. "You know us." Her voice was impossibly deep. "You slew us in the desert. You murdered our children and wives in the mine. Now you will worship us. Now you will join us. We are the Masters. We are the Ancients. We are those who rise."

"Scum," Marco whispered, staring at the young Lailani. He grabbed his gun. "Let her go! Get out of her body!" His shout was hoarse, his eyes damp. "Take me instead. Let Lailani go!"

The young Lailani laughed. A deep, rumbling laugh, a sound impossible for one so small. "Let her go? Lailani has always been one of us. We were always inside her. It was we who impregnated her whore of a mother. It was we who lurked inside her throughout her childhood, keeping her frail body alive. It was we who broke her soul. It was ..."

The older Lailani stopped listening. She knew that Marco would be fine. She remembered this day. Remembered that he had subdued her.

Serenity, she thought, reactivating her chip.

Marco and the younger Lailani began to grapple. The older Lailani inched forward. She grabbed Elvis and tugged him back into the shadows. He moaned, chest lacerated, blood seeping over his uniform. He blinked up at her.

"De la Rosa?" Elvis whispered, struggling to cling to consciousness.

"Hush!" she whispered, dragging him. "Keep playing dead!"

By the plasma pipes, only a few meters away, the younger Lailani was squeezing Marco's throat, laughing maniacally, her eyes filled with the madness of the scum.

You'll be fine, girl, the older Lailani thought, tears in her eyes, looking at the monster she had been. *You'll get a chip installed. You'll be cured. I promise you. Hang in there.*

She pulled Elvis to his feet behind a network of pipes. She stared up into his eyes.

My God, it's really him, she thought. The same face from her memory. The nose sharp. The sideburns long. Her friend. Benny "Elvis" Ray.

He frowned down at her, clutching his bleeding chest. "Lailani? How?" He peered around the pipes to where the younger Lailani was still strangling Marco. "But—"

"Shush! I need your blood." She grabbed his wounded chest.

When he began to scream, she covered his mouth with her other hand.

She worked quickly. Using his blood, she painted a trail toward a pit full of pistons. She ripped off Elvis's shirt and tossed it over the guardrail. Once power was restored to the ship, those pistons would begin to pump out an inferno of fire. Marco would think that Elvis, wounded, had fallen inside, had been incinerated.

She grabbed Elvis's hand. "Now come with me." She pulled him toward the door and shoved him into the corridor. "Marco will be fine. Move!"

As Elvis stumbled forward, Lailani stepped through the doorway too.

She paused.

I shouldn't. Oh God, I shouldn't. Paradoxes and destroying the universe and everything. But … Oh, dammit.

She peeked back into the engine room, her helmet still covering her head. She lifted the visor. She shouted, "Don't let Sofia fall!"

Kneeling over Marco, her claws wrapped around his throat, the younger Lailani looked up.

Marco kicked the girl off.

The older Lailani grabbed Elvis and dragged him away.

The ship swayed as the Scum King bellowed outside. She could see his claws and scales through the portholes. Elvis and she kept running, heading back toward the airlock. The ship thrummed as, back in the engine room, Marco managed to reactivate the plasma cannons.

"We're back in business!" rose a voice from above—young Addy's voice. "Eat fire!"

Lailani and Elvis leaped into the airlock. The *Miyari* shook. Plasma was blasting out from her cannons, slamming into the Scum King. The creature bellowed.

Lailani ripped open her backpack and shoved the extra spacesuit, jet pack, and helmet at Elvis.

"Get dressed. Now!"

Plasma roared out again.

Lailani and Elvis leaped out into the storm.

They soared through the crimson clouds as behind them the *Miyari* fired her cannons, blasting the massive alien king. They flew around funnels of gas and sparkling electricity. They flew as lightning crackled around them, as thunder boomed, as the winds whipped them.

"What the fuck is going on, de la Rosa?" Elvis shouted, voice muffled behind his helmet. "And why the fuck are there two of you?"

"Shut up and fly!"

Behind them, the Scum King let out a final bellow. When Lailani glanced over her shoulder, she saw the *Miyari*'s cannons tear through the creature, cracking its ribs, filling its innards with flame.

Strangely, she felt pity for him.

Is he my father?

She pushed the thought away. She looked ahead. She kept flying.

Soon the *Miyari* vanished behind her and Elvis. All was the storm, orange and deep and burnished gold and blinding white. Endless. No ground below. No sky above. Nothing but these hellish fumes.

And there ahead, a beacon—a flash of light. They flew toward it. It emerged from the storm before them. A small starship, far smaller than the *Miyari*. A ship with a dragon and rainbow painted on its hull. The *Ryujin*.

Its airlock opened, and HOBBS stood there, gesturing for them. His voice rang through the storm.

"Hurry, mistress! We must go back!"

Lailani grabbed Elvis's hand. They flew together, jet packs leaving trails of fire, and all but crashed into the airlock.

HOBBS slammed the door shut, and Lailani raced into the cockpit. She grabbed the controls, spun the *Ryujin* upward, and shoved down the throttle. They soared upon a jet of fire, rising from the storm. They breached the atmosphere with a shower of spurting, crackling, burning gasses.

They flew through space.

Lailani sighed in relief and removed her helmet. For a moment, she just breathed.

From the hold, Lailani heard Elvis's voice.

"Will somebody tell me what in tarnation is going on here? Who the fuck are these creepy-ass dolls?" He burst into the cockpit. "Dammit, de la Rosa! What the hell is going on? And—" He frowned and stared at her. "De la Rosa?" He leaned closer. "Is that really you? You look … different. Your hair. It's longer. And your face. It's different somehow, it's …"

The face of a woman, no longer a girl, she thought.

"HOBBS!" Lailani said, ignoring Elvis. For now, she had to focus. "HOBBS, can you open a portal back home?"

The robot stood behind her, manipulating the hourglass. "All ready, mistress. Shall I rock?"

She nodded. "And/or roll."

The robot tilted the hourglass.

The portal opened.

They flew through time and space and a thousand visions of what might have been.

They reemerged.

They shuddered, the dreams fading.

They floated through silent space.

"Mistress, we are back," HOBBS said. "Once more, it is the year 2153."

Elvis was pale. His hands trembled.

"I saw myself," the boy whispered, voice choking. "When we flew through that tunnel of light. I saw myself dying." He looked at Lailani. "I saw you rip out my heart. I saw ... I saw a decade of lost life. I ..."

He fell to his knees in the cockpit, clutching his bleeding chest.

Lailani set the ship on autopilot.

"Come, Elvis, into the back room." She placed a hand on his shoulder. "Let's get that nasty scratch patched up."

She took him into the hold, and the other robots moved aside. Lailani spent a moment tending to his wounds—wounds she had given him ten years ago, wounds still fresh and bleeding.

"Lailani." Elvis gulped, looking queasy. "I'm scared. What the hell is going on? Where are we? What did that robot mean about 2153? He meant 2143, right? Right?"

She placed a final bandage on his chest. She kissed his cheek.

"Elvis, it's a long story. And it begins with me ripping out your heart."

For long moments, she spoke. He listened silently. She told him about how she was one percent alien, a hybrid designed in a scum lab, placed as an embryo into a human woman to be born on Earth, to be raised human, to become a drone waiting to be activated during the war. She told him how she had sabotaged the *Miyari*, how she had crashed the ship, and how she had killed him. How the HDF had placed a chip in her skull, keeping her evil at bay. And how, for ten years, the guilt had filled her.

"I had to make it right," she said, tears flowing. "I had to save you. To bring you back to me. Because I couldn't live with myself as a murderer. I had to save you and redeem myself."

Finally she finished her tale. Elvis looked at her, pale, and his fingers shook. He exhaled slowly.

"Wow," he finally said.

Lailani nodded, eyes damp. "Wow."

And suddenly she was sobbing. She embraced her friend. He was still just a kid. Scrawny. So young. By God, just a boy. She wept against his shoulder.

I found some redemption. You are alive. You are alive. Finally, you're here. Finally, a part of me is healed.

"Lailani." Elvis spoke softly. "So ... you have a time machine."

Lailani nodded. "Yes."

334

Elvis was silent for a moment, looking at his lap. When he raised his eyes again, they were damp. "It was almost a year ago. Well, eleven years ago now. My girlfriend. She died in a car crash, and maybe we can go back, and—"

"No." HOBBS stepped forward. "We have already ruptured spacetime. Perhaps beyond repair. Look." He pointed out a porthole. "Look!"

They crowded around the porthole and stared.

It looked like a crack in the universe. A black rift where no starlight shone.

"A rent in spacetime," Lailani whispered. She looked at HOBBS. "Fuck. Is this it? The whole destroying-the-cosmos event?"

HOBBS's eyes were dark. He kept staring.

"The rent is still small," the robot said carefully. "It does not seem to be spreading. But we must not time travel again. It is too dangerous. We have damaged the universe itself." The towering robot shook his head. "Your friend was not meant to live, mistress. Yet here he is, ten years after he was meant to die. The cosmos is unhappy. And the cosmos tore open."

Lailani gulped. "It's … just a teeny, tiny little tear. Many kilometers out in space. Nobody will even notice. Right, HOBBS?"

"I do not know, mistress. I am not an expert on these matters. The grays are the true masters of time travel. We are not. We cannot see all that they can." He looked at her. "I would suggest that we destroy this hourglass."

She stared at him. She raised her chin. "No."

The robot seemed almost to scowl. It shocked her, even scared her.

"Mistress, we must," HOBBS said. "We—"

"We need this hourglass," Lailani insisted. "We need this *weapon*." She took a deep breath. "The grays are the masters of time travel, you said. They are enemies from the future. If Earth is at war with those creatures, we'll need a time machine of our own. HOBBS, we're not destroying this hourglass." She took a deep breath and reentered the cockpit. "We're taking it back to Earth."

The *Ryujin* flew, leaving behind a hellish planet, a nightmarish moon, and a rift in the cosmos.

CHAPTER EIGHTEEN

"Father!"

Ben-Ari pushed down on the throttle, and her mechanical horse burst into a gallop. As the battle raged around her, covering the plains of Mongolia, she rode toward her father. The bruised and bloodied man knelt. He seemed barely alive. He gazed at her, panting, one eye swollen shut. His arms and legs were chained.

"Not too close now!" Abyzou said, smirking.

The Gray Prince stood within his mecha, amusement in his eyes. The mecha was shaped as a great scorpion, large as a dragon. Abyzou's body was visible inside the scorpion's chest, protected behind a sheet of glass. The mechanical arachnid loomed over Ben-Ari's father. Its metal stinger rose, large as an oak.

"That's close enough, girl," Abyzou said. "One more step, and this stinger bursts through your father's chest."

Ben-Ari hit the brakes. The robotic horse she rode froze several meters away from her father. They faced off on the hill: a human woman in body armor, wearing a jet pack, riding astride a robotic horse; and the Gray Prince, deformed and wretched, within a metal scorpion suit the size of a T-rex. Between them knelt Colonel Yoram Ben-Ari.

My father, she thought. *The man I once hated. The man who gave me his ship, who helped me fight the marauders. The man I dare not see die now.*

Father looked up at her.

"Einavi," he rasped. Blood caked his dusty hair. "I ... I fought them. I remembered what you said. About fighting for Earth. I came back. For Earth. For you."

She sat on her horse, her fists trembling around the controls. She stared up at Abyzou. Her eyes burned. She spoke through clenched teeth.

"What do you want?"

The scorpion inched closer. The stinger rose higher, ready to strike. From inside the mecha suit, Abyzou stared at her. He grinned, half his smile melting into the ruin of his wounds. Shards of his broken skull were visible, piercing the flesh. She had hurt him last time they had met. She had hurt him badly. But if his body was frail, his scorpion suit was not. It was larger, faster, deadlier by far than the robotic horse she rode.

"I offer you this deal," Abyzou hissed. "The life of your father ... in exchange for yours."

"Don't do it!" Father cried, and Abyzou swung his arm. The scorpion's claw moved in tandem, slammed into Father, and knocked him down.

Every instinct in Ben-Ari screamed to leap off her horse, to run to her father. She forced herself to stay mounted, to stay still. She did not break eye contact with Abyzou.

"I have a better deal for you!" she said. "You call off your hosts, and you flee this world with your tail between your legs. In exchange, I will offer you mercy." She bared her teeth. "If you remain, I will kill you."

Abyzou laughed, the sound dripping with pain, jangling the shards of bone in his cheek.

"Still you do not understand, Einav," the Gray Prince said. "We are your children. You are our blessed mother. It was you who marooned the Nefitian monks on a desert world, destroying their starships. You started their evolution. You left the monks to grow harder, stronger, wiser, to evolve into us." Abyzou clenched his fists, and the scorpion's claws tightened. "You created the Sanctified Sons. You gave rise to Nefitis, my mother and your goddess. For that, she seeks you. For that, you may sit forever at her table, ruling this world at her side!" His eyes shone. "Instead of a miserable wretch, screaming in chains, you can become a goddess! Join us, Einav. Join us and your father shall live. Join us and you will be spared the eternal torment Nefitis has promised you. Join us now as the peak of human evolution rises, and you will rise with us!" He leaned forward, eyes narrowing. "Refuse, and your father dies now. Refuse, and instead of sitting at Nefitis's side, you will scream upon her altar as her claws rip out your organs. This is your choice. Eternal glory or eternal damnation."

She stared at him.

He's not sure he can win, she thought. *That's why he makes this offer.* She tightened her jaw. *He's scared.*

She looked down at her father. He knelt on the ground, chained, beaten, but he met her gaze with clear eyes. And she knew what he wanted her to do. How he had always taught her to live.

He has always loved Earth more than he loved me, she thought. *He expects me to place Earth first too.*

She looked back at Abyzou. She sat tall on her horse. She had discarded her empty plasma rifle. She held two new weapons now. In one hand, she held an assault rifle taken from a dead infantrymen. In the other, she held an electrical rod she had taken off a dead gray warrior.

"You call yourselves the pinnacle of human evolution!" she said. "I call you decayed, wretched, and evil. Yours is the path we will not take! I look around me at the world. And I see in humanity cruelty, greed, violence. I see fear, superstition, hatred. I see men and women stabbing others in the back. I see ideologies of bigotry and violence crush the meek under their heels. I see a world overrun with sin." She spoke louder. "But I see nobility too! I see sons and daughters willing to dedicate their lives—and their deaths—to save their families. I see poets and painters create art to inspire millions. I see sacrifice, honor, and valor. I see the ugliness of humanity but our beauty too, what we can become. You and your kind have succumbed to the base instincts inside humanity. You let compassion die out, and you replaced it with malice. That will not be our path! Let your presence here be a warning to us, a vision of what we could become. We will not become you, Abyzou. We will choose the path of honor." She spoke more softly now. "A young species we are. We have only dipped our toes into the cosmic ocean. We still have so much to learn, to explore, to become. You showed us the path of shadows. We will choose the path of light."

Abyzou sneered. His scorpion reared. "Then you choose death!"

The mechanical scorpion swung its tail.

Ben-Ari galloped, tried to stop it, but she was too far.

The scorpion's stinger burst through her father's chest.

Ben-Ari halted on her horse, staring, tears in her eyes, terror in her heart.

The robotic scorpion raised its tail, lifting Father off the ground. The colonel hung, skewered upon the metal. The scorpion flicked its tail, tossing Father down the hill.

Ben-Ari screamed and charged on her horse toward Abyzou, firing her rifle. Her bullets slammed into the glass plating, but it withstood the assault. Abyzou grinned, and the scorpion raced toward her on its mechanical legs.

An instant before the two machines could crash together, Ben-Ari reared on her horse, lifted her electrical rod, and held it forth like a lance. Bolts of electricity flew out, slamming into the scorpion. Ben-Ari veered and rode around the mecha, feeling like a medieval knight battling a dragon.

Electricity raced across the scorpion. Within the mecha, Abyzou screamed as the bolts shocked him. His skin sizzled. He swung his body around. His scorpion mecha spun in tandem, lashing its tail.

Ben-Ari charged, ducked under the swinging tail, and thrust her electric rod again. She slammed the tip against the scorpion, then released another bolt of electricity.

Inside the mecha, Abyzou howled. Smoke rose from him. Ben-Ari leaned into her rod, keeping it pressed against the scorpion. As electricity flowed into her enemy, she made eye contact with him.

"It's over, Abyzou," she hissed, releasing another pulse of electricity. "You and your mother lost."

He swung his arm.

The scorpion's metal claw, as large and thick as a street lamp, swung into her horse.

Both Ben-Ari and her robotic mount flew.

They flipped in midair. Ben-Ari cried out and leaped off the horse. She hit the ground and instantly scurried away. The mechanical horse slammed onto the ground only centimeters away.

It had almost crushed her. It did crush her electrical rod.

The scorpion reared above the fallen horse, claws extended. Abyzou cackled within, his skin burnt away, his eyes blazing with maniacal fury.

Ben-Ari loaded a new magazine into her rifle.

The claws swung.

She leaped back, and the claws slammed into the soil.

She fired her rifle on automatic, emptying the magazine. Bullets slammed into the scorpion, doing it no harm.

The claws slammed down again, and she leaped back. Damn it! She wanted to call for some aid—artillery and armor backup—but the other forces were all engaged in their own battles. She snarled, loaded another magazine, and—

The scorpion spun around, lashing its tail.

The great metal whip, as thick as a tree trunk, slammed into Ben-Ari.

It cracked her armor and tossed her into the air.

She seemed to fly forever.

She crashed onto the ground, unable to breathe.

The blow had shattered the side of her suit, armor built to withstand bullets and the inferno of atmospheric reentry. If she survived until tomorrow, her body would be covered in bruises. She struggled to her feet, gasping for air, able to inhale only thin whiffs. It felt like she had cracked a rib. She hit her communicator. She needed some backup, dammit! But the communicator buzzed uselessly, crushed in the assault. Her jet pack sputtered, its engine dead.

The tail swung again.

She leaped aside, and the scorpion's stinger, still red with Father's blood, sank into the soil.

She grabbed a grenade from her belt and hurled it.

She leaped behind her fallen horse, hit the ground, and covered her head.

The explosion rocked the hill. Chunks of earth and grass pattered onto her. When she rose again, she gazed at the scorpion.

The massive machine still stood. A single crack appeared on the glass shielding Abyzou. The scorpion mecha was otherwise undamaged.

The claws reached down and lifted the mechanical horse.

Ben-Ari ran.

Abyzou tossed the horse, and Ben-Ari leaped aside. The horse grazed her arm, chipping her armor, and she screamed. She fired her rifle, aiming at the crack in the glass. Her bullets glanced off harmlessly. One bullet ricocheted and hit her leg, leaving a deep dent in her armor. She cried out in pain.

I can't beat him, she realized. *He's too strong.*

Abyzou grabbed her in his metal claws. He lifted her, and she screamed, thrashing in his grip. He tossed her against a boulder. The stone cracked. Ben-Ari slumped to the ground, head spinning. She gasped for air.

Abyzou lifted the boulder and swung it into her.

Pain exploded. White light flared.

She hit the ground.

For an instant, she couldn't see. She lay sprawled on blood-soaked soil. Her head tilted, and she saw the battle below the hill.

She saw that humanity was losing.

More saucers were arriving. Fresh battalions of grays were spilling forth, covering the land. Tanks burned. Entire human brigades lay fallen. No more human fighter jets flew. Ben-Ari watched as a laser beam flew from a saucer, carving through lines of human artillery. Corpses burned.

We will all die.

The visions flashed before her: humanity's warriors fallen, the survivors enslaved.

I will not live as a slave.

She struggled to rise.

The scorpion lashed its tail, knocking her back down. She lay on her back, head ringing, chest aching, no air reaching her lungs. Abyzou lifted the boulder, then slammed it down onto her arm.

Her armor shattered.

Her bone—only recently broken while battling Marino—snapped again.

She screamed.

She tried to rise. The boulder pinned her down. She lay, dizzy with pain, close to passing out.

Abyzou nodded. He leaned over her, towering in his mecha suit, a scorpion above an ant.

"Poor ape," he hissed. "So weak. So frail. Bones so fragile."

He reached down. With his mechanical claws, he caressed her helmet. Ben-Ari howled and fired her gun with her free arm. Her bullets hit the glass shielding, unable to pierce it. They ricocheted back onto her. One bullet shattered her visor, nearly blinding her. Glass stung her face.

Abyzou laughed. "Still you fight. Even now, your army crumbling, your body broken, your father dying in a puddle of blood. Even now you resist." He grabbed her rifle with his metal claws, then tossed it away. "You would have made a good goddess. Instead you will make a marvelous slave."

She struggled to speak. "I … will never … serve you."

Inside his suit, Abyzou sneered. He swung open the front of the mecha, then climbed out of the massive metal scorpion. Even outside his machine, he was still imposing, over seven feet tall. He was a wretched creature, his skin burnt and peeling, half his face shattered. Only several hearts still beat on his chain; the rest had burned away. Yet despite his injuries, he seemed to feel no pain, no weakness. He reached down, wrenched off her helmet, and grabbed her head.

She was too weak to fight him. The boulder still pinned her down. Beneath it, her arm was crushed, useless. Abyzou leaned down closer until his face was only centimeters away. His drool dripped onto her face, sizzling hot. His nostrils flared as if he were savoring her scent.

"I will show you," he hissed, and his grip tightened on her head.

His black eyes bored into her.

And she screamed.

Inside his eyes, she saw it. The homeworld of these creatures. Their dark city and their goddess upon her throne. Millions of gray troops were mustering there. Countless saucers filled the sky above them, spreading beyond the horizon.

"Now you see," Abyzou hissed. "We have sent only a drop from our might against you. The bulk of our fleet still awaits. You have seen but the first and smallest wave of our invasion. And your fleet is gone! Your army is crumbling! You cannot resist us. You can only serve us."

Every word was agony, rasping at Ben-Ari's throat. "I ... would rather ... die."

He leaned down and licked her cheek. He laughed. "My mother will not let you die, Einav. Not for many thousands of years. Not until you are a broken, miserable shadow of life, too mad to even beg for death. We have ways of extending your life ... and making it so, so painful. I will take you to Mother now." He cackled. "First I will free you from this rock."

He straightened and drew an ugly curved blade.

"No!" Ben-Ari cried.

The blade swung down and severed her trapped arm.

She screamed.

Her blood spurted.

She was free from the boulder, but the agony was too great. She could not rise. Only scream.

Abyzou placed a foot on her chest, pinning her down, as if she had the strength to rise. He drew a device from his belt. Her eyes widened when she recognized it.

A blowtorch.

He ignited it. And he sprayed its flame against her stump, cauterizing the wound.

She screamed. She passed out. She woke and screamed again.

Abyzou grabbed her with both hands. His hands were so large. They engulfed her. He lifted her, and her feet dangled. She hung in his grip like a rag doll. His hideous, broken face grinned before her.

"And now, Einav, it's time to meet Mother."

Her eyes were rolling back. Her life was fading away. Her rifle lay across the hill. She had no more grenades. No more weapons. After surviving so much, to end here, in such a defeat . . .

I'll never see my friends again, she thought. *I'll never see Marco and Addy and Lailani. Never see my dear professor.*

As her consciousness was slipping again, she thought of him. Her dear, kind professor. The hours she had spent in his study. With a man who was not a warrior. A man who was kind. A teacher. A friend. Somebody who could become a soul mate.

I miss your books. Your lessons. Your science. I miss you.

The professor smiled in her vision. He nodded.

You know what to do, he said.

She shook her head. *You told me I could not. Not here. Not on Earth.*

He stared at her steadily. *You must.*

She wept. *It's too dangerous.*

War is dangerous, the professor said in her vision. *You can do this. I believe in you, Einav. I love you.*

Tears in her eyes, she reached to her side. She hit a button on her armored suit, and a compartment opened on her thigh, used for storing ammo. Inside she still carried it: the wormhole generator.

The disk was gone. She held the heart of the device: a metal component, the size and shape of a heart. Inside it—an azoth crystal.

She had not wanted to use it. She had taken it only for the most dire of emergencies. A doomsday weapon. An azoth crystal bent spacetime itself, the fabric of the universe. It was used only in space, far from any world. And this wormhole generator didn't merely bend spacetime; it ruptured it, tearing a pin-sized hole through it.

If she opened a wormhole here on Earth, it was likely to split the planet in two.

It was a weapon more dangerous than a hydrogen bomb. A weapon that could destroy Earth.

"What is that?" Abyzou hissed. "What are you holding, ape?"

Hanging in his grip, she gazed into his eyes. "It is doomsday," she whispered. "A day for death. Or a day for victory. Einstein once said that God does not play dice with the universe." She smiled shakily. "I do."

She aimed the wormhole generator at Abyzou and turned it on.

Nothing happened.

Abyzou's eyes narrowed. And he began to laugh.

"Is this your doomsday weapon?" He tightened his grip on her, crushing her armor. "You have failed, Einav! You—"

"Eighty percent," she whispered.

"—you will scream for all eternity in—"

"Ninety percent," she whispered.

"—and your screams shall echo in the halls of—"

On the device's display, the characters appeared: *100%*

And the wormhole materialized.

It was narrow. Only a few atoms wide. It punched but a pinprick through Abyzou's face.

And then it began to suck in the rest of the skull.

With a shower of blood, Abyzou's skin and flesh ripped. His skull crumpled inward and blasted out in a thousand pieces.

Ben-Ari fell to the ground.

The world thrummed.

The sky turned red.

The ground cracked.

The air shrieked. Deafening. The howl of ten thousand demons. Thunder boomed as the sky split open.

She clung to the device. She held it firmly with her one remaining hand. In the vacuum of space, it had barely vibrated. Here it was like holding Satan's hand.

The wormhole stretched outward. It ate through the scorpion mecha, pulling it inward, belching it out. The wormhole stretched farther. It slammed into a saucer, crumpling it, ripping it out of existence.

Ben-Ari was wounded. Badly. Dying. But she rose to her feet, still clinging to the wormhole generator.

"Doomsday," she whispered.

Her tears flowed, and she swept the device from side to side, lashing the wormhole like a sword the length of the cosmos.

Wherever the beam swept, reality shattered.

Saucers were sucked into the wormhole, shattered, and fell. Hundreds of saucers bent, split open, and blasted shattered pieces across the cosmos. Remains fell burning to the ground.

Ben-Ari lowered her beam.

The device thrummed in her hand, nearly tearing free. It was dangerous. Too dangerous! If the wormhole hit the ground, it could dig a hole through Earth. The planet itself could curve in on itself, then shatter. Doomsday. Doomsday.

I believe in you. You can do this.

The voice of the professor. Of her friends. Of her father. Of the millions who had fallen.

She lowered the beam, bringing it but a meter above the surface.

And she swept it from side to side, plowing through the lines of gray warriors.

Thousands of chariots. Thousands of grays. The wormhole ate them all. Their burned, mangled remains fell.

She released her finger from the button, deactivating the device. The funnel faded away. With wisps of light, the wormhole vanished.

Ben-Ari dropped the generator from her trembling hand. It thudded onto the ground.

Your father is dying, Abyzou had said. She remembered. Dying. Not dead.

She tried to walk. She fell. She crawled. She reached him on the hillside. Her father.

He lay in the grass, a hole in his chest. His skin was ashen, his eyes sunken.

"Einavi," he whispered, voice hoarse.

"I'm here, Father." She crawled closer and placed her hand on his cheek. "I'm here."

His breath was shallow. Blood speckled his lips. Every word seemed a struggle. "Einavi, I'm sorry." His tears fell. "I'm sorry that I wasn't a better father. A better man. I'm so proud of you." His voice was so soft she could barely hear. "I'm so proud. I love you so much."

"I forgive you," she whispered, trembling, weeping. "I forgive you, Father. I love you."

He gazed into her eyes, and he smiled, and he breathed no more.

She lay down beside him, her arm gone, her breath slowing. She closed her eyes.

Voices flowed from the muffled afterlife.

"It's her! The Golden Lioness!"

"Major Ben-Ari! Major, can you hear me?"

"Doc! Doc, we need you!"

They held her. But she slipped away. There was no more pain. Smiling softly, she faded into blackness.

CHAPTER NINETEEN

Marco's jaw unhinged.

Here inside the ancient mecha—a living Taolian!

The alien looked as ancient as his home. His mane was long and white, and golden fur coated his weary, wrinkled face. Heavy brows shadowed his sad amber eyes. His mouth was missing the fangs depicted on statues of younger Taolians. He stood stooped over, holding a staff. An orange robe draped across him, richly woven, embroidered with red dragons, and his slippers curled up to points. An amulet hung around his neck, its right half shaped like a sunburst, the left like a moon.

"Greetings, children of Earth," the Taolian said. "I am Ling, son of Xe Shuan, Guardian of the Holy Empire of Taolin Shi, defender of her fallen-yet-eternal king."

Addy waved. "Yo. I'm Addy. Got any tacos around here?"

Marco stepped forward, placing himself between her and the Taolian. He bowed his head. "Forgive us, sir. We did not realize you live here. We did not mean to disturb you." He glanced up at the old alien, wonder growing in him. "We did not realize that anyone survived the flood five hundred years ago."

The old Taolian nodded, eyes sad. "A few of us did. Now only I still live. Come, my friends. I will serve you food and tell you old tales. Five hundred years?" Ling shook his head sadly. "I did not realize it had been so long ..."

Ling took them to what he called Kaiyo's Heart, a room in the mecha's chest. Scrolls hung on the walls, displaying delicate calligraphy and watercolor landscapes. Bamboo dividers separated the room into four chambers. One chamber seemed dedicated to meditation. Marco saw a soft pillow to sit on, a bronze bell, and— surprisingly—a copy of Baba Mahanisha's *The Way of Deep Being*. One chamber was a bedroom, another a dining room. The fourth chamber contained bronze statues of a Taolian woman and three children.

"You've been living here all this time?" Addy asked. "For five hundred years?"

Ling nodded. "I was a young soldier when our world flooded. A pilot of this vessel. I watched the waves." His eyes dampened. "I watched the water flood the world I had vowed to protect. And for five centuries, I did not abandon my post. I remained true to my charge. I still defend my world, even if all its splendor is drowned."

Addy's eyes softened. She stroked the old alien's mane. "You must have been very lonely."

"My family lived with me at first." The Taolian looked at the bronze statues. "They are still with me."

"They're beautiful statues," Marco said. "Beautiful ways to remember your family."

The old Taolian raised his bushy white eyebrows. "Statues? No, child of Earth. These are not statues. They are my family."

Addy leaned closer to Marco. "He's a bit loony," she whispered into his ear.

Despite his age, Ling's ears were sharp. "Loony? No, child. I am but a practitioner of the old ways. My wife and children chose this fate. They entered a deep state of meditation. And I entombed them in bronze. They are still there, still inside, still alive. Oh, their hearts have stopped beating. Their bodies inside are now nothing but bone. But those are mere physical things. Their souls are alive inside the bronze shells. Their souls will remain there for eternity, deep in meditation, at peace."

Marco and Addy shared a glance. He saw the horror in her eyes. He felt it too. To bronze your wife and children? To leave them to die horrible deaths because of some superstition?

"You mean, they were *alive* when you bronzed them?" Addy whispered.

Ling nodded. "They are living still. In spirit. Their souls are eternal."

Marco felt like gagging. He could not imagine a more horrible death. But then he remembered Kemi. He remembered how the yurei had placed her soul into a shell. Perhaps he was hasty to judge.

"But here I'm babbling on like a forgetful elder!" Ling said. "Come, friends, come, let me serve you food and tea."

He led them to a low table, and they sat on cushions. Marco volunteered to help, and they brought out steaming tea and a dish of seaweed and fried fish. Ling explained that the mecha had a water filtration system, and that he could find all the food he needed in the ocean. As they had suspected, there was indeed another door—a small airlock in the mecha's helmet, only a few meters below the water's surface. From there, Ling could retrieve water, catch fish, and soak up sunlight.

"Mmm, my appetizer is delicious!" Addy said, gobbling down the meal. "What's the main course?"

Marco cringed. "Addy, you just ate the main course. For all three of us."

Her cheeks flushed. "Um ... Poet! Go fishing!"

Ling laughed. "There is more, my children. Much more. I forget the appetites of youth."

Marco nodded. "Addy eats like a teenager. An elephant teenager."

"I do not!" She bristled. "Elephants only eat peanuts, and I eat lots of things." She raised her chin triumphantly. "I knew something you didn't."

"Actually, Addy, elephants consume a varied diet of—"

"Smarter. Than. You." She nodded.

Marco turned back toward the old Taolian, who was serving more fish and tea. "Ling, does this mecha still work? Can it fly?"

"Indeed it can," Ling said. "I have dedicated my life to maintaining it. It is aging, perhaps. And it has lost some of its luster, and I have become too old to oil and polish the deepest gears. But it can still fly. Still fight."

Marco felt another burst of hope.

We found a mighty weapon. A way to fight the grays.

"So why did you stay here?" Addy said, looking through a porthole at the water. "You could go anywhere! Find a nice dry world! Maybe one with other aliens." Her voice softened. "You spent so long here ... Didn't you ever want to leave?"

"Many times." Ling lowered his head. "I was tempted. To find another world. Even to visit my friend, Baba Mahanisha, on Durmia. Yes, children. He is my friend. Does that surprise you?" He laughed softly. "We are both the last of our kinds. Both too proud to leave. He remains on Durmia, guarding his temple, even though all else lies in ruin. I remain here on Taolin Shi, for I have sworn to guard my planet, and I am still bound to my vows. Two aging soldiers. Two stubborn old fools."

Marco glanced at Addy. She bit her lip, sadness in her eyes. He looked back at Ling, and he spoke softly.

"Ling, I'm sorry to tell you this. Baba Mahanisha has passed away. We were there with him. He was peaceful at the end."

Ling looked up, and his bottom lip wobbled. His eyes dampened. He lowered his head, and a tear flowed.

"This grieves me. He would visit me here every year. He would place coins on the seabed in memory of the fallen. Such guilt filled him for what he had done." Ling wiped his eyes. "It was Baba Mahanisha who flooded this world, who destroyed

Taolin Shi. But only because I had destroyed his land, flying this mecha in war." He shook his head, tears flowing. "Two old fools. Two old soldiers who should have died long ago."

Addy embraced the old Taolian. "We are all fools as soldiers. We are all mad when the fire rages." She kissed his wrinkly cheek. "We only grow wise once peace has come, once it's too late, once the fire has already burned us. You are no fool." Embracing the Taolian, she looked at Marco. "You are a veteran."

She's speaking to Ling, but also to me, Marco thought, smiling sadly. *Yes, she's smarter than she lets on. Maybe she's right. Smarter than me.*

"Ling, you speak English," Marco said. "Do you know much about Earth?"

"My people visited Earth thousands of years ago," Ling said. "My own ancestor, a noble warrior, joined the expedition. A great Earthling king met them, and they spent many days together, learning about each other. A descendant of that great explorer, I have studied all that I could about Earth."

"China," Marco said in wonder, gazing around at the hanging scrolls. "Your people visited China. You inspired their culture. Or they inspired yours."

"Perhaps," Ling said. "Many of those legends are lost. Yet I know that my ancestor wrote words of much praise about Earth, that he saw your species as having great potential, great wisdom, but also too much aggression, too much fear. Much like the Taolians. Much like the Durmians." The old alien reached out and held their hands. "Learn from us, children of Earth. Learn from

Baba Mahanisha and old Ling. Learn from our worlds that are gone. Do not let this happen to Earth."

Marco thought about the new war. About the grays, a future race of highly evolved humans. Somehow, this war seemed more shameful than the ones before it. This was not humanity fighting against evil space bugs. It was humanity fighting against itself, against its own greed and wickedness.

Perhaps this is the war in which we carve out our evil, reject it, slay it, Marco thought. *A war between the good and evil within us.*

He spoke to Ling, and he told him about the wars against the scum and marauders, of the war against the grays, against the wickedness of man. He spoke for a long time as Ling listened.

"And so we've come here for aid," Marco said, completing his tale. "To find the fabled mechas. To use them to defeat the grays—to reject this dark path of evolution. Will you let us take the second mecha, the one that is empty?"

Ling patted his hand. "You will take both. One for you. One for Addy. You face the great choice I did not. The fork in the road. One path leads to light, a path along which humanity can grow wiser, nobler, bring peace and knowledge and art to the cosmos. Another path, one of fear and hatred, that leads to the grays. For the sake of life, for all life is holy, and for the sake of my ancestors who visited your land—take these mechas. And strike out the evil."

Addy frowned. "But Ling! Your vow! You vowed to remain and guard Taolin Shi."

He nodded. "And I shall. I will not fly with you to Earth. I will remain in Taolin Shi." He turned to look at his bronzed family. "With them."

Addy gasped. "Ling! You're not going to …" She covered her mouth. "Turn into a statue?"

Marco cringed. The thought of the wise old Taolian coated in bronze, rotting away inside his shell, chilled him. He wanted to respect the alien's culture, but how could he stand by and watch such horror?

"Ling." He placed a gentle hand on the Taolian's shoulder. "We do not wish to doom you to death. Gift us only one mecha. Or fly with us. You needn't die for our war."

Ling smiled and placed his hand atop Marco's. "I will not die, child. This way, I will live eternally. This is why I have clung on to life for so long, the last of my kind." Tears flowed into his mane. "Finally I will have eternal life. Will you help me? Will you pour the bronze atop my form, and will you place my family and me in our ancient temple? You will be giving me the gift of immortality. Of eternal blessing."

Marco took a deep breath. Witnessing such a ritual was bad enough. But to participate?

"Ling, I—" he began.

"For five hundred years, I've lived here alone," Ling said. "I have perhaps another few years in me. Maybe less. Don't let me die an old man, lonely, ashamed. I give you the gifts of Kaiyo and Kaji. Give this gift to me."

Marco nodded, eyes damp, lips tight. "Tell me what to do."

Ling nodded. "Come with me."

He led them to a prayer room in the mecha's belly. An idol rose on an altar, shaped like a Taolian monk in deep meditation. The materials for the ritual were already here: chunks of raw bronze, cauldrons to melt it, and plaster to form a cast.

It was here that he must have embalmed his family, Marco thought.

Addy glanced at Marco. She leaned closer.

"Poet, I don't know about this," she whispered. "It feels like murder."

"More like assisted suicide," Marco said. "Maybe we should stop this."

But Ling was going ahead with the ritual. Embers glowed at the idol's feet, and Ling warmed swirling green tea. He downed the cup.

"I drank the holy pine needle tea," he said. "The poison is now in me. It will guide me gently to the world beyond. It will purify my body, so that the worms and maggots cannot touch me. Come, children. We don't have long. Help me melt the bronze."

Marco and Addy shared another glance.

I don't like this, Marco thought. *I want to respect other cultures. But this feels wrong. Gruesome.*

Then he thought back to Earth, to his own people. He thought back to the military hospitals he had been in. He remembered seeing mortally wounded patients, their limbs and faces blasted off, blind, mute, deaf, burnt, living in agony. Yet kept alive. Kept in agony for years because of the terror of death.

Are we any less brutal? Are our death rituals any less horrifying?

He nodded. "We'll help him, Addy."

It was a long ritual. Ling chanted prayers for hours, and he drank more of the poisonous tea. He seemed to feel no pain. His meditation deepened, and he entered a trance.

And Marco and Addy followed his instructions. They applied the plaster cast. They poured the molten metal. And when their work was done, he sat before them, cross-legged, embalmed. Coated in bronze, Ling appeared peaceful, a soft smile on his lips. Inside, he was surely already dead.

"May your soul live forever," Marco said. "Here in the world you vowed to protect. Be with your family. Be at peace."

He and Addy put on their spacesuits. They carried Ling and his family out into the water. They placed them inside a temple on a hill, facing an archway with a view of a coral reef.

Marco and Addy hovered for a moment in their spacesuits, gazing at the statues.

"Poet," Addy said.

"Yeah?"

"When I die, can you turn me into a statue?"

He sighed. "No, Addy."

"But why? I want to be a statue!"

"I'll bury you inside a hot dog statue, how's that?"

They began swimming back toward the mechas.

"I like that idea," Addy said. "Can the hot dog be holding a bottle of mustard and pouring it on himself? And I can hold a sign that says: 'Too hot to handle.'"

"Fine, Addy."

"And can you be buried beside me inside a giant hamburger?"

"No, Addy."

She pouted. "But I don't want to be lonely!"

"I'm not being buried inside a hamburger."

"Fine, fine!" Addy said. "How about a giant taco?"

"Addy!"

She grinned. "And the taco can have googly eyes and look a little like you. And it can be holding a sign that reads: 'You taco to me?'"

"Addy, shut up."

"Or maybe a giant banana statue that's saying: 'I find you a-peeling.'"

"Addy, I'm going to bury you in a statue *right now* if you don't shut up."

They reached the mechas. Addy shot barnacles and clay off the female mecha, found an airlock, and entered it. Marco returned to the male mecha. As he took the elevator up to the head, he found himself humming "The Girl from Ipanema." Damn Addy getting her damn elevator music stuck in his head.

He reached the control room in the mecha's head. He couldn't begin to comprehend all the monitors, panels, and holograms that filled the place. He would have to learn on the fly.

He approached the exoframe that stood in the center of the room—a metal suit roughly his size.

He climbed in.

Once his four limbs were in place, the suit tightened around him, bits and pieces snapping into place. Marco wasn't a large man, but Taolians weren't very large either, and the suit adjusted to fit perfectly. A helmet closed snugly around his head, and for a moment, all his senses vanished.

He floated in silent darkness. Held within the suit, he even felt weightless. Marco had heard of sensory deprivation tanks. This felt similar, the losing of the senses.

Yet all our senses sit atop awareness, he thought. *I learned that from Mahanisha. In here, I am pure consciousness.*

And then, slowly, a world began to wake up.

At first, his sense of touch—dryness to his skin, like scabs covering his body. Then his hearing—the muffled sounds of water, the songs of whales, the scurrying of fish. His sight remained dark, but many other senses awoke. His sense of weight—massive now. His sense of balance, of being. The feelings of his limbs, as long as starships. The heat in his belly, engines awakening, gears turning.

He was Marco. But he was also Kaiyo the mecha. He was this ancient god.

And he could move.

At first, movement was hard. He was embalmed like Ling, engulfed in clay and barnacles. But his muscles awoke from their ancient slumber. No, not muscles—gears and working pistons and grumbling engines. He moved one arm, and chunks of clay shattered and fell to the seabed. He raised one leg, tearing free from his bonds. He shook his head, and clay shards fell, revealing the sea.

He saw the second mecha ahead. Addy was operating the machine, tearing off the layers of clay, revealing a goddess in golden armor. Kaji shone in the water, tall and proud, gazing with the face of a lioness. In her hand, she held a mighty sword.

Her voice filled Marco's head.

"Hey, dumbass."

Marco took a step across the seabed. The water swirled around him. He raised one of his massive hands, large enough to crush a car, and waved. Fish scattered and water swirled.

"Hey, dingbat," he said.

The female mecha stepped forward too, tearing her colossal feet out from the clay. Addy spoke again, her voice emerging from speakers in Marco's helmet.

"Finally, you're no longer short!" she said.

"I'm just amazed you squeezed into that mecha, what with all the hot dogs you've been scarfing down," Marco said.

"Shut up and let's fly." Addy paused. "So, Poet—how do we fly these things?"

"You didn't read the manual?" Marco said.

She snorted. "Poet, the only books I've ever read are yours and *Freaks of the Galaxy*. And I skimmed through the boring parts of yours."

"Hey!"

"Well, your books need more freaks in them!"

Marco groaned. "I'll make you the main character in the next one."

"That's more like it."

He took a deep breath. Flying. How did one fly this machine? He explored with his awareness, moving it across his body—and the body of the mecha. Under Baba Mahanisha's tutelage, Marco had spent many hours scanning his body, moving his consciousness from toes, to calves, to knees, letting each part exist in awareness while the rest faded. He found that now, using the same technique, he could explore the mecha—using nothing but his awareness. That awareness was like a little passenger moving through the great machine, observing. Using this technique, he could access the control center around him, could pull up information. Holographic displays appeared before him, but the language was foreign. Even if he could find the user manual here, he couldn't read it.

But if I can explore this machine with my awareness, move its limbs with my awareness, why not fly?

He raised his chin. He gazed upward toward the surface of the water.

Fly.

Deep inside him, engines rumbled.

Jets extended from his back; he saw them in the holographic diagrams.

Fire blazed.

And he flew.

His head burst from the sea, dripping water and seaweed. His engines grew hotter, and soon he was soaring—a massive machine, as large as humanity's largest warships. He blasted through the sky. Numbers and speedometers flashed before him in a foreign language. He soared through clouds. The roar and clattering was deafening. He felt like a pea inside a shaken can. His joints ached. He felt his awareness fading, moving back from the machine into his own small body.

"Woo! Poet!" Addy laughed. "Poet, I can see you! We're doing it! We're flying!"

Marco saw her. She was soaring nearby, body straight as an arrow, arms held upward.

"I feel sick!" he shouted over the roaring engines.

"Hold your hands up like me! Pretend you're Superman. Your body's too crooked."

As his suit kept rattling, Marco raised one arm, then the other. He pressed his hands together like a diver, then pushed his legs together and rose onto his toes. He kept his body—and by extension, the mecha's body—as flat as possible.

The rattling eased. He flew faster, smoother. He and Addy soared together.

They burst out from the atmosphere into open space, and the stars spread around them.

They kept flying, freeing themselves from Taolin Shi's pull. They flew through space, side by side, two ancient gods.

"For the first time in centuries, Kaiyo and Kaji fly," Marco whispered. "The dead have risen again."

"And these machines will *fight*," Addy said. Her golden mecha gazed at Marco, sword in hand. "*We* will fight. We will fight the grays and anyone else who dares attack us. Poet, we are now the greatest warriors Earth has known. And it's time to go home."

CHAPTER TWENTY

Ben-Ari lay in her hospital bed, sipping chamomile tea, watching the news on her small television set.

A reporter was interviewing a mustached colonel. They stood in the devastation of Mongolia, and the camera panned across the battlefield, showing the husks of tanks, chariots, saucers, and starfighters.

The reporter spoke, voice solemn. "Was it here, Colonel, on this very field, that Major Einav Ben-Ari opened a black hole and sucked in the grays?"

The colonel harrumphed. "I cannot discuss what military tactics the HDF utilizes. Suffice to say that Major Ben-Ari's actions turned the tide of the battle. Bear in mind there are still sporadic battles breaking out across the globe, but the HDF is handling the threat. In Eastern Europe, our artillery division has been—"

The reporter interrupted. "Colonel, is it true that Major Ben-Ari nearly destroyed the planet? Opening a black hole in the middle of—"

Ben-Ari switched the channel. But the next station was showing a news report too. An image of her appeared on the screen. A caption below it read: *Major Ben-Ari: Heroine or Madwoman?*

She flipped the channel again. Every station was reporting on the war. She had fought in the epicenter, but the grays had invaded other locations on Earth too. Some violence still raged, but the HDF was gaining ground quickly. The battle was won.

But the war, Ben-Ari knew, was only beginning.

She thought of the vision Abyzou had shown her. Pain stabbed her.

She grimaced and glanced at her stump. It was wrapped in bandages, and a morphine drip was taming the pain. But she still felt a phantom arm. Still felt it crushed.

She looked away. Finally she found a channel showing something other than war coverage. She spent a blissful ninety minutes watching *Lost in Love*, a romantic comedy about a couple marooned on a tropical planet. Her favorite part was their pet monkey.

This is the first time I've gotten to relax in years, Ben-Ari thought. *All I had to do was save the world three times and get my arm chopped off.*

A knock sounded on her door. She placed aside her cup of tea, expecting another visit from her nurse.

"Come in!"

But the visitor was a stranger, a tall man wearing a black suit, a black tie, and black sunglasses. He surveyed the room, pulled out a sensor, and swept it across the walls.

"Are you looking for rodents?" Ben-Ari said. "Or are you ghost hunting? I'm not sure about mice, but by the way it creaks, I could swear my bed is haunted."

The man silently retreated from the room.

A moment later, another man entered.

Ben-Ari smiled.

"Mister President."

President James Petty still looked horribly uncomfortable in a suit and tie. He had worn only military uniforms for four decades, had risen to command fleets. Today he commanded the world.

He looks handsome in a suit, she thought. *Though I'll never convince him to lose his military buzz cut.*

"Einav!" Petty held out a bouquet. "For you."

"Flowers?" She scoffed. "You should have brought me chocolates!"

He seemed flustered for a moment, but Ben-Ari laughed, and he smiled. It was so rare to see him smile.

He sat down by her side, and now his smile faded. "Einav, talk to me. You fought these creatures in the darkness. You studied them. You were inside one of their ships. Tell me everything. Tell me what we're facing."

Her head spun. She was weary. She was so weary. The morphine was wearing off, and she pressed the button on her dispenser, releasing another boost. She sighed in relief. It was good stuff. Almost as good as chamomile.

Through the haze of painkillers, she spoke to Petty.

She told him everything she knew.

She spoke of Yarrow, a green, lush world, of visiting a colony of hardy farmers missing its children.

She spoke of flying to a cruel desert world, a harsh land where a pyramid soared. Monks lived there, worshiping Nefitis, an ancient Egyptian goddess. She told Petty how she had found Yarrow's missing children there—children that seemed a hundred years old, inflicted with progeria. Children the monks had used as guinea pigs in their time machine. A time machine they were building to return to Egypt, to hear Nefitis speak.

Voice steady, she told Petty how she had destroyed that time machine, destroyed the monks' starships, and marooned them on their desert world. No technology. No way to leave. Their secret lair had become their prison.

And she told Petty what happened next. What she had learned.

"Over the next million years, the monks evolved on their desert planet. They grew taller. Smarter. Stronger. They became the grays. From among them rose a queen, wretched and cruel. They finally invented their time machine. It took them a million years, but they finally invented it. Their queen traveled back in time to ancient Egypt, revealing herself to the Egyptians. She became Nefitis, the goddess the monks worshiped. A self-fulfilling prophecy, in a way. She formed a circle in time."

Petty listened silently the whole time. Finally he spoke. "And now the grays—these evolved humans from the future—want Earth. Our Earth."

Ben-Ari nodded. "A million years from now, Earth is destroyed. A wasteland. Inhospitable to life. The gray I captured aboard the *Lodestar* told me. Earth only lasts another thousand years from the present day before pollution destroys it." She sighed. "So the grays came here. Using their time machine. To take our world. To make it their own. They were human once. They see Earth as their birthright."

Petty frowned. "Why Earth now, then? Why an Earth that's already polluted, that's already filled with an army that can resist them? Why not travel back to the days before humans even existed? Or if they want slaves, why not travel back to ancient Egypt again, where they'd face swords and arrows instead of cannons and starfighters?"

"Because they can't," Ben-Ari said. "Not anymore. Not since I marooned the monks. If the grays conquered Earth a million years ago, or a thousand years ago, or even just one year ago—I wouldn't be around to maroon the monks. And the monks wouldn't have evolved into grays. If they conquered Earth before their exile, they would blink out of existence. So they came now. To a time when Earth is still reeling from two galactic wars, a time when we're weak."

Petty nodded. "All right. So time travel is possible. So we figure it out. We travel back in time and prevent you from marooning the monks. Hell, we can just go to those monks now. They're only a few months into their exile. We kill them. We stop their evolution. We—"

"We can't," Ben-Ari said softly. "The grays were too clever. They placed themselves in our past. They landed in Area 51 and Roswell. They landed in ancient Egypt and helped build the pyramids. They attacked me in space, and I captured one on my ship—never knowing it allowed itself to be captured." She sighed. "If we kill the monks now, yes, we'd prevent them from evolving into the grays. Which means Area 51, Roswell, and all those other events will not have happened. Which creates paradoxes in our lives. Which can unravel spacetime itself, more thoroughly and dangerously than my wormhole generator. It could undo Earth." She shook her head. "No, James. We can't kill the monks. We can't undo this. It's too late. Professor Isaac taught me something. That you can't change the past. We must look only to the future."

"And what lies in our future?" Petty said. "What do these creatures plan now?"

She propped herself up in bed, felt woozy, and lay back down. She glanced at the timer of her morphine dispenser. The damn thing was locked for another hour.

"Another invasion," she said weakly, trying to ignore the pain, the dizziness. "A hundred times stronger than the assault they already hit us with. Before he died, Abyzou showed me … a vision. A glimpse into his world. I saw gray armies. A huge fleet. They plan to hit us again. Maybe not today. Maybe not tomorrow. Professor Isaac told me that it's dangerous to open such large rifts in time so close together. But sooner or later—maybe in a year, maybe in only a month—the grays will open another portal. And they will attack again. And they will hit us harder than we've ever been hit."

Petty stared at her in horror. "We have no warships left. Earth is undefended. Even if we have a year, it's not enough time."

"We have one ship," Ben-Ari said. "We have the *Lodestar*." She propped herself up in bed, ignoring the pain in her phantom limb. "Why did you send her away, James? During the attack, you said you had a mission for my ship. You sent her fleeing from battle. Why?"

Petty stepped toward the window. He gazed outside. They had given Ben-Ari a room with a view of the Pacific, and Petty spent a while gazing at the ocean. Finally he spoke.

"I sent the *Lodestar* away to serve her original purpose." He looked back at her. "She was never meant to be a ship of war. She's a ship of HOPE, the Human Outreach Program for Exploration, not the Human Defense Force."

Ben-Ari nodded. "I know. You built her for exploration. But you also gave her weapons. Because you knew that someday I might need them. And I did. We all did."

"For exploration?" Petty nodded. "Yes, I suppose. That was part of it. That was how I could enlist famous scientists such as Noah Isaac and that long-haired Alien Hunter. But the *Lodestar*'s true purpose, Einav, is diplomacy."

Ben-Ari smiled thinly. "You might have noticed that my idea of diplomacy is charging headfirst into a hostile fleet, getting my arm chopped off, and then activating a doomsday device to slaughter a hundred thousand of my enemies."

"A useful skill at times," said Petty, struggling to stifle his own smile. "Yet the *Lodestar* is the last of our major starships. When the grays attack again, she cannot hold them off herself. We need to enlist aid. We need to join the Galactic Alliance."

The Galactic Alliance. Yes, Ben-Ari had heard of it. Humanity had discovered that distant league of civilizations only last year. It had barely made the news, not with the gray assaults, but she had been listening.

Ben-Ari pushed herself up in bed, winced in pain, and lay back down. "James, we're not nearly advanced enough. The Galactic Alliance? We'd be like a gorilla asking for a seat in the zoo's boardroom."

"Then this gorilla better put on a suit," Petty said, uncomfortably adjusting his tie. "Einav, the Galactic Alliance is the premier peacekeeping force in the Milky Way. Every spacefaring civilization worth its salt is a member. They have powerful pacts of protection. If any hostile race—creatures like the scum, marauders, or even the grays—attacks one member, the rest of the Galactic Alliance is sworn to defend that member. If we can join the alliance, we'd have powerful allies. When the grays attack again, they would not be attacking Earth alone. They'd be attacking a member of the GA. They'd be incurring the wrath of a mighty organization with massive fleets. That is how we defeat the grays. Earth cannot fight alone. We need allies."

Ben-Ari sighed. "I don't know, James. The Galactic Alliance accepts civilizations far more advanced than ours. Their members have built Dyson spheres around their stars. They have colonies on many star systems. We humans have only a handful of colonies. We barely have any ships left. What do we have to offer them?"

Petty smiled. "We have Captain Einav Ben-Ari."

"Not even all of her, not now." She glanced at her missing arm and winced. The phantom limb still ached. Why the hell wasn't more morphine available?

"The *Lodestar* is idling right now on the edge of the solar system, undergoing repairs. She'll soon be ready to fly into interstellar space again. While you recover, Commander Isaac will captain the *Lodestar*. He will lead the starship to the Galactic Alliance headquarters, where he will present our application for membership, and—"

"No." This time Ben-Ari forced herself to sit up. She stared into the president's eyes. "I'm going. The *Lodestar* is my ship. I will lead her on this mission."

He placed a hand on her shoulder. "Einav. You're hurt. You lost an arm. You—"

"It's 2153, James. Getting a new arm is like getting a crown for your tooth." She rose to her feet. "We still have a handful of shuttles, yes? I'll catch the next one back to my ship." She swayed and placed a hand on the wall. "I'll rest on our way to the Galactic Alliance headquarters."

Petty sighed. "You are a force of nature, Einav Ben-Ari."

She nodded. "Like a hurricane. Or black hole."

He stared into her eyes. "Bring us back hope, Einav."

"I always do." She saluted.

Lips tight, he returned her salute. "Godspeed, Captain Einav Ben-Ari."

She grabbed the flowers. "I'm taking these with me. Now if you really want to win me over, will you grab me some chocolates from the shop?"

* * * * *

Through the window of her shuttle, Ben-Ari gazed at her. Her ship. Her pride. Her home.

The ESS *Lodestar* had seen better days. Her hull was still cracked and punched full of holes. Her figurehead was dented. Her paint had burned off. But her engines were still humming, the exhaust pipes glowing blue. The *Lodestar* was shaped like an old sailing vessel, the kind Captain Cook would have used to explore the world, for she sailed the cosmic ocean, seeking new lands. And new hope.

Engineering crews were bustling across the hull, soldering, painting, making Ben-Ari's ship whole again.

As I am whole again, Ben-Ari thought.

She moved her new arm and flexed her new fingers. Some amputees chose showy prosthetics—claws, hooks, or elaborate steampunk limbs filled with brass gears. Ben-Ari had chosen a prosthetic that looked like a regular arm and hand, the right size and proportions. But instead of coating it with artificial skin, she left the metal bare. Her new arm was slick and silvery, stronger than her old arm had ever been. With this prosthetic, she could beat a champion arm-wrestler. A control panel on the forearm let her bring up a holographic monitor, which she could use for work or recreation—check stats, communicate with her crew, view maps, or access a library of books and movies.

I don't need to hide my handicap, she thought. *I'm proud of my sacrifice. I'm more whole than ever.* She smiled wryly. *And my old arm couldn't load up holographic operas.*

The arm contained a hidden compartment too, which she could open with her thoughts. She opened it now. Inside rested an old derringer. The small pistol was dear to her. Her old Bat Mitzvah present from her grandfather. The grizzled old man, a retired general who had fought in the Cataclysm, had died shortly after her twelfth birthday. The gun was her memento from him. Ben-Ari had never fired the derringer in battle. It was small and not very powerful. But she had held onto it. It was her first weapon. It was precious. She closed her arm's compartment, sealing the gun inside.

When she stepped into the *Lodestar*, her bridge crew was waiting in the corridor. They all applauded.

"Crikey, she's turned into a bloody cyborg!" Fish said.

Ben-Ari frowned at the Australian. "Lieutenant Commander Fishburne, put on your uniform. I told you not to wear shorts on my ship. And cut your hair and get rid of that shark-tooth necklace."

The Alien Hunter grinned. "Oh, I was worried for nothing. She's still a full robot." He pulled her into his arms. "Good to have you back, sheila."

She sighed but couldn't stifle her smile. "It's good to be home, Fish."

She walked farther down the corridor to where Aurora stood. Well, stood was perhaps the wrong word; the mollusk crawled across the floor, wriggled upward, and extended one of her eight tentacles. Colors flashed across the pilot's body. Her translating device, held in another tentacle, emitted the English.

"Welcome back, mistress of dark waters. The ocean was cold and dark without your guiding light."

Ben-Ari shook the extended tentacle. "And the ocean would be impossible to navigate without you adjusting my sails."

She walked past other officers and crewmen—engineers, navigators, biologists, geologists, maintenance workers, security guards, chemists, and technicians. After twelve years in the military, Ben-Ari was used to her subordinates standing at attention and saluting. It still felt a little strange, even after a while in HOPE, that they shook her hand and smiled.

But that's why HOPE exists, she thought. *To shake hands.*

At the end of the corridor stood Professor Noah Isaac. He frowned at her, arms crossed.

She stood before him. "Professor."

He glowered. "You opened a wormhole on Earth, despite my warnings."

She nodded.

"You nearly died," he said.

She nodded again.

"And now, after all your recklessness, you come here to relieve me of my command."

She nodded a third time.

The professor's eyes softened, and he pulled her into his embrace. "Thank you. Thank you. For everything—thank you."

She laid her head against Isaac's shoulder. "Are you ready to go exploring?"

He held her close. "Always. Just … promise you won't try to destroy the universe."

She grinned. "Maybe only a few solar systems."

He sighed. "That's the best I could hope for, I suppose."

They stepped onto the bridge. It was still mostly shattered. Many of the viewports were missing. Crews were at work, fixing the cracked walls, installing new monitors. In time, the bridge would resemble a planetarium again, offering a full view of space all around them, even beneath their feet.

Yet one large viewport was still functional. Through it, she could see the stars. It was only a monitor displaying a feed from a camera mounted on the hull, but it seemed so real, as if Ben-Ari could just reach out and grab those stars. And they were beautiful. Despite everything, they were beautiful.

Daniel Arenson

Aurora slithered into the pilot's seat, and her tentacles reached out to her eight control panels. The professor manned the science station. Ben-Ari settled into her captain's seat, and an ensign brought her a cup of tea. Chamomile. Perfect.

"Are you ready, Aurora?" Ben-Ari asked.

The mollusk turned toward her. "Where shall we swim in the cosmic ocean, mistress of dark waters?"

"To find hope," Ben-Ari said. "To prove our worth. To shake hands."

And when the enemy strikes again, she thought, *may many hands rise against it.*

She flexed her new, metal hand. And she thought of how Kemi had lost her hand too. She thought about how Kemi had fallen, how so many millions had died, how millions still lived. Still depended on her.

Ben-Ari closed her metal fist.

I will not let you down. I reach out one hand in friendship. The other will remain a fist.

The *Lodestar*'s warp engines rumbled. They blasted out toward the stars.

The story concludes in …

Earth Eternal (*Earthrise* Book 9)

NOVELS BY DANIEL ARENSON

Earthrise:
Earth Alone
Earth Lost
Earth Rising
Earth Fire
Earth Shadows
Earth Valor
Earth Reborn
Earth Honor
Earth Eternal

Alien Hunters:
Alien Hunters
Alien Sky
Alien Shadows

The Moth Saga:
Moth
Empires of Moth
Secrets of Moth
Daughter of Moth
Shadows of Moth
Legacy of Moth

KEEP IN TOUCH

www.DanielArenson.com
Daniel@DanielArenson.com
Facebook.com/DanielArenson
Twitter.com/DanielArenson

60250731R00231

Made in the USA
Middletown, DE
28 December 2017